M000206940

Once A Welder

a Novel

Jim Brennan

This is a work of fiction and the names, characters, and incidents are products of the author's imagination, or are used fictitiously and are not to be construed as real. Certain long-standing institutions, agencies, and public offices are mentioned, but the characters and occurrences involved are wholly imaginary.

ISBN 978-1-946702-72-2

Copyright © 2023 by Jim Brennan

All Rights Reserved. No part of this book may be reproduced in any form or by any electronic or mechanical means including information storage and retrieval systems without permission in writing from the publisher, except by a reviewer, who may quote a brief passage in a review.

Published by Freeze Time Media

For Joanne

and

To the men and women who worked at the Philadelphia Naval Shipyard and all who labor in dangerous jobs on waterfronts around the world.

"All the good guys are dead."

Jimmy McKee

"I know you can take care of yourself, Jimmy, but these people are powerful, and ruthless. Be careful."

Jackie Reddi

"I am truth."

the homeless man

Once A Welder

Part I

The Waterfront

Chapter I

In for Life

July 1976
Philadelphia, Pennsylvania

Jimmy McKee folded over a handrail, heaving hot air and drool into a deep pit. His stomach churned from the stench of a blackish-yellow goo oozing around human bone. A boilermaker stood next to him, sobbing as smoldering remains were lifted from an escape trunk on the USS Belknap. What had been a nineteen-year-old painter less than fifteen minutes ago was a lifeless heap inside a metal bucket normally used to haul scrap, rusted valves, and trash.

A hand rested on Jimmy's shoulder. "You okay, buddy?"

The guy who guided him away from the horror wore the white hardhat of a foreman, though he looked much younger than other bosses in the shipyard. He sat Jimmy down inside the project management trailer on the pier, poured coffee into two Styrofoam cups and handed him one.

"Apprentice?" he asked.

"Second year," Jimmy replied, taking a cautious sip of the lukewarm coffee.

"Is this your first?"

"First what?"

"First person you saw killed in the shipyard."

"Yeah," he said, remembering back to orientation. He thought the safety pitch was a ploy to sell life insurance. Fifteen months ago, he didn't understand all the ways the body of a human being could be mutilated in a place where thousands of tons of steel were cut, forged, bent, and assembled into a tanker or destroyer.

"It's impossible to know the stories of all twelve thousand people who work down here," said the foreman in a reassuring tone. "But we're all connected." He paused to let Jimmy process his words. "Everything you do affects everyone else."

"Thanks," said Jimmy, not sure what he was thanking him for.

The foreman imparted bits of waterfront wisdom disguised as small talk then slid a thin booklet across his desk.

"Be safe out there," he said.

Feeling about as settled as he could after seeing death, Jimmy took a last sip of coffee. As he stood, he glanced at the cover of the booklet. In the short time since the foreman pulled him from the darkness, he didn't mention anything about religion.

"Thanks again," he said, slipped the booklet into his back pocket and left.

By the end of the day, Jimmy learned that the dead painter was a first-year apprentice named Charlie Dickinson. The following week, he recognized his picture in the Beacon, the shipyard newsletter, as the guy he once made a bet with on an Eagles game while they pissed in urinals next to each other in the shithouse. The article cited OSHA's preliminary investigation, which found that a hose used on the graveyard shift was never disconnected from a gas manifold and the valve had cracked open. Charlie climbed down a ladder that morning through invisible combustible gas, cigarette dangling from his lips, an open can of paint attached to his tool belt. He planned to paint a storage compartment. Instead, he became a fiery pool of flesh and tissue six decks down at the bottom of a four-by-four-foot escape trunk.

And you can't look away.

You can't look away because that's your brother at the bottom of the trunk, but it could be you. You don't smoke but Charlie does, and you could have been climbing down the ladder a deck below him and would have been covered with flammable paint inside a four-by-four steel trap filled with oxygen even before Charlie's burning body crashed into yours and took you with him. You have a stake in Charlie's death, and you have a stake in the pipefitter's negligence, because you are all from the same tribe, and when a tribal member burns to death, part of you dies with him.

~

Before Jimmy McKee's twenty-first birthday, he'd seen a man burnt to death, a rigger crushed by a propeller, and a fellow apprentice lose his left eye when a grinding wheel exploded in his face. He accepted exposure to carcinogens, hearing loss, impaired eyesight, and loss of life or limb as job hazards, nothing more. News reports about accidents, injuries, and deaths at the shipyard gave him street cred he couldn't have earned hanging out in corner bars in the sanitary white bubble of Mayfair, the blue-collar neighborhood in Northeast Philly where he grew up. He wore bruises and burns with pride and told friends how it felt to work underneath a ship resting on concrete keel blocks, looking up at thousands of tons of steel within inches of your head, imagining the concrete pulverize, and getting squashed like a bug.

Witness a death on the job, and one of two things happen: you either look for a new line of employment, or you're in for life, like the mafia. It's sacred being present as life drains from a co-worker, watching him gasp for one last breath before surrendering to the great unknown. It's also impossible to keep from envisioning yourself in their place, watching your own spirit drift from your body while your wife, kids, loved ones, or partner are at home, waiting for you to walk in the door.

Return to work after a coworker is killed, and you see things you never saw before. A two-ton pump suspended from a crane with wire cables seems precariously unstable as it passes overhead. Welds on high-pressure steam pipes look defective. You imagine a hint of acetylene in the air you breathe.

Working side-by-side with men in life-threatening conditions, relying day-in and day-out on the person next to you to secure a thousand-pound load or shut off a combustible gas valve, forges a bond that goes deeper than in other professions. Witnessing death forms a brotherhood, a family, a tribe. A tribe of boilermakers, pipefitters, and ironworkers who sustain lacerations, bruises, and amputations.

A tribe that embraces danger that would make most men shit themselves.

~

Jimmy seemed to remember that it rained the night of Charlie Dickinson's wake when it started to drizzle outside McKinley's Funeral Parlor on Girard Avenue. A guy with thick wrists and a beard too straggly to hide his baby face tilted his umbrella so Jimmy could duck underneath.

"What a way to go, huh?" he said, in a way that the sounded like he needed someone to talk to.

"Yeah," Jimmy agreed, and then more to himself, "but nothing like the painter who got killed on the Belknap."

"You saw him get killed too?" the guy asked, moving the umbrella to cover more of Jimmy's head.

Jimmy described the stench and gruesome image when they pulled Charlie out of the escape trunk three years ago in a way that made Mark Witherspoon's death seem rather ordinary. It was pure coincidence that Jimmy was working overtime the serene Sunday morning Mark was killed.

Or maybe it was fate.

It had just been a small crew of riggers, a few machinists, a crane operator, and a propeller suspended from a crane 150 feet above the dry dock floor. From the pier, the thirty-two-ton nickel-aluminum-bronze casting silently swaying a few inches in any direction was undetectable with the naked eye. But as the casting closed in on the hull of the sixty-thousand-ton ship, that undetectable sway was the difference between life and death for the thirty-eight-year-old rigger with five sons and a daughter he taught to bait a hook when she was three.

"It was a nightmare in slow motion," said Jimmy, sounding more like a veteran than a third-year apprentice.

The *Beacon* article memorialized Mark as a family man who coached Little League, but it didn't mention how safety-conscious he was on the job, or that he didn't make mistakes. There was nothing about the night shift worker who left the wheels unlocked on the portable staging the riggers used to maneuver the propeller into position. The staging rolled just enough to put Mark between the hull and the propeller as it swayed ever so slightly and crushed his chest against the side of the ship like a wafer. Mark's limp 230-pound body slid onto the twelve-inch planks twenty-five feet above the dry dock floor where he lay for twenty minutes while they lifted the propeller back to the pier and lowered a bucket to get him.

They rushed him to the hospital, but he never had a chance.

It was raining harder by the time Jimmy got to the door of the funeral home. The umbrella man waited for Jimmy to step inside before he folded the umbrella and followed him in. Jimmy stroked mist through his hair as he got in the next line, a drier line where he looked at photos of Mark's life: on the beach with his family on vacation, drinking in a pub with his buddies, fishing with his little girl. The little girl was here and looked the same, except now she stood with her arms around her mom's waist next to her father's casket. Jimmy didn't know her dad. He just happened to be in the same place when his life ended.

Jimmy thought he heard sniffling. When he turned around, umbrella man looked shaken.

"You know," said Jimmy, placing his hand gently on the man's back, "I've come to learn the best way to deal with these things is to accept death as a condition of employment."

Umbrella man stared at Jimmy like he'd handed him a precious gift, when all Jimmy did was share a hard lesson he'd learned on his own: how to survive another day working in a crucible and come out whole.

But Jimmy was naïve. He had only been exposed to tangible dangers, things he could see, smell, and touch. He had yet to learn about the more sinister perils of working on the waterfront, unimaginable hazards typically reserved for the underworld and white-collar criminals, with consequences that could change or even end lives.

Chapter II

HEART & SOUL

Jimmy's respect for ships bordered on reverence. He'd experienced an overwhelming awe the first time he descended into a dry dock, stood with his feet planted firmly on the concrete floor, and looked up at sixty-thousand tons of steel arching above like it was about to swallow him. Since then, he treated ships like they were living organisms, vessels that housed a crew of seamen and transported them from the shores of one continent to another, protecting them from storms violent enough to rip an entire city off the face of the earth.

And if a ship was a living, breathing organism, the boiler was its vital, beating heart. Without boilers, a ship was a hunk of metal driftwood.

Boilers fascinated Jimmy, and he made it his business to know as much about their construction and operation as the boilermakers, maybe more. One job in the rear of the boilers was particularly mysterious to him, and the longer he worked in the fire rooms, the more his curiosity grew. Nobody ever went near the job while it was in progress, which only heightened his fascination. He would wander behind the boiler near the end of the shift to watch the two welders working the job, men he had seen around but never met. They never showed up at morning muster when the boss handed out jobs. It was if they were assigned a covert mission. One of the welders they called Snake because his lanky build enabled him to contort into tight spaces. The other, a grandfatherly-looking man with silver hair, he found out later was named Chuck.

One day, Chuck lifted his shield after finishing a weld and caught Jimmy watching. "What's up, kid?"

"What are you working on?"

Chuck motioned with his head. "Come take a look."

As soon as Jimmy started climbing onto the staging erected behind the boiler, he felt heat radiating from the preheated metal. He looked inside one of a series of four-inch holes bored through the outside of a long, thick metal pipe. There were rows and rows of small tubes, hundreds of them. A perfectly symmetrical weld was on each tube in rows of four from the bottom of the pipe to where the guy had just welded, and from that point to the top the joints were open, requiring weld.

Jimmy pointed inside the hole. "What are those small pipes?"

"Superheater tubes. Each one carries twelve hundred pounds of steam."

Jimmy looked at the equipment he used—an extended welding rod holder, what welders called a "stinger," a pneumatic deburring tool and wire wheel. They were specialty tools not used for other welding jobs. "Looks complicated."

"Takes years to learn how to weld these things," Chuck said, "but if you're taught the right way and you persevere, you get it."

~

The firebox—a large brick-insulated compartment lined with rows of vertical tubes spaced inches apart carrying water heated by a fuel oil fire—was the raging, glowing soul of a boiler. When a boiler is in operation, a glass window on the side of the firebox provided a view of hell and damnation.

Feedwater entered the boiler at ambient temperature and was heated until it produced steam that spun turbine blades which in turn rotated propellers on the ends of long shafts and thrust tens of thousands of tons of steel through thousands of miles of ocean. Steam produced by the boilers drove pumps that generated electricity and circulated water and fuel. Saturated steam traveled into a superheater through an inlet header, then raged through hundreds of smaller chrome tubes before discharging through an outlet header as superheated steam. A rupture in any one of the hundreds of superheater tubes during a ship's operation would release enough energy to fry everything in a compartment the size of a two-story house. It would cut a human being in half.

Installing superheater tubes was an intricate process of setting a one-and-a-quarter-inch diameter tube inside a hole bored through a two-and-a-half-inch thick chromium header. The tube was then expanded with a rolling machine until it was tight against the inside of the hole. There were 256 superheater tube ends per header arranged in sixty-four rows of four and two headers per boiler for a total of 512 welded joints.

Boilermakers worked twelve-hour shifts around the clock installing superheater tubes. Once they finished, insulators wrapped the headers with induction heaters and insulated blankets, then preheated the metal. The preheat process was a precise science of incrementally raising the temperature of the metal until it reached four hundred degrees, then allowing the heat to saturate the headers for four hours before welding began. A reverse process was followed when welding was complete, slowly lowering the heat until it reached ambient temperature. Welders wore heat-resistant gloves and leather sleeves to protect their skin from serious burns.

Superheater tubes were configured in rows of four inside the header, a ten-foot vertical cylinder. Welders had to reach inside a four-inch diameter hole with a welding rod held with an elongated stinger—a custom-made tool that could reach the inside surface of the header—and pour molten metal from a ten-thousand-degree arc into a beveled tube joint. The finished welds were required to pass one hundred percent Non-Destructive Test or NDT inspection, a magnetic particle test that detected cracks and other defects, before the boilers were pressurized to twenty-two-hundred pounds per square inch during a hydrostatic test.

The welding process was rigid, and there could be no deviations. Welding under such repressive conditions twelve hours a day, seven days a week required a steady hand, concentration, stamina, and dedication. Each step had to be followed to exact specifications. Preheating was essential to eliminate moisture. Moisture in chromium steel caused cracks, cracks caused catastrophic failure, and catastrophic failure during boiler operations killed people. Boilermakers told stories about boiler explosions that spewed superheated steam across a fire room and scalded eight or ten or a dozen sailors to death.

Chapter III

BOILERMAKERS

Boilermakers were to the shipbuilding trades what boilers were to ships—essential, complex, powerful, and combustible. They were a breed that labored long and hard over decades to earn a reputation as crude, profane, hard-drinking brutes. It was a reputation in which they took tremendous pride. Ripping apart and reconstructing boilers was grimy, dusty, and hazardous grunt work, but boilermakers were indestructible. Falling debris, choking smoke, and oppressive heat couldn't deter them. In a trade best described as equal parts miner, rigger, ironworker, bouncer, and wildfire hotshot, they thrived inside fireboxes filled with mortar residue, and in thirty-inch diameter steel vessels preheated to hundreds of degrees. Chipping out brick with a pneumatic hammer in confined spaces required raw strength, steel nerves, concentration, stamina, perseverance, and care. The unrelenting hammering of metal against metal was deafening. There were no so-called *gravy jobs* dismantling and building boilers.

Alcohol was the boilermakers' medication, motivation, their kryptonite. Booze also sparked ingenuity, especially when they were devising ways to sneak beer onto the job. Fiberfrax, material used to insulate between tubes and brick, came in five-gallon buckets, the perfect size to fit two six-packs on ice when empty. Most afternoons it was a safe bet that for every two buckets of Fiberfrax carried down to the boiler room and passed inside the firebox, one was filled with beer. Non-boilermakers knew the unwritten rule for afternoons in the firebox: keep out.

Jimmy's relationship with boilermakers was inadvertent, then interchangeable, and finally, irreversible. It wasn't much different than handling a firearm: intimidating at first but becoming more familiar with time and experience. It started the day he was welding angle iron in the bilge and Doug Skate, a thin, unrefined, chain-smoking, cowboy-boot-wearing foreman boilermaker, coughed, "Hey, kid, could you tack a couple plates for me under the boiler?"

Jimmy climbed out, slid under the boiler and welded two plates that had been holding up the boilermakers' progress. Doug was impressed by the way he navigated the tight quarters with finesse and at the end of the shift asked Jimmy's boss if he could work with his men the next day, which stretched into the remainder of the week. Soon, Jimmy had a permanent assignment in the boiler rooms, and after only a few weeks, he was invited into the firebox for a Friday afternoon drinking session, the equivalent to being inducted into a secret society.

~

Jimmy became close friends with Vince Murphy, a wisecracking street corner guy from Southwest Philly. He was tall, had long brown hair, and a crafty smile: a lady-killer in an industrial jungle. He was good-natured and funny as hell, able to break up fights with a jibe that would have everybody laughing so hard the combatants would forget what they were fighting about. Vince was second-generation boilermaker. His father, who went by the name Old Man Murph, was a journeyman who always carried a thermos-full of coffee heavily spiked with Jameson and ran the biggest bookie operation in the shipyard.

On a sweltering August Saturday working overtime, Jimmy watched a wiry kid they called "Cajon" carry trays of brick and load them into the firebox. He was hauling metal bar stock up and down ladders and then shoving four-inch tubes into steam drums. At the end of the shift, Cajon rolled the sleeves of his soiled tee-shirt to his shoulders exposing fresh tattoos on muscular biceps, one a replica of Robert Indiana's LOVE sculpture, the other a pair of boxing gloves strung over a nail.

"You box?" asked Jimmy.

"Since I was eight." As if reading Jimmy's don't-bullshit-me expression, he added, "My dad started taking me to the gym when I was six. Managed me to a Golden Gloves championship when I was nineteen."

"So your old man's a boxer, too."

"He fought for the lightweight title in '59. Got screwed because he was a Jew."

"That sucks."

"Yeah, a little early for his time, I guess." Cajun grinned. "But I got the best manager in the world."

Jimmy respected that, the way he talked about his father. It gave him a good feeling, more like a good kind of hurt.

Chapter IV

SPECIALIST

Many considered Snake the best welder in the shipyard, but he was also a drinker and a womanizer. It was a miracle he made it to work some days, the way he'd stay out all night, showing up in the morning smelling of whiskey and then go on to lay perfectly uniform welds.

Snake's work was reliable, but the woman he picked up at a topless bar one night and took to a fleabag motel wasn't. He dozed off sometime before dawn, and she took his car keys, stranding him in the middle of the Jersey Pine Barrens with no way to get to work.

Chuck waited until nine o'clock, and when Snake didn't show, he went to the foremen trailer and told his boss he needed a partner. Colin Hanagan had supervised more superheater tube jobs than any foreman in the shipyard and knew that Snake and Chuck were the only two welders in the gang who were qualified. But Colin had a different way of looking at things than other supervisors. He had assigned Jimmy to difficult jobs as an apprentice, having him squeeze into confined spaces to weld electrical connectors that penetrated pressurized compartments. In Colin's mind, the job was training for welding superheater tubes.

"Take Jimmy McKee down and indoctrinate him on the job," he told Chuck.

Chuck liked the idea of a young apprentice taking such an interest in the job. He took time and care to explain to Jimmy the temperamental nature of chromium steel and gave him tips on things like how to angle the welding rod and weave it across the open joint in a circular motion to keep it from cascading. That afternoon, he let Jimmy weld his first joint, and then another.

When Snake returned the next morning and saw Jimmy behind the boiler welding, he yelled, "What the hell you doing on my job?"

"Easy, buddy," Chuck intervened. "I asked Colin for a partner when you didn't show up yesterday."

Snake stormed out of the fire room and up to the office ready for a battle, but Colin stood firm and explained that it was time to break in new blood. Jimmy remained on the job. Had any other foreman attempted such a move, Snake would have lodged a complaint with the superintendent, but nobody questioned Colin.

"I miss one goddamn day," Snake sulked, and went back down to the fire room.

Colin slipped Jimmy into the welding school the next week for a qualification test. He passed on his first attempt. Over the next several weeks Jimmy, Snake and Chuck alternated welding superheater tubes every row or two. Snake slowly accepted Jimmy, recognizing his talent and commitment.

It didn't take long for Jimmy to settle into the life as a specialist welder. He fashioned himself a surgeon, operating on boilers and restoring life to an ailing ship. After several weeks working twelve-hour shifts behind the boilers, he felt like he lived in a fire room. The stench of oil and rust was engrained into his skin and nostrils and seeped into his subconscious. Pneumatic grinding echoed in his brain. He saw thousands of tubes in his sleep and dreamt of the pains-taking slow and steady circular motion of a welding rod, the arc burning at ten thousand degrees fusing the end of the tube to the superheater header. He woke at four-thirty every morning for countless weeks, drove south on the dark, empty Schuylkill Expressway, descended back down into the fire room, walked behind the boiler and began welding another row of tubes. Hours went by as he welded row after row. Work and dreams converged.

~

Jimmy was officially a journeyman when he first crossed paths with a twenty-year old apprentice boilermaker named Tommy Homes. Tommy's loose strawberry locks and freckles gave him the appearance of an adolescent. A razorblade had never touched the milky skin of his face. But he had a thick neck and torso, the physique of a weightlifter, and he attacked his work as if he was fighting for his life. He labored with single-minded purpose that humiliated anyone working around him into pulling their own weight. He didn't trash-talk or curse, but he didn't take any shit from anyone, even Beast, the street corner thug from South Philly who was built like an M-1 tank and tormented anyone he didn't think respected him.

But the thing that set Tommy apart from his coworkers was the thing that impressed Jimmy the most: he wasn't a follower. He'd nurse a single beer while the other boilermakers pounded down six-packs in the firebox and crushed the empties on their forehead. They nicknamed him "One-beer Tommy," though nobody had the balls to call him that to his face. Tommy knew it and didn't give a shit. He'd stop at a dive bar with the gang after work and debate sports and local politics, just sipping that one beer while everyone else was raising hell. One time at the Tin Brick, a stevedore pub on Water Street, a boilermaker they called Clunk started throwing darts at dockworkers. A bouncer with a head the size of a steer evicted the whole gang. On the way out, Jimmy picked up Tommy's beer and shook it.

It was still full.

The day he met Tommy, Jimmy was setting up to weld superheater tubes when he overheard Doug Skate's whiskey-strained, antagonistic voice coming from inside the boiler. When he distinctly heard the word "daddy," he walked around the front of the boiler and stuck his head inside the firebox. Tommy had two fists-full of Doug's shirt with Doug jammed against the brick wall.

"You ever mention my old man again, I'll beat you're brains out," Tommy growled.

Doug looked to Jimmy for help.

"I didn't see nothing," said Jimmy, and pulled his head back out.

At the end of the shift, Tommy caught up with Jimmy in the parking lot and thanked him for backing him up.

"Like I said," remarked Jimmy, nonchalantly, "I didn't see nothing."

"No, I mean it. That could have been a problem for me if Doug decided to press the issue."

Jimmy shoved his hands in his pockets and looked off at the water tower at the far end of the parking lot, recalling the disdain he'd heard in Doug's voice, especially the irreverence in his tone when he said "daddy." It set off flashbacks of his own dad, a non-union roofer in Philadelphia during the 1960s, a job more dangerous than handling suspicious packages for the bomb squad. Non-union contractors were fed scraps from John McDuffy's table, the Roofer's Union president who controlled new construction and large commercial renovation contracts in the city. Jimmy was in fifth grade when a dilapidated building his dad was working on Market Street downtown collapsed. He clung to the belief that his father was alive the entire thirty-five hours it took to recover his body buried under debris.

Jimmy didn't see Tommy slam Doug into the brick boiler wall that day. He saw Tommy slam McDuffy against the wall, along with the courts, the lawyers and judges.

"Fuck Doug," said Jimmy.

~

Despite his age and their strained relationship, Doug trusted Tommy enough to lead jobs, and Doug didn't trust anyone. Tommy was his most reliable mechanic for installing boiler tubes, like the slugger a manager sent to the plate with the score tied in the bottom of the ninth with two out. For more than a year, Jimmy spent days and weeks side-by-side with him, going from ship to ship doing the most critical and tedious work on the waterfront. During that time, they became closer than soldiers in a foxhole waiting out a bombing. In the barren bowels of a ship, they shared stories and secrets they never told anyone else. On the surface they were an unlikely duo—Tommy, a newlywed with plans for a family, and Jimmy, single and more comfortable with a bunch of guys in a dingy saloon. But they were from the same stock, blue-collar to the core. Work ethic and decency bonded them, as well as their shared aversion to bullshit.

Though only four years separated the two, Tommy looked up to Jimmy like an older brother. He took his advice ever since the day he threatened Doug in the firebox and Jimmy had his back. Jimmy told him that day, "Don't respect anyone who doesn't earn your respect."

When the boilers on their second destroyer passed NDT and hydrostatic test with a ninety-nine percent acceptance rate, Jimmy and Tommy got the reputation as best welder/boiler-maker superheater tube team in the shipyard, a changing of the guard. On their next ship, the USS Mehan, they set a goal to pass inspections with zero defects—one hundred percent acceptance.

Chapter V

MAN VS. MACHINE

Welder specialist was the most secure job in the shipyard. Certainly more secure than any other trade, white-collar profession, and arguably even more stable than the shop superintendent. Welder specialists possessed the unique skills that ensured pipes carrying twelve hundred pounds of superheated steam didn't rupture and kill an entire crew and cause millions of dollars in damage. Absent their talent, the ship did not sail.

Three weeks into the USS Mehan overhaul, rumors began circulating about an automated welding process being tested on the boiler tubes of the USS Talbot, a frigate dry-docked on the other side of the shipyard. The rumors became more pervasive with time, the stories more improbable. Depending on the source, a process they called Maestro Fusion was anywhere from two to five times faster than manually welding the tubes.

Jimmy thought the stories were overblown, especially when he heard the new process substituted the standard preheat procedures with a two-minute preheat cycle.

"I'm no welding engineer," he told Tommy one day behind the boiler, "but the reason for preheating chromium is to prevent it from cracking. We wrap the headers in insulated blankets and preheat them to four hundred degrees for hours before we start welding." He pointed to the side of his head. "It doesn't make sense."

"What doesn't make sense to me is all the secrecy," said Tommy. "All we're hearing is rumors."

"You'd think the guys working the job were under a gag order or something."

Tommy got quiet, noticeably quiet, like he was holding something back. "I'll ask my old man," he finally said.

Jimmy stared at him. "What's he got to do with it?"

"He's the boilermaker superintendent."

"Your dad?" Jimmy had no idea that Skip Homes, the old school, no-nonsense, by-the-book boilermaker superintendent, was Tommy Homes, Sr. He wore a white shirt and tie to work every day, even days he boarded ship and toured the boiler rooms.

"That's why I got in that fight with Doug in the firebox."

Jimmy thought back to the day of the incident, the antagonistic *Daddy* taunt that initially caught his attention. "You never mentioned it before."

"I don't want to be known as the superintendent's kid," said Tommy. He left out the part about his strained relationship with his father, that whenever they talked shop, it turned into a screaming match. Nevertheless, Tommy was curious enough to ask him that night.

Half the morning passed the next day before Jimmy asked Tommy if he'd talked to his dad.

"Yeah," said Tommy. "He got all defensive when I asked him about the Maestro Fusion process. Stuck up for the Navy like he usually does." He paused, shifted gears. "But he told me a lot of shit I didn't know. He said the Talbot wasn't the first ship they tested the process on, and that Philadelphia was actually the third shipyard. They already used it in San Diego and Hawaii." Jimmy rolled his neck from side to side like a boxer loosening his shoulders before a fight. "According to the old man, if the Navy's successful in Philly, an east coast shipyard, they plan to write the process into the NAVSEA engineering manual and mandate it be used on all of their ships."

"Son of a bitch," Jimmy blurted, at the mention of NAVSEA. The Naval Sea Systems Command was responsible for delivering all ships to the Navy and had final say on any manufacturing processes. "The Navy wants to replace us with a machine." He felt the pressure of his livelihood being threatened, and imagined looking for a new line of work and starting all over again. "No wonder the assholes are keeping everything a secret."

"You know," said Tommy, in a reserved tone, "me and the old man been having these heated arguments lately. Almost came to blows not long ago when I accused him of being too loyal. I told him he was afraid to question his bosses, that he followed orders regardless the consequences, even if it hurt his men." He looked Jimmy in the eye. "He didn't come off that way talking about Maestro Fusion. He defended the Navy like I expected him to, but I got a sense his heart wasn't in it."

~

Jimmy graduated from his apprenticeship with a guy they called the Professor because he quit college one semester short of an engineering degree to work at the shipyard. The Professor had the reputation as an eccentric, always taking up causes nobody in Philadelphia ever heard of, like boycotting grapes in support of migrant farm laborers from California. The Professor was the only shipyard welder assigned to work on the Maestro Fusion job. He worked alongside shipyard engineers and company reps as well as metallurgists and engineers from NAVSEA headquarters in Washington.

After work on Friday afternoon, Jimmy waited for him at the end of the caisson at Dry Dock #4 where anyone working on the other side of the shipyard would have to pass to get to the parking lot. He spotted the Professor among a crowd funneling across and watched him duck into the scrum pretending not to see him.

"Hey, Professor," Jimmy shouted, too loud for him to ignore.

"Jimmy," said the Professor. "Long time, no see."

Jimmy sidled up to him. "Walk with me," he said, giving him no alternative. "What are you working on?"

The Professor was illusive, so Jimmy got specific and asked about the Maestro Fusion process. The Professor gave short, cryptic answers, and the more Jimmy pressed him, the more evasive he became.

"What's with you, Francis?" said Jimmy, knowing the Professor hated his given name.

"What do you mean?" asked the Professor.

Jimmy leaned close to his face. "How does the Maestro Fusion machine weld in a few minutes what it takes fifteen, twenty minutes to weld manually? And how the hell does it preheat a two-and-a-half-inch thick chromium header with a two-minute preheat cycle?"

For a man who prided himself in spewing long explanations full of technical jargon, the Professor didn't have a coherent answer. Jimmy stared at him, determined to wait him out. Avoiding eye contact, the Professor finally said, "Ask the engineers."

"That's it?" said Jimmy. "You're telling me to ask the engineers?" He scowled at the Professor the way Ali glared at Sonny Liston after he knocked him to the canvas.

"Traitor," Jimmy muttered.

~

The job on the Mehan rolled into another weekend, four twelve-hour shifts. Mid-morning on Monday, George Sputz wandered around behind the boiler. George, a forty-something welding engineer who sported plaid shirts, a tie, a pocket protector, and nerdy glasses that slid down his nose when he performed inspections, was the guy who oversaw and provided guidance for welding processes on high-pressure systems. He acted as liaison between the head of the shipyard metallurgy and welding engineering department, and NAVSEA engineers. The boilermakers mostly ignored the tall, lanky techie, except Vince Murphy who did dorky impersonations of the way George addressed guys working in the fire room saying, "How goes it?" George would laugh along with the joke, genuinely, as if Vince was the funniest person in his otherwise serious life.

Jimmy lifted his welding shield, saw George, and smiled. He'd befriended the engineer years ago after seeing through his nerdiness. He considered him an honest, misplaced, authentic gentleman. In return, George explained complex engineering and metallurgical phenomena in terms Jimmy could comprehend. Consequently, Jimmy understood the theory behind filler metals, welding arcs and the effect of environmental conditions that other welders couldn't care less about. George became sort of a mentor to him.

"Where you been hiding, stranger?" Jimmy said.

"On the Talbot," said George.

Jimmy raised his head. "The Talbot, huh?"

"Yeah, they're testing a new welding process."

"I've heard," said Jimmy. "Maestro Fusion." He paused, sensing an opportunity. "Well, here's my theory," he continued, and described the elaborate preheating and welding process he had followed for as long as he'd been welding superheater tubes.

"You sound like an engineer," George remarked.

"You taught me well," said Jimmy, then eyed George closely. "So tell me how this automated process circumvents such a complex preheat process without cracking the tubes?"

George didn't answer right away, and when he did, he looked uncomfortable. "It doesn't circumvent it. It replaces it with an abbreviated process."

"An abbreviated process?" said Jimmy. "How about you explain this abbreviated process to me."

George started to describe how the robotic machine made two sixty-second revolutions with the electric arc to heat the metal, then he began to stammer before breaking into academic mumbo-jumbo about formulas and equations that wasn't convincing anyone. Jimmy was irritated at George's attempt to defend the process, but at the same time he felt sorry for putting him in an awkward position.

"George," he interrupted. "Stop it."

"Look, Jimmy. This thing's being directed by NAVSEA in Washington. I'm not happy with it. And I know Mr. Strunk isn't either."

Joseph Strunk, George's boss, was a legend in the shipyard, a throwback from the World War II era. Some people didn't think he really existed because the only time he ventured outside the lab where he wrote procedures and conducted tests was when he was summoned to the shipyard commander's office. Nobody had ever seen him on a ship. George was Mr. Strunk's eyes and ears, his agent and ambassador. Strunk wrote the processes, directives, and instructions, and George implemented them. Jimmy got to know Mr. Strunk when he was on a four-week appointment in the metallurgy lab during his apprenticeship. The top metallurgist and welding engineer in the shipyard took a liking to Jimmy. He seemed to appreciate the way Jimmy questioned him and gave him unsolicited opinions. He told Jimmy to call him Joey while the engineers, even the supervisors who worked for him, addressed him as Mr. Strunk.

Jimmy knew everything George told him was bullshit, because he knew Mr. Strunk wouldn't authorize a welding process that could jeopardize the shipyard's reputation, or its survival.

Chapter VI

AUTONOMY

Shipbuilding had been a fixture on the Philadelphia waterfront since the nineteenth century, the hammerhead crane a landmark in South Philly since its completion in 1919. Locals who knew nothing about the shipyard would point at the three-hundred-fifty ton capacity crane from halfway up Broad Street and talk about it like it was a favorite relative. Airline pilots used it as a navigational landmark to guide them to the runways of Philadelphia International Airport. A journeyman shipwright they called Samurai Sammy stood on the flight deck of an aircraft carrier each day at lunch waving homemade orange wands, convinced that planes would wind up in the Delaware River if they missed his directions.

Arched above the shipyard entrance between two brick columns at the foot of Broad Street, *The Navy Yard* was wrought in eighteen-inch iron letters. To Jimmy it wouldn't have mattered if it read "Military Factory" or "Admiralty." Ships were ships, huge steel vessels with boilers and engines and reduction gears and propellers, and shipyards were places where skilled tradesmen built and overhauled the mammoth structures. He never gave the Secretary of the Navy's signature on his paycheck a second thought.

Until the day during his apprenticeship when he was climbing out of the water drum on the lower level of a fire room, and someone said, "Hey, kid, weld this."

Lying on his back on the deck plates, all Jimmy could see was a bulbous belly about to burst out of a blue button-up navy shirt. He pushed himself onto his feet and came face-to-face with a bald five-foot-five, grease-covered sailor.

"What?" Jimmy said, unsure what the man was referring to.

The guy raised his hands. One held an angle iron, the other clutched a valve handle.

"I said 'weld this.'" He lifted his fat arm and pointed to a stripe on his shirtsleeve indicating his rank like he was showing off his first tattoo.

The stripe meant nothing to Jimmy, who could feel his face getting warm. "Are you asking or telling?"

"I'm ordering."

"Then go fuck yourself," said Jimmy.

The sailor's face swelled. "I'm gonna report your ass to your boss," he shouted.

Jimmy had no time for politics, positions, or titles. He judged people by how hard they worked, what they contributed to the job. In his mind, a trainee who finished twenty feet of carbon steel weld in a shift had more value than a shop instructor or a captain. The Navy might have been his employer, but the shipyard commander and military hierarchy were just people to him. They had their job, and he had his. He gave one hundred percent every day. His conscious was clear.

Jimmy leaned close to the sailor's face, and said, "You can tell the president for all I care."

The sailor stumbled backward into the front wall of the boiler, then turned and ran up the ladder.

Jimmy remembered the feeling of autonomy he had that day. He was a yardbird, the fabled nickname shipyard workers had adopted decades ago, and proud of it.

~

It was a wonder that a kid who grew up in Forksville, Pennsylvania, two hundred miles from an ocean with a population one hundred and forty, would join the Navy. The largest body of water Boiler Technician Louis Robert Smitt had ever seen was the Delaware River when he hiked the Appalachian Trail the summer of his junior year in high school. Hiking was his escape from a dysfunctional childhood. He was a timid kid who'd jump at loud noises and instinctively raised his hands when his foster father yelled because oftentimes it was accompanied by a beating. After a school nurse found bruises covering his body, he was placed in the care of a second foster family, but wished he was back at his first home once the sexual abuse started.

Smitt grew to hate the name Louis because that's what his perv foster father called him when he came home drunk late at night and wandered into his bedroom looking for some gratification. He retreated into books. He'd take gadgets apart and reengineer them to be more efficient or something completely different. Not long after his twelfth birthday, he was rescued by a big-hearted man everyone in town called Griz who showed up in court and saved him from going to the youth detention center. Griz discovered the young man had a sharp and inquisitive mind. He just needed purpose in life.

Smitt found that purpose the day he graduated from high school and walked into the Navy recruiting office and took an oath to serve God and country.

Jimmy had stayed clear of sailors after his run-in with the fat man in the fire room, but he couldn't ignore the boilermakers the day they were making fun of Smitt's speech. It started with one of them impersonating the kid's long, drawn out words, then more chimed in.

"Yo," yelled Jimmy, and threw them a hard look. The guys shut up and he thought that was that.

His impression of Smitt as a meek, defenseless kid changed when Beast called him a faggot. Instead of wallowing in intimidation, the insult short-circuited a switch inside the kid's brain. In deliberate, measured words, he said, "Call me that again, and I'll fillet the skin off your balls and stick it down your throat."

Beast exploded toward Smitt but Tommy reached out and horse-collared him at the same time the kid pulled a blade that defied the physics of fitting into a pant pocket.

Smitt nodded at Beast, and in a calm, menacing tone said, "You be right sure I will."

Beast looked between the kid's thirsty eyes and the blade he rotated between his nimble fingers like it was an extension of his hand, its sharpened edge gleaming in an overhead light. Beast glowered at the young boiler tech, and when Tommy let him go, he walked away.

The strangest thing about the encounter was that a navy officer watched the entire confrontation from the control room window and made no move to intervene. Commander Bradley Stevens was a well-schooled man, earned a master's degree in the leadership program at Georgetown University, and then coasted through assignments onboard ship doing just enough to get by. He punched the ticket, as he liked to say. Other officers despised him because of his quick ascent through the ranks, but he was so steeped in affluence and spoils that he was immune to inhibition. Nobody respected him after rumors circulated about the nepotism behind his stature. If such rumors were true, being on the wrong side of Stevens would be a career ender. At his core, he was a coward and used his authority as a defensive mechanism. He was quick to smack down anyone who questioned his authority or showed resentment of his position, whether it was real or imagined.

To compensate for lack of character and technical experience, he used people, and after seeing the way Smitt handled himself with the much bigger boilermaker, Stevens thought there might someday be a roll he could play. Sort of an insurance policy. At the end of the day, he called Smitt aside.

"Yes, sir," said Smitt.

"That incident you had with the boilermaker this morning."

"Yes, sir," he said, defensively. "I can explain…"

"No explaining necessary," said Commander Stevens. "I liked the way you handled it."

Smitt looked confused that a commander in the United States Navy would approve of him pulling a knife on a civilian. "Thank you, sir. I had to defend my honor."

"Honor's important to you, huh?" asked Stevens, seemingly impressed hearing the young man talk about values with such conviction.

"The most important thing in the world, sir. That and patriotism. I couldn't live with myself without honor and patriotism."

"I like that," said Stevens, while reading at the name printed on the breast of his shirt and looking at the stripe on his sleeve. "I like that a lot, Third Class Smitt."

Chapter VII

SLEP

One hundred forty miles south of the shipyard, a protracted battle was playing out on Capitol Hill between Senator Marlon Hawkins from Pennsylvania and the Virginia delegation. At issue was a five-hundred-million-dollar contract for the Service Life Extension Program or SLEP on the USS Saratoga. The overhaul was scheduled for twenty-eight months, and the winner would be assured the three follow-on SLEP overhauls, equating to almost a decade of work. The contract would have a huge economic impact, ultimately pumping millions of dollars into the economy of either Philadelphia or Norfolk.

Lobbyists roamed the hallways on Capitol Hill, pressing Congress for funding and contracts to place their constituents' systems on ships. Across the Potomac River and a three-minute drive south from the Pentagon, corporate salesmen in tailored suits and buffed loafers worked the Crystal City offices at NAVSEA headquarters, convincing program managers the systems produced by their defense contractors were the most lethal and cost effective. It was a grand escapade of wining and dining senators, congressmen, admirals and captains at exclusive five-star restaurants, on lush fairways of exclusive country clubs, or in waterfront condos in the Caribbean, before whipping out the ten-karat-gold Cross pen to sign on the fine line of a multi-million-dollar contract for this electronic suite, that high-frequency radar, or these main steam turbines. Place your John Hancock right here for an automated superheater tube welding contract that will save the Navy tens of millions of dollars per ship.

It didn't matter that the Navy was planning to transition to a nuclear-powered aircraft carrier fleet, or there were still conventional aircraft carriers that would remain active for decades and require regular overhauls to maintain readiness. Program managers were eager to evaluate cost reduction proposals to keep conventional ships in the fleet for as long as practicable. The highest return on investment system for savings were the boilers, the beating heart of the ship.

And nobody knew that better than Admiral Lawrence Foley.

Admiral Foley was the senior military officer in Navy acquisition and one of the most influential voices in the defense acquisition community. His fights with the Senate Arms Service Committee over funding to field the V-22 Program were legendary, and he alone was credited with saving the program.

Five years before his distinguished military career would come to an end, the admiral shifted his attention to a civilian career by cultivating a relationship with Johnny Neumann, former Secretary of the Navy, who had retired and started a company he named Maestro Fusion Corporation. The company designed and manufactured advanced technology robotic welding machines. They had pioneered a revolutionary automated process for welding high-pressure piping systems, the most sophisticated of which was for superheater tubes. The process had proven successful on ships in the warm climates of Hawaii and San Diego, where the sun always shined and the daytime temperature rarely dipped below seventy degrees. The company's recent success welding boiler tubes on two destroyers at an east coast shipyard was part of Admiral Foley's plan to update the NAVSEA engineering manual and mandate the process be used on all its vessels. But the sitting Navy Secretary insisted on completing boilers on an aircraft carrier on the east coast first, as irrefutable proof.

Foley was on first name basis with many lawmakers on the Hill from years of testifying on Navy acquisition programs. He was shrewd, a detail man who always did his homework. He knew that Johnny Neumann was a native Philadelphian, and lobbied Congress to award the SLEP program to the Navy Yard. Before the Navy's decision and after a round of golf at the Arlington Army Navy Country Club, the admiral shared his vision with Neumann.

"I'm laying the groundwork for the Saratoga overhaul to be done in Philadelphia, Mr. Secretary," said Foley. Watching Neumann's eyebrows arch, he plowed forward. "This is the opportunity of a lifetime for your company. If the Maestro Fusion process is successful on an aircraft carrier, as I'm sure it will be, NAVSEA will have no alternative but to write the robotic welding process into the engineering manual."

"I don't know, Larry," said Neumann. "Philly's not Hawaii. We're still a year or two away from adapting the process for temperate climates." He looked at Foley. "Have you ever been to an Army-Navy game in Philly? It snowed last year."

The admiral had run the plan through his head so many times that he recited it with total conviction. "I've seen to it that the boiler work is scheduled to be done in the summer. All we have to do is get one ship under our belt on the east coast to prove the process will work anywhere on the globe. That'll give your tech folks time to come up with a solution for the preheat issues. By the time the Forrestal arrives in a few years it'll be documented in the NAVSEA engineering manual."

"Too risky, Larry," the former Secretary responded. "You know there's always unforeseen problems that come up in a complex overhaul like the Saratoga. If the job runs into November or December, we'd be screwed." He paused, then added, "I'm not putting the company's reputation on the line."

"Trust me, Mr. Secretary," Foley said. "The company's reputation won't come into question. I guarantee it."

Neumann gave Foley the steely look of a man who once commanded the Navy. "Tell me how you can guarantee it, Admiral."

"Listen, Mr. Secretary," Foley began, and went into a pitch he'd been rehearsing for years. If the overhaul extended into the winter months, he'd have industrial size space heaters strategically placed in the boiler rooms to simulate conditions in Southern California. Then he went into the details, describing the eight boilers on the Saratoga like the Secretary had never set foot on a ship—two boilers in each of the four fire rooms, 512 superheater tube joints welded on each boiler for a total of 2,048 tube ends in the forward, or FWD, fire rooms which would be welded using the traditional manual method by hand. That would leave the 2,048 tube ends in the aft, or AFT, fire rooms to be welded with the robotic welding machine. Foley would have NAVSEA engineers collect and analyze cost, schedule, and test data to document the superior quality and cost savings of the automated Maestro Fusion process.

"Once the Navy sees millions of dollars in savings," Foley concluded, "they'll be compelled to amend the engineering manuals and mandate that Maestro Fusion be used on all future contracts for ship construction and overhaul."

Foley watched Neumann as if he could hear the *cha-ching cha-ching* of millions of dollars in revenue calculating in his head.

"At a cost of seven and a half million dollars per boiler," said Foley, "the company will make thirty million dollars for the Saratoga's four boilers. On future SLEP contracts, Maestro Fusion Corporation will earn sixty million for all eight boilers."

"And you guarantee everything will run smoothly," said Neumann.

"Just leave it to me, Mr. Secretary."

The decision to award the Saratoga boiler contract to Maestro Fusion Corporation was the first step in Admiral Lawrence Foley's grand scheme. Step two was to amend the NAVSEA engineering manual to mandate the Maestro Fusion welding process be used on all Navy boilers. The third and final step, Foley would line up the future SLEP contracts in exchange for the Chief Operations Officer job at Maestro Fusion Corporation after he retired.

~

Jimmy's contempt for authority, especially for men in high positions who used the workingman as pawns in their thirst for power and wealth, was rooted in the loss of his father at such an early age. Union bosses didn't intimidate him. Neither did sailors with stripes on their sleeves or flag officers. Jimmy held John McDuffy, President of the Roofer's Local, responsible for burying his dad under tons of debris while working on a dilapidated building that collapsed in downtown Philly. He'd never met McDuffy, but knew he was a thug from newspaper articles he'd read about his extortion and strong-arm tactics, like when he ordered hundreds of his men to firebomb the Valley Forge Sheraton Hotel construction site being built by a non-union contactor.

Jimmy felt no remorse when he heard that a hit man posing as a flower deliveryman walked into McDuffy's house around Christmastime and splattered his brains all over his white kitchen wallpaper while his wife watched.

Instead, he felt a sense of justice.

Chapter VIII

THE RECRUITS

T he year 1980 was a seminal one for the city of Philadelphia: The Eagles went to the Super Bowl, the Sixers went to the NBA finals, and the shipyard embarked on the four-hundred-million-dollar SLEP overhaul of the Saratoga. Thousands of journeymen and trainees were hired, and the apprenticeship program was revitalized. For the first time since Rosy the Welder worked at the shipyard supporting the war effort for World War II when employment rolls topped 40,000, women were hired in modest numbers, adding diversity to the skilled trades. Bakers were hired as sheet metal mechanics, barbers and hairdressers took on work as pipefitters, and laborers toiling in scrapyards along Passyunk Avenue became ship fitters, boilermakers, and welders. They succeeded by applying their indigenous blue-collar work ethic to their new environment.

The shipyard ramped up technical and support professions as well. There was a need for instructors to train the new employees who'd never been onboard a ship, plus endless calls for more planners, schedulers, inspectors, and managers. Job announcements were released for promotion opportunities in numbers nobody had seen since the war.

The Saratoga spent its first year at the Navy Yard under the scalpel of welder's torches, getting ripped apart in the dry dock. Large access holes were cut into its shell to remove equipment that was either scrapped or sent out to manufacturers for overhaul or upgrade. The workforce grew to nearly twelve thousand, the highest level it had been in decades. On year two of the twenty-eight-month overhaul, the carrier finally started to come back together.

~

At the beginning of a twelve-hour shift, the only sounds heard onboard ship were like the murmurs of a slumbering beast: the hiss of leaking air manifolds, water or fuel rushing through piping systems and discharging into the bilge, random thrumming from a job five hundred feet away, and the natural yawn of sixty-thousand tons of steel expanding and contracting with the temperature. Graveyard shift workers were still tucked inside alcoves, stealing some shuteye. The ship wouldn't come alive until day shift workers arrived.

Jimmy was setting up his gear on the lower level when he heard footsteps on the stainless-steel grates above. He looked up and saw Kenny Essington climb scaffolding into the overhead and begin to weld a twelve-inch pipe joint. In this peaceful time of day, he thought back to his first encounter with Kenny when the young, lean guy with skin the color of an eight-ball barged into morning muster and unleashed a tirade on the foreman, Harry Gillis, about a white shipyard run by white bosses. He glared at Harry like he was trying to disintegrate him with concentration while accusing him of being part of the white conspiracy that never gave a black man an opportunity. Harry was an old timer, experienced, smooth and unshakable, and as he defused the tension with his calm, Kenny's lips parted, exposing gleaming white teeth and a smile Jimmy felt from the other side of the compartment. Kenny's theatrics worked; he was now up on the scaffolding welding X-ray quality pipe.

Guys who worked the regular eight-hour shift would be funneling down the ladder pretty soon. It would get loud, hectic. Jimmy put down his gear, climbed up into the overhead, and when Kenny lifted his welding shield, his eyes widened, surprised to see someone inches away.

Jimmy patted the pipe, and said, "Twelve hundred pounds of main steam. A pinhole leak will cut a man in half. Failure during operation could cook a fire room full of sailors like steamed shrimp."

Kenny's eyes were deep and serious. "You're the first person who ever explained to me how critical this work is."

"You haven't been working with the right people," said Jimmy, and went on to tell him that he'd been teamed up with some of the best welders in the shipyard when he was an apprentice. As he talked, he realized the opportunity he'd been given being teamed up with Chuck and Snake at such an early age.

And there wasn't one black superheater tube welder in the shipyard.

~

Boiler Tech Louis Smitt had been transferred to the Saratoga shortly after it arrived in Philly. He hoped to stay with the carrier after it was re-commissioned and went out to sea so he could be part of a team operating the boilers and troubleshooting problems. He spent his days climbing in and out of fireboxes, superheater cavities, water and steam drums, but mostly he kept to himself. Nobody bothered with him, and it seemed none of the other sailors even knew his name.

One morning Kenny was watching him loop a rope around heavy valves, tie knots and lower them to the deck below.

"Hey, brother," he said, "you're a magician with a rope?"

Smitt looked over at him. "Just something I picked up hunting and camping back home," he said. He looked at his hands, and lowered his voice, adding, "Knowin' your knots comes in handy, bein' a boiler tech."

"Being a what?" asked Kenny.

"A boiler tech. That's sailor language for boilermaker. We operate the boilers out at sea. Do repairs and stuff." Smitt mindlessly spun a single bowline. "Can't tie no bow knot like you do with your shoes when you're securing a two-hun-dred-pound valve in the overhead. Thing falls it'll crush your head like a melon."

"Can't argue with that," said Kenny.

It was an unlikely conversation between a young guy from the streets of North Philly and an unworldly kid from Forks-ville, Pennsylvania. Louis confided in Kenny, told him he was dyslexic and that sailors made fun of him because he talked slow and stuttered. They called him a hick.

His expression turned serious, and he said, "Me and you. We're more alike than I thought, I guess."

"What do you mean?" asked Kenny.

"People treat you different because of the way you look. People treat me different because of the way I talk."

Kenny stuck out his arm next to Louis's. "Yeah," he laughed, "it's funny how alike we are."

Smitt opened up to Kenny more than he had with anyone he'd ever known, except for the man he called Griz. He told Kenny how he started working on cars when he was eight years old, dropped out of high school after his junior year to work in a garage, and became a master mechanic. Smitt loved cars and would go on and on about his 1968 Dodge Charger that he dropped a 440 engine into, painted black and took first place in competitions at Beaver Springs Dragway.

~

"I don't want those guys using the Maestro Fusion machine getting too far ahead of us," said Colin, "so I'm gonna make two teams to weld superheater tubes on the forward fire room boilers."

"You think we can keep up with four guys welding?" asked Jimmy.

"Not the way they're talking. But I'm thinking they're going to run into problems when it comes time for inspection."

Jimmy probed his boss' expression. "Cracks?"

Colin nodded.

"So who do you plan to recruit?"

"I'm going to team you up with Chuck, and Snake with Denny Yorko.

"They should be able to keep up," said Jimmy, and restraining a smile, added, "if they can stay sober."

Denny was a younger version Snake, excellent welder but unpredictable once he got drinking. Also like Snake, he was an enigma, a drunk with the concentration and eye-hand coordination required to weld superheater tubes. He'd stumble to work stinking like a beer-soaked barroom floor, then weld for twelve hours. Every weld would pass one hundred percent NDT.

Jimmy lobbied Colin to break in Kenny welding superheater tubes as an insurance policy in case Denny went on a drunk and disappeared for a few days. Colin rubbed his chin hard like he was trying to remove a layer of skin, looked Jimmy square in the eyes, and said, "Good idea."

When Jimmy broke the news to Snake, he made a face like he'd just ingested rat piss.

"I'm not working with that spook," he said.

"I'm going to pretend you didn't say that," said Jimmy.

"Do all the pretending you want. I'm not working with him."

"Nobody said you have to," said Jimmy. "He'll work with me."

"What, are you auditioning to be a social justice activist?"

Jimmy let the comment settle. "Name one black guy welding boiler tubes, Snake."

"That's because none of 'em have any talent," Snake shot back.

"That's bullshit," said Jimmy.

"If you want to give some black guy a chance, why him?" asked Snake. "The guy's got an attitude. He's rebellious. Everyone in the shipyard knows about the shit he pulled on Harry."

"Yeah," said Jimmy, coming right back at him, "and now he's a damn good X-ray pipe welder."

Snake seemed worn down from the argument.

"He's not a bad guy, Snake. Really."

Snake stared at Jimmy for a long time, before he said, "I don't care what you do, just don't drag me in on it."

"Don't worry. This is on me."

~

Not a business on earth could increase employment by three hundred percent and not experience growing pains, especially a complex operation like shipbuilding. Taking bakers and cops and hot dog vendors off the street and training them to be pipefitters and welders and boilermakers was a feat that rivaled raising the dead, or at least making the lame walk. Production superintendents anticipated schedule slippages. Schedulers planned workarounds to alleviate their impact, while foremen dealt with contingencies.

Admiral Foley refused to accept any deviation in the schedule. He was a tyrant. He'd fly up from Washington, storm into the shipyard commander's office and threaten him with demotion if his aircraft carrier missed a schedule date by a single day. He was furious when the superheater headers manufactured by Babcock & Wilcox arrived at the shipyard in August instead of June. It took two weeks to install them onboard ship, and six weeks to fit and roll the superheater tubes. He was a madman waiting for welding to begin.

Chapter IX

THE STAKES

In wintertime, yardbirds called the waterfront the tundra. During prolonged sub-freezing temperatures, the Delaware River froze over, double-digit inches of snow weren't unusual, and cars refused to start. Gusting winds made crane lifts dangerous, machinery and older workers broke down, their insulated clothing keeping them warm for only so long. Some laborers broke wooden pallets and fed them into empty fifty-five-gallon drums to keep fires blazing to combat sub-zero temperatures. Clouds of hot breath preceded workers, moist skin stuck to frozen metal. Snow, sleet, rain, and daylight ceased to exist below the hanger deck of the Saratoga. Lifeless in the bottom of the dry dock the ship sat like a beached whale, its belly a steel icebox.

The stakes were high when it came to welding boiler tubes on the Saratoga. It would be the first time shipyard welders competed head-to-head with robotic welding technology. If the robot was successful in the frigid east coast weather, the Navy would update the engineering manuals and mandate the Maestro Fusion process be used on all future ships. The most prestigious welding job in the shipyard would cease to exist. Experienced welders with families and kids in school, and who coached Little League would be sent out to pasture by a robot.

For Admiral Lawrence Foley, the stakes were even higher. He'd convinced his boss, the Secretary of the Navy, that the automated process would reduce the welding time by more than 50 percent, saving tens of millions of dollars. And he guaranteed Johnny Neumann, the former Secretary, that he would simulate climate conditions of Hawaii and San Diego in the AFT fire rooms so the Maestro Fusion process would work flawlessly.

"After the success of the job," he promised Neumann, "a steady stream of multi-million-dollar contracts will flow to Maestro Fusion Corporation."

In the admiral's own mind, it all translated to six-figure bonuses to the man who engineered the coup and retired to become the company's Chief Operations Officer.

~

Insulators worked feverishly in the FWD fire rooms, wrapping the chrome superheater headers for welding. While the headers were being brought up to four hundred degrees, Kenny helped Jimmy run welding lines, install heating canisters to keep the welding rods dry, and set up staging to reach the upper rows of tubes.

Back AFT, the Professor worked with Maestro Fusion Corporation engineers and NAVSEA tech reps, ensuring procedures were followed in preparation for the robotic welding machine. They watched boilermakers polish each tube until inspectors could see their reflection in the finish, and they measured each joint to make sure they fit within thousandths of an inch toler-ance. It took more time than the company estimated to install the space heaters, sanitize the headers, and fit the joints so the sophisticated equipment would operate properly.

As November wore on, temperatures dropped to record lows. The Thanksgiving Day Parade marked the first snowfall in Philadelphia that year. Welding began in the FWD boiler rooms the following Monday. The Professor began with the Maestro Fusion process four days later. The admiral was enraged.

~

Old Man Murph started a pool, placing odds on which process would finish first, the date they'd finish, number of NDT failures, and how many tubes would leak during hydrostatic test. He assigned odds to each boiler: two each in Fire Room #1 and Fire Room #2 that would be welded manually, and two each in Fire Room #3 and Fire Room #4 welded using the Maestro Fusion robotic welder. He created over-and-under bets that Maestro Fusion would finish two days, one week, or two weeks before manual welding. The smart money was on the automated process to finish first, but more money was placed on the manual process than expected.

Old Man Murph explained the disparity this way: Philly was the city of underdogs, where Eagles' fans would bet on the home team even if they were on the downside of 50-1 odds. Money shifted so often that Murph had to adjust the odds daily.

As information dribbled out of the fire rooms, more money poured in. It took only one week to complete boiler 3A with the Maestro Fusion process. Jimmy and Chuck hadn't completed half of boiler 1A, and Snake and Denny trailed slightly behind on boiler 1B. The Professor had a jump on boiler 3B before the boilers in Fire Room #1 reached the halfway point. Everybody wanted a piece of the action, which had grown into thousands of dollars. Old Man Murph set the cutoff for taking bets when welding began in Fire Room #4.

With about a dozen rows remaining on the boilers in Fire Room #1, Jimmy ordered that the boilers in Fire Room #2 be preheated so there wouldn't be any delays. Colin stepped back and let Jimmy take charge, which psyched up his teammates.

Word spread that the boilers in the AFT Fire Rooms had completed before the boilers in Fire Room #2 reached the midway point. Quality Assurance, or QA inspectors, began NDT in Fire Room #3.

More than twenty rows still remained to be welded on both boilers in Fire Room #2.

Melancholy pervaded the workforce, as if they were witnessing the death of a way of life. Jimmy ignored the pessimism, ordering Chuck and Snake to keep their heads up and weld. Denny followed their lead. Jimmy made a calculated move and added Kenny to the mix.

Everything got quiet as NDT inspections progressed on boiler 3A. The glowing stories about the robotic welding process slowed down for the first time since the job began. Progress reports from back AFT dried up. Old Man Murph couldn't get updates for his gambling operation. Jimmy used the silence as motivation, figuring if Maestro Fusion machine was going well, progress reports would be leaking out like water from a cracked dike, but now that the reports had dried up, something had to be going wrong.

Jimmy alternated with Kenny welding tubes in the final rows of boiler 2A, and eventually set Kenny loose on his own. He observed from a distance, analyzing Kenny's demeanor, how confident he looked. He seemed completely unintimidated by the job.

When he finished a row, he turned to Jimmy, and said, "You're up."

Jimmy leaned in and looked at his welds, shook his head, and said, "You're good. Keep going."

Later in the afternoon, Chuck lifted his welding shield, and said, "Finished." He was surprised when he turned and saw Kenny on the staging across from him.

"I'm on the last row," Kenny reported.

Chuck looked down at Jimmy who shrugged and said, "I'll get the boilermakers to lower the heat, and then run up and tell Colin to call the inspectors to get ready to NDT."

Momentum shifted once inspections began in Fire Room #1. Boiler 1A flew through NDT with no defects, and when the inspectors started boiler 1B, rumors began circulating about cracks in the tube welds back AFT. By the time the inspectors completed 2A, there was talk about preheating the AFT super-heater headers and doing manual welding repairs.

Boilermakers hooked up air and water hoses for the hydro-static test in Fire Rooms #1 and #2. The Hydro pumps chugged and strained pressurizing the FWD boilers, and when the gage reached twenty-two-hundred psi the inspectors found no leaks.

Old Man Murph paid the guys who placed money on the underdogs. Jimmy made a killing.

~

Weld repairs in the AFT fire rooms finished a week after the FWD boilers passed inspection, but when they were pressurized for hydros, leaks sprung like a punctured garden hose: six in #3A, a dozen in #3B, seventeen in #4A, twenty-one in #4B. The AFT superheater headers had to be drained, wrapped in insulated blankets and preheated, and the cracks had to be ground out and rewelded.

Jimmy, Chuck, Kenny, Snake, and Denny had welded 2,048 tubes without one defect, and none of them were asked to help make repairs on the AFT boilers.

Admiral Foley was a wild man about the weld failures and schedule delays. He admonished Mr. Strunk for dereliction of duty, though he'd been a vocal critic of the automated technology since it was proposed to the shipyard. He threatened to fire the welder and boilermaker superintendents. The only people spared from blame were NAVSEA engineers and technical personnel from Maestro Fusion. The admiral was determined to keep information about the Maestro Fusion failures from getting out to the public.

Chapter X

SEA TRIALS

"Critical path" was shipyard jargon for managing the ship overhaul schedule. The critical path included key milestones that had to be met for the ship to progress to the next phase of the overhaul. Missing a milestone would impact delivery of the ship. Sea trials was a key milestone on the Saratoga critical path.

After two years of tearing the carrier down to its skeleton, sand blasting its hull and tanks, replacing and upgrading key electronic and mechanical components, and refurbishing the boilers, the ship went out to sea for its operational test six weeks behind schedule because of the superheater tube weld failures in the AFT Fire Rooms.

Specialists from the skilled trades went on sea trials to repair anything that broke down or leaked so operational tests wouldn't be interrupted. Tradesmen worked twelve-hour shifts, but were on call when they were off duty. Sixteen, twenty, even twenty-four-hour shifts weren't unusual. Saratoga's sea trial was scheduled for ten days.

Jimmy was one of four welders on the sea trial team. The

week before the ship sailed, Colin called him to his office.

"Butch is looking to recruit a younger welder for foreman," said Colin, referring to the welding shop superintendent Butch McMann. "He's going to put out a job announcement next week."

"Don't look at me," said Jimmy.

Colin raised a hand like a cop directing traffic. "Slow down, Jimmy. Don't be so quick to shut out an idea." Jimmy's instinct was to rebut his boss, but instead he listened. "Look at Harry, God bless him. He's been around since they used lute and rivets on wooden ships. The shop needs young blood with open minds to supervise new processes and technologies." Colin was actually older than Harry, but had the mind and heart of a much younger man.

"Welding is what I do, Colin," said Jimmy. "I love working on things that peoples' lives depend on."

"You love the work now because you're twenty-five," said Colin. "Look at Chuck. He loves the work too, but he's sixty-three. He has bad knees and a bum hip. Watch him after he's been jammed against a hot header for ten hours, he comes out limping like a cripple."

Jimmy stood, thinking. "I just can't see myself away from the action," he finally said.

"Listen to me, Jimmy," said Colin, in his elegant Irish lilt. "You can only weld so many pipe joints. As a foreman, you have a hand in on every weld in a fire room, or a number of fire rooms." He put a hand on Jimmy's shoulder. "You get to teach young welders the right way to do things. Even more important, you get to teach them the right way to approach the job, and to take pride in their work."

Jimmy had never heard anyone describe a supervisor's responsibilities in such terms. After losing his dad at a young age, he never had an adult advise him so caringly.

Colin suddenly winced.

"You okay?" asked Jimmy.

"I'm fine."

"What is it?"

After momentary silence, Colin said, "You can't tell anyone."

"You know you can trust me."

"They found a spot on my lung."

Jimmy's legs got soft. In the midst of their work—the banging, the dirt and the danger—he never realized how close he'd become with him. Boss or no boss, he had the urge to embrace him.

"What's that mean?" he asked.

"They're evaluating treatment options."

Jimmy took a deep breath and exhaled a stream of distress. "I'll apply for the foreman job if you promise me you'll be okay," he said.

Colin smiled.

"Deal."

~

To an F/A-18 pilot on a flyby at the speed of sound, the Saratoga appeared a steel fortress slicing through the Atlantic. But in the heart of the ship, more than a dozen decks below the mast, trouble began brewing shortly after the vessel hit breakwater at the mouth of the Delaware Bay.

Fifty miles off the coast, there was a drop in pressure in the AFT boilers. The crew investigated and found seven superheater tubes leaking in boiler 3A, and then twelve in 3B. The report from Fire Room #4 was bleaker: fifteen leaks in 4A and twenty-two in 4B. All four AFT boilers had to be taken off-line, two at a time so that the ship could continue operations. The headers were preheated, and the leaking tubes plugged by welding machined steel pins into the tube ends. Then the boilers were brought back on-line. The process took twelve hours per boiler. Sea trials had to be extended two days so the crew could get all eight boilers back up for the power run, which was the full capacity demonstration of the propulsion plant.

The captain took the ship two hundred miles off the Virginia coast before giving the order to open the boilers to full throttle. Fifteen minutes later, sixty thousand tons of steel were cutting through the seas at thirty knots or nearly thirty-five miles per hour.

The inertia vibrating through the steel excited Jimmy. He climbed the ladder out of the fire room, navigating passage-ways to more ladders until he reached the flight deck. When he cracked open the hatch, the force of the wind made a sucking sound.

He stepped outside the island.

Standing on the flight deck, Jimmy had the sensation of riding a metal surfboard three football fields long. He shifted his feet to keep his balance as the ship performed figure eights and ovals five miles in diameter. Feet planted on Saratoga steel, infinitely closer to the heart of the ship than an F/A-18 pilot, he wasn't fooled by the unfathomable power of the behemoth. After welding twelve hours a day seven days a week for six weeks, he was intimately connected to the superheater tubes. They'd become as much a part of him as blood pumping through his arteries. He could feel they were stressed, so he was stressed. He sensed the tubes straining to break free from the headers the way a desperate, obese man feels an imminent heart attack.

~

Joey Strunk considered himself a blue-collar guy even though he taught night classes in Material Science and Engineering in the Masters of Science program at his alma mater Drexel University. He never used PhD, P.E. after his name. And he never flicked ashes from his non-filtered Camel. Rather he let them spill onto his white button-down dress shirt, some into the breast pocket where he kept a notebook and yellow number two lead pencil with an unused eraser. If he owned more than one tie, they were all navy blue with tiny, imprinted anchors. His crewcut was flat like the flight deck of an aircraft carrier. Mr. Strunk spoke in a low tone, emphasized the points he made by raising an eyebrow. His pencil was his authority, and sarcasm was his way of scolding. Nobody questioned his judgment on metallurgical matters: not peers, superintendents, nor shipyard commanders. He outlasted five of them.

While the ship was out at sea, Mr. Strunk stopped in the shipyard commander's office and proposed conducting a study to determine the cause of the Maestro Fusion welding failures. The shipyard commander said he would need the Navy's approval to commission the study, and when he called NAVSEA Headquarters with the request, he was told the Navy already contracted with a Washington consultant to do an independent review. Strunk knew what that meant: a "beltway bandit," what they called hundreds of well-connected D.C. consultants. And he knew that an "independent review" was analogous to hiring a bunch of bureaucrats to deliver a desired outcome, or, in other words, paying to influence the study and write your own conclusions.

Strunk had been skeptical of the Maestro Fusion process from the beginning. He never told the shipyard commander that he'd written a memo to the commander of NAVSEA in early 1980, before the first Maestro Fusion contract was awarded, stating that the process was "unproven, with potential flaws" and "required more analysis." The memo made its way to Admiral Foley and never went any further. Had the Navy done their due diligence and employed objective, untainted welding engineers and metallurgists, they would have discovered that the process *was* flawed.

Admiral Foley kept the memo as a reminder of Strunk's dissent, figuring it might one day be useful. What the admiral didn't anticipate was Joey Strunk commissioning his own study that produced raw test data and documentation proving that welding chrome headers without the proper preheat procedures resulted in a phenomenon called "hydrogen embrittlement," a condition that caused cracks that made their way to the surface of welds under pressure.

Chapter XI

CHESS

Butch and Skip Homes had been ordered to be in the shipyard commander's office at nine o'clock. Neither was given an explanation. On the ride over, they debated the purpose of the meeting. When they arrived and found they were the only ones invited, they had a hunch.

Captain Flask looked grim when he waved them in. "Admiral Foley wants to meet with us in the Pentagon tomorrow."

"About what, Captain?" asked Butch.

"Commanding Officer of the Saratoga refused to accept his ship unless the tubes in the AFT boilers are replaced," said Flask.

Butch lowered his head and shook it, regretting he hadn't taken a stronger stance against the automated technology and its abbreviated preheating cycle. He glared at Skip, and said, "That fucking machine."

~

Admiral Foley, Commander of the Aircraft Carrier Fleet, picked his Pentagon office for the meeting as a power move. His suite once belonged to Admiral Hyman G. Rickover, the tyrannical father of the nuclear Navy, and was a stark and imposing museum of Naval artifacts that commanded attention and respect.

Captain Cahill, the Saratoga's commander, was already in the admiral's office when the Philadelphia contingent arrived. A coffee cup was on a table next to Cahill, and when he got up from his chair to greet them, he left a well-worn impression of his ass in the leather.

The admiral pointed at a sofa for Captain Flask and his superintendents to sit, like a dog trainer directing canines. Foley remained standing, took a few steps toward his desk and stroked a model of the USS Nautilus, the first nuclear submarine, which Rickover had planned and supervised the construction.

"Excellence, gentlemen," said Foley. "That's why we're here today. To talk about excellence."

The Philadelphia contingent looked at one another. Captain Cahill stared straight ahead. "We're not going to leave this room until we settle this superheater tube dispute, everyone understand?"

"Yes, sir," came in unison, except Butch who left out the *sir*. The admiral didn't miss it.

Foley nodded in Cahill's direction. "Captain Cahill."

"Admiral, I'm being asked to accept a ship that just went through the most costly overhaul in Naval history and has fifty-six plugged superheater tubes. I have very little confidence in the boilers and propose all the tubes be replaced in the AFT boilers."

Foley swooshed his lips side to side. "I get your point, Bobby," he said. Butch lurched like an electrical charge shot through him at the sound of the admiral addressing Cahill by his first name. Foley gestured toward Flask. "What do you have, Captain?"

"Sir, the remedy in the NAVSEA manual is to replace only the plugged tubes," Flask said, definitively. "Replacing all of them would be a waste of taxpayer money."

Cahill jumped in. "If they would have been done right the first time, we wouldn't be having this discussion," he said. "Your men didn't properly prepare—"

Flask cut him off and dug the balls of his feet into the thick rug. "I'm not going to sit here and listen to you try to hold the shipyard responsible for a welding process NAVSEA mandated," he said. "There wasn't one reject in the tubes my men welded in the forward boilers, and not one leak during the hydros." Flask knew he was risking disciplinary action, but he couldn't restrain himself. "If anyone's responsible for the defects in the AFT boilers, it's the Navy."

"The Navy, huh?" said Foley, massaging his jaw like it was a relief valve. Captain Flask had led men through hostile waters in Vietnam with the boldness of a mercenary, but in the Navy a captain had to eat an admiral's shit and like it if he ever wanted to make flag officer, especially a vindictive prick like Foley. "I don't know how you got so goddamn disillusioned, Captain, but you're an officer in the United States Navy, and you'll follow orders, or you'll be managing a storeroom on the Samoa."

The admiral compromised and ordered the shipyard to repair the plugged superheater tubes before the ship was re-commissioned. As an insurance policy to protect his investment in the Maestro Fusion welding process, he commissioned a Graybeard Panel to conduct an investigation into the cause of the leaking superheater tubes. The panel leader was a retired admiral who owned a consulting firm in Crystal City, and the members were former commissioned officers.

~

Doug Skate had been more ornery than usual at being shut out of the AFT fire rooms after the tube repairs were done. Early one morning, he shot down the ladder into Fire Room #1.

"Tommy!" he yelled, motioning him to a corner of the room. Doug waved Jimmy off from following them.

"He's good, Doug," Tommy insisted.

Doug looked between the two, then started. "Navy investigators are inside the superheater cavity back AFT looking at the tubes," he said. "I'm hearing they're trying to pin the leaking tubes on the shipyard."

"What?" said Tommy. "How?"

"That's what I want to find out," said Doug. "Go back and snoop around and see what you can find out."

"You got it," said Tommy and took off up the ladder. No matter what anyone thought about Doug—that he was obnoxious, a drunk, whatever—when it came to boilers, he was a genius and passionate. Skip Homes trusted his judgment on boiler matters more than he trusted his own. And Doug supervised preparation of every tube on all eight boilers before they were shipped from the shop to the fire room and installed, so there was no doubt they were pristine and rolled as tight as a baby's ass.

Fire Room #3 was a ghost town except for a few boiler technicians and a chief inside the control room. Tommy climbed back up the ladder, walked down the passageway and went down into Fire Room #4. Standing on the upper-level deck plates, he heard a loud voice coming from behind the boiler, and as he snuck back, it burst into shouting.

"If I hear you try to blame the robotic process again, you're going to be looking for a job, young man." Tommy looked down and saw an older man with a flash of white hair sticking out from under an unmarked hard hat with his finger in George Sputz's face. "You people do studies and come up with whatever bullshit conclusions that fit your needs!" He shook his fist. "I have certified data from two shipyards as evidence that Maestro Fusion is proven technology. If it didn't work in Philly, it was because of shoddy workmanship, improper cleaning, half-ass fitting, and sloppy rolling!" The man took a second to calm himself, and a decibel lower, he added, "And if I hear otherwise, you'll never set foot on another Navy ship."

Tommy turned to leave and tripped over a pipe. It rolled to the edge of the catwalk and crashed down to the lower level. The man looked up, and they locked eyes. The last thing Tommy saw before he turned and ran were silver stars on the man's shoulder reflecting off an overhead light.

"Get back here!" he screamed, watching Tommy double-time up the ladder.

~

The plugged tubes the shipyard repaired passed NDT and hydro-static test. On a Wednesday, with spring on the horizon, Captain Flask invited the superintendents and senior managers to the Officer's Club for drinks to celebrate the Saratoga leaving the shipyard. While they hoisted beers, the carrier was steaming south along the Atlantic coast and different tubes began to leak, so many that by the time it reached its homeport in Mayport, Florida, it had exceeded the allowable threshold for plugged tubes stated in the NAVSEA engineering manual.

The next day there was another more serious leak: an information leak on Capitol Hill about the nearly half-billion dollars spent on an aircraft carrier with leaking boilers. Senator Hawkins called the Pentagon, demanding the problem be resolved. Within an hour, the order traveled from the Secretary of the Navy to Admiral Foley.

"Fix it!"

~

Admiral Foley called his second meeting for a Saturday morning in Philadelphia, this time in the shipyard commander's office. Butch and Skip Homes sat with Captain Flask in his office, sipping cups of coffee. Captain Cahill sat outside in the waiting room. When Admiral Foley showed up at 9:01 a.m., Cahill stood and followed him into Captain Flask's office.

Admiral Foley held up the report prepared by the Graybeard Panel. "Gentlemen, I'm holding a study conducted by some of the greatest minds in naval propulsion who have concluded that the Navy Yard was derelict in their duty by improperly preparing the superheater tubes for the automated welding process. Based on their experience and professional judgment I've decided that the superheater tubes on all four boilers in the AFT Fire Rooms will be ripped out and replaced in Mayport, Florida this summer." He gestured toward the shipyard commander, and said, "Captain Flask, begin planning," then turned and walked out. Captain Cahill stood and followed him.

"Ambush," seethed Flask, through clinched teeth. Foley had traveled to Philadelphia on a Saturday morning for a five-minute meeting to pass down a premeditated verdict. The Saratoga was within the guarantee period, the period of time after ship delivery when the shipyard was contractually obligated to repair guaranteed work found defective, which included the power plant. Flask had no recourse. He looked at his superintendents, and said, "That's what that was. An ambush."

The only other person to see the Graybeard Panel's report was Johnny Neumann, the man whose company pioneered the automated welding process, when Admiral Foley took him to dinner that evening and explained that the failures had been caused by the shipyard's inferior workmanship. Neumann had no choice but to accept the study's findings and conclusions.

~

Butch, Skip, and Flask remained huddled in the commander's office discussing the tiger team they'd assemble to send to Mayport. On the surface, it was a boiler job like many others the shipyard had conducted in the past: ripping out tubes, installing new ones, preheating, welding and inspection. Yet they all knew this wasn't business as usual. This would be the most scrutinized job in their history. The shipyard's reputation was on the line. For that matter, its survival. The Virginia delegation still held animosity over losing the congressional battle for the SLEP program and would undoubtedly use the boiler failures to try to persuade the Navy to reevaluate their decision and send future carriers south. The USS Forrestal was already dry docked at the Navy Yard, but two more aircraft carrier SLEPs had yet to be awarded, nearly a billion dollars in contracts, and Norfolk was the Navy's home turf.

Chapter XII

PROMOTION

During the first week in May, the temperature reached the mid-eighties every day, hotter than in San Diego. Hotter even than it was in Honolulu. Jimmy was back working a civilized forty-hour week on the USS Forrestal. He showed up for work one morning and was surprised to find Harry running muster.

"Where's Colin?" Jimmy asked.

Harry ignored the question and said, "Butch wants to see you in the front office." Jimmy stared at him, a torrent of conflicting thoughts running through his head. "Right away," Harry added.

Butch was on the phone when Jimmy showed up at his door. The usually boisterous superintendent was in a listening mode, nodding his head like he was taking orders. He waved in Jimmy and pointed to a chair across from him. It was easy for him to picture Butch during his semi-pro football days, with his wide shoulders on a six-foot-four frame, even sitting behind his desk.

"That was the shipyard commander," said Butch, hanging up the phone. "We gotta send a tiger team to Mayport." Jimmy wasn't surprised after hearing all the rumors about leaks on the Saratoga after it left the shipyard. "And I want you to run the job."

"Run the job?" said Jimmy. "I'm not a foreman."

Butch walked around from behind his desk.

"You are now," he said, extending a hand. "Congratulations."

Jimmy offered his hand like he was about to pet a junkyard dog showing its teeth. "I'll need a day or two to think about it."

"What's there to think about? It's a great opportunity. You'll be the youngest welder ever to be promoted to foreman."

"Big deal," said Jimmy, unenthusiastically.

"You're twenty-five, kid. Three years removed from your apprenticeship. The average age of a foreman in the shop is fifty-three."

Jimmy remained apprehensive, mulling the challenge, the implications.

"The bottom line is," Butch paused, "I need you."

"What do you mean?"

"I trust you, Jimmy. And I need someone I trust to supervise the job in Mayport."

Initially, Jimmy felt proud, but then his blood starting to percolate. "But I didn't work the AFT Fire Rooms. I never operated the Maestro Fusion machine." He looked around the room. "Why isn't the Professor here?"

Butch eyed Jimmy in a way that left no doubt he appreciated his passion. "We're going to weld them manually," he said, "the way we would've done them in the first place if they'd listened to me."

Jimmy digested the words. It was the first time he'd heard Butch come out and say he didn't support the Maestro Fusion process.

"Crazy, isn't it?" said Butch. "They blame the shipyard for shoddy workmanship, maintain that Maestro Fusion is the future, then tell us to go down Mayport and weld the tubes the old-fashioned way." He laughed. "Assholes want their aircraft carrier back."

"I'll tell you what's crazy," said Jimmy. "If the tubes were welded during the summer on schedule, they probably would've gotten away with it."

Butch stared at Jimmy. "Hmm. You're right."

The conversation lapsed. "How about Colin?" asked Jimmy. "He knows more about managing a boiler job than anyone in the shipyard."

Butch's expression turned sullen. "Colin can't go."

The words hit Jimmy like a punch in the gut. "Did his condition worsen?"

"You know?"

Jimmy nodded.

"His wife left a message on my answering machine. I called her when I got in this morning. She told me he was coughing up blood after dinner last night. She took him to the hospital, and they kept him. He starts radiation today."

A vacuum sucked Jimmy back to his childhood, the abandoned feeling when his mom told him his dad wouldn't be coming home anymore.

"Okay," he said. "I'll go to Mayport."

"A lot of prep work is being done," said Butch. "They're ordering a couple thousand new boiler tubes, equipment, and all the shit that goes with it. The tiger team will leave the beginning of August. I'm going to have a meeting sometime in the next few weeks, so think about who you want on the team."

"I already have a pretty good idea," said Jimmy as he got up to leave.

Butch nodded. "Good."

Jimmy was halfway to the door when Butch called after him. He turned around. "Yeah, boss?"

"Between me and you, the shipyard commander told me there's some powerful people in the Pentagon trying to use the boiler tube failures to move the SLEP program to Norfolk. If that happens, it'll give 'em a reason to BRAC us."

BRAC was the death rattle to shipyard workers. The Base Realignment and Closure Commission reviewed military instal-lations before deciding which ones to close. Once the commis-sion started evaluating a facility, it was only a matter of time.

"Bastards!" Jimmy spit out, realizing they were in a fight for survival. "They can't do that because of something that was their fault, can they?"

Butch shrugged his big shoulders. He looked as tired as Jimmy had ever seen him.

"Jimmy, the Navy owns the shipyard. They own the ships. They can do whatever they want."

Chapter XIII

THE DRAFT

Jimmy had no foreman orientation, no management classes, and no mentoring. That also meant there was no time for politics or resentment from older welders who might hold a grudge because they considered themselves more deserving.

He showed up at muster wearing a white hard hat that designated supervisors and a clipboard he grabbed off someone's desk to keep his roster and work orders. After he handed out jobs, he headed down the fire room. On the way down the ladder, he heard Doug ranting, launching expletives like machine gun fire. He asked what was going on, and Tommy told him that Hank Peachtree was picked over Doug for the tiger team. Jimmy laughed because Doug hadn't been picked to travel for the shipyard since he went missing on a two-day drunk ten years ago on a tiger team. Hank was reliable, even-tempered, and arguably as knowledgeable about boilers as Doug. He was young for a foreman at thirty-eight, and the type of guy who could talk his men into thinking the grimiest job in the fire room was an honor.

Jimmy first met Hank on the Belknap the day the painter was burnt to death in the escape trunk. Hank noticed how the gruesome accident had shaken Jimmy and slipped him a paperback booklet titled *Word of God* that contained a prayer and meditation for each day of the month. Hank was inconspicuously religious with a wickedly sarcastic sense of humor, a combination that chipped away at Jimmy's repulsion for self-professed preachers who tried to push their beliefs on people. He didn't use profanity, instead relying on curse words he invented, like crank hole, stiff stick and peanut balls. And he was an intellectual, an oxymoron for a boilermaker, two semesters away from becoming the only foreman on the waterfront with a master's degree, which he did entirely by attending night classes.

Jimmy and Hank deliberated on the makeup of the tiger team as carefully as general managers of professional football teams selected draft picks. Talent was paramount. They couldn't afford rejected welds or leaks. Temperament, too, was a key factor. They wouldn't have time to deal with volatile egos and bullshit like settling arguments and breaking up fights. And each member of the team had to have character that would leave a favorable impression of the shipyard nine hundred miles from home. Chemistry was their endgame. One asshole on the team could sabotage the game plan. Still, they were realists and knew Butch and Skip Homes would have the final say in the selections.

The sheer numbers making up the team required going beyond the *talent-plus-character* formula into a pool of *talented-but-temperamental*. Like musicians, artists, and athletes, some of the most talented craftsmen were some of the most eccentric, personalities like Keith Richards, Jackson Pollock or Terrell Owens, or a combination of all three. They were the type that possessed a gene averse to convention and weren't settled unless they were following their own asymmetric path, if they could be settled at all. Throw oppressive heat, dirt, dust, grime, and eardrum-shattering noise into the equation, top it off with alcohol, and you had a shipyard specialist.

Jimmy and Hank designated their non-negotiables: guys they refused to go to Mayport without. Hank had four boiler-makers he wouldn't leave behind. Tommy Homes would be his pusher, the go-to guy he'd rely upon to keep progress moving forward. Jerry Yorko, the young, experienced boilermaker, was skilled at troubleshooting malfunctions. Cajon, the Golden Glove had a win-at-all-cost attitude from his experience punch-ing his way out of corners. Finally, there was Vince Murphy, who would keep an upbeat tempo cracking jokes and breaking balls through the drudgery of twelve-hour shifts seven days a week for twelve weeks.

Jimmy had two non-negotiables: Chuck, indisputably the best welder in the shipyard, and Kenny Essington, a selection that would stun everyone, but one that Jimmy was ready to go to bat for. The last two slots were a toss-up between three other welders.

~

Hank hadn't calculated how much marriage and a newborn had changed Tommy Homes until the young boilermaker told him he wasn't going to Mayport. After several attempts to recruit him, Hank got so frustrated that he gave up and began considering other boilermakers to be his go-to guy. When Jimmy heard, he told Hank to wait until he talked to him.

Jimmy waited to get Tommy alone in the firebox.

"Twelve-hour shifts, seven days a week, Tommy," said Jimmy. "That's a down payment on a house, or the start of a college fund for your daughter."

"It's not about the money, Jimmy. I don't want to be away from my wife and little girl for that long."

"You'll be so busy you won't have time to miss them."

Tommy shook his head. "You have no idea, buddy."

"I have no idea about what?"

"Jimmy," Tommy said, choosing his words carefully, "you gotta get a life before you wind up married to the shipyard."

Coming from anyone else, Jimmy would have told him to go fuck himself, but Tommy's words carried weight, and he was right. The shipyard *was* his life. He wasn't sure what to say, and the best he could come up with was, "Bring them with you."

"What?"

"Some of the other boilermakers are bringing their wives. It'll be a vacation for them."

"My wife will never travel with the baby."

"Listen, Tommy, the shipyard's reputation is on the line," Jimmy confided. "Our future. Hank needs a guy who can push the gang on night shift, and you're the guy."

Tommy looked to be thinking of another way to say "no." "We're baptizing our daughter in October," he said. "The job's not scheduled to finish until November."

"We'll fly you home for the christening," said Jimmy in desperation. There was a long pause. "Well?"

"I guess I got to tell you."

"Tell me what?" said Jimmy.

"We were going to ask you to be the godfather."

Jimmy's eyes shot open. He grabbed Tommy in a bear hug, and when he let him go, he said, "That's it! We'll both fly home."

~

Hank was relieved when Jimmy told him that Tommy was onboard, until he told him about the promise he'd made.

"How the hell could you promise him he could fly home?"

"Because I'm the godfather and I'm going to fly home with him."

Hank shook his head. "You think Butch'll go for it?"

"If he wants me to go, he will," said Jimmy.

"You got balls, McKee."

Jimmy laughed. "Big deal if we miss a day or two," he said. "We'll almost be finished by then anyway."

"You're crazy," said Hank.

~

Jimmy couldn't wait to ask Kenny to be on the tiger team and was dazed when he responded, "I don't want to be no token black guy on the job."

"Where the hell did that come from?"

"Why else would you ask me?"

"Because every weld you did on the Saratoga superheater was perfect. And once you got going, you finished a row of tubes faster than I did." He stared Kenny down. "For Chrissake, even Snake was impressed, and he's not your biggest fan."

"Butch good with me going?" said Kenny.

"I don't give a shit who's good with you going," said Jimmy. "But yeah, Butch is good with it."

An awkward silence between the two, then that trademark smile spread across Kenny's face. "Okay, my man. If you want me on the team, I'm in."

Jimmy opened his hand. Kenny clasped his palm and pulled him in.

~

Package deal. That's what Jerry Yorko called it when he told Hank he wouldn't go to Mayport without his brother Denny. Jimmy flat out refused. He'd already knocked Snake off the list because he was on the tiger team with Doug the time they went missing for two days. He wasn't about to replace one drunk with another. But blood was blood, and this was twin blood. Same color hair and eyes, height, weight, and physique, the twins were indistinguishable, until Denny started drinking. The first few beers, he was the life of the party telling stories and jokes, but at some point, his face would begin to list, and he'd get this look where his eyebrows bulged and his stare turned into a laser. He'd become suspicious of anyone he didn't know, narrowing his eyes like a juror at a suspect after viewing photos of a mutilated victim. And the more he drank, the less he trusted people he *did* know.

Hank couldn't get Jerry to budge. It was either both of them or none of them. He told Jerry to talk to Jimmy.

Jerry promised Jimmy he'd keep tight reigns on his brother. Jimmy wavered, impressed by Jerry's loyalty and the way he cared about his brother. It wasn't that he didn't like Denny. He just didn't like him when he was drinking. Realizing he was in a no-win situation, he made a deal.

"If I have to send him back to Philly, you're going with him."

"I'm good with that," said Jerry.

~

Jimmy was so furious when he saw Snake's name back on the tiger team roster that he stormed into Butch's office. "It's either me or Snake."

Butch finished a note he was writing before looking up from his desk.

"Sit down, Jimmy."

"No, Butch. You're not going to calm me down with one of your *ra ra, go get 'em* pep talks. I already conceded to take Denny Yorko because his brother refused to go without him. I'm not taking two drunks."

"How'd it work out for you on the Saratoga?" asked Butch.

"Big deal. He stayed sober for a few weeks. We could've pulled guys from other ships if one of them disappeared. If one of them goes on a drunk in Mayport, we'll be a thousand miles away."

"I'll talk to them personally."

"Oh, you'll talk to them personally. That'll solve everything." Jimmy caught himself when Butch's chest inflated, his biceps tightening around his sleeves. "I feel like you're setting me up to fail, Butch."

"It's my decision, Jimmy. If anything blows up, it's on me."

Jimmy trusted Butch, and by the time he left the office, his boss had him convinced that without Snake there'd be little chance the tiger team would be a success.

Chapter XIV

BON VOYAGE

The Sons of Ben Franklin on Cross Street in South Philly was a large room with hardwood floors, fake pine paneling, a drop ceiling, a long oak bar and a kitchen equipped with an industrial stove and refrigerator. The bathroom had a porcelain wall for a urinal and trough at the floor with running water and a solitary toilet in the corner stripped of partitions. Above the sink, a medicine cabinet held a half tube of a brand of toothpaste that hadn't been produced since the 1950s, and tucked in the corner, for no reason anyone could remember, was a tub that looked suited to bathe livestock.

Boilermakers, welders, and a few pipefitters, insulators, electricians and riggers dribbled in, one or two at a time. The crowd was predominantly white, except for Kenny, a black pipefitter named Russell, and a rigger they called Ironman. Juan, a boilermaker and former professional baseball player who made it to Triple A but was never called up to the bigs, was one of two Hispanics. Also among the gang were two female graduate apprentices, one a pipefitter, the other an electrician. Jimmy perked up when Hank walked in with his wife, Rose.

He ordered them both drinks: rum and Cokes without the rum.

The hall had the atmosphere of a union meeting: forty-some people laughing, cursing, drinking, talking Phillies, Flyers and Sixers, and arguing about what place the Eagles would come in next season. Heads turned when Butch and Skip Homes walked in at quarter past eight. Butch wore an Eagles jersey, jeans, and a baseball cap. Skip had shed his trademark tie, but still had on the white dress shirt and black slacks he wore to work that day.

Butch said something to Skip before heading to the bar for a beer. He turned around, leaned his back against the bar and took a long gulp while looking out over the crowd.

"Okay, men," he said in a commanding voice, then paused until everyone shut up. He nodded in the direction of the two women, and added, "And ladies." That brought a few laughs. "You folks were picked for the most important tiger team in shipyard history. Forty-four of you will travel to Mayport to rip-out and replace two thousand boiler tubes in the AFT boilers on the USS Saratoga." He looked around the room. "Huey," he said, gesturing toward boilermaker General Foreman Huey Kortez, "will be general foreman overseeing the job."

Huey was a legend, twenty-two years in the Navy, rising through the ranks from seaman recruit to chief engineer before retiring and being hired by the shipyard. Nobody knew more about managing men and reconstructing boilers than Huey, and his was hands-on knowledge, accrued in the bowels of a ship. He once saved the lives of six of his sailors by pulling them from an incendiary fire room after an explosion in the West Pacific. Huey raised his hand, and someone started a chant, *Huey, Huey, Huey.*

When the crowd settled down, Butch introduced Jimmy and Hank as the day and nightshift foremen. "The best management team the shipyard ever assembled," Butch boasted. Jimmy, unsure whether the paperwork for his promotion to supervisor had even been processed, tried to keep a straight face.

Butch nodded to Skip Homes in the back of the crowd, and when he introduced him, the hall became still. Tommy's dad was the statesman for the production trades in the shipyard, a rare, dignified presence in the territory on south Broad Street known for rough characters. The shipyard commander relied upon him to brief politicians and flag officers visiting from Washington.

"A lot of eyes will be on this job, gentlemen," Skip began. "Don't be surprised if an admiral or two visits you in Mayport, maybe a congressman, at any time of day or night. Be respectful if they ask questions. You're representing the shipyard. The impression you make will go a long way." That was it. To the point. Professional. He looked back to Butch and nodded.

"One last thing," said Butch. He paused and rubbed his jaw. "The boiler tube failures put the shipyard under a microscope, and frankly, I think we're getting a raw deal." The pronouncement pulled everyone's focus onto him, except Jimmy who watched Mr. Homes lower his head and walk toward the back of the room. He looked uncomfortable with the change in direction of Butch's message. "You guys welded the tubes on four boilers without one defect, and you didn't make the decision to use that damn robot to weld the AFT boilers."

"That's what I'm talking about!" someone shouted.

"So go to Mayport and show the Navy how it's supposed to be done." Yeah's came from several people. "You were picked because you're the best of the best, so show the outside world what Philly's all about. Have pride in your blue-collar, Philadelphia heritage." Butch raised his head looking for Mr. Homes to join him but couldn't see him in the far corner of the room. He returned his attention to the crowd, raised his beer, and shouted, "Philly Pride!"

"Philly Pride!" rang out from the crowd, over and over.

~

Kegs were drained, the bottom of shot glasses slammed the bar, workers argued and laughed and debated and argued some more. The night was in full swing, like a platoon before going into a war zone. Plans were made, groups of young guys renting houses, while older and more solitary men opted for hotel rooms or apartments. They decided who'd drive nine hundred miles, so they'd have their own car, who'd fly down and rent a car, and who'd carpool with whom.

Vince Murphy was on his fifth beer when he struck a deal with Hank to let one of the nightshift guys take orders and pick up lunch for the entire backshift gang while they were working in Mayport. He had all the details worked out: they'd choose one guy who'd take the orders at the beginning of each shift, then around midnight would drive to a restaurant, place the order, and bring back dinner for the troops. Hank agreed on the condition that Tommy, the most reliable boilermaker on the backshift, would be the runner. It was a decision he'd regret for the rest of his short life.

Part II

Mayport

Chapter XV

850 MILES SOUTH

S udden gusts jolted Flight 4355 sideways. The aircraft dropped, leveled, then jolted again. Passengers gasped, digging their fingernails into armrests and darting nervous looks at one another. Jimmy had never been on a plane. In fact, he'd never been farther from home than Wildwood at the Jersey shore. His dad's brother Bobby would take him on weekends the summer after his father was killed in the accident. The plane's turbulence thrilled him, reminding him of riding the rollercoasters on the boardwalk while Uncle Bobby and his friends were drinking and playing poker. He'd always pick the rides with the steepest inclines, the most treacherous curves and the most exaggerated inverted loops. He never braced himself. Rather he'd cede to the danger, drinking in the thrill of being thrown around. With each ride, he dared fate.

The wheels of the aircraft scorched the tarmac of Jacksonville International at one o'clock. After it jerked to a stop at the gate, he stood and funneled down the aisle behind the line of passengers and off the plane into the terminal. He followed signs for Ground Transportation and caught the shuttle to Enterprise

Car Rental Agency where he waited in yet another line until a skinny kid with long, black hair waved him to the counter. He glanced at Jimmy's paperwork, and said, "Another Philly guy, huh?"

While the kid processed the papers, he recommended restaurants and watering holes even though he didn't look anywhere close to legal drinking age himself. He handed over the keys to a Ford Escort, gave Jimmy directions to the hotel, and said, "Don't leave Atlantic Beach without trying the Farmstead. Open twenty-four hours and has the best fried chicken in the state."

When he walked outside, Jimmy shielded his eyes against the glare. He flipped down the sun visor before he started the car, then pulled out onto Atlantic Boulevard heading east. He scanned the road, taking inventory of motels, bars, adult bookstores, an auto parts store. He did a double-take at a drive-in window at MAX Liquors.

Except for the receptionist who checked him in and a custodian emptying trashcans, the Sea Turtle lobby was empty. He took the elevator to the twelfth floor and fished the room key from his pocket on the way down the hall, then unlocked the door and pushed it open with his foot. Two steps inside, he dropped his bag and stared out the glass door across the room at a bright turquoise backdrop resting on sparkling aqua. He walked over, slid open the glass doors and stepped onto the balcony. *They put me up here and expect me to go to work?*

In less than a minute, he went back inside, kicked off his sneakers, and left without unpacking. Three boilermakers checking in at the front desk didn't see him as he scooted across the lobby behind them and headed outside toward the beach.

A sign posted at the trailhead to the dunes read "Sea Turtle Nesting Area" with a list of instructions for protecting the habitat. If Jimmy hadn't stopped to read it, he would have thought the hotel was just another tired name for a seaside resort, like the Dauphin or The Breakers. He continued to the beach, conscious not to disturb sea turtle nests or crush any eggs or hatchlings. Midway to the ocean he looked back at the hotel and counted to the twelfth floor where a woman draped towels over the railing and a man stood smoking a cigarette a few balconies away. From this distance, both were the size of dolls. He brushed the bottoms of his feet against the warm sand all the way to the water, then stood, letting remnants of waves wash back and forth until his feet disappeared. It didn't seem a minute before he was ankle-deep in sand. The surface of the water appeared to be at eye level. He felt buoyant and extended his arms, shifted his weight like a skateboarder leaning into a turn, imagining he was a seafarer.

Sharp-pitched squawking echoed in the distance. He looked out over the water and watched a line of dots parade across the sky from the north. The closer they got, the louder their barks and the larger they became, until the dots were tubular bodies with swooping wings that propelled them forward.

Suddenly, the first bird dropped from the sky, followed by her trailers. They accelerated in their dive, wings spread five or six feet across. A dozen or more tight, plump bellies leveled off and skimmed so close to the water that Jimmy filled with a soothing, almost giddy sensation. Some had throats bulging with prey. He clicked them off in his head—one, two, three—and just before they passed him, a single pelican broke ranks and headed in his direction, gaining speed and velocity, its beady eyes ringed with bright orange circles. As the missile zeroed in on him, the wet sand covering his feet turned to concrete. Jimmy froze and was about to cover his head in defense when the great bird veered left and flew back with the others. He watched until it was a single dot in a string of tiny dots fading into the sky, its form dwindling, then finally vanishing.

Something inside Jimmy stirred. He thought about the turbulence that pummeled the aircraft on the way to Florida, tons of metal and equipment and electronics and humans bouncing around like a ping pong ball. A bird weighing mere pounds had to be subject to exponentially more turbulence, yet he'd never seen anything so graceful, so majestic.

So peaceful.

Faint laughs and shouting broke his concentration. He twisted his feet loose from the sand and turned toward the hotel. A gang of rowdies was drinking, cursing and shoving by the pool. Parents carted children away from the commotion, and other guests evacuated. In those precious peaceful moments by the water, Jimmy had forgotten about the tiger team charged to perform heart surgery on the USS Saratoga. It was a crude reminder that the war would begin tomorrow: twelve weeks of hammering hardened steel tubes into chrome headers, chiseling excess metal from welds, breathing smoke and fumes, picking steel burrs from skin and out of eyes. It would be a battle for respect and dignity—for vindication.

For these twelve weeks, the welders would fight for their survival.

~

The four-thirty alarm was more than an hour earlier than Jimmy woke up back home, but in Philly he didn't have to get a temporary ID and decal for a rental car. At the red light on Atlantic Boulevard, he stretched his arms and craned his neck, willing himself to wake up. As he yawned, he spotted a 7-Eleven up Third Street. When the light turned green, he swerved left.

Jimmy poured a coffee, grabbed a V-8 out of the fridge and handed a man of Middle Eastern descent working the cash register a twenty. The man-made change, and with a slight, respectful bow, said, "Many thanks, my friend."

"Thanks to you, chief," said Jimmy, but the man's graciousness had caused him pause. "Hey, I'll be around the next couple of months. I'll see you tomorrow."

"Do I detect a Philadelphia accent?" the man asked, with a warm smile.

"You have a good ear," said Jimmy.

"Sailors come in from all over. I can tell Boston, New York, Philadelphia," he laughed slightly, and in an exaggerated Southern drawl, added, "Mississippi and Louisiana."

Jimmy laughed along with him. "See you tomorrow, chief."

Chief winked. "Okay, boss."

The air was still outside, the sky black. No other cars were in the parking lot, none passed on the street. Jimmy climbed into the car, took the lid off his coffee and blew steam onto the windshield. He looked up and down a deserted Third Street, noting the medial strip dotted with palm trees, a church steeple a couple of blocks away. He turned the ignition and pulled out of the lot, the serene image of Third Street receding in his rearview mirror.

About a mile down Atlantic Boulevard, a sign for the Naval Station pointed right. Jimmy followed the arrow onto Mayport Road, a wide boulevard with four empty lanes and darkened stores on either side. The businesses spread out the farther he drove, eventually giving way to single one-floor houses on disparate size lots and pickup trucks and campers parked in dirt driveways. On the other side of Wonderwood Drive, the last major intersection, there were mostly vacant lots full of trees and overgrown shrubbery.

When he rolled down the Escort's window, the scent of ocean washed in. He stuck out his arm, opened and closed his hand, collecting invisible salt particles from the air. The sky turned from a supernatural shade of cobalt to sapphire, and as the sun pushed toward the horizon, its billions of tons of energy pulsating just beyond the earth's curve, Jimmy's own energy swelled inside of him. He rarely thought about his father, but at this moment he wished he could tell him about the aircraft carrier, the high-pressure tubes he welded that could cripple a sixty-thousand-ton warship if they failed. He wanted to tell the world about shipyard welders who performed miracles with a ten-thousand degree arc.

~

An armed marine stood erect at the gate with his palm extended at the oncoming vehicle. Jimmy slowed to a stop, flashed his shipyard ID. "I'm with the tiger team from Philadelphia working on the Saratoga."

The marine pointed to the small brick building off to the right. "You're going to need a decal for your car."

Jimmy pulled into the lot and parked. Inside the building, a muscular marine stood at a filing cabinet with his broad back facing Jimmy. "We don't open until six," he said, without turning around.

Jimmy looked at the clock on the cinderblock wall that read 5:54. "You're kidding."

The Marine continued what he was doing. A few minutes later, he shut the file cabinet and disappeared into an office. He was oblivious to Jimmy's glare when he came back out at exactly six, took a seat on a stool behind the counter, and said, "What could I do for you?"

Jimmy pushed his paperwork across the counter. The marine glanced at the papers, and said, "Philly, huh?" He looked up, and asked, "You the guys who fucked up the Saratoga?"

Jimmy could feel his blood vessels throb, everything in the room tinted scarlet. "The Navy fucked up the Saratoga," he said. "We're down here to do the job the way it should have been done in the first place."

The hint of a smile crept across the marine's face, which pissed Jimmy off even more, then it struck him that the marine's words hadn't come out in a Southern drawl. "Marlin from Harlem," said the marine, offering his hand.

Jimmy studied Marlin's face as he shook a huge hand with a palm as rough as pumice. "Jimmy from Philly."

"Listen to me, Jimmy from Philly," said Marvin. "People down here talk a lot of shit. Don't pay attention to anything they say." He leaned in, the whites of his eyes accenting his dark skin. "The only thing that matters is that the Giants and Eagles kick the shit out of the Cowboy's this season."

"Now you're talking," said Jimmy.

Marvin handed him back his paperwork along with a car decal and temporary Naval Station ID.

"You be careful down here," said Marvin. "And watch out for the rednecks."

~

The Saratoga rose high above the wharf across from the parking lot, a floating city complete with stores and galleys and sailors and the capacity to hold enough warplanes and ordinance to annihilate a metropolis. Jimmy sat in the Escort, staring at the gray monster, before getting out and climbing the gangway to the hanger deck. He looked around but didn't recognize any faces, so he walked out onto the aircraft elevator. The sun pushed above the horizon, casting a soft yellow sheen on the shoreline across the Saint Johns River. Forklifts speeding around behind him spewing exhaust couldn't make enough noise to drown out squawking seagulls. He walked back inside and watched cranes set pallets loaded with equipment and material close to the fire room accesses so they could be transported to the jobsite. A small group of men, some with NAVSEA etched on the side of their white hardhats, gathered on the other side of the hanger bay.

Jimmy started in their direction. *Keep your friends close and your enemies closer*, he thought. As he closed in on them, he recognized George Sputz who was conspicuously avoiding eye contact.

"Morning, gents," said Jimmy. "I'm Jimmy McKee, the day shift foreman."

A few of the men nodded their heads in acknowledgement. A middle-aged man with a serious face wearing a white button-down shirt and holding a clipboard extended his hand. "Ralph Munson, Chief Engineer, NAVSEA. Admiral Foley sent me down to keep an eye on the job."

The name didn't ring a bell, but he was suspicious of anyone from NAVSEA. "Great," said Jimmy, clearly unimpressed. "If you take a look at the superheater welds down in Fire Room #1 and #2, you'll see that you won't have much to keep an eye on."

Munson had no response, nor did anyone else in the group. George looked uncomfortable.

~

At muster, Jimmy directed his men to get the gang boxes full of tools down to the fire rooms, run the welding lines and air hoses, and set up the heaters and staging. He spent most of the morning organizing office space in the command trailer in the hanger bay, reviewing process instructions and checking material and equipment orders. After lunch, he went down the AFT fire rooms to inspect the Maestro Fusion welds before the tubes were ripped out. He started at the bottom row of the inlet header of boiler 3A and worked his way up sixty-four rows to the top, then climbed back down and repeated the process on the outlet header. When he finished, he moved to boiler 3B and started over.

The welds were tight and uniform. *A work of art,* he thought.

Next, he went to Fire Room #4 and found the welds in 4A and 4B identical to those he'd just inspected. Balanced on a twelve-inch plank positioned to reach the upper rows of 4B superheater, a voice came from above.

"Figured you'd be checking out the job."

Jimmy looked up at Tommy staring down at him. "Guilty as charged."

"How do they look?"

"Perfect," said Jimmy. He shined his flashlight back inside the header, leaned in squinting, and then looked back up at Tommy. "The welds look perfect, but so many of them leaked. The cracks must be microscopic." He climbed out from the cavity onto the upper level and looked Tommy in the eye. "If a welder and a boilermaker could figure out that bypassing the preheat cycle would cause the tubes to crack, why couldn't a bunch of engineers at NAVSEA?"

"That's what I'd like to know," said Tommy.

"That's what I asked Sputz a few months ago."

"What'd he say?"

"He gave me a load of metallurgical mumbo jumbo that wasn't very convincing." He looked to be replaying the conversation in his head. "I don't think he even believed the bullshit he fed me."

Tommy's expression conveyed an unspoken language they shared, and his silence urged Jimmy to continue.

"This trip's gotta be costing them a mint," said Jimmy, "and they blame the shipyard so they can keep using that piece of shit robot welder." He tightened his lips and blew a short burst of breath out his nose. "Someone's driving this train, Tommy. Someone with a lot of influence."

Tommy's eyes shot wide.

"What is it?" asked Jimmy.

"Remember the day Doug came down the fire room and told me to see what I could find out about the Navy blaming the shipyard for the boiler leaks?"

"Yeah."

"Some guy was behind the boiler in Fire Room #4 chewing George's ass out. He threatened him, said if he didn't say the leaks were caused by the shipyard's shoddy workmanship that he'd have him fired."

"You know who he was?"

"Never saw him before. He was an older guy with a bunch of stars on his shoulder."

Chapter XVI

SMELL OF BLOOD

The job got off to a quick start. Forty-four tradesmen—welders, boilermakers, pipefitters and electricians—were jammed onto one shift, removing structures and piping interference to clear the way for re-tubing the boilers in two fire rooms. The new replacement tubes delivered from the manufacturer were set in the hanger bay, ready to be polished and prepped for installation. Friday afternoon, Huey started down the ladder into Fire Room #4. He stopped before he got to the bottom and watched people bumping into each other, then turned around and climbed back up and waited in the command trailer for his foremen to show up at the end of the shift.

"Time to split into two gangs," said Huey. He nodded to Jimmy. "Your guys report Monday morning, five-thirty." He looked at Hank. "Tell your gang to report five-thirty Monday afternoon for a turnover. I want our guys talking to each other at the change of shifts. Your job is to make sure the lines of communications are open, and guys are talking through problems: what's working, what's not. We'll go around the clock until the job's done. I want to be out of here in early November."

Jimmy had decided before he left Philly that he'd team Kenny with Chuck to weld on dayshift and let Hank deal with Denny and Snake on the backshift. He knew Hank had the patience to deal with them if their behavior took a detour. Plus, Hank had that divine intervention thing on his side, and probably packed a few *Word of God* booklets. Jimmy figured he'd need them.

~

Jimmy's men infiltrated the AFT fire rooms Monday morning, brandishing torches, pry bars, mauls, and pneumatic tools. They filled the compartments with smoke and debris while they ripped out the old superheater tubes. Hank's gang followed up on second shift, and in one week the boilers that had generated twelve hundred pounds of superheated steam to propel the Saratoga down the Eastern Seaboard had transformed into an industrial warzone. By the end of week, three of the boilermakers had wrestled, hammered, and cursed new tubes into place, rolling them tight against the inside of bored holes. Insulators wrapped the headers with induction heaters and insulated blankets and preheated them to four hundred degrees. With nine days remaining in August, welding began on dayshift.

Chuck and Kenny each welded nearly two rows on their first shift, completing almost sixteen tube joints between them. Denny and Snake were right behind them, finishing nearly as many on nightshift. It took a couple of days for both shifts to settle into a flow, but once they did, they could knock out four rows per twelve-hour shift, thirty-two tube joints per day.

The temperature in Jacksonville teetered near one hundred degrees for the fifth day in a row. Eight decks down behind the boilers, it was easily twenty degrees hotter. Microscopic metal burrs shot from deburring tools and implanted into sweltering flesh, smoke clung to matted hair, sweat seeped through soaked clothes. Though nobody complained, Huey sensed tension. There was an edge in tone, a thrown tool, expressions of dread. He called Jimmy and Hank together Friday afternoon before Jimmy left at the end of dayshift.

"I'm thinking of giving the gangs off Labor Day. Let them blow off a little steam."

"Can't say they haven't earned it," said Hank.

Jimmy looked back and forth between the two of them. "Really?"

"What do you mean?" said Huey.

"We haven't been here a month," said Jimmy. "If you want to give the guys a day off, put something out in front of them as an incentive."

"Like what?" Huey asked.

"Tell them if they finish a boiler by a certain date, they can have a day off."

"When did you become such a prick?" asked Hank.

"I'm just being realistic," said Jimmy. "I know these guys. I know how they think, and how some of them get when they're drinking, and that's what they'll do on a day off." Jimmy could see he had them thinking. "And down here, away from home? Three weeks after we got here? Next, they'll want a day off in two weeks, then we'll be working six-day workweeks."

Huey rested his hand on Jimmy's shoulder. "What's the worst that could happen? Someone gets in a fight, gets lumped up? Comes back with a busted lip, a black eye? It'd get a few laughs,

and everyone would get back to work. It'd be good for morale."
He scratched his cheek, and his expression slowly turned serious.
He looked at Hank. "Jimmy does have a point, though."

Hank shrugged. "I guess."

"How about this?" said Huey. "How about we reevaluate the
end of each week? See where we're at." He looked at Jimmy. "I
don't want these guys getting too burned out. They'll get sloppy.
So *you* let *me* know when you think it's time for a day off."

Jimmy shook his head. "Got it, boss."

~

Skeet's Café was a typical local hangout: smoky, noisy, and
close to water like the Tin Brick. But the scent of salt air and
squawking pelicans were no comparison to the stench of refineries and pigeon shit on Water Street. Skeet's had four pool tables
and two dart boards, and it was only a two-minute walk from the
Sea Turtle. The jukebox leaned heavily toward country western,
and there were a shitload of Southern drawls. Jacked-up pickup
trucks and Harley-Davidsons lined the curb out front, patrons
smoked weed outback. It became a meeting place at night for
the single guys on day shift. Some of the married guys stopped
from time to time. Most of the guys were content to respect the
locals' turf, but a few, mostly Beast, had an insatiable urge to
claim their own real estate.

Everyone on dayshift agreed to meet at Skeet's after work on
Labor Day. On his way over, Jimmy took a detour and headed
to the beach. He crossed the dunes, and midway to the water,
he was distracted by the sun glinting off a pair of gold-rimmed
sunglasses. The guy who wore them had taut, black skin that
glistened at the edge of his ripped muscles. He had on cut-off

jeans frayed at the knees, a red bandana, and walked with a swagger. The contrast of his skin against a beach full of white people gave him the appearance of a mythical character.

As the distance between them shortened, he flashed his white teeth at Jimmy. "Thought you'd be at Skeet's."

"Needed to clear my head before I go sit in a smoky bar listening to cowboy music," said Jimmy.

"Listen to city boy slammin' country music," Kenny laughed.

Jimmy gestured toward the bar. "How about we go over and hang out for a little bit?"

"I don't drink."

"Who said anything about drinking?" Jimmy asked, at the same time looking for signs that Kenny was kidding. "We'll shoot a game of pool."

"Yeah, right," he said. "A brother is going to hang out in a bar south of Mason-Dixon with Confederate flag decals on pickups out front."

The words stung, the bitterness and sarcasm buried under humor. Jimmy felt stupid. "I…"

Kenny put up his hand. "Don't, man," he said. "It's okay." He gave Jimmy a tight-lipped smile. "That's just the way it is.

~

Many of the guys who brought wives and kids volunteered for the backshift, figuring they could spend the days with their family, enjoy the beach, and play with their kids in the pool, then catch some shuteye before they went back to the ship. The plan worked for a few weeks: back to the hotel after a twelve-hour shift, out at the pool by nine, kids shouting and laughing as fathers threw them high in the air making huge splashes when they hit the water.

Then there were guys like Rhino who drank after work whether it was nine a.m. or p.m. He'd suck down beers in the pool, four or five kids clinging to his three-hundred-fifty-pound frame while he waded through the water pretending to be a sea monster. There he would be, a sixteen-ounce can in one hand, flipping the kids one by one into the water with the other. Kids loved the Rhino. He taught many of them how to swim. Around noon each day, he'd wander down the beach with a small cooler and a folding chair and pass out until it was time to go back to work.

Vince Murphy made an appearance each day around ten, stood waist-deep in the water surrounded by kids, and told ridiculous stories with cartoonish characters based on their fathers. He'd go on for about an hour, then leave them laughing hysterically and take off for the beach where he'd drink a few beers, set the alarm on a small wind-up clock, and fall asleep. When the alarm went off, he'd wake up Rhino and they'd go back to the hotel and get ready for work.

Work, play, pool, beach, alcohol, start over again—life couldn't get any better.

~

Snake had avoided Jimmy since they arrived in Mayport, either by being conveniently out of sight or hiding among the crowd. As the weeks drug on, tension mounted, and after Hank gave out jobs at the change of shifts one afternoon, Jimmy called him over.

"You've been avoiding me since we got down here."

"I'm not avoiding you," said Snake, unable or unwilling to look Jimmy in the eye. Jimmy didn't answer, just waited. A painful minute passed in silence before Snake slinked from his six-foot-four frame. "It's just… well, you were right."

Deep wrinkles spread across Jimmy's forehead. "Right about what?"

"Kenny," said Snake.

"Kenny?"

"Chuck says he's a great welder." Snake bowed his head like a child apologizing to a parent for some transgression. "And I hear he's not a bad guy."

"Yeah," said Jimmy, resisting the urge to goad. "He's not bad."

~

The job churned around the clock for three weeks after Labor Day, with twenty-one twelve-hour shifts each day and night. For five hundred and four hours, it was work, drink, sleep, and repeat. By mid-September, productivity increased to three rows of tubes per welder each shift and sometimes more. Jimmy estimated they'd complete welding on all four boilers in less than four weeks, which would take them into mid-October. He factored in a week for NDT inspectors to check the welds, another few days for the hydrostatic tests, and a week or so to reinstall interference, wrap up loose ends, and pack up the gear to travel back to Philly. If everything went according to his calculations, they'd complete the project before Huey's early November end date.

On Thursday afternoon of the third week in September, Huey walked into the trailer.

"Hey, boss, I was doing a little math," said Jimmy. "We're going to finish the job the beginning of November. How about we give the guys a breather on Sunday?"

Huey smiled at his young foreman. "Are we going to make early November?"

"Guaranteed," said Jimmy.

Everybody won on the deal. Jimmy took control, Huey got a chance to disappear and hit the links, and the guys got a day off.

For seven weeks, Jimmy marveled at the drive-in window every time he drove past MAX Liquors on Atlantic Boulevard: the ease of pulling up, ordering a bottle of liquor, perhaps a drink, and going on your merry way. He couldn't imagine such a thing in Philadelphia. Each time he drove past he'd shake his head and think to himself, *It's just too easy.*

Then, on Thursday of the tiger team's seventh week in Florida, the afternoon he recommended giving the gang a day off, he found out how easy it was.

~

Kenny's demeanor didn't invite people to engage him, and nobody ever accused him of going out of his way to make friends at the shipyard. None of that mattered to Lucy. Sunday morning, their first day off seven weeks, he was lounging on a chair by the pool when the five-year-old wandered over and stood beside him. It was hard to tell if he was awake or asleep with the dark glasses he wore, so she just stood and stared until Kenny lifted his shades.

"What'cha looking at, girl?"

"You're really black," she said.

Kenny looked down and patted his six-pack abdomen. "How about that," he said, shimmying up in the chair. "You know what?" he asked, breaking into a smile. "You're pretty smart."

"How'd you get so black?" she asked.

"Darndest thing," he said, his eyes widening as if witnessing a miracle. "God made me that way."

A woman hurried over.

"Leave the man alone, Lucy," she said to the little girl, and then to Kenny, "I'm sorry."

"Nothing to be sorry about," Kenny laughed. "Me and Lucy are good."

The woman offered her hand. "I'm Liz," she said, "my husband is one of the pipefitters. Lucy's usually getting ready for bed by the time you guys get back from working dayshift."

"Kenny Essington," he said, shaking her hand. "I'm pretty much a hermit after work anyway."

Lucy looked up at her mom. "Can Kenny come to the alligator farm with us?"

Liz smiled at her daughter. "I'm sure he has better things to do."

"Alligator farm?" said Kenny, raising his eyebrows. "They don't have any of those in North Philly."

Lucy pulled on Kenny's cutoff jeans. "Please. Please."

Kenny looked into her innocent eyes. "It's up to your mom, Lucy," he said.

When Liz saw that Kenny was serious, she said, "There's a bunch of us going. You're welcome to join us."

"Well, I guess that's it. I'm going."

"We're meeting in the lobby at noon," said Liz.

~

The moms gave the dads the day off to kick back by the pool or on the beach. At the alligator farm, the twenty-eight-year-old ebony-black man wearing a silk black tank top and matching bandana got more suspicious looks walking around with a group of white women and kids than Rhino, who somehow got roped into the trip by his swimming students. Uncontaminated by stories of a black radical from the shipyard, the moms found Kenny a charismatic young man the kids swarmed like a teen idol, and money he didn't waste on booze and carousing, he spent buying ice cream and treats for the kids.

By noon, the sun was directly overhead, and the thermometer was inching toward one hundred degrees. Nobody except Kenny had noticed Rhino laboring his three-hundred-fifty pounds around the farm, trying to keep up with the group.

"Theo!" suddenly echoed through the farm.

When everyone turned, they saw Kenny had wedged himself between the boilermaker's slumped body and a wooden post to keep him from falling. He eased Rhino to the ground, looked into the crowd that had gathered, and said, "Someone call an ambulance." He placed his hands around Rhino's thick neck, leaned down face-to-face, and whispered, "Stay with me, buddy." By the time the paramedics arrived, his skin was ashen and clammy. Kenny insisted on riding in the ambulance with Rhino, and though the paramedics said no, he wound up in the back anyway.

Gruff, fearless Rhino lay listless staring at the light in the ambulance ceiling, a clear oxygen mask barely covered his mouth and nose. Even as the paramedic hooked up the intravenous and checked his vitals, Kenny never took his hand off Rhino's shoulder, never stopped giving him advice on how to improve his condition, eating more fruits and salads, cutting back on beer and whiskey. By the time the ambulance pulled up to the emergency entrance at the hospital, the fright was gone from Rhino's eyes.

~

The wives gave Jimmy a rundown of the afternoon at the alligator farm when he arrived at the hospital. He looked around for Kenny, and when he caught up with him, he asked, "How'd you know his name was Theodore?" in a tone that sounded as if he himself didn't know Rhino's name.

"That's his name, man," said Kenny, matter-of-factly.

The answer was so simple, so obvious, yet forty-four shipyard workers had to travel nearly nine hundred miles to learn what Kenny Essington knew from simply having a real, honest conversation. All they had to do was abandon their preconceptions and become like a five-year-old to realize Kenny had more intimate conversations with Theodore Snipes, a.k.a. Rhino, than any of them had ever had amongst themselves.

Kenny didn't fit into a clique. Perhaps that's the reason people confided in him. They felt their secrets were safe, like with a priest in a confessional.

~

Beast showed up at Monday morning muster sporting a swollen lip, purple eye, and a prideful smirk.

"Get stuck in a revolving door?" Jimmy asked.

"You should see the other guy," said Beast. Vince told a different story, one where Beast was a punching bag for a four-hundred-pound biker who rode down from Georgia with his biker buddies. Beast started talking his street-corner shit, making a terrible miscalculation that the bikers would be intimidated by a South Philly thug. According to Vince, Cajon got in more shots than anyone on either side. He was also the only one who walked away unscathed.

In the end, Huey's prediction was right: the guys came back to work after a day off with the fervor of tigers that smelled blood. The two shifts melded into a continuous rhythm of industrial progress and determined forward motion. They were kicking ass and could feel it. Already more than a week ahead of schedule, they were confident that every weld was perfect.

The tubes on both boilers were completed in Fire Room #3 by the last week in September. NDT inspectors accepted every joint without one defect. By the beginning of the second week in October, the tubes in boiler 4A were complete, and welding started on 4B. Jimmy projected to complete welding and NDT on all four boilers by the end of the following week. After the heaters were removed, it would take a few days to prepare the boilers for hydro, pump them to almost two thousand pounds per square inch, and check to make sure there were no leaks. Once the hydros were signed off, it would take about a week to reinstall the interference they removed, break down the equipment, and pack the gear. The gang would be traveling home to Philly in early November.

~

Eleven weeks, twelve hours per day, seven days a week looking at rows of one-and-a-quarter-inch tubes with only one day off. Welders walked off the ship at the end of a shift in a trance. They saw circular holes in their sleep. Trips to the bar at night gave way to chilling out on the hotel balcony with a cold six-pack. Most guys went to bed before midnight. During the day, the crowd at the pool dwindled to mostly wives and kids.

Huey called an all-hands meeting at shift change Monday afternoon. It would be the first time he'd been on the ship that late in the day in weeks, and rumors flew like starlings: one about the shipyard closing because of the boiler tube screw-up, another that Huey was being fired or even the Saratoga being sold for scrap.

Everyone was milling around outside the command trailer when Huey stepped off the gangway. He walked straight across the hanger bay into the center of the crowd. Everyone got quiet.

"Senator Hawkins is planning to visit on Friday." The guys looked at each other not knowing if that was good or bad. "The senator's the ranking member on the Senate Arms Service Committee, he fought to get the SLEP program in Philadelphia. Word is that he's pissed about the Navy blaming us for the Maestro Fusion fuck up, and he's determined to clear our reputation so future aircraft carrier overhauls are done in Philly. He plans to tour the ship, get an update on the job, and then have an all-hands meeting with all of us."

A glimmer of hope. A spark to push the welders to finish boiler 4B in the next four days—tight but doable.

Chapter XVII

INTRUDER

Nightshift was a state of mind—an emotion, an aura, a mood. It was tranquil, free of interference and aggravation. Guys signed up for nightshift to try it out for a month or two and retired forty years later without ever coming off. To dayshift workers, those conforming members of society who lived in full view of the establishment, nightshift workers were phantoms, names on a turnover sheet, with no description, personality traits, interest, or redeeming values. Nightshift workers were ghosts. Dayshift left their jobs at four o'clock in the afternoon, went home, ate dinner, watched a ball game, caught a movie and went to bed, and when they returned in the morning their jobs had progressed, as if by magic. Nightshift was the background beat, the base for the rhythm of the shipyard symphony.

Nightshift was the yin to the dayshift yang.

An ominous air disrupted the rhythm during the third week in October. Backshift workers began to fidget and sneak anxious peeks over their shoulder like they were in the crosshairs of a sniper. Jimmy shot up in the middle of the night soaked. He smelled acetylene, saw the yellowish charcoal of melting flesh. It was a recurring nightmare he had any time he sensed danger since he saw the painter burnt to death when he was nineteen.

The only non-tradesmen who'd been in the Saratoga fire rooms on the backshift since August were NDT inspectors and an occasional engineer, until the hit man arrived at three o'clock Wednesday morning.

He looked to be in his sixties, white-haired and dressed in blue overalls, surveying the upper level of the fire room like a vulture circling prey. A much younger man, tall and lean, followed close behind, bodyguard-style. They descended the ladder to the lower level and walked behind boiler 3B.

"Who authorized you to be in Florida?" the white-haired man exploded, when he saw the engineer in the superheater cavity.

George Sputz had kept a low profile ever since his run-in with Admiral Foley back in Philly. In Mayport he hid on the backshift. He should have known that Senator Hawkins's visit would prompt the admiral to fly south and snoop around the boilers in the middle of the night. "My boss, sir."

"Doesn't anyone in Philadelphia talk to each other?" the admiral asked angrily. "I told Strunk I never wanted to see you on an aircraft carrier again." His hand trembled as he wiped spit off his lips. "Pack your bags and get the next flight back to Philadelphia or I'll have you fired too."

Fired? The word kick-started George's brain. In all the years he had worked for Mr. Strunk, his boss never once mentioned retirement, yet in the few short months he'd been in Mayport he announced he was calling it quits. *Fired?*

There was only one way into the superheater cavity and one way out, and Foley and his goon were blocking it. Cornered. Survival. George scurried out, and as he squeezed passed the admiral, papers fell out of his back pocket. Foley picked them up. Rage filled the old man's eyes as he glared at the front cover: *Hydrogen Embrittlement of Chromium Alloy by Joseph Strunk*. George ripped the papers out of the admiral's hand and took off around the front of the boiler.

Foley took chase but was out of breath by the time he got to the ladder. He held the handrail gasping as he watched George disappear.

"That's an unauthorized study!" he screamed.

George shouldered the fire room door and ran into Tommy who was about open it on the second deck. Frantic, he grabbed Tommy's shirt and pulled him down the passageway into a compartment.

"What the hell's going on, George?"

George put a finger to his lips when he heard the fire room door open. They listened to footsteps outside the compartment as they slowed, then silence.

"Admiral Foley's onboard," George whispered. There was no way of telling the admiral had slipped into an adjoining stateroom and pressed his ear against the bulkhead listening to their exchange. "… I was going to give this to Senator Hawkins at the all-hands meeting," he said, handing Tommy the study, "but the admiral ordered me to go back to Philly."

"What is it?"

George shook his head. "It's better you don't know," he said. "Just make sure it gets to the senator."

The only sounds for the next couple of minutes were the vibration of generators, the hum of transformers, and air sifting through a split gasket. George cracked the compartment door and peeked into the desolate passageway. He squeezed Tommy's bicep and nodded, then snuck out and hurried toward the hanger bay ladder. Tommy shoved the study under his belt and pulled his shirt over it, then headed in the opposite direction to the fire room. The stateroom door slit open as he went by. The admiral stepped into the passageway at the same time Tommy pulled open the access door to the fire room. Their eyes locked at twenty feet. Foley squinted the way a big game hunter zeros in on his prey through a scope, hitched the corner of his mouth, and winked.

~

The nightmare was too disturbing, too real, and though Jimmy tried to get back to sleep it was futile. The command trailer was empty when he arrived at four-thirty. The air was tense, like a courtroom right before a verdict is read. He expected Hank to be busy documenting the job status: problems, what to look for, all the information he typically included in a turnover sheet. Instead he found half-written notes, a pen dropped in a notebook, chairs pushed out haphazardly like storm troopers invaded and hauled everyone off to the brig.

The door swung open and the white-haired man in navy blue coveralls stomped in, a tall young lackey half of a step behind. He walked up to Jimmy, and asked, "Who are you?"

"Jimmy McKee, dayshift foreman."

"Foreman, my ass," the man said. "If there were a competent foreman in Philadelphia, we wouldn't be in this mess."

He scanned the trailer looking for more victims, then back at Jimmy. "Who's your boss?"

Judging by the way the lackey was brushing dust off the old man's coveralls, Jimmy figured the guy was important, which meant nothing to him. He was debating whether to tell the guy to get lost, when the old man shouted, "Did you hear me ask you a question, boy?"

Jimmy's muscles tensed, visions of the fat third class boiler mate who ordered him to weld an angle iron when he was an apprentice flashed through his head. He clenched his fist, glared at him, and said, "Yeah, I heard you."

"Yeah?" the old man burst. "Is that the way you address an admiral?"

Jimmy didn't know if admiral was above or below captain, and he didn't care. And it didn't matter that Foley was a flag officer because he didn't know what a flag officer was. Jimmy grew up on the streets, a working grunt who hung in corner pubs, rooted for the Phillies, Eagles, Sixers and Flyers and worked his way up from apprentice to foreman by breaking his balls in dry docks and bilges. He loved his work, loved the shipyard, and took pride in his trade. The day the tiger team tore open the boilers in Mayport, the fire rooms became blue-collar turf—his turf. This was where he practiced his trade, his craft. This *was* who he was. And the little old stocky man with white hair who called him "boy" didn't address him with respect. Jimmy didn't take orders simply because someone had bars or stars on their shoulder.

It took every ounce of restraint Jimmy had to keep from spitting in the old man's face and knocking the big pussy behind him on his ass. Instead he turned, and walking toward the door, muttered, "Fucking asshole."

"What'd you say?" Foley exploded, just as the door slammed. He ran over, opened it, and screamed, "I'll have you fired!"

~

Huey was made for moments like this. He thrived on them. The long-distance phone call at five a.m. from his boss back in Philadelphia. Under his breath, he chuckled, listening to Skip Homes's distressed voice as he explained that one of his foremen called a four-star admiral a fucking asshole. An F-bomb had never fallen from the lips of Hank Peachtree, so he knew it was Jimmy. And Admiral Foley was the only four-star who'd set foot on the Saratoga during the boiler controversy. Refereeing one-sided fights, evening the odds between a professional and an amateur, was how Huey earned his salary.

In his best impersonation of sounding concerned, he said, "I'll handle it, sir."

Less than an hour later, Huey was schmoozing the lackey standing guard outside the captain's stateroom where the admiral was camped out, convincing him it was an urgent matter. The stateroom was an impressive display of leather, cherry wood, and carpet, the paneled walls decorated with enough paintings to fill the wing of an art gallery, including a three-by-four-foot image of the *Battle of Hampton Roads*. Huey wore the long sleeve khaki shirt from his Navy days he packed just for such an occasion. He rolled up his sleeves as he strolled in, flaunting tattoos on his forearms: USN superimposed over an anchor with USS Ohio scrolled across the top on the left, a fully rigged tall ship on the right.

"Admiral Foley, sir," Huey began. He briefly acknowledged Jimmy's transgression, peppering his dissertation with old master chief lingo, comparing his foreman's dedication with that of a chief engineer. He dropped a few names every Navy man recognized and respected before segueing into salty bars where commissioned officers hung out on Malta and Lisbon, and when he saw the glint in Foley's eyes, he began massaging the four-star's ego, describing the passion of Philly shipyard workers and their motivation to get the admiral's boilers shipshape and return *his* carrier to the fleet.

Foley nodded what seemed his acceptance. Slowly his brow furrowed, and he asked, "How about the other kid?"

Huey's expression said he didn't follow him. "What other kid?"

The admiral stared through Huey to something indiscernible. "Never mind," he said. "You're dismissed."

~

Everybody on the backshift had been below decks when Huey snuck onboard in the dark, and it was inconceivable that he was in the captain's stateroom when Jimmy caught up with Hank in the trailer a few minutes before six.

"You guys finish last night?" Jimmy asked.

Hank sat staring at the wall. "No," he said.

"What's with you?"

"Denny disappeared before lunch and never came back."

Jimmy stood stone-faced for a few seconds. "Tell Chuck and Kenny to finish up," he said, and turned toward the door.

Hank grabbed his arm. "Don't do anything stupid, Jimmy. The job's almost done."

Jimmy pulled away. "I got business to attend to," he said, and disappeared out the door.

Hank followed him, pleading. "Denny's been doing good…" It was unlikely Jimmy heard him as he ran down the steps and jogged off the ship to the parking lot.

Jimmy was lucky he didn't get pulled over by a cop on his way to Denny's motel. He jumped out of the car and pounded the door of this room, and in between series of knocks, he pressed his ear against the door. Silence. He made a fist and knocked with the meaty bottom of his hand. More silence. He kicked the bottom of the door so hard it vibrated from the lock to the ground. Still no answer. The veins in his neck pulsated. He smelled Denny inside the way a shark smells blood. He alternated between kicking and pounding until he sensed movement inside, not a human but a creature struggling to stay alive.

He looked around, picked up a large landscaping rock, lifted it with both hands and hurled it at the door splintering the jamb and sending woodwork across the room.

Denny rolled over in bed, and groaned, "What the f…"

Jimmy ran straight at him, grabbed his shirt and shook him.

"You go out and get drunk at the most critical time of the job! What the hell's wrong with you?"

Denny covered his head with his hands. "I can't take it anymore," he sobbed. "I just can't take it."

The words stunned Jimmy. "Can't take what?"

"The pressure," Denny said, and when he put down his hands, tears were streaming down his face. "It's too much. I can't handle it."

Jimmy let go of him. After a few moments, he sat next to him. He waited for Denny to stop crying, then in a calm, even voice, he said, "Go to the airport and get a plane ticket home. We'll talk when I get back to Philly."

~

Eight years tearing ships down to their skeleton, working double shifts, weekends. Coworkers maimed and killed. Vessels steaming down the Delaware River to the bay and out to sea. This was the classroom in which Jimmy based his thesis. Ships and boilers were real, tangible. He touched them and burnt his flesh on their metal hulls. He spent his days the way he spent his life, laboring with specialists in the skilled trades, conferring with engineers and inspectors. He might have been the youngest foreman in the shipyard, but he wasn't naïve.

The debate with George Sputz a couple of years ago behind the boiler on a destroyer echoed in his brain, the engineer's monotone voice as he halfheartedly justified how the Maestro Fusion process preheated the chromium headers in two minutes opposed to the manual process which took more than twenty-four hours. *George didn't believe it himself.* During his tour of the metallurgy department as an apprentice, Jimmy remembered Joey Strunk explaining the qualities of metals and the susceptibility of certain metals cracking if proper preheating procedures weren't followed.

Metals like chromium steel.

Jimmy's calculus about the reason the tiger team was in Florida crystalized.

~

A body suspended in space, falling backward, arms and legs flailing, down, down into the abyss. Long, heavy, rotted timbers

119

fall and crash into darkness, burying the man under granular roofing cinders, rusted nails, brick, mortar, and wrought iron. A black limousine with tinted windows approaches the wreckage and slows as it passes the mountain of rubble. The back window slides down, and John McDuffy rolls a thick Cuban cigar from one side of his mouth to the other with his teeth, removes it with fingers that have perfectly manicured nails, and blows smoke rings out the window. Benjamins fly from stuffed pockets, leaving a trail down Market Street.

Chapter XVIII

STATEROOM SCHEME

T he hatch to the bridge swung open at nine a.m., and in walked an ensign who looked too young to shave. The commanding officer stood at the windshield, hypnotized by the view of St. John's Point across the basin. Having recently completed his in-grade requirement at commander and promoted to captain, Bradley Stevens had been installed on the Saratoga specifically for the retubing of the carrier. It was meant to be a temporary appointment: early August to early November. The position was a proxy and an unusual assignment: no formalities, no change of command ceremony, and oddest of all, no backlash from the previous CO, Captain Cahill. He would never command the ship at sea, for he was miserably unqualified. But all that mattered to Captain Stevens was that every swinging dick onboard obeyed his orders.

"Captain, your presence is requested in your stateroom, sir."

The captain turned, looked the junior officer up one side and down the other.

"By who?" he asked, belligerently.

"I can't say, sir," said the ensign, with obvious strain in his voice.

"Do I have to remind you that you're addressing the captain of the ship?"

"No, sir. Sorry, sir."

"So who wants to see me?"

"Sir, I was ordered only to tell you to report to the captain's stateroom."

By this time, Stevens knew only one person could be summoning him with anonymity, and the only time *that* person came to see him was when he needed something. Not to give him advice, share experiences that might help him, or just tell him that he was proud to see him at the helm of an aircraft carrier in the United States Navy. The captain also knew that the ensign was in a no-win position.

"This is the last time I'm asking. By who!"

The ensign looked around the empty bridge, put his hand to the side of his mouth, and just above a whisper, said, "The admiral, sir."

The captain exhaled the triumphant smirk of an interrogator who'd broken a suspect.

~

Bradley Stevens was intelligent as a child, but he was spoiled and had a laziness borne of privilege. He placed in the top quartile of his class at the Naval Academy, but could easily have been one of the top ten had he applied himself, and if he had the determination of a leader, maybe the top two or three. He was also naïve, too naïve to acknowledge that every ship he'd ever been assigned and every promotion he'd ever received was orchestrated. He'd been manipulated as part of a plan, a grand scheme that would one day require payback to a man who was behind every move since his acceptance into the academy.

Admiral Foley was sitting back in one of the cushioned leather chairs with his hand wrapped around a coffee cup when Captain Stevens walked in.

"I didn't know you were onboard, Admiral."

"I'm not," said Foley, stoically. "Sit down."

Captain Stevens sat across from him. "Is everything okay, sir?"

"What are your aspirations, Bradley?"

"Finish this assignment, get over to the Pentagon, and eventually compete for general officer," he said, reciting the list like a POW drilled to state name, rank and serial number.

"Compete," the admiral sniggered. "You never competed for anything in your life."

"What do you mean," the captain protested, before catching himself, and adding, "Sir?"

"Wake up, young man. How do you think you got in the academy?" The admiral's expression conveyed the pleasure he took watching a subordinate squirm. "You don't really think you'd be a captain if it wasn't for me, do you?"

Stevens straightened in defense of his rank, and said, "I'd be commanding this ship with or without you."

The lame protest brought a smile to the admiral. "That's the first time I ever heard you sound something like a leader," he said, but unable to restrain himself, he added, "a little tentative, but it's a start." He looked the captain in the eye. "So you think you can get to the Pentagon and make general officer on your own?"

"I know I can."

"Well," said the admiral, letting the word hang for a few seconds, "I have a test for you."

"I'm listening," said Stevens.

"I have a mission that is more important than anything you've ever done, and possibly anything you'll ever do for the rest of your career." He placed the coffee aside and leaned forward in his chair. "If you pull it off, you'll be rewarded handsomely."

"Go ahead, sir," said the captain.

"Maestro Fusion Corporation is close to signing a sixty-million-dollar contract with the Navy to re-tube the Forrestal. I'm planning to retire at the end of the summer to become the company's Chief Operations Officer, but we've hit a snag."

"A snag?"

"Yes," said the admiral. "The reason I'm going to work for the company is to save millions of dollars to build a strong national defense, and to care for our honorable veterans. And it's all about to be jeopardized."

In all his years in the Navy, the captain had never been so engaged, so motivated as he was listening to the admiral's dissertation about sabotage, ideology, traitors, and patriotism. So spellbound by the man who'd made a career of motivating and manipulating people, that when the admiral asked for his help, he blurted, "Whatever you need, sir!"

Foley's lips tightened into something resembling a smile. "I knew I could count on you."

Captain Stevens's response had been pure emotion, an instinct to impress the admiral. He had volunteered without

understanding what had been asked, and as the master manip-
ulator described what he meant by "eliminate the threat," the
captain's enthusiasm turned to trepidation, then panic. His
cowardly disposition surfaced, and his mind went into a tailspin.
He tried to think of someone he could recruit to do his dirty
work, someone he could trust to commit an act so heinous he
was incapable of committing it himself.

Chapter XIX

THE HUSTLE

A ristocrats are bred in an impenetrable bubble called privilege, sheltered from hunger, violence, and poverty, where they are safe and secure as an embryo in a mother's sac. They are a breed comfortable in plaid Bermuda shorts and shirts sporting insignias flaunting brands acceptable to members of their exclusive club. Isolated from the outside world, this rare order of individuals is oblivious to the boundaries of its influence, full of the type who believe they could escape a beating by a gang in a dark alley by simply telling them their rank, title, or annual income.

~

In Captain Stevens's judgment, the speed with which the young ensign had collected intelligence on Third Class Boiler Tech Louis Smitt demonstrated senior officer potential. The dossier the ensign had compiled about Smitt included a note that the boiler tech hustled pool at night, and not in the usual sailor hangouts where beers were two for a buck, but in a local hangout by the beach where the locals made real money working construction, repairing cars, or on the docks and drove pickups, muscle cars, and motorcycles.

Bradley Stevens walked into Skeet's Café that night, immune to the stares from tattooed and bearded men who shifted on their stools, watching the clean-shaven guy decked out in a pinstripe Polo shirt tucked into pleated navy-blue shorts. The officer brushed the back of his hand under his nose to repel the stench of stale beer.

Smitt didn't recognize the captain in civilian clothes until Stevens offered to buy him a beer. "Sir, I never expected to see you in here," he said, unable to conceal his surprised.

"Why's that?"

Smitt looked embarrassed. "Just surprised, that's all," he said, as if realizing honesty would do him no good. He was quick to change the subject. "What a coincidence we wind up on the same ship again, huh?"

"Pure coincidence," said Stevens.

"And a captain. Congratulations, sir." A few minutes of small talk, shipboard life and the next port-o-call, then Smitt asked the captain if he'd ever played eight ball. Though tennis was his sport, he obliged. Smitt kept the score close, missing shots he'd easily sink against anyone else, before beating his CO on the last shot. Stevens was about to order another round when he noticed Smitt's beer was still full. "You didn't touch your beer," he said.

"I don't drink, sir."

"You should have told me. What *do* you drink?"

"Club and lime," he said. "People mistake it for gin and tonic." He winked, and added, "Part of the hustle."

Stevens ordered the drinks, and while they waited said, "So when are you up for promotion?"

"The end of next year, sir."

"Second Class, right?"

"Correct, sir."

"You can drop the 'sir,'" said Stevens. The drinks came, and he took a sip of his beer. "What if I told you I could get you in for first class boiler tech in the spring?"

"Sir?" said Smitt, as if he wasn't sure if he heard him right. "This coming spring?"

Stevens grabbed his beer and gestured to an empty booth in the back of the bar. Smitt followed the captain and slid in across from him.

"I'm leading a critical mission," said Stevens, and went on to tell him about a conspiracy, a traitor, and a top-secret mission involving tens of millions of dollars for national defense and s benefits. The entire time he spoke, he was thinking about the day he looked out the control room window in the fire room of a destroyer and watched the young boiler tech pull a knife on a boilermaker and threaten cut off his balls. He leaned in, and confided, "And I need the help of a patriot."

Chapter XX

MILESTONE

There's a school of thought that if you take tiny screws, springs, armatures, gears, regulators, levers, pallets, a faceplate, and a few other intricate odds and ends, place them in a capsule, and rotate it around and around, at some point, say a million years from now, all the parts will fall into place and become a functioning stopwatch. People who subscribe to such a theory would likely believe that Kenny Essington would become a superheater tube welding specialist and wind up in Mayport, Florida on night shift with Snake. All the pieces fell into place: the job was near completion, Jimmy sent Denny packing for Philly, and Kenny volunteered to work a double shift to help Snake finish welding the boiler tubes before the Senator Hawkins visit.

At 4:57 a.m. on Thursday, Kenny lifted his welding shield and flashed his signature smile at Snake.

"Finished," he said, announcing the 2,048th superheater tube was complete.

Snake nodded his approval. "I'll go tell Hank to begin lowering the heat."

After an unsettling twenty-four hours, the momentum shifted back in the shipyard's favor. Now, when Senator Hawkins visited on Friday, Huey could report that welding was complete, NDT inspections had begun, and the hydrostatic tests would start before the weekend was out.

The boilermakers had plans of their own, and they elected Vince Murphy to pitch their idea to the boss. With less than an hour left in the shift, Vince caught Hank alone inside the boiler inspecting welds. "Almost two weeks ahead of schedule. Not bad, huh boss?"

Hank smelled a con. "Get to the point, Vince."

"We've been stuck in this damn fire room for twelve hours a night with only one day off in two months, and not one person bitched."

"You sound a little winey right now," said Hank.

"The guys would feel appreciated if they were allowed off the ship to go to lunch for a change." Vince waited for a reaction, and when he didn't get one, he pressed on. "One night out of how many? Let me see, eight weeks, seven days a week…"

"I can do the math, genius," said Hank.

Vince put his arm around the boss's shoulder. "Listen, Hank, a couple hours away from the job is just the thing these guys need. It'll put 'em in a good frame of mind for the senator's visit."

"We'll see."

"Come on, boss. I know 'We'll see' means it'll never happen."

Hank ran his fingers through his hair. "Okay, Vince. When you guys come in tonight, five guys, and that's it. You pick them, but Snake can't be one of them."

"You're awesome, Hank," said Vince, walking away with a hop in his step.

"One more thing, Vince," called Hank after him.

Vince stopped and turned. "Whatever you want, boss man."

"Tommy drives."

"Sounds reasonable to me."

The guys on nightshift had found out about the Farmstead from Jimmy who found out from the kid from Enterprise Car Rental. The week after Huey split the tiger team into two shifts, Tommy started picking up takeout from the restaurant, but he'd never eaten in. The guys loved the southern fried chicken, and nobody from Philly had ever heard of smothering it with honey, the same way Southerners had never heard of covering soft pretzels with mustard, but once they tried it, they never ate it any other way. When Tommy told them the place had a bar that was open until two a.m., Farmstead was a unanimous decision.

~

Jimmy was in the trailer Thursday morning reading the night-shift turnover when Tommy walked in. "Remember our deal?"

"Of course, I remember our deal," said Jimmy. He lifted the lid off his coffee and blew steam. "What was it?"

"The christening!" said Tommy, so loud that two inspectors at the other end of the trailer looked up.

"Easy, buddy," Jimmy laughed. "I'm kidding. I cleared it with Huey and Hank before we left Philly. Did you get your plane ticket?"

"I'm going to call the airline before I come to work tonight. I'll fly out tomorrow after the all-hands meeting with Senator Hawkins."

"Skip it," said Jimmy. "The senator's not going to miss you."

"What are you going to do?"

"I'm flying up on Saturday afternoon. I'll meet you guys in church Sunday morning and fly back for work on Monday."

Tommy looked to be in deep thought. "There's one more thing."

"What's that?"

A commotion broke out at the trailer door. They both turned as Kenny walked in with Snake. Vince and a few boilermakers were close behind.

"Kenny," said Jimmy, "I heard you guys finished last night."

"You sound surprised," said Kenny.

"Not at all," said Jimmy. He looked at the clock. "Shit! I gotta go muster my guys." He got up and started for the door, but stopped and turned back to Tommy. "I'm sorry, Tommy. What were you starting to say?"

"Hydrogen embrittlement caused…" Tommy started.

"Hydrogen what?" Jimmy interrupted.

Tommy looked at him with a blank stare, as if not knowing where to start. There was too much to tell him in a minute or two, about Mr. Strunk's study that George Sputz had given him the night before, the chromium alloys, the Maestro Fusion preheat cycle and Philadelphia's harsh winters. Tommy wanted to tell Jimmy that *Hydrogen Embrittlement* caused the chromium tubes to crack, but it was too complicated to summarize in a few moments. "I'll tell you tonight."

Chapter XXI

Minor League

Huey stood outside the trailer near the end of dayshift, arms folded like a bouncer at the door of a seedy nightclub. Jimmy could tell by the way his eyes zeroed in on him that he was in for an earful. He'd been expecting it.

"How about we take a walk?" said Huey.

"Can I write my turnover for Hank first?"

"You come with me." Jimmy prepared his defense as he followed his boss out to the fantail. Huey turned and faced him. "You got something you want to tell me?"

"About the asshole who said there aren't any competent supervisors in the shipyard?"

"You know who that was?"

"I don't care who it was, Huey," said Jimmy, louder than he meant to. "He showed me no respect. And he had no respect for the shipyard. None of us. Not you. Not the guys who've been down here breaking their balls for ten weeks …" The rant would have gone on forever if he hadn't noticed a trace of a smile on Huey's face. "What?"

Huey put his hand on Jimmy's shoulder. "I love your passion, kid. I really do." The smile disappeared. "But here's the thing. That asshole happened to be Admiral Foley. He pulls a lot of weight in the Navy, a lot of weight in Congress. He has influence in where ships are overhauled. You don't want to piss him off." Jimmy gave a reluctant half-nod. "Sometimes you got to eat shit to win. It's part of the game."

Jimmy thanked Huey, knowing he could have been disciplined.

"Shit," he said, suddenly.

"What?"

"Tommy had something he wanted to tell me when he came in tonight."

"Don't worry about Tommy. I'll tell him you'll see him in the morning. You go back to the hotel and relax."

~

Treadmill: four-thirty wake-up, shower, 7-Eleven for coffee, drive Mayport Road, muster, work a twelve-hour shift, a few beers, go to bed, four-thirty wake up, start over. Seven days a week, week in and week out. The schedulers estimated the job would be done in twelve weeks once the welding began. The team had already cut more than a week off the schedule and were poised to cut more. The dayshift planned to celebrate completion of welding at Skeet's, but Jimmy was burnt out, stressed from the grind and the bullshit. His nerves were frayed from alcohol. He needed alone time, not another night of drinking. He'd seen posters around the hotel and on some storefronts about a minor league baseball team, the Jacksonville Suns, and thought he'd drive out to the stadium, sit in the bleachers and take in a game. Dry out for a night. Chill.

That evening, Jimmy drove west on I-90 to Sun Stadium. By the time he got there, the parking lot was packed. He could hear the announcer reading the team lineups over the public address system as he cruised up one row and down another before finding an open spot near the cyclone fence in the back. Straggling tailgaters a few cars away dressed in NASCAR caps and t-shirts offered him a beer. Jimmy declined, but they insisted. *Just one,* he told himself, popped it open and took a couple gulps. He chitchatted a few minutes, then chugged the rest and said goodbye. He entered the stadium in the bottom of the first inning, passing concession stands with neon Budweiser and Miller High Life signs, and walked down to his seat a few rows behind the first base dugout. The last of the day's sun reflected off a gold globe on top the flagpole in center field. Seagulls circled swaying palm trees beyond the outfield fence. His seat was so close to the field, he could hear the players curse in the dugout and see dust rise when their spit hit the dirt.

The Suns were up 2-1 in the third inning when a vendor walked down the steps and turned at the rail in front of him.

"Cold beer!" shouted a man who looked to be in his seventies, couldn't have weighed a hundred pounds and had a tray of beers balanced on his shoulder. "Ice cold beer!" The gleam in his eye met Jimmy's, who nodded and pulled a twenty out of his pocket. Whether it was his thirst, the sun sparkling in the outfield, the warm, dry breeze, or just plain magic, that first sip of beer was enchanting. He nursed it into the fourth inning before getting up to take a piss. On his way back from the men's room, just inside the tunnel that led to his seat, was the concession stand. He fought the temptation as he walked past, then began to waver, turned, and went back for another beer. The visiting team had tied the game by the time he got to his seat in the top of the fifth.

In the seventh inning, the old man with the tray of beer returned. Jimmy pulled out a wad of bills and bought another. The score remained tied into the ninth inning when the Suns catcher hit a walk-off home run to win the game.

Jimmy was surprised to see the concession stand still open on his way out of the stadium. Ass dragging from long hours of work and all the alcohol he'd consumed, the beer taps glimmered like a mirage. He walked over and ordered one for the road.

Outside the stadium, he stood scanning the parking lot trying to remember where he'd parked. He walked straight ahead, looking left and right down each row, and when he got to the cyclone fence, he turned and started back. He took a long gulp from his cup, licked the foam from his mustache, then started up the last row to the end and back down the next row. Cars were emptying out of the lot, and by the time he got to the middle of the second row from the back, he found his Escort sitting between two empty spaces.

Jimmy fumbled the keys out of his pocket, scratched the paint on the door trying to get the key in the lock before dropping them on the ground. He placed the cup on the roof and got down on his hands and knees, patting the ground. After a few seconds, he reached under the car and found them. He stood and opened the door, climbed inside and stared into oblivion, recapping a night he'd planned to purge his system of poison. Instead, he was as drunk as he would have been had he gone to Skeet's with the boilermakers. Just before he pulled out, he reached out the window and grabbed the beer off the roof, put it between his legs, and drove off.

Jimmy kept an eye on the speedometer and was careful not lift his cup too high as he cruised east on the interstate. About halfway back to the hotel, he saw tiny red and white lights flashing in his rearview mirror. He white-knuckled the steering wheel, and as the lights grew larger, he started getting paranoid, envisioning himself handcuffed in the backseat of a police cruiser. The inside of the car illuminated, brighter and redder, almost blinding him until a patrol car sped past. After the cop disappeared down the road, he grabbed the beer from between his legs, polished it off in one long gulp, and tossed the empty cup down a grassy embankment.

Brake lights funneled into a single lane up ahead. Flashing lights reflected off cars and billboards into an open field. Four tires stuck up from an overturned car in a ditch on the side of the road, and as Jimmy got close, he could see the roof submerged in water. The stench of steam, burning rubber, and oil saturated the muggy air. A piercing scream came from inside the car. Less than twenty feet away, rescue workers tried to pry open the car door. Stop and go traffic crawled, people rubbernecking. The car in front of him stopped, and he jammed his brakes. A police officer looked over, raised his flashlight, and walked toward the car. Jimmy reached between his legs, forgetting he'd already gotten rid of the beer.

The policeman beamed the flashlight in Jimmy's bloodshot eyes, then leaned in the window. "You okay, buddy?"

"Yes, sir."

The cop dropped his head, looked back at the car in the ditch, and said, "Get the hell out of here."

The remainder of the ride back to the hotel went without incident before he hit the curb at the parking lot entrance and the car jumped onto the blacktop. He pulled into an empty space facing the ocean, shut off the engine, and exhaled a long sigh of exhaustion. An alcohol-influenced buzz droned in his brain until he nodded off, for minutes, or hours.

An explosion catapulted Jimmy out of his seat. He threw open the door and stood outside steadying himself on the car, looking around, feeling as though the earth had shifted under him. It took several long, painful seconds before he realized he was in the parking lot of the Sea Turtle. Deep breaths of salt air slowly stimulated his brain. Waves washing back and forth against sand in the distance eased him. But nothing could erase remnants of the cataclysm that had woken him.

~

The elevator groaned to the twelfth floor and the doors cranked open. The narrow corridor looked like a prison scene from a vintage black and white movie. He opened the door of his apartment and out of habit grabbed a beer from the refrigerator, walked over, opened the sliding glass door and stepped onto the balcony. This was the night he'd chill, the night he'd abstain from alcohol and clear his head. He was drunk with another beer in his hand.

A large shadow crept into his peripheral vision, and when he turned, a pelican floated up from his left and hung suspended on the other side of the railing, so close he felt he could reach out and touch its long beak. The huge bird rotated until it was face-to-face with him, its beady orange-ringed eyes drilled into his own.

Jimmy had never seen anything so beautiful, so peaceful, so free.

"I envy you," he mumbled. The pelican turned, releasing him from its spell, and veered toward the sea. He'd felt inferior and hypocritical, holding the beer in the presence of the magnificent creature, and in one fluid motion he wound up and threw the bottle as far as he could. The force with which he threw it gave him a sense of emancipation, and as he watched it disappear into the dunes, he felt as if he'd rid himself of a great burden.

"I envy you," Jimmy repeated into the darkness, and with that he went inside, laid down, and drifted into a deep sleep. Faraway, waves crashed in long lines of white foam and dissipated down the coast.

~

Jimmy oscillated between two worlds: the world of welders and boilermakers filled with smoke, dust, sweat, cursing, alcohol, testosterone, and the world of the pelican, where saltwater waves cleansed white sands, and glorious creatures glided between heaven and earth.

The two worlds were real to Jimmy, and for two months they coexisted, intertwined, and then, in an instant, exploded.

Chapter XXII

FARMSTEAD

Louis Robert Smitt had more reason to abuse drugs and alcohol than any kid in Forksville, Pennsylvania, but at an early age he chose to abstain. He didn't want to deaden the pain of his foster father's beatings, or the torment of his next foster father's sexual abuse. He used the assaults and rapes to strengthen his resolve to make something of himself. What, he didn't know, but something. The night Captain Stevens walked into Skeet's Café and recruited him for a top-secret mission to eliminate a threat to funding for national defense and veterans' benefits, he found that something: a patriot.

Louis Smitt killed a deer bow hunting when he was fourteen. Gutting the one-hundred-eighty-pound mammal with a nine-inch Buck knife in Loyalsock State Forrest was his first religious experience: the sacred sensation of its warm blood running down his arms, between his fingers, and dripping into the blessed earth, and the awe of holding its intestines in his hands, watching the faint pulse of its heart fade, fade, fade until it was still. It was an image he might have had in mind the day he threatened to fillet Beast in the fire room.

~

The night Jimmy got drunk at the Jacksonville Suns' game, Smitt drove out the Naval Station gate and onto Mayport Road. At the traffic light at Atlantic Avenue, his hands started to tremble, and he felt disoriented. He slid the gearshift into neutral and tried to steady himself until the light turned green. The car behind him beeped. With unsteady sweaty palms around the steering wheel, he shifted into first and let up on the clutch, made a left and pulled into a strip mall where he parked, lowered his head and tried to calm his breathing.

"You okay, buddy?"

A few seconds passed before Smitt raised his head and looked out the window at an older black gentleman stooped eye-to-eye with him.

"Yes," he said. "I mean, yes, sir. Thank you, sir."

The old man patted him on the shoulder and walked away. Smitt opened the console, took out his hunting knife, and turned it over and over in his hand. The knife dropped onto his lap, and he jumped out of the car like burning coals had fallen on him. He stood leaning against the door with his forehead pressed against the roof. People going in and out of stores made wide arcs around him. He was spooked by the prying stare of a young girl on the sidewalk, so he climbed back in, started the engine and pulled out of the parking space. He drove slowly toward the end of the lot where there was a backup, cars inching along every minute or so, before suddenly realizing he was in line at a drive-thru window.

"What could I get you, handsome?" asked a woman with cherry lips and blonde hair that waved six inches above her scalp.

Smitt looked between the woman and shelves full of liquor bottles with names he couldn't pronounce. He had never allowed a drop of liquor touch his lips, but he'd never committed to ending the life of a young man he'd worked with in the boiler rooms either. He pointed to a bottle of clear liquid, and said, "I'll try one of those."

The woman put her hand on a bottle. "This one, honey?"

"Yes, ma'am."

"You have good taste," she said. "This here's my favorite tequila." Smitt handed her a twenty and she smiled.

"That'll be thirty-two-twenty-five, good looking."

He reached back into his pocket and took out another twenty. She handed him change and said, "Now you come see me again, you hear?"

Smitt repeated "Yes, ma'am," and drove to the parking lot exit. He stopped and picked the knife up off the floor, put it back in the console, then pulled out onto Atlantic Boulevard. About a mile down the road, he made a right onto Third Street and drove south through Jacksonville Beach onto Ponte Vedra Boulevard. Modest homes turned to estates: extravagant mansions with wrought iron gates, stone driveways, fountains, and terra cotta roofs, some sapphire, others teal. He cruised past Sawgrass Country Club, and as he continued down the coast along A1A, the disoriented feeling he'd had earlier resurfaced. The farther he drove, the more anxious he became until he pulled over at the Guana River Aquatic Preserve.

Emergency break engaged and engine idling, he reached over to the passenger seat, grabbed the brown paper bag and rolled down the top so that only the bottleneck stuck out. He unscrewed the cap, closed his eyes, and in one deliberate motion took his baptismal swig of alcohol. His entire body quivered, and when he opened his eyes, a million brilliant diamonds sparkled against the aqua blue water. He took a second sip and twisted the cap back on, shifted into gear and headed south.

The tequila was warm in his belly by the time he got to Saint Augustine Beach. Young people roamed sidewalks that alternated with front lawns of homes. Restaurants and pubs lined both sides of the street: a custard stand, taco shack, and a biker bar. He pulled into the dirt parking lot of a brightly painted shack called Peachy Peachy on the left side of the street, got out and went inside. He'd been hustling pool in bars since he was fifteen, but this was the first time he'd ever ordered a beer. Oblivious to the barmaid's smile, he took the pint outside and walked up to the beach, crossed the sand, slipped off his shoes and let saltwater wash over his feet for the first time in his life.

As the warm sea water touched his toes, he had the sensation of being baptized.

He scanned the horizon, imagining himself an apostle on the Sea of Galilee awaiting guidance, then looked down at the pint glass in his hand and remembered his mission. He lifted and drained it in one long gulp, and his thoughts shifted back to the conflict, the threat, the leftist radical, enemy of freedom and liberty depriving veterans of tens of millions of dollars for health care. He was a patriot called to duty. Dusk turned to night. He flipped the empty pint glass over and jammed it in the sand, walked back to the parking lot and climbed into his black Charger and started the engine. Steady again and focused on his mission, he pulled onto the street and headed north.

Cruising along A1A, windows down, salt air blowing through the bristles of his short hair, the reflection of the moon shining against the Intracoastal Waterway, he pulled the bottle of tequila from between the console and his seat and took a swig. The lights of Jacksonville Beach flickered in the distance as he approached Ponte Vedra. Time to survey the hunting ground.

Back in the bustle of a beach resort, he made a left on Beach Boulevard, a right on Penman Road. A few minutes later, he pulled into the dark parking lot Captain Stevens had described. Black on black. He circled the lot once before pulling into a space in the corner farthest from the restaurant.

The staging ground.

Smitt grabbed the neck of the tequila bottle and took a long swig. He closed his eyes and envisioned Tommy pulling up to the restaurant, going inside to pick up dinner for the welders and boilermakers, and walking out to the car after midnight. As he opened the car door, Smitt would emerge from the darkness, shove the hunting knife into his back, jerk it upward, slicing his stomach and intestines and, finally, piercing his heart. Quick and clean.

~

Louis Robert Smitt had no frame of reference for his tolerance for alcohol. The strongest beverage he'd ever drank before the night of the operation was Coke. As far as he could tell, the effects of drinking two beers was no different than drinking a six-pack or a bottle of tequila. He had played pool against guys who drank beers all night long and could still clear the table. Some even got sharper with the amount of alcohol they drank.

Smitt didn't know his brain was operating differently than it had his entire sober life as he sat surveying the Farmstead with almost an hour to kill. *Why sit in a parking lot*, he thought, *when I could sit at the bar and leave before Tommy Homes arrives?* He opened the console, took out the hunting knife and slid it into his calf holster. He got out and marched into the Farmstead.

The clock behind the bar read eleven-thirty when he ordered his first beer, and as he sipped he vacillated between calm from the tequila and the frantic realization he would end the life of another human being in less than an hour. At eleven-thirty, he ordered a second beer, and the closer the big hand on the clock crept toward midnight, the more effort it took to control his nerves. Not even the half-bottle of tequila and the beers eased the apprehension of Tommy walking through the door, nor did it reduce his distress about killing someone he knew. This wouldn't be plunging a hunting knife through the heart of a deer in the forest, but of a young man with whom he had a strange connection from the day Tommy horse-collared Beast during the confrontation in the fire room. And then, just as he was about to waver, Captain Stevens's words daunted him: *Tommy Homes isn't a boilermaker, he's a left-wing radical... He'll deprive Veterans of millions of dollars in benefits... Patriotic duty... Patriotic duty... Patriotic duty...*

Smitt drained the beer and lifted the glass toward the bartender.

Instead of giving him a refill, the bartender said, "How about you have something to eat, fella?"

Through an alcoholic haze, Smitt stared at the short, thick man in front of him, silver jewelry on every finger and both wrists. His forearms were covered in faded tattoos. Chest hair bushed from a blue and white print shirt opened to just above his navel, his black belt was full of colored stones. He put his hand firmly around Smitt's beer glass, as if his question about ordering something to eat wasn't a question at all. Smitt glanced at the clock on the wall above the mirror behind the bar.

Eleven-fifty-five.

"Fuck it," he said. "I gotta get out of here." He pulled a wad of money from his pant pocket as he got up, threw a twenty on the bar, looked around and walked toward the men's room in the back.

Feet straddling the sides of the urinal and staring at the wall in front of him, he groaned a long sigh of relief. Before he was finished emptying his bladder, someone walked in and started pissing in the urinal next to him. Smitt shook the last few drops into the porcelain bowl and went to the sink to wash his hands.

A few seconds later, the water in the sink next to him gushed on. "Hey, man. What's up?"

Smitt turned and looked through bleary eyes. "Huh?"

"You okay?" the guy asked.

"Uh, yeah," he said, squinting to focus. "Just caught me off guard. What's your name again?"

"Denny," he said. "Denny Yorko. I'm here with some of the guys."

Smitt looked confused. "I didn't see anyone from the ship."

"We came in the restaurant entrance," said Denny. "Stop over and have a beer with us. We're celebrating. The welders finished the boilers today."

"I gotta early day tomorrow."

"Come on, man, just one," said Denny, but Smitt was already out the men's room door. Denny hurried after him. "At least say 'hi' to the guys."

Smitt scrambled toward the exit. On his way past the opening to the dining room, he slowed and peeked at a table of boilermakers in the back. Denny put his hand on Smitt's arm. "Just one…"

Smitt ripped his arm away and made a fist. "I said no!"

Patrons at the bar hushed. Denny put his hands up and backed away. "Okay, okay."

Smitt looked back into the restaurant. He locked eyes with Tommy for a split-second, then took off for the parking lot. He opened his car door and climbed behind the wheel, pulled out the half-empty bottle of tequila and took a long swig. He sat brooding, more conflicted than he'd been since leaving the Naval Station. He thought about Tommy's perseverance and dedication when they worked the same fire room back in Philly, and realized that, in a way, Tommy reminded him of himself. But Tommy was a left-wing radical determined to deprive the military of tens of millions of dollars to protect freedom, liberty, and the welfare of cherished veterans. It was all in jeopardy because of a fraudulent report he was going to give to a United States senator tomorrow.

Patriotism. God and country. The greater good.

No. Smitt's purpose was still clear: eliminate the threat. It was a mission for a special operator or a Navy Seal.

A patriot.

But now there were six of them, and Smitt agonized over how to eliminate one without taking out all of them. He took another long slug of tequila to erase any trace of feelings he had about shoving a hunting knife into the traitor's back. He opened the car door and got out, walked across the parking lot and ducked behind a dumpster in the corner of the dreary strip mall.

~

From the pile of chicken bones and empty beer bottles left behind on the table, it looked as if the celebration had been going on for days instead of hours. Everyone filed outside, except Vince who stopped to order two six-packs for the road, and Tommy to pay the bill and apologize to the waitress for his idiot friends. Denny stumbled down the steps and his brother, Jerry, caught him at the bottom and led him to the car. Jerry had kept his brother sober enough to weld for eight weeks but felt guilty that Jimmy had to break into his apartment and order him to go back to Philly. He shoved Denny into the front seat and squeezed in next to him. Cajon and Kenny hopped in the back and locked the doors. Vince walked out with the six-packs and banged on the window.

"Let me in, assholes." Kenny and Cajon giggled inside like children.

Tommy came out a few minutes later and stood on the top step, laughing at Vince screaming into the back window. As he started down the steps, Smitt inched out from behind the dumpster and scurried through the darkness in a crouched position. He reached into his calf holster as he closed in on Tommy, and when he straightened, he was in the direct line of sight with Vince who faced Tommy looking over the car roof.

"Tommy!" shouted Vince.

Tommy turned quickly and was startled to see Smitt, who panicked and ran back around the corner of the strip mall. Tommy stared into the darkness for a few seconds, then looked back at Vince, and said, "What the hell was that all about?"

Vince chugged his beer and tossed the empty can. "That dude's strange."

Tommy opened his door and got in. Cajon unlocked the back door but refused to give up his window seat, so Vince hopped over him next to Kenny and popped open another beer. Tommy looked at Denny next to him and regretted not kicking him out of the car back at the Naval Station, but his mood lightened when he noticed Jerry's arm around his brother like a guardian angel. The image in the rearview mirror was of Vince wedged between Cajon and Kenny, chugging a sixteen-ounce Busch. Vince had fulfilled his role on the tiger team exactly the way Tommy had planned, maintaining buoyancy in an oppressive environment. And Cajon might've been a welterweight, but he outworked heavyweights in the boiler room. Then there was Kenny, Jimmy's non-negotiable, who came to Mayport with a reputation as an angry black radical, but won everyone's respect as a talented welder with an irresistible smile and engaging personality.

Tommy rolled down the window and inhaled a deep breath of satisfaction at being part of this team of characters who'd accomplished one of the most physically and mentally demanding jobs imaginable. He smiled, turned the ignition and pulled out onto Third Street, looking forward to flying home tomorrow to christen his little girl.

Smitt ran from behind the building, got into his Charger, and kicked over the 440-horsepower engine. He kept his lights off until he pulled onto Third Street and followed Tommy from a block and a half behind. Tommy was cruising along when suddenly he flicked his turn signal and made a left into a 7-Eleven. Louis slowed as he drove by and watched the car empty out. He went another block and a half before he pulled into a Baptist church parking lot, shut off his lights and turned to face the 7-Eleven. Tommy's rental car sat alone outside the store. Louis sat with the engine idling in neutral.

The feeling of dread returned, and he fought to keep from descending back into brooding.

"I'm a patriot," he told himself. He wrapped his hand around the tequila bottle and repeated out loud, "I'm a patriot," then even louder, over and over, spit spraying on the windshield. "I'm a fucking patriot!"

Three of the boilermakers came out of the store and got into the car. Kenny and Denny horsed around in the parking lot, pushing and shoving, jockeying for seats in the car. Jerry got out and shoved Denny back against the console up front, Kenny hopped in the back.

A minute later, Tommy came out.

Louis lifted the bottom of the tequila bottle toward the heavens and drank until it was empty. He stretched his arm out over the passenger seat and threw the bottle out the window against the brick wall of the church, shattering glass everywhere. He slid the gearshift into first, let up on the clutch and inched out of the parking lot. He crossed the street and sat with the engine idling at the curb. When Tommy's taillights turned on and the car eased to a rolling stop at the parking lot ramp, Louis revved his engine and crawled up the street.

The moment Tommy's front wheels touched the asphalt of Third Street, Louis popped the clutch, unleashing the fury of 440 horses. The engine screamed, and the front wheels jumped off the ground. He shifted into second, and the speedometer hit fifty miles per hour before the end of the block. He shifted into third at seventy miles per hour, and by the time Tommy's car was in the middle of the northbound lane, the Charger was a ninety-mile-per-hour stealth fighter with the headlights off at two a.m. that no boilermaker or welder ever saw.

Chapter XXIII

MAYPORT ROAD

Jimmy rubbed his face in a vain attempt to erase the images in his mind: drunk at the concession stand, searching the parking lot for his car, crawling on all fours like a dog looking for his keys, the cop shining the flashlight in his eyes, the overturned car, his dad. He pressed his palms against his temples.

"My fucking head," he pleaded. A petition, a prayer.

He sat up, shifted to the side of the bed and faced the sound of squawking seagulls filtering through the sliding glass doors, waves washing against sand. Even in the dark he could feel the vastness of the ocean, sense an emerging sunrise that greets the honorable as well as the vile. He covered his face with his hands and saw beady eyes ringed in orange staring at him.

"I gotta quit drinking," he said.

~

A cold shower, coffee at 7-Eleven, salt air blowing in the face driving along Mayport Road. Kettledrums pounded inside his head—*thump, thump, thump*—echoing the news Chief had just told him about an accident in the middle of the night. Jimmy slowed at the guard shack and flashed his ID at Marlin who avoided eye contact as he waved him through the gate. Marlin from Harlem who broke his balls every chance he got since finding out he was from Philadelphia on his first day at the Naval Station. Marlin the marine, as aloof as Chief had been.

The Saratoga looked different when he pulled into a parking space across from the wharf. The same sixty-thousand tons of steel afloat in the basin was fastened to the same moorings it had been secured to ever since he arrived twelve weeks ago, but on this day, it sat lifeless, like a sunken ship on the ocean floor that had become a reef for tropical fish and marine biologists to explore. He could picture steel hulls deformed by unforgiving seas, ruptured pipes sticking out like straws from a thick milkshake, and twisted iron caused by eighty-foot waves. Salvagers would exhume artifacts and relics to piece together stories of the people who constructed and sailed the great fortress.

Jimmy forced himself out of the car and walked up the gangplank. The men and women of night and day shifts, who had worked twelve hours on/twelve hours off for months and saw each other every day at the five-thirty shift changes, milled around like strangers in a bus terminal. The gang seemed larger than usual, as if everyone needed to be present to watch the dayshift foreman arrive. Even from a distance, Jimmy could tell it took great effort for them to avoid looking at him. Each morning, nightshift workers would laugh at stories the dayshift told them about the night before, playing darts at Skeet's, like the fight Beast started with the locals that ended in black eyes and rounds of beer. Once Jimmy assigned, jobs they'd settle down and go to work.

But today was different.

Snake broke from the rest of the gang like he'd lost a bet. He walked up to Jimmy, and said, "Huey wants to see you in the trailer."

Jimmy made his way to the trailer without acknowledging Snake or the others, climbed the steps and opened the door. Huey sat on an upside-down wastebasket, looking like a prize-fighter on a stool after losing a unanimous decision. His eyes were puffy and swollen. Not lack-of-sleep swollen but crying swollen. Before that moment, it would have been impossible for Jimmy to picture barrel-chested, tattooed, blustery Huey crying.

"Sit down, Jimmy," he said, softly.

Huey was the kind of warrior you'd pray would jump in your foxhole when you were being pounded by enemy fire. He defended his men against everyone: superintendents, Navy brass, politicians, the press. Fuck with Huey's men, you fuck with Huey. Jimmy would've done anything for him.

"I'd rather stand," said Jimmy, because he sensed he was about to hear grave news, and he had to know whether he could take a knockout punch. He wanted to prove to Huey that he was worthy to be in the foxhole with him.

Huey tightened his lips in a way Jimmy had never seen. "We lost a few of our boys last night."

The words didn't hit Jimmy with the force he'd expected, maybe because he figured it out in the twelve-minutes he had cruised Mayport Road analyzing Chief's indifference. Or maybe Marlin confirmed his suspicion by avoiding eye contact at the gate or the way the ship listed at the pier.

"What happened?"

"Hank let some of the guys go out for something to eat in the middle of the night. You know, a little reward for finishing up the welding." His head dropped like his spine had suddenly collapsed. "Four of them didn't make it back."

Jimmy asked Huey who was in the car. *Beast? Denny? Am I close?*

Huey stared at the floor. Long moments passed. He raised his head and looked to the back of the trailer like he was hoping the four guys would walk in and tell him it was all a prank, that they'd staged the whole thing. The blood. The body parts.

"I don't know how they can tell how fast the car was going," he said to no one.

"Who?" asked Jimmy. "What?"

"Cops called me about two-thirty. I get here, and investigators were talking about tire marks and car parts or some shit. They calculated the sailor that hit our boys was going ninety miles an hour before his car went airborne and hit a tree. Lopped off a chunk of bark eight feet off the ground." Huey looked at the ceiling of the trailer. "The car flew eight feet in the air and hit a fucking tree."

Uninterested in sailors and tire marks and flying cars, Jimmy pressed him, "Who was in the car?"

"Vince and Denny Yorko were sitting in the middle of the front and back seats." The vacant words came from a man still processing what had happened. "Luck of the draw, I guess. Sandwiched between guys who wound up being cushions and saved their lives." He shook his head. "The roof peeled off and Murph flew out. Landed on a lawn on the side of Third Street."

Huey never looked at Jimmy while he went on and on about kids and families and obliteration. He wasn't looking at anything.

"Who didn't make it, Huey?"

Chapter XXIV

Laborers' Tears

F our hard hats set atop of four pair of work boots arranged in center-front of the stage. Beast choked back tears, placing a nameplate in front of each set.

Kenny Essington.

Jerry Yorko.

Cajon.

Tommy Homes.

It took six men to lift a half-inch steel plate onto two huge wooden spools that would be used as an altar. Chuck welded together two lengths of one-inch-round stock for a crucifix the riggers hung from an overhead beam with a chain fall. Snake directed a dozen or so guys arranging folding chairs in rows of twelve, six on each side of an aisle. Father Leonard, the Catholic priest who married Tommy and his wife, flew down from Philadelphia to preside over the memorial Friday evening.

The sun cast a tangerine sheen across wisps of clouds outside the open hangar bay door behind the altar. The water was cobalt blue. Father Leonard stood behind the altar and welcomed believers and non-believers, encouraging every one of them to share in the sacred bread, to sip His blood, a practice clergy purists considered a sacrilege. He read a passage from Luke, a message of comfort that descended like a soft snowfall on hardened shipbuilders who wept openly, hugged one another and choked on feeble attempts to console their fellow tradesmen. Losing a brother-in-labor was devastating.

Losing four of them was more than they could bear.

Jimmy sat in the front row between Huey and Hank. A heavy burden weighed on him for convincing Tommy it was his duty to be a member of the tiger team. He was tortured by the passionate plea he made to Kenny to go, not as the token black guy, but because he was worthy. Twenty-three-year-old Cajon would never find out if he could make it in the ring as a professional. Jerry Yorko, the good twin, gone. Denny and Vince would be in the hospital for a long time, but at least he'd see them again.

A deep hollow feeling sucked inside his chest at the sight of Tommy's distraught mother on the other side of the aisle. Mr. Homes looked frail, his skin ashen, a black suit coat draped over his withering frame. Tommy's wife, Peggy, stayed home with her infant daughter, Danielle. There would be no christening on Sunday.

On his way back from communion, Jimmy felt like he was floating above the hanger bay looking down on the service. He scanned the crowd: mostly shipyard workers, some wives and kids who'd come on the trip with their husbands, Butch, a few sailors, a camera crew from a local television station. He caught a glimpse of George Sputz hiding in the back. Senator Hawkins stayed around for the service after the all-hands meeting he held with the men earlier in the day. At the meeting, the senator promised that the Navy Yard wouldn't be held responsible for superheater tubes that failed because of a machine the Navy forced them to use.

Jimmy scoured the crowd for Admiral Foley, who'd stormed the trailer two days ago and addressed him as "boy." He looked for Navy brass and Maestro Fusion Corporation company reps. Their absence was more conspicuous to him than those in attendance. He looked back at the empty hard hats and work boots of his dead friends, who had traveled to Florida to repair boiler tubes welded with a flawed robotic machine and developed by a company that didn't have the decency to send one representative to pay their respects. It took every ounce of his strength to keep from screaming.

He wiped his hands over his wet eyes, and when he removed them, Tommy stood on the altar in front of him holding a pile of bloodstained papers. Jimmy shuddered. He turned to Huey, and said, "What happened to the sailor?"

Huey quivered out of a trance. "What?"

"The sailor who drove the car that killed our guys. What happened to him?"

"They said he was on life support. Lost both legs. An eye. Took a million stitches to sew him up." Huey hesitated, as if debating whether to tell him more. "Didn't sound like he was going to make it."

Jimmy chewed the inside of his cheek. "They oughta pull the plug."

Jimmy left his seat and walked toward the back of the hanger bay before the final blessing was over. Each stride was deliberate, with increased purpose, and by the time George Sputz saw him coming, it was too late. Jimmy didn't offer his hand or any pleasantries, words of sorrow or remorse.

"Why did they use that fucking robot?"

"Jimmy," said George, but nothing else came out. "Tommy," he stammered, about to cry. "I'm so sorry, Jimmy."

"What do you mean, 'You're sorry?'"

George fidgeted, crossed his arms to keep from shaking. "It worked in the shop, Jimmy. And in San Diego."

"It was December in Philly, George," Jimmy said, louder and angrier.

"That's what we told them, Jimmy."

The admission stunned Jimmy. "What do you mean?"

Looking uncomfortable talking with so many people around, George gestured for Jimmy to follow him off the ship. At the end of the gangway, he made a U-turn and walked down the wharf.

"Okay, George," said Jimmy. "What the hell's going on?"

"You have to promise you won't tell anyone what I'm about to tell you."

"Start talking, George," said Jimmy, fidgeting with impatience.

"Jimmy, I'll get fired."

Jimmy slammed his fist into George's chest. "Fuck getting fired," he seethed. "I got four dead friends because they were down here fixing boilers that had no reason to be broken. And you're worried about getting fired?"

George rubbed where Jimmy had hit him. "Mr. Strunk commissioned an internal study. We did research that proved the automated preheat cycle wouldn't work in the cold weather.

Every way we looked at it, the engineering didn't support it. The Navy's process was flawed."

"Then why the hell did you guys insist on using it?"

"We didn't. Mr. Strunk sent our findings to the Navy in a memorandum."

"I don't get it," said Jimmy, looking bewildered. "Strunk writes the processes and procedures for every welding job in the shipyard. Why would they use it if he proved the process was flawed?"

"Maestro Fusion was mandated at the highest levels in the Navy. They told Mr. Strunk if he couldn't make it work, they'd replace him with someone who could. The next thing I knew, Mr. Strunk retired."

"Who's *they*?" demanded Jimmy.

Tears streamed down George's face.

"Give me a fucking name!"

"Admiral Foley," said George.

Chapter XXV

BLOODY BOOT

After the memorial, Huey told everyone to take the rest of the day off. On the way back to the hotel, Jimmy prayed for the hope and optimism he once felt driving along Mayport Road, that intoxicating feeling he got when he breathed the salt air as the sun radiated on the other side of the horizon. A black Charger rocketed from out of the abyss and annihilated that hope, along with the life and dreams of four young men. Back in Philly, an infant waited to be lowered into baptismal waters.

A car horn jolted Jimmy from his malaise when the traffic light turned green. He made a left onto Atlantic Boulevard and saw Enterprise Car Rental on the next block, remembered the contract for his Escort was about to expire and pulled into the lot. He parked and stared at the blue cinderblock wall feeling detached, a sensation that stayed with him after he shut off the engine. He took the contract from the glove compartment and got out.

The door made an irritating sifting sound when he pulled it open, like a cracked gasket on a vacuum. A vending machine breathed a monotonous hum on the other side of the room. Wide blue fabric tape strung from pole to pole, creating lines for invisible customers. Jimmy had an eerie sense that he wasn't alone, a feeling that didn't pass when a kid walked out from a half-opened door at the far end of the wall and stood behind the counter.

"Can I help you?" he asked.

"I need to extend my contract," said Jimmy, pulling it from his back pocket and laying it on the counter.

The kid took the papers and began to enter information into a computer. After a few seconds, the tapping on the keyboard slowed. He peeked at Jimmy without raising his head, then stopped typing altogether.

"You're from Philadelphia," he said, with trepidation.

Whump, whump, whump echoed from somewhere. Maybe it was the vending machine. Maybe it was inside his head. Or maybe it was from the netherworld.

"That's right," said Jimmy.

Sweat formed in the creases of the kid's forehead. "Did you know the guys who were killed in the accident on Third Street?"

Their eyes connected like magnets. "I did."

Though he seemed to want to say more, the kid shut down.

"What is it?" Jimmy asked.

"I … I …" he said.

Jimmy reached across the counter and grabbed his forearm. "Come on, buddy. What do you want to tell me?"

"The…the car…" The kid paused for breath. "The car those guys were driving … It's impounded in our garage for the investigation. It's locked in a separate room in the back."

The words sucked every molecule of air from the room. Breathing sounded magnified like it came from a woofer. Heartbeats were bongos. Blinking eyes were the windshield wipers of an eighteen-wheeler swishing through a monsoon. That eerie feeling made sense now—the cracked seal of the door, the hum of a vending machine, the kid appearing from a back office.

There was a presence inside the building.

The kid looked at him. "Do you want to see the wreck?"

The words sounded sublime, like electronic music throbbing from a grave, filtering through six feet of soil, slithering from between blades of grass. The kid turned, walked to the end of the counter and opened a door leading into the adjoining garage. Jimmy followed him because he had no choice. They made their way between cars and pickups scattered around the floor in various stages of maintenance. Mechanical lifts suspended vehicle carriages exposing exhaust systems, universal joints, and transmission casings. The smell of grease and oil got stronger and more pervasive the further they went until they reached a sectioned-off portion in the back of the shop. The kid opened another door, stood aside, and said, "Take as long as you need." He turned and left.

Jimmy stepped inside the inner sanctum, the Holy of Holies, separated from all that was real by all that was sacred. A mausoleum of twisted metal and anguish sat in the middle of the room, a distorted form that was once a Chevrolet Impala. A conglomeration of buckled metal, shards of glass, shredded fabric and melted rubber. The hardtop roof was peeled back like the pop-off lid of a can of corn. He leaned closer to the car and stuck his head above what was once the driver's seat. The metallic taste of blood saturated his tongue. A faint pulse emanated from the walls, soft breathing, and when he looked across the crypt, an infant lay cooing.

Jimmy shut his eyes, covered them with his hands to concentrate. He prayed for guidance, a message, and when he opened them, under the gas pedal, soaked in dark coagulated maroon liquid, was a work boot. He reached down and pulled, but it was jammed, so he leaned in further and took it in both hands. He jerked it loose, stumbled backward, and slammed his head into the cinderblock wall. He slid to the floor, the boot clutched to his chest. The cooing stopped.

The infant was gone.

Jimmy sat alone on the garage floor with Tommy's blood-soaked work boot pressed against his cheek. He rubbed the sodden leather against his flesh, savoring the taste of blood that doused his tongue. He'd never been this intimate with Tommy when he was alive.

It became clear to Jimmy that Tommy's daughter would grow up without a dad because greedy men had a lust for power and money that eclipsed the oath they'd taken to preserve freedom. These miscreants made a down payment on their lucrative lifestyles with the blood of four hard-working men who labored to keep their warships operational. Avarice amassed in Jimmy's saliva, and he spit their poison out on the floor.

~

In the real world, people lived in row homes, and a fifth grader who lost his dad in an industrial accident got a job to help his mom with bills while company owners and lawyers profited by gaming the system. In the real world, the spark of a cigarette ignited a gas-filled trunk and caused a flashfire that melted skin onto the bones of a teenage painter. In the real world, the shift of a breeze rocked a thirty-ton propeller suspended from a crane just enough to crush the father of six young children.

Jimmy lived in the real world, where actions had consequences.

Chapter XXVI

PELICAN SOARS

Images of the wreckage haunted Jimmy on his ride back to the Sea Turtle. Funeral procession music piped into his head, and cars that passed him on Atlantic Boulevard were driven by corpses. He felt chilled though the temperature on the Florida National Bank sign read 101.

He hurried through the lobby of the hotel without making eye contact with anyone, took the elevator to the twelfth floor, and went to his apartment. Once inside, he went to the refrigerator, stooped to get a beer, and a large shadow blotted out the sunlight. He felt as though he was being watched. He stood, and on the other side of the balcony railing, a pelican hovered with its beak pointing directly at him, its pouch stretched like it held an entire season's bounty. Its miraculous wings spread against the blue sky.

Jimmy walked across the room, slid open the glass door, and stepped outside. Spellbound by beady eyes, he remembered the parade of pelicans that skimmed the water on the beach the day he arrived in Mayport. Now he stood nose-to-beak with the majestic creature, weighing twenty pounds or more, its wingspan more than six feet, as it floated regally in the updraft. Pitch-black eyes circled with thin, orange rings pierced his own, making him feel self-conscious. The gaze forced him to examine his conscience, as if she knew more about him than he knew about himself. Without moving its wings, the goddess soared into the heavens, as if summoned by the almighty.

Jimmy's grip on the beer loosened and crashed onto the balcony. In one swooping motion, he swept it under the railing with his foot. Seconds later it splattered on the sidewalk below. He sat on one of the outdoor chairs and contemplated the pelican, the improbability of creation, the universe, his existence, and why he would wake tomorrow and witness the miracle of another sunrise while four of his brothers would not. He couldn't keep from returning to the reason he and forty-four of his fellow-shipyard workers traveled 850 miles south of Philadelphia: the unproven robotic welding process, the Navy blaming the shipyard for the leaking boiler tubes, and the tiger team welding the new tubes using the old manual method.

None of it made sense.

Day turned to night before Jimmy went back inside. He opened the refrigerator door and filled his arms with the beer that remained, walked back out to the balcony railing, and let go. The bottles disappeared into the darkness, and as he turned to go back inside, the glass crashed twelve stories below.

~

Voices were muffled inside a rectangular chamber, and there were hazy images of orbs covered with hair: three in front of him, two to his right, one to the left. The orbs turned out to be people, and the one behind a steering wheel had wide shoulders and tight curly hair. The other two in the front looked identical. Slurred speech came from the one in the middle. An arm reached down next to him and pulled a beer from a cooler on the floor. Someone wearing bright red boxing gloves sat to the right of the person with the beer. A large feel-good smile full of gleaming white teeth flashed in the dark on the left. A green arrow on a dashboard clicked on and off.

On, off, on, off.

Click-click, click-click.

"No!" he shouted, but there was no sound. He yelled louder. "Nooo!" Still muted. He screamed, "Don't turn!" A searing light blinded him.

An explosion.

Everything remained intact when it was all over. Tommy, Denny, and Jerry were still up front. But when Tommy turned around and asked for a beer, his face was a veneer of flesh with no eyes, nose, or mouth. Denny wore the invisible expression of the feeble-minded. His brother Jerry's face was flesh casing. Vince pulled a beer from the cooler and looked grateful. Next to him, Cajon's face hid behind boxing gloves. Kenny's teeth were no longer polished, and the orb on his shoulders was missing orifices.

Jimmy shot up dripping sweat. He sat shaking for a long time before he threw his legs over the side of the bed, lowered his head into his hands, and sobbed in the dark. Sobs droned until they were overtaken by the sound of crashing waves. A breeze kicked the window curtains toward him, the air dried his skin. He got up and went to the refrigerator for a beer but there was none. He remembered dropping them and was glad.

He was thankful his head was clear so he could feel the full breadth of his sadness. He welcomed anguish to feed his fury.

He filled a glass with water and went out and sat on the balcony. He watched millions of stars shimmer against the ocean. Every conversation he'd ever had with Tommy funneled through his head. The one that stuck was Tommy telling him to find a girl or he'd wind up married to the shipyard.

The constellation took the shape of an old man sitting alone in a room, sipping a flat Guinness, eating blueberries, and watching a Phillies game. He kept the box score in a beat-up notebook with yellowed pages. Old shipbuilders who'd lost limbs and contracted asbestosis staggered around, dragging oxygen bottles on carts behind them. A newspaper on a table was opened to the obituaries. One simply read, "Jimmy McKee: Welder." Six people showed up at his funeral: a rigger who'd been crushed, a painter with charred skin, and four faceless men.

Chapter XXVII

HOMEWARD BOUND

Not a single boilermaker, welder, insulator, electrician, or pipefitter considered Huey's offer to take the weekend off. Every one of them showed up early Saturday morning and went about their business, as solemn as monks. They all hurt inside, afraid to be idle or left alone without purpose. They needed to be near one another, even if they didn't say a word for twelve hours. Simply being in the proximity of their brothers-in-labor was therapy. It reinforced the feeling that someone cared.

Huey told Jimmy and Hank to cut their gang in half by Monday. A skeleton crew would reinstall the interference that had been removed and take care of any loose ends. Already four men short on the backshift, Hank didn't have to cut as many people as Jimmy. Those not picked to stay began packing gear into gang boxes to be shipped home. They'd be on a plane to Philly on Tuesday.

By the end of the week, NDT inspections were complete without one failure on the 2,048 tubes. The boilermakers sealed the boilers and hooked up the hoses to the hydro pumps over the weekend. On Monday, they began pressurizing the boilers to eighteen thousand psi. Boiler inspectors from NAVSEA and the ship's crew crawled through the superheater cavities with flashlights and mirrors, checking every welded joint and mechanical seal for leaks.

Hank spent the backshift alternating between keeping an eye on the inspectors and completing paperwork in the trailer. Five o'clock Wednesday morning, he left the trailer for the fire room to check the status for the turnover. He climbed down the ladder and walked past Beast without saying a word. When he rounded the boiler, he saw the beam of the master chief's flashlight bouncing from tube to tube inside the cavity of boiler #4B.

"How do they look?" asked Hank.

The master chief looked at Hank and gave him the thumbs up. Final inspection was complete.

It took another week to touch up the work areas, wrap up the equipment and pack the remaining gear. The last members of the tiger team returned their rental cars and shuttled to Jacksonville International Airport two weeks before Thanksgiving.

~

Jimmy imagined an angel looking down at the clouds from his window seat on Flight 1990 from Jacksonville to Philadelphia. He thought about the night at the Sons of Ben Franklin, the last time that every member of the tiger team was together, drinking beer and listening to Butch tell the gang they were picked because they were the best of the best. He'd been petitioning them to show the world what blue-collar, Philadelphia waterfront heritage was all about. Tommy's dad distanced himself from the camaraderie when Butch pumped his arm into the air and led the chant.

Philly Pride! Philly Pride! Philly Pride!

More than three months had passed since that night, and the words Jimmy couldn't get out of his head was Butch saying the shipyard was "getting a raw deal," the same words used by Senator Hawkins. Butch and Tommy had been suspicious of the robotic welding process from the beginning, when rumors circulated about it being tested on the other side of the shipyard. They were distrustful of the way it was treated like a convert operation. The Professor avoided questions about the process. George Sputz stammered.

Thirty-five thousand feet above the Atlantic Ocean, Jimmy heard a whisper in the clouds: Tommy's voice, as clear as if he was in the seat next to him. Even in a whisper, Jimmy could hear the urgency. He vowed to get to the bottom of deaths of Tommy, Kenny, Cajon, and Jerry, and to avenge those responsible.

Part III

Post Mayport

Chapter XXVIII

HOME BITTER HOME

No feeling in the fingers, legs numb, brain paralyzed. The image of a man falling through space, buried under tons of rotted lumber. A twelve-year-old gets a job to help his grieving mother who works day and night to make ends meet. The end of innocence. A continuum of jobs beginning at Newt's Grocery Store delivering packages, and ending as shipyard foreman. He moves into a one-bedroom apartment in Tacony after his mom dies of a broken heart.

The ring of a phone was an electrical charge that stimulated the brain. Light seeped through the window blinds. "Hello."

"Jimmy?"

The voice was familiar. "Butch?"

"You okay?"

"Yeah," said Jimmy, unsure. He looked at the clock radio on the nightstand. It was almost eleven. "I'll be in before noon."

"No," said Butch. "I just wanted to check on you. You've been through a lot, kid. Take the day off. Rest up the weekend and we'll get caught up on Monday."

Jimmy hadn't missed a day work since he started his apprenticeship, but he didn't have the will to argue. He grabbed the blankets, pulled them over his head and slept until Saturday.

~

Jimmy knew he had to get back to the shipyard, his refuge, but dreaded answering questions about the accident. Lights that outlined Boathouse Row shimmered on the Schuylkill River as he drove south on the expressway Monday morning. Hundreds of pill-shaped oil tanks dotted the Sunoco refinery when he emerged from the Twenty-sixth Street tunnel heading toward the back entrance in Southwest Philly.

He was relieved the nightshift foremen were out checking jobs when he walked into the office. Dayshift wouldn't show up for another hour.

This was his final chance to decompress before the madness began.

He scanned a large diagram of the USS Forrestal master schedule posted on the wall. The shipyard was in the rip-out phase of another twenty-eight month, half-billion-dollar overhaul. Unlike commercial construction, experience was no guarantee that the second project would go smoother than the first. There was no way to predict if the thickness of the steel hull would meet minimum specs until the ship was in dry dock, and no way of telling whether pipes submerged in fuel and water tanks were deteriorated beyond repair, or if turbine blades inside heavy cast metal casings were broken or bent. Likewise, it was impossible to determine if the internal structures of the rudders were rusted until the ship was out of the water.

The Forrestal was a skeleton of a ship resting on keel blocks with huge swaths of steel cut out of its hull. Engines, reduction gears, main feed pumps, and auxiliary machinery had been removed and sent out to vendors for overhaul. Damaged pipes, angle iron, deck plates, insulation, asbestos, and cable had been scrapped. The Forrestal was Humpty Dumpty being prepped to be put back together again.

Nobody approached Jimmy about the accident that morning. Well, one guy kind of did in the context of a general *"how'd the job go?"* But after Jimmy told him they finished two weeks ahead of schedule, the guy asked, "Anything else?"

Jimmy struck him mute with a glare. It wasn't that he didn't want to talk about it as much as *he* knew that *everyone else* knew what happened. They'd read about it in the papers, saw it on the news, and got bits and pieces from other guys on the tiger team. But they heard that Jimmy had seen the impounded car and wanted to hear the gory shit about the mangled wreck, like how the roof had been ripped off or if there was still blood inside. Jimmy knew more than any of them but spoke the least. He'd done time in the sanctuary, the Holy of Holies. He'd held the relic—Tommy's work boot—and still had the metallic taste of blood in his mouth.

~

The message light on the phone was blinking when Jimmy got back to the office later in the morning. Butch wanted to see him right away. Temperatures had plummeted on the waterfront. Blustery winds that pushed him across the caisson reminded him of a year ago, when they started welding superheater tubes right after Thanksgiving. He blew warm breath on his hands when he arrived at Butch's door. The boss was on the phone. He waved Jimmy in, gestured to a chair across from his desk, and told whoever he was talking to that he had to go.

"Hate to drop this on you your first day back," he said, apologetically, "but I need you to keep an eye on the boiler work in all four fire rooms."

Jimmy's eyes narrowed. "Colin's not doing good, is he?"

"He's going to be out for a while."

"What's the prognosis?"

"He says he's going to be fine," said Butch. "But the chemo's kicking the shit out of him."

Jimmy braced himself against the weight of Butch's words. After losing his dad at such a young age, Colin had become a role model. Colin told him things other welders never talked about, like Irish musicians and writers and the importance of reading and education. Joking around, Jimmy would call him the Renaissance Welder.

He put his hands on the armrests to push himself up out of the chair. "I gotta get back to work."

"Before you leave," said Butch.

Jimmy settled back down. "Yeah?"

"I wanted to let you know that I heard all good reports about you in Mayport."

Jimmy wasn't in the mood for praise. He went to Mayport with forty-four men and returned with forty. Four out of twelve thousand people in the shipyard might have only been a fraction, but they were four lives that filled him with the stuff that sustained him: Tommy's honesty and grit, Kenny's heart-warming smile, Cajon's spunk, and Jerry's loyalty. Without their collective spirit, his emotional balance was thrown out of alignment, and it would reshape his decisions about who to pick to lead jobs, who to train, and who to promote.

And now Colin was fighting for his life.

"You okay, Jimmy?"

Jimmy stared at the wall behind Butch, shivered like a gust of cold air had blown through an open window.

"It's hard to believe," he said, stood and left.

~

Jimmy climbed out from checking a job under boiler 2A and noticed someone shining a flashlight into the mud drum. The guy wore neatly ironed black pants and a button down blue and white pinstripe shirt, and a small notebook and mechanical pencil stuck out of the pocket. Engineering gear. He was of Asian descent and didn't appear old enough to drink legally.

"Looking for someone?" Jimmy asked.

The guy jumped like a grenade had rolled between them.

"Sorry," Jimmy said. "Didn't mean to scare you."

"My first day on the ship," he said, nervously.

Jimmy swatted invisible flies. "A few explosions and couple mangled bodies and you'll be fine."

The remark did little to put him at ease.

"I'm kidding," said Jimmy, offering his hand. "My name's Jimmy."

"Jimmy McKee?"

Jimmy raised an eyebrow. "How'd you know?"

"George Sputz told me about you," he said. "He said I could learn a lot from you."

"How come he's not down here with you?"

"He got transferred."

"Transferred?" said Jimmy, alarmed. "Transferred where?"

"NAVSEA in Crystal City."

Creases waved across Jimmy's forehead. "What?"

"It was weird," said the kid. "He was in the boss's office when I got in this morning, and when he came out, he gave me a quick turnover, cleaned out his desk, and took off."

Jimmy thought back to his conversation with George after the memorial in Mayport. *"They told Mr. Strunk if he couldn't make it work, they'd replace him with someone who could."* George had worked with Mr. Strunk on the study that proved the Maestro Fusion process was flawed. Strunk was forced out, and now George was transferred to NAVSEA.

"Maybe not as weird as you think," said Jimmy.

"I never saw George pissed," the young man said. "He was always under control and professional when he mentored me as a co-op student. Mr. Calm I used to call him. But the whole time he was giving me the turnover he was ranting about the Navy brass, cursing and everything. The last thing he said to me was 'Those bastards will pay.'"

~

Jimmy drove to Lankenau Hospital after work. The elevator doors opened on the fourth floor to a sterile hallway with white tile floors, light blue walls, and an ivory drop ceiling. Beeps and moans drooled out of rooms on either side of him. A gurney with a disheveled white spread thrown on top was against the wall on the left, and a stainless-steel pole holding a drip bag with thin clear tubing spiraled to the floor on the right.

Jimmy peeked apprehensively into room 615, afraid of what he might see. Two fortyish blonde-headed women who appeared to be twins stood on the side of Colin's bed. One of them looked over and welcomed him when he walked in.

"I'm Jimmy," he said, introducing himself, "a friend from the shipyard."

"So you're Jimmy?"

"Uh-oh. That sounds like trouble."

"No," she laughed. "Dad talks highly of you."

Jimmy rolled his eyes and walked to the side of the bed. He looked down at Colin, trying hard not to appear shaken at the skeleton of the man he admired more than anyone on the waterfront.

"How's he doing?"

"He's a fighter," said the other woman.

Colin opened his eyes. "Jimmy," he strained.

"How are you, Colin?" Jimmy asked, squeezing his shoulder.

"Good to see you," Colin said, brushing aside the question. "I want you to meet my girls, Maura and Colleen."

Jimmy nodded to them. "Nice to meet you."

"We've heard a lot about you," said Colleen.

Jimmy looked at Colin. "The Renaissance Welder told you about me?"

Maura laughed. "Hear what he called you, Dad?" Colin smiled. She looked at Jimmy, and said, "He doesn't usually talk shop at home."

The girls stayed for a few more minutes before saying goodbye. After they were gone, Jimmy pulled a chair next to Colin's bed. Neither of them mentioned work. Colin didn't ask about the accident, and Jimmy didn't bring it up. When Colin's speech became labored, Jimmy said, "Why don't you let me do the talking?"

Colin looked to the side of the bed and grabbed a book off the night table. He held it up for Jimmy to see. "Ever read *Cannery Row*?"

Jimmy shook his head no.

"There's a character named Doc. He's based on Steinbeck's best friend…" *cough, cough,* "Ed Ricketts."

Jimmy put his hand on Colin's arm, and said, "Easy, Colin."

"Rickets was driving home from Steinbeck's late one night, and his car got stuck on railroad tracks. His wheels kept spinning as a train barreled toward him. It totaled the car and killed him." Colin coughed again.

"Take your time, Colin."

Colin continued, undeterred. "Steinbeck did some of his greatest work after he lost his best friend."

Jimmy's eyes reddened. "Okay," he ceded. A few seconds passed before he leaned down until their faces nearly touched. "I get it. Now rest."

Colin went into a coughing fit. Jimmy was about to push the nurse's station button, but before he could Colin grabbed his hand. "You got your whole life ahead of you, Jimmy," he said. "Experience all that you can." *Cough.* "Read. Learn." *Cough. Cough.* "Do great things."

Jimmy put a finger to Colin's lips. "Rest," he said.

Colin was asleep in less than a minute.

Jimmy sat in a chair and watched him until visiting hours were over. He felt empty when he left the room, a feeling that stayed with him out to the parking lot. His mentor's parting words—*do great things*—played over and over in his head on the ride home.

Chapter XXIX

THANKLESS THANKSGIVING

Hank showed up late most days since returning from Mayport. He slept through lunch, a time once reserved for study or meditation. Jimmy noticed a slight shake in his hands, and a slurred word here and there. *Word of God* pamphlets could no longer be found on his desk. When he didn't come to work the Monday before Thanksgiving, Jimmy called his wife Rose, who he'd met at the Sons of Ben Franklin the night before they traveled to Mayport.

"Rose, it's Jimmy McKee."

"Is Hank okay?" she asked.

"That's what I was going to ask you."

"What do you mean?"

"Hank's not in work."

"He left with his lunch this morning," she said, and after a short pause. "Oh, God, I don't know where he is."

"What's going on with him, Rose?"

"I don't know," she said. "He came back from Florida a different person. All he talks about is the accident and the guys that were killed. He blames himself."

"Has he talked to anyone? A counselor? Or a priest?"

"I mentioned it to him the other day, and he told me he'd work it out himself."

"They got a counseling program at the shipyard for employees with problems. Get him back to work, and I'll take him."

"I don't know, Jimmy. Hank's proud, and he's hardheaded."

"Trust me, he'll go." There was awkward silence. "Rose, are you still there?"

"I'm here," she said, then fell silent again, but in the silence, Jimmy could hear her aching to tell him something.

"Jimmy?" she finally said.

"Yes?"

"What's Maestro Fusion?"

The sound of the company's name coming from her stunned him. "It's the machine they used to weld the boiler tubes. Why?"

"Hank keeps bringing it up. I even heard him say it in his sleep."

~

Hank believed in the goodness of people. He believed there was a higher power. He believed in the afterlife. Hank wasn't behind the wheel of the Dodge Charger that night in Atlantic Beach, and he took the precaution to ensure the safety of his men by insisting that Tommy drive, the most responsible person on the tiger team. Yet he couldn't shun responsibility for the death of his four men.

It was dark outside when the phone rang early Thanksgiving morning. Rose was on the other end and through chokes and sobs Jimmy pieced together that Hank had been in a car accident. She said she asked the police if Hank was all right, and they requested that she come to the Third Police District in South Philadelphia. Jimmy told her he'd pick her up and they'd go together.

After he hung up, he leaned over and scrubbed his face with the palms of his hands. He knew what it meant when the police asked you to come to the station instead of giving information over the phone. He wished he had the pamphlet Hank had once given him about grief, something about those who mourn find comfort. He wanted to read it again. He wanted the kind of faith Hank once had.

Rose opened the door and greeted Jimmy in a low, detached tone. She looked like she hadn't slept since he'd spoken to her a few days ago.

"I can take care of this if you want," he said.

Rose nodded. "I want to go, but I appreciate you going with me."

Neither of them spoke on the ride to the police station. Jimmy parked on Wharton Street where they sat watching people walk in and out of the front door. Rose dabbed her eyes with her shirtsleeve and got out. They walked into the station together and went up to the desk officer who pointed them in the direction of Detective McKrimmon's office. Dave McKrimmon introduced himself as he slid a couple of cheap metal chairs with plastic seats in front of his desk. He was a burley Irish guy with a big head, red nose, and amber crewcut, but had a manner that was surprisingly comforting.

"My husband," said Rose, and nothing more came out.

"I'm sorry, Mrs. Peachtree," he said, and gave her time to gather herself.

Jimmy put his arm around her while she stared into her lap. A few moments passed and she looked up, and said, "Go ahead."

"We got the call at two-thirty this morning," said McKrimmon. "The responding officer thought your husband was called into work because there was a Navy Yard decal on the front bumper. He figured he somehow lost control of the car, a malfunction of some sort, until he assessed the damage to the entrance of the shipyard. So he called us in to investigate."

"The damage was that bad?" said Jimmy.

"Obliterated the guardhouse, which was only wood, but the brick column behind it was knocked over. The column supported the iron Navy Yard sign that crushed his roof."

"He had to be moving."

"Judging from the damage, our accident investigator estimated he was doing over ninety miles per hour. We looked for skid marks that would indicate that he tried to stop, but there was none, so we impounded the car. They'll look to see if the breaks malfunctioned or there was some other mechanical problem."

When all the questions were answered, McKrimmon handed Rose a bag with Hank's belongings. Among the contents were a rosary and a pocketsize Bible. She pulled out a crumpled newspaper article and unfolded it. Jimmy looked over her shoulder at a picture of an obliterated car. Her hand began shaking and she dropped it on the floor. His eyes filled with rage when he picked it up and saw in bold print across the top: *Jacksonville Times, October 21, 1983*, and an article, "Accident Claims Lives of Four Philadelphia Shipyard Workers."

"I don't want it, Jimmy," said Rose. "You keep it."

Jimmy stared at the article long and hard, and as he read it, he saw Hank driving his car ninety miles per hour into the Navy Yard guardhouse at two-thirty Thanksgiving morning with the article about his four men being killed in his pocket.

Jimmy folded the article, and said, "I'll take good care of it."

Chapter XXX

DEAD & DISFIGURED

The line spilled out the door of McFeeley's Funeral Parlor, trickled down the steps, and meandered along City Line Avenue where headlights beamed under streetlights. Jimmy was consumed with regret for settling on a makeshift memorial on an aircraft carrier eight hundred miles from home instead of attending the funerals of his four close friends. A month later, the body of another casualty was mangled inside a demolished car on Broad Street at the Navy Yard gate.

And now this.

An hour passed before he stepped inside the funeral home and signed the register. A life chronicled in pictures glued to large white poster boards and arranged on tripods stood inside a large room filled with rows of cushioned folding chairs. Everywhere you looked, there were photos of Colin: a young Colin with a full head of hair playing with his girls on the beach at the Jersey Shore; a slightly older Colin wearing a jeff and holding up a pint of Guinness in a pub in County Clare, Ireland; and a serious Colin, standing at a podium as he read at the Philadelphia Poetry Festival. There were flower arrangements from the Irish

Center and the Ancient Order of Hibernians, a championship banner from the Derry City F.C., and third place ribbon from a national poetry competition. A lone bagpiper played "Danny Boy."

Colin Hanagan, Renaissance Welder.

It was fitting that he passed away on Christmas Eve.

Another twenty minutes passed before Colleen hugged him in the front of the reception line. "Thanks for coming, Jimmy."

Jimmy held both of her hands while looking over at the casket. "Your dad was the father I never had."

"And you were the son he never had," she said, with a smile.

Jimmy wiped his eyes with the back of his hand. He turned to Maura, hugged her warmly, then kissed her on the cheek. "I'm going to go have a word with your dad." He took the few steps and knelt at the coffin. He held Colin's cold hand and reflected on the times they'd spent together. The one that would never leave him was his visit in the hospital when Colin told him "Do great things." Colin lay molded in mortal casing, but his spirit resonated inside of Jimmy.

Jimmy got up slowly, and as he reached down and stroked Colin's face, his mind spiraled to four scorched bodies.

"Jimmy, are you okay?"

Colleen was standing next to him when he turned, and he had no idea how long she'd been there. He blessed himself, nodded to her, and walked toward the exit. He didn't see anyone standing along the wall until Huey reached out and grabbed his arm as he went by. "Hello, Jimmy."

Jimmy stopped and stared at Huey like he didn't recognize him, then at Butch who was next to him.

"Are you okay?" asked Huey.

Jimmy's eyes lit on fire. "All the fucking good guys are dead," he said, and stormed out into the night.

~

Vince Murphy lived on the edge: tackle football without pads, wisecracks to wiseguys packing heat. He commuted to the shipyard on a twenty-six-inch bike, which was no big deal except he took Twenty-sixth Street that paralleled the South Philly refineries to the back gate of the shipyard. Twenty-sixth Street was the main artery to Philadelphia International Airport, a drag strip for businesspeople and vacationers racing to catch their flight. Cars, limos, and taxicabs swerved in and out of tow trucks, pickups, and tractor-trailers vying for position at speeds exceeding seventy-five miles per hour. Midway between Penrose Avenue and the underpass to Schuylkill Expressway, cars pulled out from tiny Hartranft Street into the northbound lane, causing accidents, near accidents, and road rage. It was a dangerous stretch for an Abrams tank. Vince rode Twenty-sixth Street on a Schwinn.

Some boilermakers offered him rides while others tried to convince him to take a different route, but the thing Vince liked most about riding his bike on Twenty-sixth Street was the thrill of speeding cars mussing up his hair and their draft blowing up his tee shirt. He was an urban adrenalin junky: an extreme rock climber straddling a sheer of asphalt with hunks of steel screaming past. Something about the way Vince taunted life fascinated Jimmy, and the irony never got by him that climbing into the backseat of a car outside the Farmstead was the most dangerous feat Vince ever performed.

Jimmy left work the Thursday between Christmas and New Years and drove to Graduate Hospital where Vince had been moved for rehab after surgery at Jacksonville Hospital to repair two ruptured disks, a busted leg, and four broken ribs. It was the first time he saw Vince since the accident. The scars and stitch marks crisscrossing his face were visible from the hallway outside his room, but it would've taken X-ray vision to see the plate in his left leg and the fused discs in his spine. When Jimmy asked how he felt, Vince lied with a smile and resorted to his usual self-effacing irreverence describing his injuries. He masked his hesitant speech with wit.

Jimmy cringed at the sound of a voice that greeted him from the corner of the room. When he turned and saw Denny Yorko, he barely acknowledged him. He resented Denny for surviving the accident that took his friends, and word had gotten back to Denny that Jimmy said the wrong twin lived.

Jimmy turned back to Vince. "How you feeling, buddy?"

"The doctor wants me to stay in this dump for the first week of rehab," said Vince. "Then I can come in as an outpatient."

"You're lucky to be alive."

"I know," Vince confessed. His demeanor changed. "I was just telling Denny," he said, sounding sullen, "sometimes, in the middle of the night, I hear an explosion and feel a flash of heat. I'm sandwiched between Cajon and Kenny right before getting shot through the roof. There's blood all over the place. They're screaming, staring at me, but they have no mouth or eyes."

Jimmy knew the dream. He put his hand on Vince's shoulder. "Easy, buddy."

"Then," choked Vince, "I see that sailor…"

Jimmy blinked hard. "What sailor?"

"The one who drove the car that hit us."

The room turned still and quiet. "What about him?"

Vince gestured toward Denny. "Tell him."

Jimmy glared at Denny. "Tell me what?"

"He was in the Farmstead before the accident."

"What?"

Denny walked over and stood next to him. "I went to piss when we got to the restaurant, and he was in the men's room. He was shitfaced." He looked like he might cry. "He asked me if I was with Tommy."

Jimmy grabbed two fists-full of Denny's shirt. "Don't fuck with me!"

"Jimmy!" shouted Vince. "I saw him too. He looked in the dining room, saw us, and took off."

Jimmy let go of Denny and stared out the window, thinking about how he wanted to pull the plug on the sailor's life support when he found out he was stationed on the Saratoga. That would have been mercy killing. Now he wanted him to suffer. "What… the… fuck."

"What, Jimmy?" Denny asked.

A few seconds passed. "Did Tommy go to the Farmstead a lot?"

"He was the designated lunch runner," said Vince. "He went there every night."

~

In 1983, New Year's Eve fell on a Saturday, making Friday the last workday of the year. Most of Jimmy's gang took a vacation day. The ones who showed up didn't find their boss because he'd been outside Huey Kortez's office since six a.m.

Huey didn't smile much since returning from Mayport. His "how are you, young man" to Jimmy was unenthusiastic, and Jimmy's "about the same as you, I guess" matched Huey's emptiness. When it came to expressing feelings, Huey was a vault, but he opened up to Jimmy about his godson Tommy. Hearing the seasoned leader sob yanked at something deep inside of Jimmy. He didn't know how to console the man he usually looked to for strength.

When they both tired of depressing talk, Huey said, "So what brings you here, Jimmy?"

"You hear anything about the sailor?"

"The one who killed Tommy and the boys?"

"Yeah."

"Last I heard he was still on life support. He's fucked up. No legs, missing an eye, plate in the head. To be honest, I don't know how he survived."

Jimmy didn't say anything but looked troubled.

"Why do you ask?"

"I went to the hospital last night to see Vince," said Jimmy. "He told me the sailor was in the Farmstead before the accident."

"What?"

Jimmy nodded to confirm to Huey that he heard him right. "The sailor who drove the car that killed our guys was in the Farmstead before the accident." He let the words sink in for a moment. "Denny was at the hospital too. They were both adamant about it."

Huey shook his head. "That's too much of a coincidence to be a coincidence."

"You're goddamn right it is."

"Jesus Christ," said Huey, massaging his temples with his thick fingers.

"What?"

"The night you told Admiral Foley to get fucked."

Jimmy stared at Huey trying to make the connection. "What about it?"

"Mr. Homes found out and called me from Philly. He told me to straighten it out, so I tracked down the admiral in the captain's stateroom at five in the morning and schmoozed him."

"You never told me that," said Jimmy.

"There was no need to," said Huey. "But after I convinced the asshole what a dedicated and patriotic guy you are, he said, 'How about the other kid?' I didn't think nothing of it at the time, but…"

"But what?"

"What if he meant Tommy?"

Jimmy shook his head. "Something's not right, Huey."

"You're goddamn right, something's not right." Huey tilted his head toward Mr. Homes's office. "And then yesterday the boss tells me he went to the hotel get Tommy's stuff after the accident and his room was ransacked."

"He just told you yesterday," said Jimmy, in disbelief. "Two months after the accident?"

"Keep that between me and you, Jimmy. There's an investigation going on."

"Find out where the sailor is," said Jimmy.

Huey looked at Jimmy like he wanted to ask why, but instead said, "I will."

A faraway look came to him. "What the fuck was the sailor doing in the Farmstead?"

Chapter XXXI

POLITICS

*I*t's that one time you go against your gut. You know the business better than anyone.

You know the stats, the engineering, the nuances, the risks, the players, and they're all pointing to success. But the timing's off, and timing is everything. A recipe for failure, like sending the minor league pitching prospect to the mound in the bottom of the ninth, bases loaded, two outs in the World Series. A year or two from now the move would put you on top of the baseball world, but for once you go against your gut and helplessly watched the ball explode off a bat like it was shot from a cannon, soar over the bleachers, and out of the ballpark.

~

The New Year was bountiful for Lawrence Foley. The Graybeard Panel concluded that the leaking superheater tubes on the Saratoga were caused by shoddy workmanship at the Philadelphia Navy Yard, and the shipyard was charged for the cost of the tiger team to re-tube the boilers. Maestro Fusion Corporation raked in millions for work that had to be redone.

Admiral Foley had played more than a few rounds of golf at the Army Navy Country Club in Arlington, Virginia. Its ballroom was an exclusive venue for Navy elites, the antithesis of the shot-and-a-beer, mummer's hangout with drop ceilings and cheap paneling named the Sons of Ben Franklin. Foley had been an invited guest to legions of weddings, award banquets, and retirements, but this day was reserved for him. His name was proudly displayed on the marquee for a lavish retirement ceremony attended by admirals, senators, congressmen and CEOs. Foley sat at the head table, basking in the praise of admirers, many who came seeking favor for the day their military careers would come to an end.

Johnny Neumann stood on the veranda on a brisk, sunny afternoon looking out at the Washington Memorial rise beyond the fairway. It was where Foley first floated the idea to bid on the Saratoga boiler contract. He had mixed feelings about his decision that day. In a career where he'd held office on Capitol Hill, the White House, and the Pentagon, Neumann had earned a reputation as a man of integrity. He was clearheaded about his strengths and weaknesses, as well as the shortcomings of the people around him, and though Admiral Foley was known as a technically astute and fearless leader, trusting him on the Saratoga decision never felt right.

"How are you, Johnny?"

Neumann turned around. "Mr. Secretary," he said, extending his hand to Mark Wise, his successor at the Navy's highest post that he himself held before going into private business and starting Maestro Fusion Corporation. "Good to see you."

"And you," said Wise. "You know, I was skeptical of that welding process your company pioneered, but after reading the Graybeard Panel report Admiral Foley commissioned, I understand how the poor workmanship at the Philadelphia Navy Yard caused the leaks on the Saratoga."

"Thank you, Mr. Secretary," said Neumann, stoically. Though Foley took credit for allocating funding in the R&D budget and pushed the automated process through the Navy acquisition bureaucracy, the robotic welder was Johnny Neumann's baby. He was the one who pioneered the process and knew the engineering and science. He estimated the preheat cycle was at least a year away from being resolved and approved to use in cold temperatures when Foley persuaded him to bid on the Saratoga contract. He regretted his decision, and even though the Graybeard Panel's report exonerated his company, he was conflicted because he suspected Foley influenced the outcome.

"We've worked very hard enhancing the preheat cycle since the Saratoga," he said to Secretary Wise.

"Excellent," said Wise. "It eases my mind knowing those damn Philly welders won't touch the new boiler tubes on the Forrestal." They shared a short laugh, then Wise gestured toward the lounge. "You have a good man coming on board. How about we go have a drink with him?"

Now that his company had been cleared in the Saratoga boilers leaks, Neumann found himself in a bind to hire Foley as security to win the contacts for the remaining aircraft carriers in the SLEP program.

~

Eight a.m. on Monday, January 9, 1984, Lawrence Foley walked into his new office in Dayton, Ohio dressed in a three-piece navy-blue suit with an American flag pin on his lapel. He sat in his leather chair and leaned back, looking out at Wright-Patterson Air Force Base in the distance. He smiled as he calculated the hundreds of millions of dollars the company would make on the SLEP program, *cha-ching cha-ching,* and imagined the way he could spin his bio as the brain trust behind a Fortune 500 Company.

Chapter XXXII

CPA

The old marine barracks sat across from the back channel basin where mothballed ships, once-proud symbols of American dominance, waited to be sold for scrap metal to make bicycles and razor blades. A stone sculpture of an eagle perched on a globe and anchor, the United States Marine Corps emblem, rested atop a gypsum archway on the front of the building. The four-story brick fortress housed United States Marines during World Wars I and II. In the 1970s and '80s, shipyard workers played touch football on the eight-acre parade grounds where marines had marched. Now, Temple University leased classrooms once used to teach subjects on weaponry and battle tactics for an after-hours management program.

Jimmy had shunned advice from supervisors to enroll in the program, protesting that promotions shouldn't be contingent upon checking a box. It felt like a quid pro quo: take a class and become a bona fide manager. He pointed to Harper Simpson as an example, referring to a foreman who framed his Temple Management Certificate and hung it on the wall behind his desk, yet couldn't lead a cub scout troop through Fairmount

Park without suffering causalities. Had it not been for Colin petitioning him from his deathbed to read, learn and do great things, Jimmy never would have seen the inside of a barracks classroom.

Mick Kelly was different from any teacher he had in twelve years of Catholic school. He wore thousand-dollar suits, power ties, and cuff links that fastened his sleeves tight around his thick wrists. He had the calloused hands of a bricklayer. Kelly peppered eloquent speech and sophisticated vocabulary with expletives. By day, he was a corporate accountant for one of the largest firms in Philadelphia. He taught at the shipyard's after-hours program because his father had been a dockworker. He wanted to see for himself what life on the waterfront was all about.

Kelly didn't follow a syllabus or textbook. Instead, he told stories that were parables, each with a common theme: the line between legal and illegal was a blurred one. At the end of his third class, Jimmy walked up to him, and said, "Mr. Kelly, I like the way you teach."

Mr. Kelly could talk for two hours without coming up for air, but the unsolicited compliment from a guy who looked like he was born under a boiler caused him to simply raise an eyebrow.

"What do you like about it?"

Jimmy told him about his academic struggles growing up, how he barely graduated from high school, but that he grasped Kelly's stories. The way he put complex theories into a context made sense to him.

Their after-class talks became routine until one night, Mr. Kelly said, "How about we move these deliberations to Rocky's for a beer?"

"I haven't turned one of them down since I was fourteen," said Jimmy.

Jimmy followed Kelly's black BMW sedan to Rocky's Roast Beef on Seventeenth Street where they sat at the bar and ate roast beef sandwiches and drank frosted mugs of Schmidt's. They debated the Flyers' chances in the Stanly Cup playoffs while they watched them beat the Boston Bruins in overtime on the television behind the bar. When the game was over, Kelly turned to Jimmy, and said, "So what's your plan?"

"What do you mean?"

"Where do you see yourself five years from now?"

"Five years?" said Jimmy, eyeing his teacher to see if he was kidding. "I don't know where I'll be five days from now."

"Listen, Jimmy," Kelly said, his determined blue eyes beaming. "You gotta have a plan if you ever want to get anywhere." Jimmy watched his teacher intently. "Picture where you want to be in five years. I mean, imagine yourself in the job you want to be in. What changes you'd make. What kind of people you'd hire. How would you build your team, your business, train your people and inspire them? Do the same thing for ten years."

Jimmy rubbed the hairs on his face thoughtfully. "To be honest, Mr. Kelly," he said, "I love what I do. I really don't want to do anything else."

"First of all," he said, "stop with the Mr. Kelly bullshit. The name's Mick."

Jimmy smiled. "Okay, Mick."

"They say the man who loves what he does is a lucky man," said Kelly. "But things change. Always do. Don't lock yourself in a box." He pointed his index finger at his head. "Expand yourself, your knowledge, and your experience." He picked up his mug and clinked it against Jimmy's. "Be prepared if an opportunity arises."

The after-class sessions at Rocky's became a weekly routine. Mick told stories about corporations, profits, dirty money, hiding money, and laundering money. He talked about corporations like they were as corrupt as the mob. More corrupt.

One night, Jimmy asked him how he knew so much about crime.

"My old man didn't want me to work on the docks, said it was too dangerous," said Kelly. "So when I got out of high school, I took the test for the Police Academy and became a cop. I was the youngest guy in narcotics at twenty-four. Like that wasn't dangerous, right? I'd been shot at more times than some of my buddies were in 'Nam." Kelly turned serious. "The biggest cocaine bust I was ever involved with was funded with money laundered through a corporation with its headquarters downtown. I was so fascinated by the way the feds traced the money to the white-collar guys that I went back to school at night and got my degree in finance, then my CPA from Wharton. Nothing more satisfying than putting millionaires in prison." Kelly laughed deep and hard. "Pussies whimper like babies when they are sentenced."

Jimmy drove home that night, thinking how he never would have met Mick Kelly if Colin hadn't encouraged him to expand himself. It struck him how similar the two men were: Colin, the most independent-minded foreman in the shipyard, and Kelly, narcotic cop turned corporate finance guy. As their relationship grew, Jimmy told Mick that he reminded him of his mentor, the Renaissance Welder, who passed away. He confided in Kelly that Colin gave him the same advice about expanding himself.

"Wise Irishman," said Kelly.

~

Sessions at Rocky's became more advanced as the semester progressed. One night, Mick pulled an annual report from his shoulder bag, put it on the bar and ran his finger down a column of numbers.

"Business is revenue and expenses, plusses and minuses. Academics make up fancy names to impress commoners. Corporations pay guys like me to keep as much of the revenue as they can, exploit tax loopholes, and twist the truth. Lie. You're probably smarter than half the guys I deal with."

After he translated the language to layman terms, he pulled out an edition of the *Financial Times*, handed it to Jimmy and told him to start reading business news. It would eventually start to click. "It's not rocket science," he said.

In the classroom, Mr. Kelly covered balance sheets, debits and credits, income statements, and cash flow. When Jimmy started asking questions about amortization, capital equipment, and restructuring debt, Mick said, "You sound like you've been reading the financial pages."

"It's just numbers with fancy names," said Jimmy.

Mr. Kelly gave him a wink.

Hunkered down with a pitcher of beer at a table in the back of Rocky's a few weeks later, Jimmy said, "I've been trying to research a company and not getting anywhere."

"Where you looking?"

"I went through the list of companies on the New York Stock Exchange at the Temple library."

"Could be a few reasons," said Mick. "They could be on another exchange like the NASDAQ or the AMEX, or they might not be publicly traded. How about I check it out?"

"It would mean a lot to me," said Jimmy.

Mick had a trained ear from years of interrogating druggies and criminals, and in Jimmy's statement, he detected a trace of distress. "What do you mean?"

"The company screwed up a multi-million-dollar contract for the Navy, and I can't find anything about them."

Mick grinned. "So, what's new?"

"You don't understand, Mick." Jimmy went on to explain the robotic welding process the company used successfully in warm climates like San Diego and Hawaii, and how schedule delays led to welding chrome tubes in December on the Saratoga.

Then his voice tightened. "The job was a disaster. The tubes cracked. The boilers leaked. So we went to Florida to fix a job the company fucked up, and four of my buddies were killed."

"Jesus Christ," said Mick. "What's the name of the company?"

"Maestro Fusion Corporation."

"Let me see what I can find out."

Chapter XXXIII

MORNING MASS

Jimmy knew three things about Manayunk: it was a scrappy blue-collar neighborhood, it sat on the banks of the Schuylkill River, and there were as many bars as there were hills. He'd never been there. He'd never had a reason to until Peggy Homes asked him to meet her on a Wednesday morning for the six-thirty mass at St. John the Baptist Church. She told him the mass was for Tommy's birthday. He thought it was odd that she asked him not to tell anyone.

He got off the Roosevelt Extension of the Schuylkill Expressway at Ridge Avenue, made a right and followed it to a fork where he veered left onto Main Street that paralleled the river. Main Street narrowed into a ravine of stone storefronts, mostly antique shops, boutiques, and bars. In about a mile, he turned right onto Grape Street, stopped at the iron trellises for the elevated train, then right again onto cobblestoned Cresson Street. At the next stop sign, he heard thunder, and his Jeep shook. He leaned forward and looked up, listening as the train disappeared down the tracks. On the next block, he avoided the concrete buttress and drove up the hill to St. John's, made a wide left on Rector Street and parked at the curb next to Pretzel Park.

The church looked dark, except for the huge clock illuminating ornate hands and Roman numerals high on the stone steeple. Mass wouldn't start for fifteen minutes. He got out and admired the nineteenth century stone row homes, their closeness on the narrow street gave him a warm feeling, like he belonged. He walked up Rector to where it turned into Churchview Street and continued halfway up the hill. He stopped and looked out over rooftops at the open spandrel of the Manayunk Bridge that crossed the Schuylkill into Bala Cynwyd.

The gong of church bells sent vibrations through his bones. He double-timed back down the hill, ran up the church's marble steps and walked down the center aisle before the opening prayer was over. The meager crowd of seniors and nuns hardly justified the collection. Jimmy recognized Father Leonard on the altar from the memorial mass in Florida. There was no mistaking Peggy's full head of blonde locks in the second pew. Her daughter Danielle was next to her in a white dress with big yellow polka dots. Peggy hugged him when he slid in the pew next to her. He kissed her cheek, then leaned down and kissed Danielle on the head. Her hair was beginning to curl like her mother's. She chewed on a white rubber giraffe with large brown spots. He wondered why nobody else from Tommy's family was there.

After the final blessing, Peggy lowered her head and wept. Jimmy rubbed her shoulder until she was composed enough to talk.

"Thanks for coming, Jimmy."

"Thanks for inviting me." He looked over at her little girl. "Danielle is so damn cute I couldn't concentrate on mass."

Peggy smiled. "She's her father's daughter," she said. "She's got Tommy's energy," she looked down at Danielle, and added, "and curiosity."

"How've you been?" Jimmy asked.

Peggy seemed to drift, searching for an answer she'd never find. Moments passed. "Tommy didn't want to go to Florida."

A wave of guilt swept Jimmy as he recalled Tommy telling him that money wasn't important, family was, then Jimmy convincing him that the shipyard's reputation was on the line. "I know," he finally said.

"Something Tommy said keeps haunting me," said Peggy. Jimmy waited apprehensively. "He called the afternoon of the accident. I could tell something was bothering him, and when I asked him what was wrong, he told me he had a fight with a sailor."

"A fight?" said Jimmy. "About what?"

"He said he knew the sailor from the shipyard, but all of the sudden the guy turned on him, accused him of screwing up the boilers, like the leaks were his fault. He said they almost came to blows, but some of the guys broke it up."

Jimmy's blood churned. He was so infuriated he couldn't talk.

"Are you okay, Jimmy?

"I just..." he stammered. He could feel his head throbbing as he thought about his own fight with Admiral Foley the morning inside the trailer. He strained to remain under control. "I was just thinking of something," he finally said.

Peggy looked at him for a few seconds. "There's something else."

He looked at her and waited.

Seniors mingle nearby. "I don't feel comfortable talking here," she said.

Jimmy gestured toward the doors beneath the silver organ pipes in the back of the church. She followed him out of the pew and down the center aisle. A train clattered along the elevated rails toward center city when they stepped outside. Cars pulled out of parking spaces and pedestrians hurried down the hill toward the el stop. Jimmy nodded toward Pretzel Park and helped Peggy down the steps with the stroller. They crossed the street into the park and sat on a bench overlooking the roofs on Main Street. The weather was changing, and trees were blossoming. Spring had arrived.

"I got a package in the mail last week," said Peggy. Jimmy put his elbows on his knees, locked his fingers and looked at her. "It had ten thousand dollars in it."

He clasped his hands so tight the blood drained from his fingers. "Ten thousand dollars?" he said, taking great effort to keep his voice low. "From who?"

"There was no note. No return address. Just cash."

A flurry of schemes raced through his head. "Jesus," he said. "Have you told anyone?"

"You're the only one," she said.

Jimmy stared at the cement under his feet while he gathered his thoughts. "Not even Tommy's dad?"

"He's the last person I'd tell right now," she said.

"What do you mean?" asked Jimmy. "If anyone should know, it's him."

Peggy dabbed the corner of her eye, stroked a few errant hairs from her face and looked back at Jimmy.

"I'm sorry," he said, feeling as though he was pressuring her.

"I'm not supposed to tell anyone," she said. "So keep this between me and you."

"Of course."

"Mrs. Homes called the other day. She told me they were eating dinner in the dining room, and Mr. Homes started staring at the wall. He didn't respond when she talked to him, wasn't even blinking, like he froze. She called an ambulance, and when they got him to the emergency room, all his vital signs were functioning properly, so they had a psychiatrist evaluate him. He was diagnosed with something called dissociative amnesia. They said it's caused by trauma."

Jimmy tried to make sense of what Peggy had just told him. He was twelve when his dad was killed suddenly, and he toughed it out. Why couldn't the leader of two hundred shipyard boilermakers?

"What are you thinking, Jimmy?"

"I don't know. I just thought he was detached, like he didn't give a shit."

Peggy stiffened. "I don't know how much you know about Tommy's dad, but he's the most dedicated person I ever met in my life, and loyal. Mrs. Homes told me when he was twenty-one, he was one of the troops who landed on the beach in Normandy. He saw hundreds of men slaughtered, many of them his friends. He had nightmares for years, still does sometimes, forty years later." She paused, and in a deliberate tone continued, "Mr. Homes saw the course of history

213

change because an entire army stuck to a plan. After he got out of the military, he always stuck with a plan once it was made, like it was sacred." She noticed Jimmy staring into space. "Jimmy," she said. He looked over at her. "Tommy's mom told me that Mr. Homes never questioned the military in his life until Tommy's death. Now he's so conflicted that he's paralyzed."

A young mother walked into the park hand-in-hand with a little girl, lifted her onto a swing and began pushing her. Jimmy watched as the child soared higher and higher, the rusty metal swivels squealing to be oiled. Jimmy only heard the child's laughter. "I guess that's the difference," he said.

"What do you mean?" asked Peggy.

"What Mr. Homes went through watching his friends die is unimaginable," he said, trying to envision the blood-soaked sands of Normandy. "I was in fifth grade when a building my dad was working on collapsed. He died because the men who controlled construction jobs in the city only hired union roofers on commercial contracts where they could afford to follow safety regulations. The union leaders were in bed with politicians and corporations and kept the little guys out. Non-union contractors who didn't have the money for safety equipment got the shit jobs. They cut corners and took risks to survive. My dad's dead because he was a non-union roofer." Peggy reached over and put her hand on Jimmy's. "I don't trust anyone just because they're in a position of authority. I don't care who they are, what their title is, or how much money they have. People have to earn my trust." Jimmy looked into her sad eyes, and said, "That's the difference."

Peggy shook her head in a way that told him she understood.

"A lot about the job we were doing in Florida never felt right to me," he said. "Now you tell me about Tommy's fight with a sailor and the money with no note or anything." The squealing of the swing stopped. Jimmy watched the woman wrap her arms around the little girl, lift her from the swing and lower her to the ground. "Things just don't add up," he continued. "I'm going to find out why all of this happened and who's behind it." He kissed Peggy's cheek and stood up, leaned into the stroller and kissed Danielle who had slept through their conversation. "I don't give a shit who it is." He turned and walked out of the park.

Chapter XXXIV

ATTRITION

Jimmy had been foreman for almost nine months, and Butch had never shown up at one of his musters, until now. Butch gave no explanation, just told him to be in his office at ten o'clock, then left.

It threw Jimmy off. He was preoccupied while he assigned his men jobs. After checking a few projects, he headed to meet his boss. At nine-forty, he walked down the structural group superintendents' corridor, and someone called his name from one of the offices. He stopped and walked back. Inside the boilermaker's office, Huey Kortez was talking to Mr. Homes's secretary. Their conversation stopped when Jimmy walked in.

"What's up, Huey?"

"I talked to Captain Flask," he said. "The sailor who was driving the car that hit our boys is in rehab at Walter Reed Hospital."

"Rehab?" said Jimmy. "The way you were talking over the holidays, I thought the guy would be dead."

"I don't think anyone expected him to live," said Huey. "It sounded like he might have been there for a few weeks."

Jimmy looked bewildered. "Where's Walter Reed?"

Huey eyed Jimmy. "Why?"

"Why?" Jimmy blurted. "He killed our fucking guys!"

The secretary got up and walked out into the hallway. Huey put his hand on Jimmy's shoulder. "They were my guys too, Jimmy," he said. He nodded toward his boss's office. "Tommy's death is killing Mr. Homes. He goes in his office in the morning and doesn't come out until quitting time. He doesn't talk to anyone. Doesn't hold any meetings. It's like he's not even here."

"Does he still defend the Navy for using the Maestro Fusion machine?"

"Jimmy…"

"I want to talk to the sailor."

"Listen, Jimmy," said Huey. "Nothing good will come of you seeing the guy. And besides, he's probably under guard until he goes to trial. Why waste your time on an invalid whose gonna spend the rest of his life in jail?"

Jimmy's expression hardened. "I have questions only that guy can answer."

"Why torture yourself?" asked Huey, sounding defeated.

Jimmy wrung his hands in angst. "Did you know that Tommy questioned the Maestro Fusion process? He didn't think the preheat cycle was adequate, and he was vocal about it. Then, right before Senator Hawkins visited us in Mayport, some random sailor from the Saratoga just happened to be in the same restaurant as he was and drove ninety miles an hour into his car after he left." Jimmy was tempted to tell Huey about the money Peggy Homes got in the mail but was afraid it would get to Mr. Homes.

He stared Huey down. "Doesn't that seem odd to you?" He tapped the sides of his head. "Come on, Huey. Think!"

Huey plopped into his chair and rubbed his head with the palms of his hands. "Jesus, Jimmy."

"And then," Jimmy continued, "the company wins a sixty-million-dollar contract for the Forrestal after we spent three months fixing their fuckups in Florida."

"You don't think…"

"I don't think what?" asked Jimmy, and then louder, "I don't think what, Huey?" He looked up at the clock. "Shit."

"What?" asked Huey.

"Butch wanted to see me at ten o'clock."

"You better go."

Jimmy was almost to the door when Huey called after him. Jimmy turned and faced him. "Yeah?"

"Rumors are going around that Butch's job is on the line."

The words sent Jimmy's mind into a whirlwind. The list of shipyard workers who had direct knowledge about the Maestro Fusion job was dwindling: Tommy, gone; Mr. Strunk, forced out; George Sputz, transferred; Mr. Homes, incapacitated.

And now Butch.

~

Butch waved Jimmy in and pointed to a chair while he talked on the phone. When he hung up, he stared at Jimmy like he couldn't decide where to begin.

"That was my boss," he said. "At the superintendent's meeting yesterday, he mentioned an opening in the shipyard Program Management Office for an industry analyst with background in structures and boilers."

"Why you telling me?" asked Jimmy. He watched Butch lean back in his chair, and as if anticipating his boss taking a different approach, he said, "I'm not interested."

"At the point in your career, you should be thinking about the future, Jimmy. You don't want to be climbing around a boiler room breathing smoke and asbestos dust when you're my age. It tears you apart little by little. Look at some of the old timers."

"That's not the way I look at it," said Jimmy. "Working on the iron hardens me."

"Come back in ten years and tell me that."

Jimmy took a few moments to think, then said, "I didn't see any job announcement," referring to job openings normally posted in the shipyard newsletter. "What about interviews, applications, all that stuff?"

"All taken care of."

Taken care of? Jimmy knew that was bullshit. Program management jobs were filled competitively with resumes and interview panels, all part of a formal process. His hands felt sweaty, and when he looked down instead of perspiration he saw blood, a sodden work boot. He heard leather gloves pounding a heavy bag and imagined a wide, gleaming smile: the good twin, gone because he was loyal to his alcoholic brother. Hank took his own life because he couldn't bare the guilt. Jimmy wanted to ask Colin for advice, but all the good guys were dead.

"I don't know why you even have to think about it," said Butch, but his words sounded more like a plea. *Come on, Jimmy. Take the job. Please.*

"I'm not stupid, Butch," said Jimmy. "I'm one of the last guys around who questioned the robotic welding process. Five of them are dead. Now you want to get rid of me."

"I don't want to get rid of anyone," said Butch. "It's for your own…" he stopped in mid-sentence, looking confused. "Five?"

"For Chrissake, Butch," Jimmy spewed. Every thought he'd ever had about the accident boiled inside of him. "Those guys getting killed tore Hank apart. He blamed himself for letting them go out that night. And then he comes home and crashes his car into the shipyard guardhouse on Thanksgiving." Jimmy went on ranting about how excited Tommy was to fly home that weekend and christen his daughter, then his life was snuffed out. "What'd those guys die for?" Jimmy demanded, and when Butch didn't answer, he slammed his fist on the desk. "Money? Greed?" He shot out of the chair. Jimmy didn't want to say it because it was only a rumor he'd heard minutes ago, but the gloves were off. "And you're so wrapped up in your job, you don't even know you'll be next to get canned."

Jimmy stormed toward the door. He hated Butch. He hated the shipyard commander, the Navy and the admirals. He hated himself for not doing more to stop the carnage.

As he was about to leave the office, something slowed him. He waited for his rage to settle, turned around and stared blankly at Butch. He didn't know why, but said, "I'll take the fucking job."

~

Jimmy walked along the riverfront, still fuming, and when he got to the Forrestal he kept walking, past the boiler shop, past Pier #6, the pipe shop, Pier #2 and #1. He continued out of the industrial area, past the shipyard commander's residence with its lush green lawn and century-old oak trees to where the shipyard looked no different than a placid waterfront park anywhere. He came to a stop and sat on the sloping lawn that eased to the riverbank. Cargo ships churned peacefully through the channel. A tugboat thrust a barge upriver, spitting out ripples of water that looked like cartoon images of sound waves. A water-skier trailed a speedboat and cut across making play of the wake.

He sat thinking about his life, his father, Tommy, Hank, and the people who turned it all to turmoil. He was young, but experienced enough to know graft and greed were ingrained in every field: private industry, trade unions, the shipyard, the military, the government. It was the reason his dad died young, and his mom had to work two jobs and why he himself went to work at twelve. It was the reason Tommy, Kenny, Cajon, and Jerry never returned from Mayport. Good people working honest jobs, shit on by greedy men who gamed the system and raked in millions at the expense of the workingman.

Jimmy couldn't let it go. He wouldn't let it go. Colin's parting words to him was to do great things, and in his mind the greatest thing he could do was to honor the people he loved and lost by exposing and bringing to justice those who cut their lives short.

Chapter XXXV

THINGS FALL APART

L aws were written to be violated, regulations twisted, and rules ignored. It was the dictum of white-collar criminals and nefarious military officers who went to work in the corporate world after retirement. To Admiral Lawrence Foley, the two-year ban between retirement and going to work for a private contractor on government contracts for which he previously had influence was a joke, a *wink, wink* to ethics officials in the Pentagon. Three days after retirement, he sat behind the desk of the Chief Operations Officer of Maestro Fusion Corporation. Once he got settled, he would hire Captain Neil Crosby as the head of the company's metallurgy division.

~

Maestro Fusion Corporation's lobby was one part industrial plant, one part military museum, one part corporate headquarters. A large American flag stood proudly in the center of the spacious chamber surrounded by insignias from each branch of the military services. On the wall to the left of the flag were photos of the Commander in Chief, Secretary of Defense, Chief Executive Officer, and the corporate board. Next to CEO and former Secretary of the Navy, Johnny Neumann, was Chief Operations Officer, Admiral Lawrence Foley (Ret.). On the other side of the lobby was a mockup of a superheater header cut longitudinally to expose meticulously robotic welded boiler tubes. Next to the mockup was a Maestro Fusion welding machine with a large diagram describing key components and the process.

"You can go in now, Captain," called the blonde behind a counter who appeared to be part of the display. The young captain got up and walked down the hall to the COO's office where he stopped and knocked on the doorframe.

"Close the door behind you," said Foley, never looking up from whatever he was reading. The top button of his dark blue pinstripe vest was open, a starched white shirt underneath, initials embroidered on the cuffs, gold cufflinks. A red silk tie was knotted at his throat. His suit jacket hung on a coatrack behind him to the left across from an American Flag. Fellow board members called him Larry. Everyone else addressed him as "Admiral," including family.

The office was a shrine to the man's career, the tours, and campaigns. There were photos of the admiral with numerous secretaries of the Navy. The one with the president prominently positioned. On the wall to his left was a commissioned painting of the aircraft carrier USS Midway, CV-41, which he commandeered as a young captain. Inlaid in the lower right-hand corner was a picture of him in the pilothouse.

A lone family photo on Foley's desk reminded Captain Stevens that he was destined for the military. He never had a choice. It was the photo of a child, maybe four or five years old, standing between his mother and father at the Naval Academy, saluting. It reminded him of images he'd seen of children saluting mobile missile launchers at military parades in Russia and North Korea. The photo was taken on the kind of vacations his family took after his biological father died of cancer and his mother got remarried to Admiral Foley. She realized her mistake early on, that her second husband was a tyrant, and chose not to change her name.

"Four people," snapped his stepfather.

Stevens expected their meeting would begin like this: a barb aimed at a fault or failure on his part, rather than a hello. He was so conditioned from a lifetime of degrading remarks that he no longer heard them.

"Do we have to go through this?" said Stevens, already sounding exhausted.

"Sweep it all under the rug, just like that?"

"There's more to it than…"

"There's always more to it with you," the admiral cut him off. He looked at his stepson for the first time. "But this time I don't want to hear excuses. I entrusted you with the most critical mission of your life, Bradley," addressing him the way he did as a child when he didn't meet his father's expectations, "and you screwed it up."

"Father, I…"

The F-word caused Foley to look like someone shoved shit in his mouth. "You assured me that you had the right man for the mission," he butted in.

"You don't understand!" Bradley shot back, in a tone he'd never used speaking to the old man.

"What's there to understand? That you were tasked to eliminate one shipyard worker and your 'perfect person' took out four? What? Didn't your 'perfect person' know how to count?"

"I told you, the night of the mission, Tommy Homes—"

"Don't you dare use that name in here!" screamed the admiral, slamming his fist into his desk. "Use your head, boy!"

The captain threw his stepfather a hateful look and started over. "The night of the mission, the subject wasn't alone. My man did the best he could working with bad intelligence."

"Bad intelligence?" shouted the admiral. "Don't even think about pulling me into this!" He exhaled a gust of disdain, and in a calmer tone, he switched the subject. "I thought you said your man wasn't going to make it."

"Last I heard he was on life support."

"Jesus Christ! That was months ago." Again, his stepfather struggled to maintain his composure. "Do you know what today is?"

The captain was silent, as if he knew any answer he gave would be wrong.

"It's April twentieth! If you did your homework, you'd know it was six months to the day since the accident. Your man has been rehabbing at Walter Reed Hospital since February." The old man seemed to take great pleasure in watching his stepson squirm, even more so when there was nowhere for him to hide, no hole to crawl into. He leaned back in his chair, laid his arms on the armrest and tapped his fingers on its cushioned ends. "He goes on trial in June," he continued, his tone full of bravado. "I've seen to it that he's court martialed and spends the rest of his life in jail." He didn't say it as a statement of fact, but a decree, like a king sitting on his throne handing down a sentence. A king who knew how to manipulate his servants. "This is the last time I clean up your mess."

Stevens had become immune to the tantrums. During the admiral's brief visits home between overseas tours when he was growing up, he was the target of the old man's ridicule, resentment, and insecurities. His mother tried to shield him, defend him, but it was no use. The old man was a dictator, drunk with power from a lifetime of everyone bowing to him, saluting him, calling him "sir" and kissing his ass. In his insulated, hierarchal world, he *was* king.

"Will that be all, Father?" he asked, mimicking the tone of his twelve-year-old self, meant as a "fuck you."

"As a matter of fact, it won't," said the retired admiral, and after demeaning his stepson for half an hour, the old man threw him a bone to let him recoup a semblance of dignity. He sat straight in his chair, and in a business-like manner, declared, "Well, you did get rid of that misguided boilermaker before he ruined us. So I've worked my contacts in the Pentagon, and you're going to be reassigned to the Program Executive Officer for Aircraft Carriers. You will have decision authority for every contract awarded on aircraft carrier construction and overhaul." He leaned forward, eyes honing in like he was giving an order to fire a cruise missile. "It will be solely up to you to make sure future boiler tube contracts are awarded to Maestro Fusion Corporation. And," he paused, taking a deep breath to expand his chest, "for each contract, you will be rewarded."

Chapter XXXVI

PROGRAM MANAGER

The gears of bureaucracy prevented swift and efficient promotions. Absent intervention by influential people, they took months, sometimes more than a year. It had been only six weeks since Butch made the offer, and here Jimmy was, in the Program Management Office.

Charts and graphs hung on walls, a computer on every desk. Throughout the office, the scent of fresh air circulated, as opposed to smoke and asbestos dust. People walked around in polished shoes instead of steel-toed work boots and wore pants with ironed creases, shirts, and ties. There were no crashes or explosions. Nobody shouted expletives.

"You must be Jimmy McKee." Jimmy turned to a guy who came up to his chin, dressed in a denim shirt with a flowery tie loose at the collar. "I'm Dick Wells," he said, offering his hand. Jimmy could tell by Dick's handshake that he had spent many hours with his hands wrapped around a barbell. "Let's go to my office and I'll give you a rundown of the place."

Jimmy knew Dick by reputation. A Kensington native and former machinist, he'd played semi-pro football for the Venango

Bears and went to night school to earn a business degree. He'd made a few connections and persuaded the Program Management Office to take a chance on him. He was the first graduate apprentice ever to rise through the ranks and get hired by the PMO. After he got in, he was promoted and started opening doors for others.

Dick pointed to a chair at a small conference table and sat next to him rather than behind his desk. "I hear a lot of good things about you," he said.

Jimmy seemed surprised. "I didn't expect anyone around here to know who I am."

"Yeah, well, the ships were my training ground, too," said Dick. He pointed out the door. "Most of the folks out there are college-types. Never got a length of pipe dropped on their head or had a rusted metal burr stuck in their eyeball." He laughed, then turned serious. "That's a disadvantage, but they're professionals. I make sure they respect the men and women who work on the ships, and I make sure they write procedures so they're successful."

Jimmy walked into the office half an hour ago feeling intimidated, even a little unworthy. He thought Butch had sold him out, an administrative move orchestrated by high-ups in the Navy to eliminate another connection to the Mayport tiger team. Dick eradicated any trace of unworthiness by ten o'clock.

"After you get a handle on things around here, I'll take you to the Navy offices in Crystal City where shipbuilding programs are managed, show you around, and introduce you to some of the principals."

"Crystal City?" said Jimmy.

It sounded like a fairytale land to Jimmy, not the nerve center of Navy program management that his new boss described. Dick went on to tell him that billions of dollars in contracts were influenced and awarded on the island of offices above the underground mall of shops, restaurants, and pubs adjacent to National Airport and across the Potomac River from Washington. "Any questions?"

"What program are you going to put me on?" Jimmy asked, a question that had lingered since he accepted the job.

"Aircraft carriers."

Jimmy eyebrows perked, expecting he'd be assigned to a supply ship, an oiler, or some other rudimentary program. "I figured you'd have gotten word not to let me near a carrier."

"Yeah," said Dick, mockingly. "They might've mentioned something about that." He leaned in close enough for Jimmy to smell the coffee on his breath. "But fuck them. I run this place, and I'll put you where I think you'll fit best."

Something about Dick's response seemed personal. Maybe it was the inflection in his voice or his piercing stare. Over Dick's shoulder hung a large poster with pictures of every class of Navy ship, their specs printed under each hull. Next to the poster was a Navy organizational chart, from the secretary down to the Program Executive Officers (PEO) to their PMOs. NAVSEA directories sat on the boss's desk.

"Now you're talking," said Jimmy.

"You're goddamn right, I'm talking," said Dick. "Get settled in. This afternoon you're going to go to a production meeting on the ship with Jack Reddi."

"Jack Ready?" said Jimmy, repeating the name the way he'd heard it.

"One of our best analysts. Knows more about ships than guys who spent thirty years on the iron. Your first time out with the Program Office, I want you with someone who can show you the ropes from our perspective and introduce you to the players."

Jimmy was tempted to say that he knew the ropes and the players but didn't want to give the man who'd been his boss for less than two hours the wrong impression.

"Okay," he said. "Show me the ropes."

~

"You ready?"

Jimmy looked up at the woman standing next to his desk. "Ready for what?"

"Dick told me I'm taking you to a meeting on the water-front."

"He told me I'm going with a guy name Jack."

"Do I look like a guy?" she asked, sarcastically.

"I swear he said a…" Jimmy's voice tailed off. "He said Jack Ready." He scratched his head, then relented, "Maybe he didn't say a guy."

"I think he gets his rocks off calling me by my full name," she said, offering her hand. "My name's Jackie, as in Jaclyn, Reddi. That's R-E-D-D-I."

"I'm Jimmy McKee," Jimmy said sheepishly. When he stood to shake hands, her hazel eyes were nearly level with his own, her straight brown hair pulled back in a ponytail. "I guess I'm ready to go."

Jackie was a talker, which was good for Jimmy who felt awkward walking to the waterfront with a woman. Her pedigree put him at ease: working class, row house Philly neighborhood.

In the time it took to walk from the office to the trailer at the end of the pier between Dry Dock #4 and #5, he learned that her father was a union plasterer and her mother the first female captain on the Philadelphia police force. She had four brothers: two cops, an upcoming amateur boxer, and a cement mason, when he made it to work.

"Tells me he doesn't have a drinking problem," she said of her cement mason brother, "but has a wicked stopping problem."

She started working at the shipyard as a co-op engineering student at Drexel University when she was a sophomore and didn't hesitate to tell him she had to work twice as hard as the guys to advance. Judging by her tone, Jimmy didn't dare question her claim. He realized he didn't have much history of his own to share and wound up telling her about his father being killed when he was a kid and that his mother had passed away as well. She said she was sorry, and they walked the rest of the way in silence.

As they approached the trailer, Jimmy said, "I know all the guys that'll be at the meeting," hinting that he was an insider.

"Well, don't expect them to treat you like they did when you were on the iron."

"What do you mean?"

"You're on the other side now."

"What other side?"

She looked Jimmy in the eye. "As in, the Enemy."

"These guys are my brothers," he said, opening the door. Jackie lowered her head and shook it.

A handful of people looked up when they walked in, then went about their business. A couple of guys gave Jimmy an obligatory congratulations about his promotion, but that was it.

It reminded him of his own perception of white-collar workers when he was on the ships. Not good. When the meeting started, his *brothers* gave abbreviated answers to his questions and didn't elaborate unless he asked a follow-up question. They were uncharacteristically businesslike, even a little sarcastic, he thought. Last week seemed an eternity ago.

The only person who didn't change was Huey, who ran the meeting from the head of the table. When it was over and most of the attendees had left, he called Jimmy to the front of the trailer. He patted the seat next to him, and said, "You hear about Butch?"

"Only what you told me about his job being a little iffy."

"Yeah, well, he got shitcanned to a job in the back channel." Being sent to the back channel was the equivalent to being banished to the gulags of Siberia. "They gave him a bullshit job with no responsibility and buried him in some old building."

"Bastards!" blurted Jimmy. He sat steaming for a few seconds, then said, "Tell Mr. Homes I want to talk to him."

"Not now, Jimmy."

"Why not?"

"He's not doing well. He's…" he paused, shook his head. "It's like he crawled inside himself. Stays locked in his office all day. Doesn't make any decisions. I don't know what's going on with him."

It got quiet between them. Jimmy was thinking, *With Butch exiled and Mr. Homes incapacitated, Huey was the only civilian left in the shipyard with insider knowledge about Maestro Fusion and the tiger team.* "What about you?"

"They offered me a job at the Frankford Arsenal. Told me to either take it or put in my papers."

"What are you going to do?"

"I'm a grunt, Jimmy," said Huey, without hesitation. "It's the shipyard or nothing."

"Don't you think sticking around is risky?"

"Those assholes come after me, I'll be the last person they ever fuck with." Huey's words were full of bravado, but his body language signaled he was in a losing battle.

~

"What'd Huey want?" asked Jackie, on their way back to the office.

Jimmy was in a stupor thinking about the purge of managers, engineers, and boilermakers who'd been involved in the Mayport job. "Huh?"

"Huey," she said, pointedly. "What'd he want?"

Jimmy stopped and stared at her with a blank expression. "It's complicated," he said.

Jackie shot him a hard look. "Fuck you then," she said. "Just keep being the inside man with all of your friends who stonewalled you at the meeting." She walked away leaving Jimmy alone on the pier.

Jimmy was struck motionless by the attack. He hurried after her, and when he got close, he talked fast. "Me and Huey went through a lot of shit together in Mayport," he said. She turned and waited. "I lost four of my friends. Huey lost his godson. Everyone who knew what went on behind the job was either killed or fired or transferred, and Huey's probably next."

Jackie looked at him, seemingly unmoved by his explanation. "So here's the deal, McKee," she said. "You're in the program office now. The program office might be in the shipyard, but we don't answer to the shipyard commander. We answer to the PEO. You have access to Navy contracts, schedules, program managers, any information you need. Dick's taking you to Crystal City where all the wheeling and dealing goes on: the marketers, the schemers, backroom negotiations, stuff nobody on the outside ever sees. If anyone's in a position to find out what went down before, during, and after Mayport, it's you."

Jimmy was stunned by the lambast, and by the onslaught on intelligence. He'd never been chewed out by anyone the way Jackie chewed him out. He was defenseless. If Dick had been speaking an unspoken language during his orientation, Jackie just deciphered it. *Maybe Butch knew exactly what he was doing when he persuaded me to take the Program Management job.*

"Did you know George Sputz?" Jimmy asked.

"Jesus Christ, Jimmy," she said, sounding annoyed. "You know boilermakers and pipefitters, right?"

"Yeah, of course," said Jimmy.

"Engineers stick together just like production guys. So yes, I knew George. Actually, I knew him well. We used to eat lunch together sometimes." She paused, took some of the edge off of her words, and added, "He was a nice guy."

Jimmy stared at her, as if noticing the change of tone when she added the "nice guy" remark. "Have you heard from him since he got transferred?"

A few seconds passed. "Not a thing," she finally said.

Jimmy couldn't get himself to ask her any more questions about George.

Chapter XXXVII

BEEF & BEER

Jimmy waited for the last student to leave class on the final night of the spring semester before he got up and walked to the front of the room. Mr. Kelly was packing his briefcase, and without looking up, he said, "We need to talk."

"We do," said Jimmy. "Rocky's?"

"Rocky's."

Their visits had become routine: roast beef sandwiches, lots of horseradish, Schmidt's, usually on stools at the bar. But when they walked in the front door, Kelly pointed to a small, unoccupied table against the back wall. Conversation buzzed from every corner of the room as they wound their way through the crowd. Sixties jazz piped through ceiling speakers, Sinatra and Sammy Davis, Jr.

Kelly pulled papers from his briefcase as he sat. "Maestro Fusion Corporation is a privately held company," he said, placing them on the table.

"Okay," said Jimmy, in a way that begged for further explanation.

"That's why you didn't find them listed on the New York

Stock Exchange. They don't have the same reporting require-
ments as a publicly traded company."

Jimmy fingered the papers. "So where'd you get these?"

Kelly raised two fingers to a waitress who appeared at their
table, and said, "Just bring us a couple beers for now." Never breaking his concentration with Jimmy, he told him about a friend who
worked for the SEC, the Security and Exchange Commission, and
slid a spreadsheet on top of the papers. "Your company's not doing
bad for a relatively new company, they're in the tens of millions."

Jimmy leaned in. "Let me see."

The waitress returned with the beers and placed them on
the table. Mick waved her away. He pulled out another paper,
put it on top and pointed to a list of names. "It's not too hard to
figure out, considering this."

Jimmy looked at the paper for a few seconds, then asked,
"Considering what?"

"You see these," he said pointing to "Ret." printed after the
names of nearly every corporate board officer.

Jimmy nodded indicating that he did.

"That's what they call 'The Good Old Boy Network.'
'Ret.' means Retired Military. My guess is that these guys had
contracts lined up before they started the company."

"Good Old Boys, huh?"

"You want to know their sales pitch?" asked Mick, rhetor-
ically. "It's good for the taxpayer. Nobody knows the military
better than the military." Mick threw Jimmy a nod of assurance.
"All true, except in some cases the companies aren't qualified
to run a lemonade stand let alone a multi-million-dollar corporation."

Jimmy slid the paper closer and scanned the corporate board members. Suddenly, he smacked the table with his open hand. "Son of a bitch."

Beer shot out the top of their glasses, people around them looked. Mick calmly picked up his beer, licked the rim, and took a sip. "See something?"

Jimmy turned the paper toward Mick and pointed to a name. "See this guy here?"

Mick raised his head and looked down like he was wearing bifocals. "Lawrence Foley, USN, Ret.? What about him?"

"I know him." He hesitated a second. "Well, I know who he is. He's behind the contract I told you about, the one we were working on when my friends were killed."

Mick put a hand above his eyes and massaged his forehead. "Hmm."

Jimmy looked at Mick like he could smell the gears grinding inside his head. "What are you thinking, Mick?"

"These guys paid contractors and consultants in equity, meaning shares of the company's stock." He scrubbed the silver bristles of his beard like it helped him think. "That's not unusual for a young company, especially a private startup like Maestro Fusion. But one consultant jumped out at me." Mick caught himself. "I mean, one of them jumped out at my SEC buddy," he corrected. "He's a corporate forensic guy who investigates white-collar crime."

Jimmy eyed Mick closely, picturing him in his past life as a narcotics cop, working undercover and playing head games with suspects. "Did he say who the consultant was?"

"He did, but I don't remember," said Mick. "What I do remember is that it was a ten-thousand-dollar stock certificate for services rendered made out to an individual, no company name or firm. And it was issued in October of last year, around the time you told me your friends were killed."

"Ten thousand dollars." Jimmy rubbed his face with both hands, opened them, and said, "Jesus Christ!"

"What?"

"My buddy Tommy who was driving the car when those guys were killed, his wife asked me to meet her the other day. She told me she got an envelope in the mail with ten grand in it. Cash."

"Follow the money," said Mick.

"What?"

"The golden rule for investigating white-color crime. If you want to find out who's responsible for killing your friends, follow the money."

Jimmy looked from Mick to his beer, picked it up and took a long gulp. "Think you can get me a copy of the stock certificate?"

Mick locked eyes with Jimmy. "You said your buddies were killed working a contract that never should have been awarded, right?"

"Yeah."

"And the company paid some guy ten grand for services rendered right before they were killed, right?"

"Yeah."

"That's murder and conspiracy to commit murder," said Mick. He picked up his pint and drained it, placed the empty glass back to the table. "You're goddamn right I can get a copy of the stock certificate. I'll get you whatever the hell you need."

Chapter XXXVIII

COURT MARTIAL

On Monday, June 25, 1984, a large, testy-looking nurse pushed Louis Robert Smitt into the courtroom in a wheelchair, legless without his prosthetics. Stitch marks tracked his face like a map of the Philadelphia subway system, and his dead eye was noticeable from the bench thirty feet away. No family members were in attendance. No friends, and no shipmates. There were two spectators: a Naval officer in dress whites seated in the last row, and in the front row, a large, bearded man wearing jeans and an open-collar white dress shirt that exposed a gold chain and crucifix resting on a graying nest of hair.

"All rise," bellowed the bailiff, as the judge entered the courtroom. The gavel clapped and the trial began. Smitt's attorney pushed himself out of his chair, grabbed a cane he'd hung on the end of the defense table, and took a position in front of the five officers of the court. They listened stoically to a story about an abused eighteen-year-old foster child who joined the Navy looking for purpose in life. He jammed the end of the cane into the wooden floorboards making the point that Smitt was a young man with a dream to augment the mechanical skills he'd learned in a small-town auto shop with the competencies required as a boiler technician. That dream was snuffed out by a superior officer who recruited him for a covert mission to eliminate a saboteur to prove himself a patriot. Without presenting any witnesses to corroborate his story, nor a single piece of exonerating evidence, Smitt's attorney petitioned the officers of the court to find his client not guilty.

The prosecution dismissed the defense's case as outlandish fiction: smear campaign of a stellar Naval officer, academy graduate, captain of the USS Saratoga, a leader of men. Hidden behind smoke and mirrors was the fact that the captain was the stepson of an admiral, the man who set up the tribunal, established the charges, and selected the officers of the jury. A sham.

The jury took less than an hour to deliver a verdict: Guilty! Slam-dunk! Four counts of vehicular homicide. Life behind bars.

It would have been the end of the road for Smitt had it not been for H. W. Brockton, Attorney at Law. When Henry Wellington Brockton got a call from an old friend he hung out with on the street corners of South Philly, notifying him that someone as close as family was being railroaded by the Navy, he had an immediate connection. Brockton lost his legs to a land mine in Da Nang Province in 1969 during an ill-conceived forward assault ordered from the back lines by his commander without proper intelligence or planning. The commander was never questioned about the mission that claimed the lives of seventeen soldiers. When Henry got out of the service and recovered from his wounds, he went back to school, got a law degree, and dedicated his life to defending servicemen and women who'd been shafted by their military.

Brockton reveled in the trenches of investigation. Pick-and-shovel work he called it. He unearthed that the judge was born in Brooklyn, raised by foster parents, and served in the Army as an infantryman, and when he sensed the judge's discomfort with the verdict, he jumped in. "Your Honor, my client spent six weeks on life support and suffered permanent physical and psychological damage. Now he's about to spend the rest of his life incarcerated. Considering the incomprehensible pain he's already endured, he respectfully requests to return home to Forksville, Pennsylvania to visit his family before he reports to prison next week."

The Judge wasted no time making his decision, and when he said "Motion granted," the prosecutor jumped out of his seat. "Objection, Your Honor! You can't…"

"Sit down!" snapped the Judge. "Don't tell me what I can and cannot do!" He looked down at Smitt in the wheelchair. "This man lost his limbs while serving his country. He'll spend the rest of his life in prison." He glared at everyone sitting at the prosecution table, pointed at Smitt, and said, "Look at him. All of you, look at him! Are you going to tell me he's a flight risk? Where's a man with no legs, no money, and no future going to go?"

Had the prosecutor not relied solely on the word of Lawrence Foley that this would be an open and shut case, he would have known that Robert Louis Smitt *was*, in fact, a flight risk. Had the prosecutor taken the time to read the physical therapy records from Walter Reed Hospital about the patient's extraordinary strength on the bench press, or the one that described Smitt as "a ballerina on prosthesis," he would have been equipped to challenge the motion. And had he taken the initiative to speak with the physical therapists as Brockton had, he would have known that Smitt got around as well as most people with two legs. Instead, the prosecution remained mute.

The judge sneered at the prosecutor and slammed the gavel, then stood and left for his chamber. The officers of the court filed out after him. Brockton sat at the defense table for several minutes conferring with Smitt, and when he was done, he placed his hand around the side of Louis's head in a sign of affection. He took his cane and stood, turned to the bearded man in the front row and gave him the slightest wink before starting up the aisle focused on the Naval officer in the last row. The closer he got to the back of the courtroom, the farther the officer edged away from the center aisle. Brockton stopped at the last row, wound up his cane, and slammed it into the wooden bench before leaving.

The nurse stood from her seat, turned the wheelchair around and pushed Smitt down the aisle. A distant expression came over him when he saw the officer in the back of the courtroom. A faraway look, as if envisioning the corner booth in Skeet's Café where his commanding officer convinced him that Tommy Homes was planning to sabotage the Maestro Fusion process and only a patriot could stop him. Now, eight months later, he'd been convicted of vehicular homicide and sentenced to life and his commanding officer walked away unscathed. Smitt now knew he wasn't a patriot at all, but a naïve kid who'd been conned. A scapegoat. He jammed his hands against the hard rubber wheels, and the wheelchair jerked to a halt. He straightened his arms lifting himself out of the seat. "You'll pay for this, Stevens!" echoed from the rafters of the empty courtroom.

Stevens was terror-stricken. Transfixed by Smitt's dead eye, he couldn't look away. In the front row, a smile formed beneath the thick beard of the large man who seemed amused by the officer's fear of a man who had no chance of getting to him without his prosthesis.

"The truth will come out, Stevens!" shouted Smitt. The nurse put her hands on Louis's shoulders to keep him from falling out of the chair, then continued wheeling him toward the double doors in the back. The captain plopped into the pew, never looking up to see bearded man's scowl as he walked by.

Louis Smitt had more reason to abuse drugs and alcohol then any sailor on the Saratoga, but he didn't want to deaden the phantom pain in his amputated legs or the left eye that got knocked out of his head or the hunk of skull replaced with a stainless-steel plate. He embraced the pain, used it to strengthen his resolve to right his wrong, expose truth and bring justice to the unjust.

~

Stevens sat alone in the courtroom thinking back to the original plan. Had Smitt done his job properly, none of this would ever have happened. His life would have been easy, the way it had always been. An unnatural feeling came over him, one of empowerment, like he was a captain in the United States Navy, and for the first time he internalized what it felt like to actually be a captain in the United States Navy. The captain of an aircraft carrier! He didn't need to ask permission from anybody about anything.

Suddenly, an even more alien feeling took hold, a feeling of control. He decided he'd finally show the old man what he was made of. This time there'd be no buffer, no separation between him and the physical act. He was cutting the umbilical cord. He would be the special operator, the hit man.

"Fuck the admiral," said Stevens, to an empty courtroom.

~

Huey was waiting outside Jimmy's office when he was done work that Friday. "Come with me," he said, and started walking. They crossed the caisson in the direction of the parking lot, then turned toward the shipways and walked deep into the rising concrete structures until they were out of sight.

"What's up, Huey?"

"Did you ever visit that sailor at Walter Reed?"

"I was planning to go this weekend. Why?"

"Captain Flask called this morning. His trial was Monday. He got life like everyone expected, but the judge let him go home to visit his family before he reported to prison next week."

"Jesus Christ," blasted Jimmy. "The guy kills four people, and the judge lets him go home?"

"Yeah," said Huey. "Bleeding heart, I guess."

Jimmy stared out of the shipways at a cargo ship steaming up the Delaware. "You get the guy's name?"

"Louis Smitt. He lives in a small town called Forksville, Pennsylvania."

"Where the hell's Forksville?"

"In the middle of nowhere."

244

~

A question bounced around inside Jimmy's head all the way home, and as soon as he got in the door, he dialed Peggy Homes.

"Hello?"

"Peggy, it's Jimmy McKee."

"Jimmy," she said, sounding surprised. "It's good to hear from you?"

"Listen, Peggy, do you still have the envelope that the money came in?"

"Yes, it's upstairs in a drawer."

"Could you get it?"

"Sure. Is everything all right?"

"Yeah. I just need to find out something."

There was a tap from the receiver being placed on a table or countertop. Jimmy could hear the television in the background. It sounded like cartoons. He thought about little Danielle.

"I'm back, Jimmy."

"What's the postmark?"

"It looks like Forksville, Pennsylvania. I never heard of it, have you?"

"Not until about an hour ago."

Chapter XXXIX

FORKSVILLE

Captain Stevens had hedged that the kamikaze pilot would die from his injuries, or at least remain comatose until his vital organs shut down, but almost a year later, while Maestro Fusion ramped up for the sixty-million-dollar contract on the Forrestal, Louis Robert Smitt was spending his final days as a free man before being sent to jail for the rest of his life.

It was still dark on Saturday morning when Captain Stevens hopped in his black BMW 750i parked in the garage of his Old Town Alexandria townhouse. Before turning the ignition, he opened the console to check one last time that the magazine was loaded inside the pistol he'd bought the day of Smitt's court martial. It was the first firearm he'd ever owned. He let the weapon rest in his palm, and admired power he'd never experienced, authority that belonged solely to him. Dominance, not inherited, but rightfully his own. By the end of the day, his life would be different, better. Nothing would be in his way.

He was taking control.

He turned the ignition and revved the engine. Tires screeched when he shot out onto the street and headed north on the George Washington Memorial Parkway.

~

Four hours later Stevens found himself surrounded by mountains full of laurel and oak, though he saw only trees. Water gushed over rocks in a stream forty feet down an embankment to his left as he cruised Route 154 through Worlds End State Park. A red covered bridge came into view, and when he reached it, he made a left and drove over the Loyalsock Creek. He emerged from the other side and looked out over the small town.

"Finding someone in this town ought to be easy," he smirked. "Especially a paraplegic."

He coasted the main street and pulled into the parking lot of the Pitchfork Country Store. The clock on his dash read 0945, Navy time. There was no such thing as a.m. and p.m. growing up in the admiral's household. He opened the console and took out the pistol. The authority he'd experienced before he left Alexandria returned. He shoved the weapon under the back of his belted waist, got out, stretched his legs and walked inside.

The power Stevens had felt sitting in his BMW drained at the sight of the burley, bearded man wearing dark sunglasses and an Eagles football jersey sitting behind the counter reading a newspaper. He couldn't be sure if it was the guy from the courtroom, but if it was, he hoped the guy wouldn't recognize him out of uniform. The store was morgue-still except for the vibration of a deli case full of meats and homemade salads in the back. The guy glanced out of the corner of his eye, turned the page and went back to his *Philadelphia Daily News*. The captain figured he was in the clear.

Bearded man leaned over the counter, looked down at the Stevens's penny loafers, and said, "We don't sell fish bait."

The captain wasn't used to being disrespected by anyone other than his father, but he was in the mountains of central Pennsylvania: deer-hunting country, Red Man chewing tobacco, shot and a beer. He touched the small of his back for reassurance, and to keep from deflating into a nonentity, a nobody without a rank and title to hide behind.

"You know a guy named Louis Smitt?"

No answer, just the hum. Stevens grew impatient waiting for the guy to say something. "I said, 'Do you know Louis Smitt?'"

"The kid who lost his legs in an accident?"

"Yes," said Stevens, sounding optimistic.

The guy leaned to his right and farted. "Never heard of him."

Stevens fought to maintain a semblance of authority, fooling only himself. "I'm Captain Stevens, United States Navy," he said, thinking that pulling rank on mountain man was a power move. He fidgeted when he didn't get a reaction. "I have papers for him for his VA benefits."

Bearded man yawned and extended his hand.

"What?"

"The papers," he said, looking up at him for the first time. "Let me see 'em."

The captain fumbled for an answer, the concealed weapon unable to provide the confidence he'd hoped for. "They're in the car."

The guy tilted his head toward the door like a retriever

who heard rustling in the brush. "I'm not going anywhere." He watched amusedly as the captain rummaged behind his back.

Stevens pulled out the pistol. "Tell me where Louis Smitt is," he demanded.

"Put that fucking thing away before you hurt yourself," said bearded man.

"I'm not screwing around," said Stevens, raising his voice. "Where is he?"

"Screwing around?" said bearded man, mockingly. "What are you in third grade?" Stevens's hand started shaking. "That fucking thing goes off, I'll kill you, motherfucker!" He catapulted off the stool and darted around the counter. He reached out and grabbed Stevens's arm before he got to the door, but he broke away.

Bearded man chased after him until he got to the front porch, then stood watching Stevens fumble with his keys trying to start the Beamer. He formed a handgun with the fingers of his right hand and pointed it at the car. His scowl pushed together bushy black eyebrows that looked like caterpillars mating. A smile emerged exposing a full set of vicious teeth. The 750i burned rubber in reverse and fishtailed, just missing an army green pickup truck pulling in off the street. It was 0954.

Chapter XL

GRIZ

L evel roads outside of Philadelphia turned to rolling green hills around Quakertown which became mountains on the north side of the Lehigh Tunnel. Jimmy had the steering wheel in a strangle hold when he pulled into the tollbooth at the Wilkes-Barre exit on the Northeast Extension of the Pennsylvania Turnpike. By the time he reached the Endless Mountains in north-central Pennsylvania, he'd spent one hundred ninety-three minutes alone, thinking: first about his four dead friends, and as time drug on, about being robbed of his dad by men who drove black limousines, ate at exclusive restaurants, and smoked expensive cigars. He hadn't thought of killing another human being since the day he watched his father's casket lowered into the earth at Calvary Cemetery, until he passed a gun shop on Route 42 in Muncy Valley. But Jimmy had never even held a gun, didn't know how to load one, and didn't want to know.

If I do ever kill someone, he decided, *it will be with my bare hands.*

Twenty-six years eating, drinking, breathing, sleeping, and working in a city with a population of more than one million people of every race, ethnicity, creed, and sexual orientation didn't prepare him for the moment he emerged from the covered bridge into Forksville and saw a lone mangy black German Shepard limping down the middle of the deserted street. He crawled along at five miles per hour for half of a block before making a right into the parking lot of a country store. He cut the engine and sat staring at the three-story A-frame building constructed from what looked like wooden planks removed from a demoed barn. Except for baseball caps and denim overalls, the two old men sitting on a bench outside drinking coffee could have been casted for an old Gene Autry western.

It was half-past noon when he got out of the Jeep and stepped up onto the porch. "Excuse me, gentlemen."

"What can we do for you, young man?" said the one in overalls.

"I'm looking for Louis Smitt."

They looked at one another, shrugged, and went back to sipping coffee. In a town with a population of one hundred and forty, Jimmy suspected everyone knew everyone else, that they knew each other's business, many of whom were likely related. He thought he'd wait the men out until one of them answered. He lost. "How about you just point in the direction of where he lives?"

The other guy lifted a Styrofoam cup off the bench and shot a stream of brown tobacco juice into it. He raised an eyebrow and tilted his head toward the door. "Gonna have to talk to the mayor."

Jimmy crossed the boardwalk porch, opened to the door and went inside. The bearded guy watched him without lifting his head. "Help you?" he asked, as he turned the page of his *Daily News*.

Jimmy eyed his Eagles jersey, the team schedule pinned to the wall behind him. "You know you got a Giant's fan across the river," he said.

"Creek."

"What?"

"It's a creek. A river's big, with ships and barges and shit." He pointed out the window behind him. "That bridge out there. It goes over the Loyalsock Creek."

"Okay," Jimmy corrected himself, "across the creek."

"You stopped for gas, huh?"

"Yeah."

"Fucking Scoogie," he said, referring to the convenience store owner with gas pumps on the other side of the Loyalsock. "Should be a law against Giant's fan living in Pennsylvania."

"That's what I'm talking about," said Jimmy. "You the mayor?"

"That's what they say." He belched. "But I go by Griz."

By the look of the ferocious beast there was no reason to ask why. "I'm looking for Louis Smitt."

"Jesus Christ," he blurted. "You got papers for him too?"

Jimmy looked confused. "What are you talking about?"

"Some guy was in here earlier asking for him."

"Someone looking for Smitt?" Jimmy asked, somewhat alarmed. "What'd you tell him?"

"Told him to go fuck himself."

Jimmy swore that bearded man sounded like he'd been kidnapped from a South Philly street corner, plopped on a stool behind the counter of a country store in the middle of nowhere, and crowned mayor. "What'd he want?" he asked, to keep him talking.

"Some bullshit about the VA, had important papers for the kid." The side of the mayor's mouth rose in absurdity. "Must a thought I was stupid or something."

Jimmy sensed a sudden movement in the back of the store and when he looked, he thought someone disappeared behind the kitchen doorway. By the time he turned back, the mayor had gotten off the stool and walked around the counter. He stopped and eyed him for a second or two, then gestured for Jimmy to follow him. He opened an icebox and palmed two beers in each hand before continuing to a dining area hidden behind a long row of shelves packed with potato chips, pretzels, and pork rinds. He sat, put two beers in front of him and two on the other side of the table. Jimmy sat across from him.

"So what's the interest in the kid all of the sudden?"

"Just need to talk to him," said Jimmy, figuring by "kid" he was referring to Smitt.

The mayor rolled a toothpick from one side of his mouth to the other. "Don't bullshit me like the last guy," he said. "Nobody drives a hundred-fifty miles to talk to a kid from a town with less people than grew up on my block."

"How do you know how far I drove?" asked Jimmy.

The mayor shook his head looking disappointed. "That last asshole pulls up in a BMW 750i, walks in wearing penny loafers, calling me 'sir.' Had military written all over him. Captain Kangaroo or some shit." He popped open a beer, lifted the can, and vacuumed a sip like the opening wasn't big enough. He put the can down and ran his bottom lip back and forth against the edge of his mustache. "Nobody comes to Forksville wearing penny loafers," he said, took another short sip, and reiterated, "Nobody." He polished off the beer he held in his right hand, popped the zip top on the other with his left. "You," he said, head-pointing at Jimmy, "you pull up in a Jeep, got that Philly slang going, talk about my Eagles, I know you got something up your sleeve, but not like penny-loafer guy."

"So you think I'm from Philly?"

"Come on, man," he said, like he couldn't believe what he was hearing. "I'm from Nineteenth and Tasker." He took a brief break to reminisce. "Started coming up here hunting with my buddies after high school. They'd drink all week while I trekked through the woods, up and down mountains, cross streams. Took up bow hunting, then fly fishing, next thing I know I'm in love with the outdoors, the peace and quiet." He paused, smiled as if savoring a thought. "Me? Right?" He laughed. "Moved up here nineteen years ago and opened this joint."

Jimmy thought he had an opening to ask about Smitt, but Griz's mood shifted in a split-second. "Tell me why you're interested in the kid," he growled.

Jimmy popped open his first beer and took a healthy sip thinking of a way to settle him back down. He started talking about the shipyard and lucked out because Griz's grandfather was a rigger back in the day, which led to an exchange of waterfront stories, shipping terminals, longshoremen, and dive bars. Jimmy took a calculated risk and came clean, told him about the Mayport tiger team, the accident, and that he knew Smitt was the driver. Griz listened stoically with an unreadable expression.

"I have to tell him about my buddies who died in the accident," said Jimmy, pausing to keep his emotions in check. He took a sip of beer in an attempt to calm his voice, and added, "The pain he caused people, all of the lives he ruined."

Griz's jaw tightened. He rolled the bottom of the can around on the table before picking it up and taking another long slug, and when he put it down, he peered into Jimmy's eyes.

"Bobby's a good kid," he said.

"Bobby?"

The question seemed to mix-up the big guy. "Robert," he corrected. "The kid's middle name's Robert. I call him Bobby." It wasn't the way Griz said "Bobby" that grabbed Jimmy's attention as much as the emotion that escaped from a man who looked like he'd rip your face off if you crossed him. "He was a foster kid, moved from home to home. I adopted him after he was acquitted of killing his foster father, and he lived with me until he went in the Navy."

"He killed his father?"

"Foster father," Griz corrected him. "Fuckin' pervert molested him for years. So one night Bobby took a hunting knife to bed with him. The perv came in to rape him for the umpteenth time and Bobby gutted him like a fuckin' deer."

Jimmy shuddered.

Griz lowered his head. "When I went to see him at Walter Reed, laying there with no legs, I cried." He looked up, eyes moist. "I can tell you this, that accident killed Bobby, too."

Jimmy was conflicted by the emotion spilling from this burley guy from South Philly for the driver of the black Dodge Charger that snuffed out the lives of his friends. Something powerful and unidentifiable pulled deep inside of him—torment, anxiety… But not compassion. Never compassion. Never!

"He killed my friends, Griz," said Jimmy.

Griz glared at him. "He was just an innocent kid trying to find his way," he said. "He was gullible. He got conned."

Jimmy squinted at him. "What do you mean 'conned?'"

Slowly, almost too slow to detect, Griz's demeanor turned perilous. "We're done here," he said abruptly.

"What?" said Jimmy. "No we're not."

"If I say we're done," he said, slamming his fist into the table, "we're done!"

"What the fuck, Griz! I leveled with you."

"I've said all I'm going to say," he said. "He got conned, that's all there is to it. If you're so interested, you figure it out."

"Listen to me," said Jimmy, leaning closer. "My buddy who got killed in the accident, his wife got an envelope in the mail with ten thousand dollars in it."

"So what?"

"So what? The envelope was postmarked Forksville, Pennsylvania."

Griz pointed to the front door. "Get out of my fucking store!"

"Come on, Griz. We're both from Philly, remember?"

"I'm from South Philly," he said, like South Philly was a different country. Griz drained his beer, put the empty can on the table and crushed it with his fist. "In South Philly, talking will get you killed."

"Just tell me where I can find him," Jimmy pleaded.

Griz got up and started around the partition.

Jimmy followed him to the front counter. "I'm not leaving town until I talk to him," he said.

"He's gone. Vanished. He no longer exists."

"What are you talking about?" said Jimmy. He thought for half a second. "That's bullshit!"

Griz walked back behind the counter and slapped his palm against the *Daily News*. "Get the fuck out of my store before I do something I haven't done in twenty years," he said, then picked up the phone.

Jimmy looked between Griz and the front window where the two men on the porch stood watching. When he heard Griz telling someone on the other end of the phone about trouble in the store, he walked out, climbed into his Jeep and sat behind the wheel staring at the storefront. Something moved in the second-floor window. Jimmy looked up just as Irish lace curtains came to rest on either side of a single electric candle. It looked too nice for a storage room, or even an office. It looked more like an apartment, even a home, maybe Griz's, maybe not. An Army-green pickup pulled into the parking space next to him. A man with a beard down to his chest sat in the driver's seat with the engine idling. A minute later, a rusty orange pickup, jacked high on shocks, pulled in and parked close on the other side. The driver, easily a three hundred pounder, wore a plaid shirt with cut-off sleeves exposing Neanderthal arms. The two drivers stared at Jimmy until he backed out of the space. They both got out of their trucks and watched the Jeep pull into the street and drove toward the covered bridge.

~

Headlights flooded Jimmy's rearview mirror a few miles outside Forksville on Route 154. Bearing down on him and growing in size, the grill of an industrial dump truck looked like it was in the backseat. He veered onto the shoulder and plunged down an embankment. Tree branches whipped through the window blinding him before the Jeep came to a stop within feet of the creek. Heart pounding, he jumped out, wiped his face, and looked up at the road. The only sounds were running water and rustling leaves. He waited a few minutes for his heartbeat to slow, then got back in, engaged the four-wheel drive, shifted into reverse, and traced his tire tracks back up to the shoulder. A cinder trail disappeared into the forest on the other side of the road. Curious, he drove across to a trailhead that had once been an old mining road.

The trail gained altitude quickly, the Jeep climbing switch-back after switchback until he came to an overlook at the top of the mountain. He parked and got out, walked to the edge of a cliff, and looked across the mountains. Patches of mist were tucked into thick, endless pockets of spruce, maple and ash. The Loyalsock Creek snaked in and out of view in the valley a thousand feet below. This wasn't Wissahickon Park in Phila-delphia where he grew up. This was survivalist terrain.

Jimmy inhaled a mass of crisp, sanitary air. Awed by the vastness, he imagined an abused teenager from a small town, trekking across the valley, through dense forest in fear for his life, alone against rain, snow, cold, rattlers, black bear, physical abuse, rape. The teenager endures, persists, outlasts them all. He survives! Jimmy experienced a moment of reckoning. *Would I have survived?* He felt a sudden and odd connection with the foster child, unearthed by a bearded brute from Nineteenth and Tasker: a rough, but good and decent man with a big heart who adopted an abused kid.

What if he was right? What if Bobby was an innocent kid trying to find his way? What if he was conned?

Jimmy knew Griz was holding something back. Mick Kelly's words came back to him. *Follow the money.* A stock option for ten thousand dollars. Peggy Homes received ten grand cash in the mail. Postmarked Forksville, Pennsylvania. Smitt was the only one who would have answers. Jimmy jogged back to the Jeep, drove down the mountain, made a right onto Route 154, and floored it back to town.

Three o'clock on Saturday afternoons, the Pitchfork Country Store parking lot was nearly full. The bell above the door jingled when Jimmy walked in. He could hear customers dining on the other side of the shelving. A sturdy woman with frizzy red hair wearing a Flyer's jersey sat behind the counter with a cigarette dangling from the side of her mouth. She squinted through the smoke. "Help you, young fella?"

"I'm looking for Griz," said Jimmy.

She blew a cloud in Jimmy's direction. "Never heard of him."

The being watched feeling returned. This time, when he looked toward the kitchen, he saw a head duck behind the doorway. "Who's in the back room?"

"The cook."

He leaned across the counter. "Who lives in the room upstairs?"

She took a long drag of her cigarette, picked up the phone and dialed. A few seconds passed before she said, "Your order's ready." She hung up, looked at Jimmy, and said, "You should be getting along, fella."

"Who'd you just call?" Jimmy demanded.

She took another drag on the cigarette. "Doesn't matter," she said. "All I know is you should leave while you still got a chance."

"I'm not going anywhere until..." Jimmy saw the jacked-up rusty pickup pull into the handicap space out front. He hadn't noticed the gun rack behind the seat earlier, and when the driver reached over his shoulder for the rifle, Jimmy took off out the door. He stopped at the truck, stuck his head in the window, and said, "Your order's ready, asshole," then sprinted to his Jeep and jumped in. The Army-green pickup passed going in the opposite direction just before he got to the covered bridge on his way out of town.

Part IV

South of Mason-Dixon

Chapter XLI

CRYSTAL CITY

It was times like this, sitting on a packed Amtrak car watching passengers in business suits and dresses tap laptops with pampered fingers and manicured nails or page the *Wall Street Journal*, that Jimmy appreciated cutting his teeth climbing through bilges and welding inside preheated cast metal drums. It made him proud.

He noticed people around him watching a tall, distinguished-looking gentleman who boarded at the Wilmington stop. "Morning Joe," a ticket agent said to the man, who returned the greeting with a killer smile, rested his hand on the agent's shoulder, and gave it a squeeze as he passed on his way down the aisle to the last row. He sat with his back against the car panel and opened a *New York Times*.

"The senator from Delaware," whispered Dick, sitting to Jimmy's left and jotting notes in the margins of a report.

In a few hours he'd meet the principals in the NAVSEA office who would attend the Quarterly Production Review at the end of July. The QPR was the highest profile production meeting for Navy shipbuilding construction and overhaul programs where the status of billion-dollar contracts was presented to Navy brass, corporate executives, and a spattering of underlings and aides jockeying for visibility. The shipyard awarded the contract hosted the meeting in their executive conference room. Attendees received fancy glossed books containing charts and graphs printed on fine premium paper of Harvard Graphics presentations that were also projected on a screen. The objective of the QPR was to impress the person holding the purse strings, the one with contract authority. For aircraft carriers, that was the PEO. There was a tradition that subordinates told him only what he wanted to hear, that everything was going great, within cost and schedule estimates. Heads would bob up and down, choruses of "Yes, sir" this and "Yes, sir" that chanted like a Buddhist mantra, even as everyone knew the information presented was complete bullshit, or at least shamefully skewed.

The QPR was the dog and pony show of dog and pony shows.

Nearly two hours after leaving Thirtieth Street Station, the train made a swooping turn into a massive structure framed in stainless steel with a glass roof that covered the train platforms at Union Station.

"Welcome to fantasy land," said Dick. Curiosity wrinkled Jimmy's forehead. "The people down here don't live on the same planet we live on. They have their own lingo. They talk in acronyms. And they all tow the party line."

"You telling me to keep my mouth shut?" asked Jimmy.

"Not at all," said Dick. "Just preparing you for all the bullshit you're going to hear. There's a lot of pretenders down here, but there are just as many good people. It takes time to sort them out. Take it all in, and don't get ahead of yourself."

Jimmy nodded. "Got it."

The air breaks hissed, the train eased to a stop, and the doors opened. Jimmy followed Dick off the train, down the platform and into the terminal where they transferred to the Metro. "You're going to meet consultants and PhDs who'll try to buffalo you," said Dick, continuing the indoctrination. "Some like to hear themselves talk. A few actually know what they're talking about. You'll meet a rare one or two who worked the iron in their past lives, got their hands dirty. Not many, but there are some. Study people and listen, eventually you'll be able to read through the bullshit."

Dick's waterfront sensibilities softened Jimmy's perception that engineers and program managers were elitists. It helped him focus.

"Another thing," said Dick.

"What's that?"

"Money's the golden goose. It drives everything."

Dick's translation of "follow the money." Money meant contracts, contracts awarded to companies, companies run by people. An entire new world was unfolding before him, a world where decision makers awarded contracts for overhaul and maintenance of ships, more specifically boilers and replacing superheater tubes. He wondered how one welding process was selected over another, especially an unproven automated process that disregarded engineering and metallurgy analysis, and ignored preheat conditions that increased the risk of failure. *Who decided to use the robotic process in an icebox over an oven, Philly in January over San Diego or Hawaii?*

~

Jimmy stepped off the Metro behind Dick onto the Crystal City platform. He gawked at large rectangles countersunk into white stucco walls feeling like he was inside a giant caterpillar. The red terra cotta floor was free of trash. There was no graffiti like in the Philadelphia subway, no scent of urine. Tucked behind the turnstiles exiting the platform, a ragged soul sat against the wall cloaked in a faded brown trench coat over a gray hooded sweat-shirt. He raised his head toward Jimmy, who could barely make out the disfigured face obscured by a straggly beard. Jimmy knew the cubbyhole was his home, his turf. From the outcasts in Philly, he could count on him being in the same spot day after day. He stumbled trying to keep up with Dick while he looked back at him.

The walls brightened, and murmurs of conversation echoed down the labyrinth of tentacles that was the underground mall. He panned storefronts left to right: a tailor shop, electronic store, an Asian deli, a barbershop, restaurants, bars, a movie theater. He was dumbfounded by the bustling crowd at nine o'clock in the morning, and the diversity: mothers pushing strollers, businesspeople, military officers in uniform, stragglers. An elderly woman sat in the corner of the food court in scruffy clothes jabbering while three seats away a businessman sipped coffee reading a Wall Street Journal.

A shoulder knocked Jimmy sideways, spinning him around in the throng of people. Something deep in a bearded man's face spooked him, something familiar in a disheveled wolfman dressed in rags. Jimmy felt detached, lightheaded, as wolfman faded into the crowded underground.

A tap on the shoulder. He jumped.

"Are you okay?" asked Dick.

Jimmy worked to pull himself out of a void he'd been sucked into, perhaps by the grim homeless man in the corner, or an image buried deep inside the wolfman.

Huh?"

"Let's go," said Dick. "Captain McNally's expecting us."

~

Jimmy followed Dick into a vestibule lined with elevators. After an ascent, the elevator doors opened on the twelfth floor, and they stepped into a lobby. A young Lieutenant with brown hair pulled back in a bun walked out of an office. "Mr. Wells," she said. "Commander McNally is expecting you."

"Thanks, Blair," said Dick. He gestured toward Jimmy. "I want you to meet Jimmy McKee. He'll be representing our office at the QPR."

The lieutenant offered her hand. "Nice to meet you, Mr. McKee."

"Likewise," said Jimmy.

"We'll make our way back," said Dick. They didn't get far down the hallway before Dick stopped and nodded to a suite behind a glass wall. A sturdy looking woman with short curly red hair sat behind a desk looking like a nightclub bouncer. The door behind her opened to an office with a desk flanked by the American and Navy flags. The far wall was a floor-to-ceiling window with a view of the National Airport runways. "That's the PEO Aircraft Carriers office," said Dick. "His other one's in the Pentagon."

"Who's the woman?" asked Jimmy.

"She's the PEO's secretary, more like his master-at-arms. Her name's Rita." He turned and continued to the commander's office, adding, "Don't fuck with her."

A second didn't pass between Dick's knock on the door and McNally's booming voice. "Dick Wells, come on in!"

Dick entered, hand extended. "Commander, how are you?"

"Great, great." He looked at Jimmy up and down. "Who's this fucking guy?"

"Jimmy McKee. He's taking over the carrier program."

"McKee, huh?" said the commander, seeming to canvass his memory for dirt he might have picked up about him. He stuck out his hand, "Fucking Irishman."

Dick and Jimmy spent the next hour briefing McNally on the Forrestal cost and schedule performance, as well as the quality of workmanship. They showed him charts they'd prepared that demonstrated trends and projections. Jimmy observed Dick spar with the commander who challenged every data point and estimate. The commander wagered a beer on the final cost of the overhaul, rounding off the bet to the nearest million.

"You're way under," said Dick, of the commander's estimate.

"I don't think so, Dickie boy," he said. "They're going to save at least five million with the Maestro Fusion process."

Jimmy's muscles tensed like an electrical charge went through his chair.

McNally noticed. "What's with you?"

"The Navy didn't learn their lesson on the Saratoga?"

Dick cringed.

"What do you mean?" McNally challenged.

"They spent millions on a tiger team to re-tube and re-weld the Saratoga boilers after they failed because of that machine. What makes you think they're not going to have problems on the Forrestal?"

McNally straightened in his chair. "First of all," he said, "the Saratoga re-tubing was guarantee work. Guaranteed, my ass," he repeated, sarcastically. "Second, the boiler tubes on the Forrestal are scheduled to be welded in the summer."

"Okay," said Dick, attempting to change the direction of the discussion, "I think we should…"

McNally waved him off. "Hold up, Dick. Jimmy doesn't look like he's finished."

"So now the Navy schedules work around the seasons because of a robot?" said Jimmy. "What are they going to do if the superheater headers are delivered late again from the vendor? Wait until the winter's over and weld them in the spring?"

The commander put his elbows on the desk and folded his hands. "You're a production guy," said McNally. "I can tell. I worked construction in Chicago during summers in high school, hauled mortar and brick around in wheelbarrows." The memory seemed to bring him pleasure. "Production guys keep us squids afloat. From where I sit, they're not given the credit they deserve. I get it." He paused, narrowed his eyes at Jimmy like they were the only two in the room. "But here's the deal. If you don't follow orders in the military, people die."

Jimmy studied the commander, and the longer he studied, the harder his blood pumped. "Yeah? Well, someone gave an order to use the Maestro Fusion process on the Saratoga and four of my buddies got killed."

"Jimmy," said Dick, abruptly.

McNally raised his hand like a traffic cop. "That's okay, Dick," he said, looking at Jimmy, not mad, but not happy. A few uncomfortable seconds passed. "We're good."

Dick wouldn't have looked relieved had he known what was going through Jimmy's head, because Jimmy was thinking about the story Colin had told him about Doc, the character Steinbeck based on his best friend Ed Ricketts who was crushed to death by a train in his car. Steinbeck worked through his grief by writing *East of Eden,* his magnum opus.

Fuck it!

"It's that simple, huh?" said Jimmy.

The commander looked puzzled. "What's that simple?"

"A construction worker from Chicago can be bought that easily."

"Whoa," said Dick, making a T sign with his hands. "Time out."

"I didn't agree with the decision to use the damn machine, McKee," McNally shot back. He took a few seconds to settle himself. "The Maestro Fusion process is going to save taxpayers a ton of money someday. It just needs the bugs worked out."

Jimmy was stunned by the commander's admission that the automated process was flawed. He knew the safe thing to do would be to leave it at that, but Jimmy had no interest in safe. "So where'd the order come from?"

McNally didn't answer, but Jimmy sensed his demeanor and energy leaning in the direction of the glass suite.

Chapter XLII

PREP MEETING

Jimmy sat at his desk the next morning paging through notes from the meeting with Commander McNally. Words began running together and sentences jumbled. Lines on graphs crisscrossed and swirled and herded him into a cattle chute with rustlers wearing white cloth sailor caps, stampeding shoulder-to-shoulder. His hands and feet were shackled. A deformed, faceless man, crashed through in the opposite direction, screaming, *It wasn't me. I swear it wasn't me.* The clang of a vintage phone, with the voice on the other end sounded like an enforcer: *This is Headquarters. The new guy ain't gonna work. Get rid of him.*

Jimmy's malaise broke when he realized that the clang he heard was the ring of the phone on his desk. He stared at it while his head cleared, then picked it up, but said nothing.

"Jimmy?" It was Dick was on the other end, telling him to get in his office, right away. Jimmy was consumed with regret for blowing the opportunity Jackie had described to him: access to the people and information behind the Maestro Fusion decision on the Saratoga. On his way to the Dick's office, he thought

271

of excuses for his combative behavior and reasons he should remain on the carrier program. *I was hallucinating from fumes on the Metro. I'll call and apologize to Commander McNally, I promise I'll follow orders and make you proud.*

He knew Dick wouldn't buy his bullshit. If he got the boot from the aircraft carrier program, he would take his investigation of Maestro Fusion underground.

Dick waved Jimmy in. "Commander McNally called."

Jimmy tasted dread in his saliva, but Dick's upbeat demeanor confused him. "I figured you'd be hearing from him."

"He's scheduling the prep meeting for the QPR next week. Monday, early. Ten o'clock. You'll have to catch the early Acela."

"He still wants me on the program?"

Dick scratched his head. "What are you talking about?"

"I figured after the argument we had that he'd want someone else on aircraft carriers."

"Are you kidding?" said Dick, as if it was the most ridiculous thing he'd ever heard. "Let me tell you something. McNally hates yes men. He told me he needs a guy like you to keep the bureaucrats straight."

"Really?"

"Yeah, really," said Dick. He watched Jimmy, not saying anything but not looking like he was finished either. "Between me and you," he said, "I think you planted a seed."

Jimmy didn't intend to plant a seed by arguing with McNally, but he was glad Dick brought it up. "Anything else?"

"I'm sending Jack Reddi with you next week."

"You think I can't handle it myself?"

"You've been to D.C. once in your life, and now you want to take on the world?" said Dick, sarcastically. "Listen, Jimmy. I trust you completely, but you're new at this game. Jack Reddi's got a shitload of experience, knows the players and the playing field. It'll be a good transition. I went with you yesterday. Jack Reddi will go with you next week. You'll be on your own for the QPR at the end of the month." Dick smiled reassuringly. "Trust me, you're moving faster than anyone who ever came into this office."

~

Analysts from the program office who attended past QPRs acted like prima donnas, or mobsters bragging about people they'd whacked. Most had years of experience surveying shipbuilding programs, doing physical inspections, writing reports and going to meetings to prove themselves before the boss trusted them to represent the organization. Jimmy hadn't been in the program management business for six months, and he was on the Amtrak to D.C. for the QPR prep meeting. Analyzing cost, schedule, quality, and performance data was second nature to him, a manifestation of things he'd picked up since he was an apprentice. Purchasing, material handling, and other facets of a multi-million-dollar construction program were extensions of the business.

Twenty minutes after leaving Thirtieth Street, the train pulled into the Wilmington Station.

"You haven't said a word since we got on," said Jackie.

Jimmy was uncomfortable being accompanied, like he needed a chaperone. "You going to tell me to go F myself again?" he asked, in an awkward attempt at humor, and as the

273

words replayed in his head, he realized he was embarrassed to say *fuck* in front of a woman.

"What do you mean?" she asked.

"The first time we went to a meeting together, you told me to go fuck myself," he said, lowering his voice at the curse word. "Remember?"

She smiled and lip signed *fuck you*.

Jimmy couldn't help smiling.

Jackie pivoted from small talk to business. "The purpose of the pre-QPR is to iron out the rough spots and resolve hard issues so there aren't any surprises at the QPR. Commander McNally will chair the meeting and each organization that attends the QPR—NAVSEA, the Pentagon, and the shipyard—sends a tech rep or two. Everyone answers to McNally. When he's satisfied, he'll brief his boss, the PEO, to get him up to speed. By the time the QPR rolls around with all the big shots, everything is scripted. A real dog and pony show."

After explaining the process, Jackie went through charts Jimmy had put together for tracking the program. She pointed out things that could impact the schedule, like late material deliveries, and nuances that affected performance trends. Indicators she called them.

"You sound like you've been doing this stuff forever," said Jimmy.

"Fifteen years," said Jackie.

Jimmy's eyes widened. "Jesus."

"What?"

Caught! And again, when *you don't look that old* replayed in his head, he felt like an idiot.

"I'm thirty-four," she said, not like she was insulted as much as she was talking to her little brother. "How old are you?"

"Twenty-seven."

"So I got seven years on you, big deal."

"It was stupid," said Jimmy, attempting to wiggle out of the corner he'd backed into.

"It was," she said. Her expression turned thoughtful. "You know, you have a reputation as a bull. A guy who gets shit done. Everyone respects you. But," she paused looking like she was weighing her words, "don't take this the wrong way, but in some ways you're immature."

Jimmy was too stunned to defend himself. Stripped of his power, his manhood, all he could do was stare at her.

"I shouldn't have said that," Jackie relented.

The rest of the commute was uneventful. No gaffes, no insults, and when conductor announced Union Station, they both seemed a relieved. They'd covered a lot of ground. Jimmy had a better understanding of the program management world, and a grasp on the QPR process it would have taken him much longer to figure out on his own. They knew each other's age, and she'd stumbled upon a vulnerability. Notwithstanding the immature remark, Jimmy was glad Dick had sent Jackie along.

~

They exited the Metro at the Crystal City station and walked down the platform. The image of the homeless man Jimmy had seen on his first trip with Dick had been stuck in his head: the ragged trench coat and hoodie and the way he sprawled on the subway floor like a pile of discarded clothes. Something about the man bothered him, but he couldn't put his finger on it. He'd

275

been eager to get back for another look and waited for Jackie to pass through the turnstiles before going through himself, then stepped aside and looked back in the corner. The homeless man wasn't there.

"What are you looking for?"

Jimmy turned around and Jackie was behind him. "Huh?" he said. "Uh, nothing."

The crowd thickened as they emerged into the underground mall. He remembered making a right the last time, passing rows of shops before they came to the food court, then another right into the vestibule with the elevators. They got into an open one, and less than a minute later, the doors opened on the twelfth floor.

Blair greeted them and told them Commander McNally was waiting in the conference room. Jimmy tried to get a look at the PEO as they passed his suite, but Rita was standing in front of his desk blocking his view. He was surprised by the welcome McNally gave Jackie when they walked into the room. It turned out they'd taken contracting classes together at Wright-Patterson Air Force Base and spent a few nights at a sports bar watching March Madness. McNally laughed, telling Jackie about the debate he had with Jimmy when he came down with Dick. He actually called it a debate, though at the time Jimmy thought they might come to blows. Today McNally was all business.

"I'm going to need help putting the briefing together," he said.

"Not a problem, Commander," said Jimmy. He didn't want to get too close to McNally, but he needed him as an ally.

The small conference room got crowded in a hurry, and he wanted to get a seat at the table before they were taken. Jackie had already put her folder on the corner seat next to the commander's. Jimmy put his briefcase in the chair next to hers.

McNally started the meeting at precisely ten o'clock. The first chart wasn't on the projector screen for five seconds before a debate started, one analyst disputing the data, others defending it. McNally refereed like he enjoyed a good argument, asserted his position, then either accepted or rejected suggestions. Jimmy was in familiar territory. Shipbuilding was his home turf. To his surprise, he sided with the commander on most issues, and when McNally grilled a techie from the Pentagon about the boiler schedule, he couldn't help thinking about the seed Dick had told him he planted. His relationship with the commander might have started out contentious, but he respected him. He believed McNally did the right things for the right reasons. And the idea that McNally would rely on him to help with the briefing crystalized his thinking about every detail of the process. He'd have access to the raw data and could make changes to craft a story of the half-billion-dollar overhaul program, a story he could segue from the status of the Forrestal to the debacle on the Saratoga. There was one obstacle. Jackie mentioned that the PEO was a control freak and insisted on being filled in at every step of the process.

A plan evolved in Jimmy's head: he would make two briefs: one that the PEO would eventually authorize, and a doctored brief he would somehow have loaded onto the conference room computer before the QPR. He would make only two hard copies of his doctored brief on the computer: one for the PEO, the other for Admiral Lawrence Foley, Ret., Chief Operations Officer of Maestro Fusion Corporation.

After the meeting, Jimmy huddled with the commander and Jackie to sort through the charts and graphs. McNally handed Jimmy the charts with his marked-up changes.

"The QPR is the last Monday in July," he said. "Send the changes to me next week so I can brief my boss before the big show."

"You got it," said Jimmy.

Jackie was halfway down the hall by the time he came out of the conference room. Inside the glass suite, the PEO came out of his office, handed a report to Rita, and retreated. Rita smiled and waved to Jackie as she passed. On the way to the elevator, Jimmy asked, "Do you know the PEO's secretary?"

"Rita?" she asked. "Yeah, why?"

"Dick told me nobody messes with her."

"Yeah," said Jackie. "She's a prick."

Jimmy laughed, and when they got inside the elevator, he pushed the button for the underground. The doors closed, and it was just the two of them inside the car. "The PEO looked familiar," said Jimmy.

"He should," said Jackie. "He was the captain on the Saratoga for a while."

Jimmy knew he looked familiar, but with a crew of more than four thousand, sailors all started looking the same. Executive officers traveled in cloistered circles and were rarely seen in the fire rooms. One thing he knew for sure was that the captain wasn't at the memorial for his friends that were killed.

"That's it," said Jimmy. "Do you know his name?"

"Stevens," she said, nonchalantly. "Captain Bradley Stevens."

~

Bradley Stevens, captain on the Saratoga, now PEO Aircraft Carriers, whirled around inside Jimmy's head as he made his way through the underground. The implications. On the other side of the turnstiles, a bluesy melody distracted him. He followed the sound to the train platform and slowed when he saw a pair of crutches propped against the wall. Sitting on the floor next to them, harmonica to lips and dirty Taco Bell cup on the tile, was the person he had hoped to see. He pulled a couple of dollar bills out of his pocket, and when he dropped them into the cup, he noticed metal rods with crude attachments for feet sticking from the bottom of his brown trench coat. The music stopped and the homeless man looked up. Through a straggly beard Jimmy could see stitch marks that crisscrossed his face, and a large indentation in the side of his skull. He couldn't look away from a void where there should have been an eye. Seconds dragged like minutes, hours.

Metal wheels screeched against steel track.

"Jimmy!"

Jimmy looked up and saw Jackie at the other end of the platform, about to board the train. He jumped onto the car in front of him just as the doors closed and turned to the window watching the homeless man until the tunnel swallowed the car. He took breath after deep breath to calm himself, unsure why he was so obsessed by the vagrant. At the next Metro stop, he walked to the end of the car, opened the sliding door, stepped over the connector to the next car, and repeated until he sat heavily next to Jackie three cars down.

Jackie shifted in her seat and stared at him. He was sweaty, breathing hard, eyes aimed straight ahead. "Are you okay?"

"Huh?" Jimmy shuddered.

She stared at him a little longer. "What's with the homeless guy?"

"I don't know. He reminded me of something."

Jackie leaned back in her seat, and said, "Yeah, like a thousand homeless guys downtown." Neither of them talked on the rest of the ride to Union Station. Twenty minutes into the commute on the Acela up the northeast corridor, she broke the silence. "How about a beer?"

"Here?" asked Jimmy." "On the train?"

"Café Car," she said, getting out of her seat. She disappeared up the aisle and returned five minutes later with two bottles of Yuengling. She handed him one as she sat.

"Thanks."

Jackie tipped her bottle toward Jimmy as a toast and took a sip. "A little trivia?" she asked, as if to lighten the mood.

"Sure," said Jimmy.

"Who's Captain Stevens's father?"

Jimmy's expression was a question. "What?"

"Captain Stevens, the PEO. Who is his father?"

"How would I know?"

"Admiral Foley."

"What do you mean 'Admiral Foley?'"

"Admiral Foley is Captain Bradley Stevens's stepfather."

Jimmy grimaced like someone stamped on his foot.

"Crazy, huh?"

"Crazy's not the word," said Jimmy. He frowned at his

beer, then turned and looked deep into her eyes. "Between me and you?"

Jackie nodded. "Between me and you."

"I found out something about Maestro Fusion that's been bothering me, but I haven't been able to make sense out of it."

Jackie waited for words that seemed stuck inside Jimmy's head. Finally, she asked, "Like what?"

"The company issued a stock option for ten thousand dollars to a consultant for services rendered right before my friends were killed in the car accident in Mayport."

Jackie looked baffled. "That's really not that unusual, Jimmy," she said gently.

"Yeah, except Tommy Homes, one of the guys who was killed, his wife got an envelope in the mail with ten thousand dollars in it. Anonymous, in cash."

"Jesus!" said Jackie. She picked at the label on the bottle for a few seconds, then looked at him. "But how could you make a connection if it was cash without a name?"

Jimmy stared at her with a pained expression. "I don't know yet, but I'm working on it."

Jackie rolled the bottom of her bottle on the open tray in front of her. "People know Admiral Foley was behind the Saratoga superheater job being awarded to Maestro Fusion," she said. "And everyone knows about those guys getting killed while they were repairing the Navy's fuckups in Mayport. But nobody's got the balls to take him on. He's powerful. He's got connections in the Pentagon and on Capitol Hill." Jackie rubbed the side of her face, then looked at Jimmy. "I'm going to let you in on something."

"Go ahead," said Jimmy.

"When me and McNally were at Wright-Patt taking that class, he told me Captain Stevens hates his stepfather. I mean he despises him. What you just told me about the stock option and the money your friend's wife got in the mail, that could be criminal. I think the best way to get to the old man would be through his kid."

Jimmy tapped his bottle to Jackie's, polished it off, and asked, "Another?"

"Of course."

~

Jimmy stopped at the office on the way home from Thirtieth Street Station to get some files he wanted to review that night. It was six-fifteen when he walked in. The red message light on his phone was blinking. He pressed the button and listened.

"Jimmy, this is Huey. I heard today that the sailor who drove the car that killed our boys went missing and never reported to prison. There's an APB out on him by NIS and the FBI."

Chapter XLIII

GARAGE TALK

Jimmy shot up in the dark, soaked, terrified, and staring into the hollow eye on a disfigured face, a dented skull, rotted mangled tree roots for legs. But it wasn't the image that haunted him. There was something familiar, hidden from the light of day, buried in the earth, in the soil with Tommy and the boys.

He never got back to sleep. At four a.m., he got out of bed, called the office, and left Dick a message that he was burning with a fever and going to the doctor. He put on a pair of jeans and pulled on a dark green hooded sweatshirt, drove to Thirtieth Street Station and bought an Amtrak ticket to D.C.

For two hours, he fidgeted on the ride to Union Station, then double-timed through the concourse to the Metro. His heart thump-thumped like bongos as the railcars click-clacked out from the underground and crossed the Potomac River toward Roslyn, past Arlington Cemetery and the Pentagon. After the train pulled out of the Pentagon City station, he got up and stood by the door.

A nightmare, an impulse, and three hours later, he was in Crystal City, scouring the Metro platform. He had no plan and no idea what he would do when he found the homeless man. If he found the homeless man. The first time down he saw him tucked inside the inbound turnstiles. The second time he was on the outbound platform and had prostheses and a pair of crutches.

He was mobile. He could be anywhere.

As the train slowed, he grasped the handrail with apprehension, and when it stopped, his feet submerged in quicksand. The doors swooshed open, passengers walked around him to exit.

"Excuse me," said an elderly black woman, stepping to Jimmy's side. "Are you all right, young man?"

Jimmy nodded that he was. He twisted and loosened one foot, then the other and stepped off the train. Streams of passengers funneled from other cars and flooded the station. The doors closed behind him, and the train sped away. In slivers of space between people, a single eye lased into his own from across the platform. Seconds passed, the crowd cleared, and the homeless man remained, sitting against the wall watching Jimmy as if he'd been expecting him. Jimmy took the deliberate steps of a mountaineer navigating a narrow ledge. In his mind, it took hours to traverse the fifteen feet to the wall. He stopped when his feet nearly touched the appendages attached to the homeless man's metal rods. The earth shook, thunder echoed from inside the tube, and light shot out of the dark hole. A train exploded into the station and screeched to a stop. Passengers disembarked and herded through the turnstiles. Energy generated by thousands of tons of metal and the chaos of the mob dissipated, and in thirty seconds the underground was once again barren.

"What can I do for you, brother?" asked the homeless man.

The muscles in Jimmy's throat tightened like steel cables on a suspension bridge. He nudged the prosthesis with the toe of his shoe. "How'd you lose these?"

The man's expression turned somber as he peered down at the metal and composite extending from his trench coat. "Life's a battle, man," he said. He looked up at Jimmy. "More like a war."

Being addressed as *brother* by this vile being angered him, but his answer to the question that kept him up all night enraged him. "What kind of war?"

The homeless man pushed back the sides of his hood, exposing every centimeter of his devastation. "A war for truth," he said, cleared his throat and spit down the concourse, "and justice."

Jimmy's foot catapulted into his crutches, sending them sliding across the platform. The homeless man sat emotionless watching them spin on the tile, and when they came to a stop, he said, "You want to get those so nobody trips over them, like an elderly person or something."

After being haunted in the middle of the night by the image of a man with no legs and one eye, and tormented by Huey's message about the missing sailor, Jimmy thought he'd beat the homeless man to death with his bare hands when he found him. Instead, he stood over the person he suspected of killing his friends, holding his crutches, and when the broken human being looked up, the void that had once been an eye seemed to tell the story of his entire wretched life.

The homeless man patted the cold tile next to him, inviting Jimmy to sit.

A surreal feeling came over Jimmy as he lowered himself to the ground. He wanted to ask him if he'd ever been in the Navy, stationed on the Saratoga, or if he'd ever worked in a boiler room. Instead, he said, "Tell me about truth and justice."

The homeless man wrung his hands. "I'd love to," he said, "but the underground is nowhere to discuss such matters."

"Then where?"

"There's a garage behind a house three blocks from here, Forty-four Fern Street. Be there at seven o'clock tonight."

"What the hell am I supposed to do until seven o'clock?"

The homeless man grabbed his crutches and propped himself onto his prosthesis. "Get familiar with the battlefield," he said, and as he turned to hobble away, added, "Prepare for war."

~

Jimmy canvassed the underground. He perused coffee shops, delis, restaurants and taverns, observed patrons, scrutinized relationships. He watched a businessman and an officer huddled at a secluded table in the back of a coffee shop, passing papers back and forth and signing documents. In the afternoon, he sat at the bar at the Ale House, watching men in tailored suits celebrating with an officer in a blue blazer with a gold eagle and four bars on his sleeve, buying round after round of Redbreast.

Feeling as though he was getting a grasp on backchannel contracting, he left the underground and walked south on Crystal Drive. He sat in the lobbies of the Hyatt and the Marriott. Sharply dressed men and women checked-in with luggage and left carrying briefcases, heading to Navy offices up the street or walking to the Metro for the short hop to the Pentagon. At six o'clock, he wandered across Jefferson-Davis Highway and

South Eads Street to a sports bar on Twenty-third Street and nursed a beer until customers wearing Washington Capitals jerseys filled the stools and tables waiting for seven o'clock faceoff. When warm-ups were over, a man with a baritone voice sang *O Canada*. Jimmy finished his beer and walked outside.

The breeze made it feel colder than it was. He looked up and down the street before walking west to the corner and turning left onto Fern Street. Midway down the block, he stopped at a house with a metal forty-four nailed to a wooden post. Exhaust fans blew the scent of Chinese food from a restaurant down the alley. Lights inside the house were dim, the shades pulled. There was no movement. A single naked light bulb shined above the side door of a garage in the back of the property. He passed an old, rusted Oldsmobile with two flat tires in the driveway. Shimmying between the car and the house, Jimmy saw an illusion of the homeless man sitting behind the wheel, and for a fleeting moment, he worried he'd been lured to this dreary hideaway by a psychopath. He sloughed off the brooding and strode to the garage.

The storm door was made of sheet metal with a torn rusted screen in the bottom pane and scratched Plexiglas in the top. The sheet metal made a sharp, tinny sound when Jimmy tapped it with his knuckles. Nearly a minute passed without an answer. He imagined the legless man looking for his crutches, steadying himself, and gimping across the room. His second knock was much harder.

"Who is it?" came from a male voice inside, but it sounded different than the one he remembered from his conversation with the homeless man in the underground. And it struck him as odd that the person who'd given him the address and told him to come at seven o'clock would be asking who it was.

"It's me," answered Jimmy, in an irritated tone.

"Me who?"

Feeling as though he was being jerked around, he shouted, "It's fucking me!"

Nearly a half-minute passed before the inside door cracked. Jimmy squinted to see through the cruddy Plexiglas. The sliver of face on the inside was covered with a thick beard, and when the door opened a little wider, he saw that the man had legs. "Where's the homeless man?"

"What homeless man?"

"The one who gave me this address."

The man leaned closer to the window to get a better look, and when he did, Jimmy detected something familiar. It was the same feeling he had when he bumped into the wolfman in the underground his first time down with Dick. "What are you talking about?" the guy asked.

Jimmy grabbed the door handle and pulled.

"Go away, damn it!" He slammed the inside door, but Jimmy jammed his foot in the opening. "Go away before I call the police." Jimmy shouldered the door, but the guy's foot was wedged into the bottom inside. Jimmy crouched into a lineman stance and threw all his weight into it. The wood frame splintered, and the door swung open, sending wolfman stumbling backward across the room where a coffee table clipped his legs and he struck his head against the partition separating the kitchenette from the living room. He rolled into a ball covering his face with his arms as Jimmy ran toward him.

"Don't hit me," he pleaded. "Please, don't hit me."

Jimmy stood over him with clenched fists. "Get up!"

Wolfman peeked from between his arms.

"Get up!" Jimmy shouted again.

The man struggled to his feet in a defensive posture.

"Put your hands down," said Jimmy. He stared at the guy's stained t-shirt, then down at his cutoff jeans and bare feet.

"What are you doing here?" the guy asked.

Jimmy recognized the voice. He squinted to see through the long scruffy whiskers that covered his face. "George?"

"How'd you find out where I was?"

"I didn't. The homeless man gave me the address and told me to meet him here at seven o'clock."

George Sputz's cheeks rose, pushing his eyes into a squint. "How come you keep talking about a homeless man?"

"This handicap guy who lives in the underground. There was something suspicious about him, so I asked him where he lost his legs, and he gave me some philosophical bullshit, then told me to meet him here tonight if I wanted to know."

George stared at Jimmy like he was crazy. "You're not making any sense."

"I'm not?" said Jimmy. "Then tell me what the hell you're doing down here."

George lowered his head and said nothing.

"I asked you a question!" yelled Jimmy.

George looked up, and in a low voice said, "They fucked me, Jimmy."

"Who fucked you?"

"The Navy."

Jimmy knew the answer but wanted to hear it from George. "Why?"

"Because I knew too much."

Jimmy waited a few seconds but got impatient. "Don't stop there, George."

Words came strained at first, but once they began to flow, he seemed unencumbered. "Admiral Foley caught me with the study Mr. Strunk commissioned that proved the automated preheat procedure was inadequate and would cause the superheater tubes to crack. Mr. Strunk was on record that the Maestro Fusion process was flawed, and the admiral knew I agreed with him."

Jimmy narrowed his eyes. "You were transferred to NAVSEA and never reported, so what are you're doing in Crystal City?"

George pressed his eyelids with his fingers, released them, and looked at Jimmy. "I need a beer," he said, and walked to the refrigerator in the kitchenette.

Jimmy let out a long sigh. "Make that two."

George came back, plopped two beers on the counter, opened one, and took a swig. "Before Captain Stevens became PEO for aircraft carriers, he was chief engineer on the two ships they used as pilot programs for the Maestro Fusion process, one in San Diego and one in Hawaii. Then the old man had him stationed him in Philly for the re-tubing of the superheaters on the Dahlgren and the Talbot, both jobs they scheduled in the spring and summer. After Maestro Fusion fucked up the Saratoga boilers, he was promoted to captain and went to Mayport for the retubing."

Jimmy eyed George closely. "So you know that Stevens is Foley's stepson."

"Of course," said George, as if it was common knowledge. "Didn't you?"

"I just found out, and it explains a lot of things."

"Yeah, like the old man's an opportunist, and his stepson's a pawn." He took a sip of beer, shook his head in disgust. "You want to hear another one?"

"What's that?" said Jimmy.

"When they eliminated Mr. Strunk's position at the shipyard, they gave decision authority for welding and metallurgy to an officer named Captain Crosby, the head of NAVSEA engineering, a guy with no background in metallurgy."

"What a circle jerk," said Jimmy.

"You think that's a circle jerk," said George, nodding toward a stool at the counter, "you better sit down for this one." They both pulled stools and sat facing one another. "Remember the night Admiral Foley was snooping around when we were in Mayport?"

"How can I forget?" said Jimmy, the night Foley barged into the trailer ranting still fresh in his head.

"That was two days before Senator Hawkins was coming to visit," said George. "I was inspecting welds inside the boiler cavity, and Foley came down the fire room. I had Mr. Strunk's study with me and didn't realize it dropped out of my back pocket. He picked it up, and when he saw what it was, he went berserk and ordered me to go back to Philly. I grabbed it out of his hand and took off." George shook his head. "I don't know how he found out I gave the study to Tommy, but Tommy was killed the night before Hawkins came."

"Jesus Christ!"

"So Foley's kid gets promoted to Program Executive Officer, the old man retires and becomes chief operations officer at Maestro Fusion, the company wins a sixty-million dollar contract for the Forrestal, me and Mr. Strunk get shitcanned, and four good men are dead."

Jimmy stared at the wall across the room and talked slowly. "I get the admiral and the captain working together," he said, pausing for a long couple of seconds. "But I can't figure out how the sailor who drove the car that killed those guys is connected."

"I don't know if they are," said George, "but I'm going to find out."

It was clear to Jimmy that him and George were on parallel missions, but that George was at a disadvantage. There were things he didn't know, like the stock option, and the sailor being in the Farmstead the night of the accident. Jimmy mulled over what information to share and what to hold close.

"How do you plan to do that?" asked Jimmy.

"I'm going to blackmail Captain Stevens with the Strunk study."

"I thought you gave it to Tommy."

George seemed to drift for a moment, and his tone was dreamy as he recounted. "The night of the accident, I was up worrying about being sent back to Philly. I figured it was the end of my career. Around two in the morning, I was on my balcony and heard an explosion. I took the elevator down and ran outside, and when I saw cop cars speeding up Third Street, I went to see what was going on. As I got close, I smelled gas, then I saw car parts scattered all over the place. Vince Murphy was stumbling around on someone's front lawn like a zombie. Then I saw white sheets over bodies. I must have gone into shock because the next thing I knew, I was wandering around on the beach. At some point, it hit me that it was Tommy's rental car, and I freaked out thinking about giving him the study after my fight with Admiral Foley. Tommy's room was down the hall from mine, so I ran back to the hotel, pushed in his screen window and found the study on his nightstand. I grabbed it and took off."

Jimmy sat, mouth hanging open, the night of the accident playing out in his head. "So you…"

George waved him off. "Just before I got back to my room, I heard the elevator door open, and when I turned around Captain Stevens got off. I ducked inside my door and watched him break into Tommy's room."

"So that's who ransacked Tommy's apartment."

George nodded. "Yeah." They sat in silence for several seconds, then George said, "So I'm going to use the study to blackmail Captain Stevens to get to Foley."

Jimmy remembered Jackie saying the same thing. *The way to get to the old man was through his kid.* "But how's the Strunk study prove Foley was involved with those guys' deaths?"

"Listen, Jimmy," said George, his face swelling with anger. "I've been told the captain's an entitled brat. He had everything handed to him his entire life, prep school, the academy, the whole bit. When I get my hands on him, shove the evidence in his face and tell him he's going to prison where he'll be fucked up the ass five times a day, he'll flip on the old man in a second."

"Jesus Christ, George," said Jimmy, shocked by the rage coming from the formerly placid soul. "What the hell got into you?"

"These greedy fucks ruined my life," George choked. "They stole my career. I worked with the best engineer in the shipyard, had a position that made a difference. Now I'm living in a garage, and these people who killed good men are living like kings."

Jimmy rested a hand on George's shoulder. "Okay, buddy," he said, "I'm with you."

"Good," he said, "because I lost my clearance, and I need an inside man."

"For what?" asked Jimmy.

"To lure that asshole captain over here. I'm going to package a few excerpts from Mr. Strunk's study and some original inspection records showing the rejected welds, and I need someone with clearance to put the package on his desk. When I get him over here, I'm going to lay all the evidence in front of him—the study his old man buried, the records he forged—and I'm going to give him two choices: either cooperate, or the information will become the property of the *Washington Post*."

Jimmy took a swig of beer thinking about George's plan. It appealed to him that he wouldn't have to persuade a room full of high-ranking Navy officers that a captain and retired admiral were guilty of conspiracy and murder. That thought scared the shit out of him.

"How about we add a photo or two?"

"What kind of photos?"

"Like a shot of the car wreckage." He waited for a reaction, then added, "Maybe a photo of Tommy's daughter. An infant picture, or one from her first birthday."

"That'll work," said George. He finished his beer and went to the refrigerator for two more. He opened them and put one in front of Jimmy. "So, who do you think he is?"

"Who do I think *who* is?" asked Jimmy.

"The homeless guy in the Metro."

Jimmy had lost track of how he got to Fern Street in the first place. "The homeless guy?" Jimmy repeated to himself. "The guy's missing his legs, no left eye, face stitched together." He lapsed for a few moments. "You're going to think I'm crazy, but the driver of the car that killed Tommy and the guys had his legs amputated and lost his left eye. The reason I came down today was to confront him about being a murderer."

George gave Jimmy a sideways glance. "I thought the guy died."

"Everyone thought he died, or was going to die." Jimmy took a long sip and when he lowered the bottle he stared at George. "He was sentenced to life for killing those guys and disappeared before he went to prison."

George eyed Jimmy for a few seconds. "How the hell would he know where I live?"

His tone sounded to Jimmy more like a riddle than a question. "How the hell should I know?"

They both looked around the apartment as if being watched. George leaned close to Jimmy, and whispered, "Maybe we should meet somewhere else next time."

Jimmy nodded in agreement.

"There's an Irish Pub on King Street in Old Town called Keenan's."

"When?"

"How's Saturday at noon."

"I'll be there," said Jimmy.

Chapter XLIV

McGILL'S

"What happened to you yesterday?" asked Jackie when Jimmy walked into the office the next morning.

"I was sick as a dog," said Jimmy just as he'd rehearsed.

Jackie crossed her arms. "You didn't seem sick sucking down those Yuenglings on the train on the way home from Crystal City."

Jimmy had expected Jackie to interrogate him about missing work the day after they traveled together, but the second he looked her in the eye, he gave in. "I had business to attend to," he said, apologetically.

"Don't forget you have a brief to put together and get to McNally next week," she said, leaving him off the hook.

Jimmy was tempted to ask her when she became his boss, but he knew it would only invite her wrath. He'd dug himself a hole, now he'd be putting in some late nights to finish the brief by next week. Fortunately, the doctored brief would merely be an insurance policy in the event George's plan didn't work. "Don't worry," he said, "it'll be done."

Jackie smiled. "How'd you make out, anyway?"

"With what?"

She rolled her eyes. "Your business."

"I feel like I'm getting close."

"Good," she said. "Let me know if I can help with anything."

"Thanks, Jackie."

~

The sun had ducked behind the downtown buildings when Mick Kelly emerged from 101 Penn Center in a three-piece pinstripe charcoal suit and carrying a leather briefcase. He slowed as he approached the corner on Market Street across from City Hall and tapped a heel of his Italian loafer on the sidewalk. "Well, hello, stranger. What brings you to Center City?"

"We need to talk," said Jimmy.

Mick studied his prize student's strident expression. "I know the perfect place," he said, and continued walking.

Jimmy shadowed Mick across Fifteenth Street under the gaze of Billy Penn atop City Hall. They entered the north portal of the magnificent fortress, crossed the courtyard, and exited the south portal. Oblivious to the Broad Street crosswalk, teacher scuttled between taxicabs and busses, his student at his side. He eased into a strut down narrow Juniper Street to a back alley named Drury Street. On the left, about fifty feet up the alley, hung a sign. *McGill's Olde Ale House*. Mick walked deliberately, yet somewhat reverently, then stopped and faced a heavy wooden door framed in a masonry arch set in a brick façade. He took a few short steps, opened the door, and gestured toward the threshold with open hand. "Shall we?"

Jimmy had never been to a pub in Ireland, but the dark wood paneling, thick oak bar, and large hearth was what he imagined in places he'd heard of like Killarney, Kilkenny, or Kinsale. Mick looked around the establishment as he meandered to a small table against the back wall. He made small talk while they waited for a server, but Mick could see that Jimmy was preoccupied. "You're awful tight, young man."

"I've found out a few things since we last talked."

"Such as?"

"For one, the PEO in Washington was the captain of the Saratoga, *and* he was assigned to the ship specifically for the retubing of the boilers in Mayport."

"Okay," said Mick, like it was no big deal.

"And he's Admiral Foley's stepson."

"Hmm." It came out long and cerebral. "Now that's interesting."

"That's not all," said Jimmy.

A young woman walked up beside them, and asked, "What can I get you gentlemen?"

Mick ordered two pints of Guinness without breaking his concentration with Jimmy. "Go ahead," he said.

"I tracked down the engineer who worked on a study that proved that Maestro Fusion's welding process was flawed. He was planning to give the study to Senator Hawkins in Mayport, but Admiral Foley found out and sent him back to Philly, so he gave the study to Tommy Homes, my buddy who got killed the night before Hawkins visited."

Mick pondered a few seconds. "Pretty convincing stuff, but," he clinched his teeth, "all circumstantial."

"What's that supposed to mean?"

"It means it's dependent on other evidence."

"Mick," said Jimmy, loud enough for Mick to signal him to lower his volume. "This engineer saw Captain Stevens break into Tommy Homes's hotel room right after the accident. He had to be after the study, but this engineer got to it first."

Mick waited for the waitress to put the two stouts on the table, then reached over and held Jimmy's forearm. "Everything you're telling me is good, Jimmy. They're all pieces to the puzzle. But you need someone willing to testify under oath that either the captain or the admiral ordered the killing." He let go of Jimmy's arm and took a sip of his stout. "Proving the accident was part of a conspiracy in court is going to be difficult if all you have is a study and an accusation that a captain in the United States Navy broke into the victim's room."

"Fuck, Mick," said Jimmy, his voice weighed down by frustration. "How about you? Did your buddy at the SEC get a copy of the stock certificate?"

Mick blew out a long sigh. "This is serious shit, Jimmy," he said. "If you want the SEC to stick their neck out, they're going to want a silver bullet. An eyewitness." He paused and scratched his beard. "Look, Jimmy, knowing and proving something in court are two different things. If it was me working for the SEC, I'd be all in. But I've got to ask a friend who doesn't have a dog in the fight to put his career on the line. This isn't like an old lady tripping on someone's cracked sidewalk. This is accusing powerful people of murder. People with influence and money. If you don't have a silver bullet, like the guy who drove the car that killed your friends, who will testify under oath, my buddy at the SEC could wind up shining shoes."

Jimmy closed his eyes tight, and as he massaged his eyelids the image of a stitched-up face with a hollow eye emerged. "What if I *get* the guy who drove the car?"

Kelly nodded. "You're getting close." He hesitated a second or two. "But how would that implicate the admiral or the captain?"

"Come on, Mick," Jimmy erupted. "The stock option was issued before the accident, Tommy Homes's widow gets ten grand in the mail, and now you're going to give me shit about the guy who drove the car. I thought you were trying to help."

"All right, Jimmy," said Mick. "Calm down."

Jimmy's eyes turned to flamethrowers. He picked up a peppershaker and slammed it on the table. "Calm down? Maestro Fusion wins a sixty-million-dollar contract after these sleezeballs killed my friends, and you tell me to calm down!" He leaned across the table, his face within inches of his teacher's, and said, "Have some fucking balls, Kelly!"

Mick held Jimmy's stare waiting for the storm to recede. "Conspiracy and murder," he said, like he needed to feel the texture of the words on his tongue. "You better be right," he said. He reached into his briefcase, pulled out a folder, opened it, and slid a paper across the table.

Jimmy examined the paper, and the longer he stared, the redder his face got. He ran his fingers over the name Bradley Stevens. Under the name was a dollar sign followed by the number ten thousand. He looked up at Mick, shook the paper in his face. "This is him," he said, pointing at the name on the certificate. "The captain of the Saratoga. Bradley Stevens." Jimmy's astonishment turned to rage. "Why'd you put me through so much shit if you had this all along?"

"Preparation, young man. Training. What I put you through is nothing compared to what you'll go through if you go after the big boys. You take on these guys, you're going to take heavy fire. And make no mistake, they'll come at you with the most ruthless defense money can buy. If you're not prepared, they'll eat you alive."

"I'm going to get the driver of the car to testify," said Jimmy, as a statement of fact.

"If you get the guy who drove the car that killed your friends to testify that either the captain or the admiral ordered the killing, then we have a case," said Mick.

Jimmy picked up his beer, drank heartily, then wiped the foam from his lips. He looked straight into Mick's eyes. "You don't have a friend at the SEC, do you?"

"I was wondering how long it would take you to figure that out."

Chapter XLV

IRISH PUB

Jimmy stuffed photos and the company's financial report into his backpack and left his apartment early enough to stop in Crystal City before he met George in Old Town. He put the copy of the stock option in an envelope, folded it, and slipped it in his back pocket, undecided whether he'd share it. The drive to Union Station took two hours, where he hopped on the Metro Yellow Line through Crystal City to Huntington. He tossed his backpack on the seat next to him and stretched his legs, surprised at how empty the train was on the weekend. The train emerged from the underground, and as it crossed the Fourteenth Street Bridge, he looked out at the Pentagon thinking how easy it must be for thirty million dollars to disappear from a five-hundred-billion-dollar defense budget to fund an obscure program, like a robotic welding process that didn't work.

He stood at the Crystal City stop, scoured the landscape when he stepped off, and started walking. His stomach muscles tightened as he approached the turnstiles, and after he went through, he turned and found the area desolate. He was the only person in the walkway to the underground where the corridors of the mall were mostly empty. He stopped at the food court and bought a cup of coffee, sat and watched stragglers stroll by: a few shoppers, a bureaucrat in jeans and Chaps. At ten o'clock, he made a second round of the mall before heading back to the Metro for his final destination.

King Street station came faster than he expected. He got off and walked down the steps, realizing by the time he got out to the street that he was in unfamiliar territory. A woman noticed him looking around and asked if he needed help, then pointed him up Washington Avenue. The red brick, tree-lined sidewalks of Old Town reminded him of the historic district around Independence Hall and Carpenter's Hall in downtown Philly. He passed boutiques, antique stores, and grills on a ten-minute walk before the flag of Ireland hanging over a doorway stopped him at a white brick building with emerald green and white wainscot panels. Gold and white letters painted above the window spelled "Keenan's Irish Pub."

A few minutes past noon, he crossed the threshold and stood waiting for his eyes to adjust to the midday saloon. A round, black Guinness sign with white lettering hung on the wall next to a beveled mirror that covered the length of the wall behind bar. In the mirror's reflection, Jimmy saw more brands of Irish whiskey then he knew existed. A small group of men camped out at the far corner of the bar debated the Irish Football League. A black iron grate sat empty inside a large stone hearth against the back wall. He made his way through mostly unoccupied tables and pulled up a chair across from a man sitting alone wearing dark sunglasses and a baseball cap turned backwards.

"What'll you have?" asked George.

Jimmy nodded at the pint glass of black stout in front of him. "One of those."

George raised two fingers in the direction of the bartender. Judging by how loose he appeared, it was obvious the former engineer had a head start. "What's in the backpack?"

"The photos," said Jimmy.

"A backpack full?" he chuckled.

"So, what's the plan?" asked Jimmy, bluntly.

"You're gonna have to come up with an excuse to be down here on Friday to drop off the package. Stevens's office will be clear from ten to two while he's at the Pentagon."

"So I'm going to walk right into the captain's office?" said Jimmy. "Nobody'll be around to challenge me, check my ID or my clearance? No secretaries, aids or anything?" George's nonresponse irritated him. "What am I? A VIP all of the sudden?"

"Nobody'll be there."

"How do you know?"

"I know."

"Listen, George," said Jimmy, "you're asking me to walk into a PEO's office and put a package on his desk implicating him in a conspiracy, and all you're going to tell me is, 'You know.'" He looked George in the eye. "How do you know?"

George drained his beer and signaled the bartender for two more. "You have to promise you won't tell anyone."

"Who the fuck am I going to tell?" asked Jimmy, indignantly. He looked at a couple two tables away and pointed. "Her?" A young guy and girl looked over, saw Jimmy's enraged face across from a bearded guy wearing sunglasses, then turned away.

"Okay, Jimmy. Calm down."

"You know what, George?" Jimmy steamed. "I'm tired of people telling me to calm down." He cracked his neck to one side, then the other. "If you want me to be your inside man, you're going to have to clue me in on every detail of the operation. I have to know everything you know."

George showed no emotion until Jimmy started getting out of his chair. "Rita," he said, quickly. Jimmy looked down, turned his palms toward him, as if saying, *well?* "The captain's secretary, Rita. She gave me his calendar and promised it would be clear on Friday, between ten to two."

Jimmy leaned over and got in George's face. "How the fuck do you know Rita?"

"What do you think I've been doing down here for the last six months, jerking off?" said George, sounding belligerent himself. "I've been shadowing that asshole Stevens for months. He's been having an affair with her, so I got her alone in the parking garage one night and threatened to tell her husband if she didn't cooperate."

"She's married?" said Jimmy, slowly sitting back down.

"Hard to believe, huh?" said George, snidely. "With two kids."

The bartender appeared at their table holding two pints. "You guys okay here?"

"Yeah, we're good," said Jimmy, keeping an eye on George. After he put the pints on the table and left, Jimmy pulled the financial report from his backpack and put it on the table, then reached back inside for the photos: one of a mangled clump of metal and broken glass, a baby picture, and a picture of a little blonde-headed girl with pigtails. He put them in order on top of the report.

"May I?" asked George, reaching for the photos. He winced at the picture of the car. "How the hell did anyone survive?" he mumbled. Next, he picked up the photos of the girl, looked closely reading the inscriptions Jimmy had written: *Danielle Homes Baptism* and *Danielle Homes First Birthday*. Through the whiskers, Jimmy saw the young man he used to talk to behind the boilers: the dorky guy who patiently explained the characteristics of different types of metals or the effect of a ten-thousand-degree welding arc when proper preheat procedures weren't followed. He demystified complex theories for a welder from Northeast Philly. Sitting across from him, inside Keenan's Pub on King Street in Old Town, Alexandria, George transformed back into the caring person Jimmy once knew, the young engineer who took pride in a profession he had stolen from him. It wasn't hard for Jimmy to imagine powerful people exploiting a timid, innocent kid and robbing him of his career. He noticed mist on the rim of the sunglasses resting on his whiskers. "You okay, George?"

George nodded at the report. "What's that?"

Jimmy opened the financial report to the page listing Maestro Fusion's corporate officers, turned it to face George, and pointed at the "Ret." after the names, five including Lawrence Foley. Next, he turned to a page with columns of numbers.

"See this footnote," he said, underlining the 1983 revenue with his finger. "That's the thirty-million-dollar contract."

George sat quietly for a few moments, then pulled a manila envelope from inside his denim jacket. He opened it and took out a two-page executive summary from the study he worked with Mr. Strunk. He pointed to the conclusion about hydrogen embrittlement causing the superheater tubes on the Saratoga to crack, waited for Jimmy to read, and said, "That ought to get his attention." He organized the photos, financial report, and executive summary into a package, placed them back in the envelope and handed it to Jimmy. "There's a note inside telling Stevens to bring ten grand to the garage at eight o'clock Friday night in exchange for the evidence."

"And you think he's going to believe that you've destroyed any copies?"

"I don't care what he believes. He won't have a choice. The pressure will be on him, and he's not good under pressure. He'll have to roll the dice. I want to see his asshole twitch."

Jimmy eyed George suspiciously, like something wasn't making sense. "Where'd you come up with ten grand?"

"What do you mean?"

"The number. How'd you come up with it?"

George hesitated. "I don't know," he said, sounding unsure of himself. "He's a captain in the United States Navy. He makes good money. I figured he'd have it, or could get it in exchange for something that could put him behind bars."

Jimmy couldn't tell whether George was holding something back, so he decided to leave the stock option tucked in his back pocket as insurance. The stock option was his baby, and his alone. If everything went to shit, he'd throw it in the captain's face and tell him that he had Smitt in hiding ready to testify against him. It was a gamble on his own part. And if he *did* find Smitt, that would be the *coup de grace*, his hammer to bring down the Maestro Fusion empire and put the people who took the lives of his friends behind bars.

"Are you going to join us at the garage?" asked George.

"I wouldn't miss it for the world," said Jimmy. He took the envelope, shoved it in his backpack, then pushed his chair away from the table to get up.

"Jimmy," said George.

"What?"

"Do you think they'll put 'Ret.' after the admiral's name on his prisoner uniform?"

"We'll see," said Jimmy, as he stood. "I'll be in the captain's suite next Friday at ten-fifteen." He threw his backpack over this shoulder. "Make sure it's clear." He turned and walked out onto King Street.

~

Mick's silver bullet theory monopolized Jimmy's thoughts on his way back to the King Street Station. *You need a silver bullet, the guy who drove the car that killed your friends.* The stock option was the key piece of physical evidence linking Maestro Fusion and Captain Stevens, but if the captain didn't flip on the old man, as George swore he would, only Smitt, the driver of the car that killed Tommy and the boys, could link the captain to the murders, and therefore to Lawrence Foley.

It was as precarious as a row of dominos. Any shift would lead to failure.

The thought tormented him as the train pulled into Crystal City. He got anxious when he heard the door motor whine and shot out of his seat when they cranked open. A tense air followed him onto the platform, through the turnstile, and down the walkway into the underground mall. He walked alone through a concourse, checking every passageway in the shopping district and peeking into each store window. Coming up empty, he decided to go through the tunnel that went under the highway to the Hilton hotel. He stood in the lobby, studying guests check-in, hop elevators, and watch college basketball on a big screen at the bar, before returning to the food court and buying a cup of coffee.

He sat at a table and looked at the backpack on the floor between his legs, thinking about what was inside: the company financial report, the photos, the executive summary from the Strunk study. A clock on the wall read five. There was no trace of the homeless man. He stared into his coffee, swirled it around and around, thinking about Mick Kelly, Griz, Forksville, Smitt, everything he'd learned, and all the evidence he'd collected. The swirl of coffee turned to a funnel that sucked him down, down into the underbelly of humanity, where conmen owned beachfront properties, laborers begged from their graves for one last breath, and greed and avarice steamrolled truth and justice.

Click-clack, click-clack pried a crevasse into his spell.

He looked up and watched a silhouette emerge from the Metro tunnel. It was the outline of a man wearing a trench coat on crutches, and the closer he got the louder the *click-clack* became. Jimmy was fossilized and blinded, like a citizen of Pompeii, and all he could do was listen to the *click-clack* fade with the distance that grew between them as he continued down the mall. He prayed for the volcanic mortar to be chiseled from his lips. The coffee dropped to the floor, he slammed his fists against the table, and yelled, "Stop!"

The *click-clacking* slowed until there was silence. Jimmy turned, a veil lifted from his eyes, and what he thought was a trench coat were plastic trash bags draped over the side of a janitor's waste can he pushed on a cart. The crutches were broom and mop handles.

"Can I help you, young man?" asked the janitor.

Jimmy slumped. "No," he said. "I thought you were someone else."

The janitor turned and the *click-clack* resumed, fading as he disappeared down the passageway. On the train ride home, Jimmy thought how the homeless man had been in the underground the day he came down with Dick, and then again with Jackie. The day he came down alone, the homeless man led him to George Sputz's garage apartment on Fern Street.

But now, when he needed him the most, he'd vanished.

~

Jimmy looked down at the Chesapeake Bay from his window seat as the train crossed the bridge at Havre de Grace. He was trying to think of an excuse to take off work next Friday. No excuse would be good enough to miss the last workday before the QPR, but he had no choice. Dick would be pissed. Jackie would know he was full of shit no matter what story he came up with, but she understood his mission. He had to finish the official brief and send it to Commander McNally by Thursday afternoon. Time was running out to complete his own doctored brief. He hoped George's plan to blackmail Captain Stevens worked so he wouldn't have to use it to make his case about the conspiracy and murder to a room full of Navy brass at the QPR.

Chapter XLVI

Office Call

"Pull over at Capitol Cigars," ordered Captain Stevens, from the backseat of a black government sedan returning from Admiral Clark's retirement luncheon at the Pentagon. The driver's spiteful eyes glared into the rearview mirror as he veered to the curb. The captain jumped out and strutted into the store to buy replacements for the cigars he handed out to flag officers at the luncheon, each of them lobbying to be recruited for a position at Maestro Fusion Corporation after they retired, like Captain Crosby had. Stevens cut off the end of a cigar on his way out of the store and dropped it on the sidewalk before climbing into the backseat.

"Crystal City," he barked.

The elevator doors opened on the twelfth floor. Stevens strolled through his secretary's suite without acknowledging her, threw his coat on the sofa, and stood at his office window watching aircraft taking off and landing at National Airport. The phone rang, and when he saw it was his direct line he walked to his desk, removed the unlit cigar from his mouth and picked it up.

"Captain Stevens," he answered.

Stevens snapped to attention in his empty office at the sound of Admiral Tilly's voice. He called to thank him for the cigar, but he really called to tell him how much he admired his stepfather. Stevens hated listening to high-ranking military officers adulate the old man in the hope their words would make it back to him. He found it demeaning on their behalf and caused him to detest his stepfather even more.

As Admiral Tilly rambled, the captain was distracted by a manila envelope on his desk that he didn't recognize. He picked it up and opened it, and as he read the title on the first page he pulled out, his face turned corpse gray.

Hydrogen Embrittlement of Chromium Steel.

The next two pages were an executive summary. The final conclusion read: "The inadequate preheat cycle of the Maestro Fusion robotic welding process created a condition called Hydrogen Embrittlement causing the boiler tubes to crack on the Saratoga."

The conclusion didn't make him look as ill as the photo that slid out and landed on his desk: the picture of an infant with the caption *Danielle Homes Baptism*. A second photo dropped out of a little girl with the caption *Danielle Homes First Birthday.*

"Captain? Captain, are you there?" came from the other end of the phone. Stevens dropped the envelope, spitting a third photo of a mangled car onto his desk.

His legs gave way and he collapsed into his chair.

"Captain! Are you still there?" He attempted to answer Admiral Tilly, but most of what he said was unintelligible. He could hear desperation in the admiral's voice, and it took every bit of his concentration to ramble, "I… I'm not feeling well, sir… I'll have to call you back."

His hand trembled as he guided the phone into its holder. He grabbed his short-cropped hair and pressed his face into the desk. A few minutes passed before he lifted it.

"Rita!"

The secretary opened the door. "Yes, Captain."

"Who was in my office?"

"No one, sir."

He picked up the report, and screamed, "Someone was in my office!" He shook the papers at her. "Have you been at your desk since I left?"

"Of course," she lied, knowing that if she told him she went down to the underground to meet friends for lunch, did a little shopping, then stopped at a coffee shop for a latte, that he'd chew her out like he did whenever the mood struck. She was the only secretary in NAVSEA who knew how to handle his bullshit: by deception, lying, and satisfying him when everyone went home at the end of the day, on the sofa, the floor, and sometimes his desk. It wasn't careless leaving the captain's door unlocked. It was retribution, a payback, not only from her, but from the innocent men who were killed because of his role in the malicious and misguided plot that George Sputz told her about. So while the captain was rubbing elbows with admirals in the Pentagon, a young man who was a close friend of the dead men left the package of evidence on his desk, implicating him in the conspiracy.

Rita turned to walk out without saying another word.

"Close the fucking door," he shouted after her. He took the report and paged through it, taking note of the thirty-million footnote highlighted in green, and the "Ret." behind each corporate board member's name highlighted in yellow. A note dropped from between the pages onto his lap. He picked it up and unfolded it.

"Bring ten-thousand dollars cash in an envelope to Forty-four Fern Street tonight at eight o'clock. Otherwise this information will become the property of the *Washington Post*."

Ice gushed through his veins when he saw the signature. *Tommy Homes.*

It took tremendous effort for the captain to concentrate and organize his frantic thoughts. He had never been good in stressful situations because his entire life he knew his stepfather would bail him out. He remembered the admiral's rage at their last meeting, the way he berated him. *You'd be nothing without me!* The captain hated the bastard. He loathed to call him. This time he would handle it himself, once and for all.

Louis Robert Smitt hadn't entered Steven's mind since the day he tried to track him down in Forksville. But now, sitting in his suite on the top floor of NC-3 staring at pictures of Danielle Homes, he couldn't get the sole witness linking him to the death of Tommy Homes and the three other shipyard workers out of his head.

"Rita!" he shouted. After his second call, Rita opened the door nonchalantly so he wouldn't be mistaken that she shared his emergency. "Rita, I have a project I need done."

"Yes?" she said.

Lowering his tone, he said, "I need you to track down a third-class boiler technician named Louis Robert Smitt. He was court martialed in June and sentenced to life, but disappeared before he reported to prison. I know you have contacts in Navy intelligence. Use them. I have to find him."

"Yes, sir," she said, then, in a flirtatious tone, asked, "Anything else?"

"Yes," he said. "I need to know whatever you find out by the end of the day."

"Whatever you want, handsome," she said with a faux smile, and closed the door.

Chapter XLVII

AMBUSH

Jimmy sat sipping a beer at the sports bar on Twenty-third Street Friday evening, thinking how easy the morning drop-off had gone at Captain Stevens's office. Almost too easy.

The rest of the day he spent searching the underground for the homeless man, vexed that the invalid knew George's address and determined to find out the connection. He was convinced the homeless man was Louis Smitt and regretted that he hadn't come right out and asked him before he disappeared. Nevertheless, he would still threaten the captain and tell him that Smitt was in hiding waiting to testify against him, betting that the coward would crack. As the clock ticked closer to seven-thirty, he pulled a photo of Danielle from his pocket, kissed it, then got up and walked outside.

The walk from the bar to forty-four Fern Street took two minutes. He thought it was unusual that the lights inside the apartment were out. So was the light over the door. He started down the driveway, squeezed past the Oldsmobile, then slowed to wait for his eyes to adjust to the dark. The night ground to slow motion when he saw the screen door swaying lazily on its hinges, the rusted screen in the bottom pane ripped and hanging like the tongue of a thirsty hound.

The tinny raps of his knuckles against sheet metal pierced the moan of exhaust fans from the Chinese restaurant in the alley across the street. He banged again, this time with the meaty part of the bottom of his hand. In the stillness, he grabbed the doorknob, turned it slowly, and opened the door enough to look into the blackness. An odor reminded him of the butcher shop his mother took him to as a child.

He slid his hand across the wall feeling for the light switch, wishing he'd brought something to defend himself with other than his fists. He positioned the switch between his fingers and flicked it up.

George never mentioned anything about a ransacked apartment. Not a word about scattered belongings, ripped sofa cushions, broken lamps, or toppled drawers. There was nothing in his plan about the smell of gunpowder, and definitely nothing about blood splattered on white walls.

A bullet in the head never entered the equation.

Jimmy stood staring at the body sprawled on the floor ten feet away, clad in a blood-soaked beater shirt and boxer shorts. It had a different feel than the crushed rigger in the dry dock and the painter burnt beyond recognition in an escape trunk. In the shipyard, death was accepted as part of the job. That's why he insisted his men practice safe work habits. The only way he knew to protect himself was to eliminate risks.

But murder was different, full of unknowns and intangibles.

Jimmy stood in the doorway, thinking about the package he dropped off at the captain's office that morning, the note containing George's address.

Who else knew where George lived?

He thought about the homeless man who had given him the address, but why would the homeless man want George dead? The captain had cause.

Transfixed on George's corpse, Jimmy's peripheral vision sharpened. There were newspapers and magazines scattered everywhere, most of the furniture was overturned. Stevens ransacked the apartment, he figured, probably looking for the Maestro Fusion study and other evidence.

He stepped over a stool making his way to the bedroom, walked in and looked around. He slid his foot under the corner of an overturned drawer and kicked it up. George's shipyard badge and Professional Engineer business card flew out. He leaned over and picked them up, stuck them in his pocket, and walked back out. On his way to the front door, he crouched next to the body.

"They'll pay for this, George," he said, "I promise."

He turned out the light and was about to leave when something struck him. He stood thinking but nothing registered. He flipped the switch back on and went back to the bedroom. Under the upside-down drawers and scattered clothes was a rumpled sleeping bag. It was warm to his touch, and when he lifted it, there was a stack of papers. Sirens wailed in the distance. He stood and shoved the papers under his shirt beneath his belt. He noticed the blinds askew and lifted them. The window was wide open, the screen knocked to the ground outside. The sirens got louder, closer. He scurried out the window, ran to the back of the property, hopped the fence and ran down the alley.

A police car sped by when he came out at South Eads Street. After it passed, he crossed the street and went into a 7-Eleven and bought a cup of coffee. He handed the cashier a five-dollar bill and told him to keep the change, then went outside and joined a group of people standing on the corner looking up Twenty-third Street. Red lights reflected off windows on Fern Street. After a few minutes, he turned and headed in the direction of the underground.

On the other side of Jefferson-Davis Highway, he walked onto a grassy knoll and plopped on a park bench. He stared at glass double-doors where executives packing payoffs and bureaucrats with welcoming pockets passed day-in and day-out. He thought about schemes that made crooked businessmen and unethical Navy officers rich at the expense of taxpaying grunts like himself. *Who are the entitled?* He reached into his pocket, pulled out the ID badge and stared at George's clean-shaven face. The engineer never had a chance. Neither did Tommy and the boys. Hank couldn't live with the guilt.

Jimmy took mental inventory of the evidence. He wished he had the full Strunk study with addendums, formulas, the science, but whoever pillaged George's apartment must have taken it. He lifted his shirt and pulled out the papers he'd jammed under his belt. At first glance, he wasn't sure what to make of them. He'd seen hundreds of inspection records, but figured the ones he held in front of him no longer existed: the original inspection records from the Saratoga showing fifty-six rejected superheater tubes, signed by Joey Strunk in January 1983. It was proof that the accepted records were forged and that Admiral Foley knew the boiler tubes were faulty before the Saratoga went on sea trials. The evidence was overwhelming, but Jimmy still didn't have a witness. No silver bullet.

Not yet.

Jimmy's original plan for the QPR was back on. He had to get back to the office to finish the doctored brief and make his case about the conspiracy bulletproof. All the big shots would be in town Sunday night for the Senior Leadership Reception. The QPR was Monday morning. And with George gone, he had to figure out a way to get *his* brief on the computer in the shipyard commander's conference room. He put himself in George's shoes, remembered the strings he pulled.

He had only one choice, and it was a long shot.

~

Five minutes after midnight, Thirtieth Street Station had the feel of a Roman coliseum two millennia removed from lions and gladiators. Jimmy's foot strikes on the Tennessee marble floor echoed across the expanse as he made his way toward the corridor leading to the parking lot. He paced past rows of long wooden benches that looked like pews stolen from the Basilica of Saints Peter and Paul at Logan Circle. Half-conscious, the nightmarish image of the bullet hole in George's forehead fresh in his mind, he noticed a pair of crutches leaning against the last pew before the tunnel. A solitary figure sat at the corner of the bench, and the closer Jimmy got, the more disoriented he became. Jimmy saw a brown trench coat, two metal stubs sticking out the bottom. The man's eyes were closed: sleeping or meditating. Or acting. Jimmy walked over, stood in front of him and waited. A sparrow glided down from the top of one of the cathedral windows, flew between the art deco chandeliers, and landed on the bronze shoulder of Saint Michael in the World War II War Memorial sculpture.

Tired of waiting, Jimmy sat next to the man.

"George is dead," he said.

There was no response. A few seconds passed before the man's eye slit open.

"*I* know *you* know who I mean," Jimmy continued. "George Sputz, the engineer. Bullet in the head." He pointed to the center of his forehead. "Right here."

Though the man remained silent, Jimmy sensed emotion churn inside of him. There was a sadness in his posture and welling deep in his eye.

"He was murdered at forty-four Fern Street." Hearing the address come in his own voice shocked Jimmy. He struggled to erase the thought, but it took hold and was impossible to evict. The homeless man had given him George's address. "I know who you are," said Jimmy.

The homeless man stared at the pew in front of him. "Do you?"

"I do." Jimmy looked at him. He knew what he wanted to ask, what he had to ask, but was muted once again by the force and intensity of homeless man's wrecked body, his disfigured face, the void that was once an eye. He fought to regain his composure. "Tell me how you lost your legs."

"I told you. Life's a battle. That's all you need to know."

Jimmy's rage lifted him from the pew. "I don't have time for your bullshit," he said. He stuck his finger in the homeless man's face. "Tell me…"

Homeless man grabbed the end of the pew and propped himself onto his prosthesis. He balanced himself face-to-face with Jimmy, eye-to-dead eye. The void in his skull struck Jimmy with the wrath of a ninety-mile-per-hour flamethrower.

"A battle," he repeated, wickedly, "for truth, for justice. You can either standby and watch like a weasel or be a warrior and jump into the ring."

"You're a murderer," Jimmy seethed. "You were at the restaurant the night of the accident. You drove the car that killed my friends!" His eyes narrowed, waiting for some sign of acknowledgement, waiting for a sign of anything. And though he had no way of knowing how the money got to Peggy Homes, he charged, "And you were paid to do it. You didn't deserve to live!"

The homeless man stood more stable than he'd ever had on God-given legs. "Who are you to judge me? God?"

"You righteous motherfucker!" spewed Jimmy.

"You cast judgment on me?" the homeless man shouted back. "A welder too timid to battle the no-good bastards who ordered the killing of Tommy Homes? The greedy lowlifes who considered Kenny, Cajon, and Jerry Yorko collateral damage?" Jimmy was dazed by the sound of his deceased friend's names coming from the invalid. "You hand down a verdict on a naïve foster kid who sacrificed limbs and an eye for sham patriotism and do nothing about the conmen who orchestrated the scheme, the dredges who got wealthy at the expense of working men? Why? Because they're in powerful positions? Because they have titles like captain and admiral?" He spit on the marble tile. "And you call yourself a man?" The truth struck Jimmy powerless, and all he could do was watch as the homeless man pick up his crutches. "What are you going to do, Jimmy McKee, stand by and watch like a coward? Be complicit by your silence? Or are you going to jump in the ring and be a warrior?"

Jimmy watched the homeless man turn to walk away. "Wait!" he shouted. The man turned back around, and they stood staring at one another, simmering. "I need you to testify."

Moments passed in stillness. The sparrow soared from Saint Michael's shoulder, across the vast expanse, and landed on the back of the pew.

"You don't need me, Jimmy McKee," he said. "You're on your own."

Every emotion that had accumulated over the past twelve months came crashing down on Jimmy—the tiger team, the violent accident, Tommy's blood-soaked work boot, and now the driver of the murder weapon abandoning him. *You're on your own.*

Jimmy felt suddenly alone, confused and rudderless. "How'd you know where George Sputz lived?" he begged, like it was the most urgent question he had ever asked.

"The same way I knew you'd come back to the underground the day after you looked into my dead eye," said the homeless man. "Good men can't walk away from truth." He stepped closer, embraced Jimmy without touching him. "Look at me," he said. Jimmy didn't understand because he *was* looking at him. "Look at me!" he demanded.

Between the force of his voice and the power of his words, Jimmy felt like he had entered the homeless man's world.

"I am truth!"

Tension melted. Jimmy glowed with something that could have been respect, even reverence, but as the homeless man hobbled across the grand concourse, it slowly returned to rage. "I need you to testify," he said behind him. And as the distance grew, he shouted, "If you abandon me, I swear I'll track you down and kill you!"

Chapter XLVIII

PARANOIA

Captain Stevens sat brooding in his office on a quiet Saturday morning, alone except for the Naval Academy diploma on the wall and the American and Navy flags flanking him, but they provided no comfort. The rush he'd felt firing a bullet into the head of the one person who could link him to the Maestro Fusion conspiracy vanished almost as quickly as it came. Now he was obsessed by the glimpse he got of someone jumping out a window and hobbling away before he could run outside and catch him.

He tried to convince himself that an invalid wanted by NIS and the FBI could never have navigated from a small town in rural Pennsylvania to Crystal City without being sighted. The wretched fugitive would spend the rest of his life on the lam. The last place he'd come to is Crystal City, across the Potomac from D.C. *What harm could he do to me anyway?*

But the harder Stevens tried to convince himself Smitt posed no threat, the more paranoid he became. He imagined Smitt chasing him through the underground, hiding behind pillars in the parking lot, peeking out of his office closet. Smitt taunted him in his sleep. Stevens was trapped, a hostage. He trusted no one.

"Rita!" he shouted, but she wasn't there. Nobody was there on the weekend. He was suspicious that she played a role in the package being left on his desk while he was attending Admiral Clark's retirement ceremony at the Pentagon. She told him her sources said Louis Robert Smitt fell off the face of the earth.

"Nobody disappears," he muttered, then jammed his elbows on his desk, lowered his head into his palms, and exhaled a long, "Fuuuuck."

~

Saturday was like any other day to Lawrence Foley. Up at 0400 hours, salute the flag on the wall above his bedpost, jog three miles, shave, shower, and stop for a *Washington Post* on the way to the office. Only now instead of the Pentagon it was in Dayton, Ohio. He could have dressed casual but chose to wear a three-piece suit. Tomorrow, he would fly to Philadelphia and be introduced as Chief Operations Officer of Maestro Fusion Corporation instead of admiral.

He walked into his office, hung his suit jacket on the coatrack behind is desk, and sat in his leather executive chair. He leaned back and propped his feet on his desk, opened the *Post*, and, as he had for decades, canvassed it from front to back. A small article buried on page twenty-two caught his attention. "Man murdered in Crystal City." He scanned the article until he reached the last paragraph, dropped his feet to the floor, leaned forward and read it out loud.

"The victim was identified as George Sputz, former engineer at the Philadelphia Navy Yard."

Foley's brain went into overdrive. Tommy Homes, and now George Sputz. The welding foreman who ran the dayshift in Mayport flashed into his mind, the disrespectful bastard who told him to go fuck himself. He supervised the welding job on the Saratoga. He knows the whole story. If he only knew his name. Foley went into admiral mode. Strategic thinking. Outwit the enemy. He scrolled through his Rolodex, still had the number for Huey Kortez, office and home. No answer at the office, so he dialed his home.

"Huey," came from the receiver after the fourth ring.

"Mr. Kortez, this is Lawrence Foley, retired Admiral. We spoke in the captain's stateroom on the Saratoga." Huey lowered the receiver and threw it a questioning look while Foley went on and on about having never thanked the welding foreman for the outstanding job he did getting the Saratoga back out to sea. He wanted to send him a token of his appreciation. "If you could just give me the young man's name."

"Certainly, Admiral," said Huey, a grin still on his face after just listening to the disingenuous prick's spiel. "The foreman's name is Freddie MacIntyre."

"Freddie MacIntyre," he repeated, with great satisfaction. "Thank you, Mr. Kortez. You are a true patriot."

~

Foley hung up, then picked the receiver back up and dialed the office of the Program Executive Officer in Crystal City.

"Stevens," answered the ragged captain.

"The shipyard engineer that I sent home from Mayport was murdered in Crystal City last night."

"I know," said Stevens.

"You know?" said Foley, so stunned by his stepson's admission that he was struck silent for a second or two. "Well, son," he continued, as if he might be proud of him, "*we* missed one."

"What do you mean?"

"There's one person remaining who knows the background of the Saratoga job. The welding foreman who worked the dayshift in Mayport. His name is Freddie MacIntyre. *We've* got to take him out."

"Yes, sir," mumbled Stevens, and hung up. Stevens knew what the admiral meant by "*We've* got to take him out." He meant that *he* had to take him out. It was the coded message of a mob boss ordering a hit, and he was the hit man.

What's one more? thought Stevens as he buried his head in his desk, covered it with his hands, and said, "Doesn't it ever end?"

~

While Foley was on the phone telling his stepson to get rid of Freddie MacIntyre, Huey dialed Jimmy McKee, trying his office first since the Forrestal QPR was on Monday.

"McKee," answered Jimmy, curious anyone would be calling him at the office on a Saturday.

"Jimmy," said Huey, his voice his introduction, "I just got an unusual call."

"From who?"

"Admiral Foley."

"What'd that asshole want?"

"He wanted to know the name of the welding foreman in Mayport."

"For what?"

"Gave me some bullshit about never thanking you for your work on the Saratoga. Says he wanted to send you a token of his appreciation."

"Yeah, right," said Jimmy. "What'd you tell him?"

"I gave him your name."

"What!"

"I told him your name's Freddy MacIntyre."

"Freddy MacIntyre? Where'd you come up with that name?"

"It's a character in one of the books I read my grandkids."

Jimmy chuckled. "Good job, boss."

"What I'm telling you, Jimmy," said Huey, his tone turning serious, "is be careful. I wouldn't put anything past that asshole."

~

Stevens sat alone in his office. The Senior Leadership Reception was tomorrow night at the Shipyard Commander's Hall in Philadelphia, and the Quarterly Production Review Monday morning. This would be Stevens's first QPR as the PEO in charge of aircraft carrier construction and overhaul, and the first Lawrence Foley would attend wearing a civilian suit as Chief Operations Officer of Maestro Fusion Corporation. All the principals would be eager to hear about the progress the company had made welding the superheater tubes on the USS Forrestal. Stevens thought how easily his stepfather commissioned the Graybeard Panel to come up with the conclusions he needed to absolve the company and advance his interest. The old man outmaneuvered them all. He always did, and he always won. And now, alone with his paranoia, he worried about a paraplegic and a welding foreman.

Chapter XLIX

Reception Gone Awry

Jackie Reddi spent the weekend in the Poconos visiting friends and didn't get back to her Fairmount apartment until late Sunday afternoon. A large manila envelope stood out among junk mail scattered on the floor under the mail slot inside her door. The Alexandria, Virginia postmark grabbed her attention. She dropped the rest of the mail on the dining room table on her way to the kitchen, opened it, and pulled out a report. Bold letters on the cover page spelled out *Hydrogen Embrittlement of Chromium Steel*. The handwriting on the accompanying note looked familiar.

Jackie,

I hope you are well. You have always been a true friend and are the one person in the world I trust. I'm sending you the enclosed for safekeeping. In the event anything happens to me, please give it to Jimmy McKee. He will know what to do with it.

Best wishes,
George Sputz

Jackie knew about the Strunk Study but had never read it, until now. The conclusions were clear evidence that the cracks in the superheater tubes were caused by the Maestro Fusion process, but a memo inserted behind the last page was damning. Dated January 1980 and addressed to Admiral Foley, it documented Mr. Strunk's objection to using the Maestro Fusion automated welding process on the Saratoga without further analysis and tests.

Admiral Foley knew the process was flawed before welding began.

Jackie hadn't seen or heard from George since he was transferred, and the tone of his note sounded like he was in danger. The murder of a reclusive thirty-something male in Alexandria, Virginia was hardly newsworthy in Philadelphia. Jackie figured if George was in danger, so was Jimmy, and she knew he was attending the Senior Leadership Reception for the Forrestal that evening. Captain Stevens and Lawrence Foley would be there, as well as other influential people who profited from the Saratoga boiler contract.

Jackie went to her bedroom and changed. She grabbed the report and memo on her way out, hopped in her car, and headed to the shipyard. Attendees had already begun to arrive when she got to the Officer's Club, and her name wasn't on the invitation list. She put up a valiant, though futile fight with the Master at Arms, threatened to have him demoted though she had no authority to do so, and called him an asshole before leaving and hunkering down across the street to plan her next move.

~

It was Jimmy's second time at the Officer's Club. The first was the night he made journeyman at the union hall down the street. Him and a gang of welders broke in through a kitchen window after it closed, chased shots of Tullamore with draft beers, then trashed the place. Those were the good old days when he was a working grunt, a specialist who welded high-pressure pipe with the nimble hands of a brain surgeon. He missed those days and would have done anything to take back the past year. If he turned down the foreman job and declined joining the tiger team, he wouldn't have talked Tommy and Kenny into going to Mayport.

But life's clock ticks in one direction, and he was playing the hand he was dealt.

Jimmy kept a low profile standing among a group of civilians in the back corner of the bar. He couldn't remember ever running into Stevens face-to-face at the PEO office and had a good sense that Foley wouldn't recognize him. Still, he used the crowd as interference.

"You lost?"

He recognized Commander McNally's voice before he turned. He was glad to have an ally occupy the space next to him, or at least an impartial party. "Where can a guy get a Slim Jim around here?" asked Jimmy.

McNally laughed. "Where's your boss?"

"Prior commitment," Jimmy lied.

"I don't blame him. By the way, thanks for putting the brief together. You did a decent job for a first timer."

"Thanks," Jimmy quipped. He gestured toward the other

end of the bar. "I can't place the guy in the suit talking to the shipyard commander."

"That's Lawrence Foley. Last time he was here he was an admiral. Now he's Chief Operations Officer at Maestro Fusion Corporation."

"Didn't recognize him without the stars on his shoulder," said Jimmy. Three officers in close-cropped haircuts and gaudy graduation rings surrounded him. One patted the retired admiral on the back while the others exchanged handshakes. "Does everyone kiss his ass like that?"

"Anyone who wants a corporate job after they retire."

The officers followed the senior Foley to the head table and waited for him to sit before they took seats themselves. Jimmy sensed McNally's mood shift and followed his gaze to Captain Stevens walking through the door directly to the bar.

"He must be stressed," said McNally.

"How can you tell?"

"He ordered whiskey on the rocks. Usually orders bridge club drinks. Martinis, pina coladas, shit like that." Jimmy let out a silent laugh. "Fucking guy's losing it," added McNally. "Tells me not to let in a guy named MacIntyre."

The name jolted Jimmy into high alert. They were on to him but had his name as the alias Huey had given him.

"Watch this act," said McNally, as Stevens made his way to his stepfather's table.

"What act?" Jimmy asked.

"The captain pretending he gets along with the old man," said the commander. "Puts on a big show because he's indebted to him."

The story George had told Jimmy played out in front of him, about how old man Foley promoted his stepson to positions that protected his investment in Maestro Fusion Corporation. *The old man's an opportunist. The kid's a pawn.*

"Speaking of acts, time for me to put on one of my own," said McNally. He picked up his drink and walked to the head table.

It was as if Stevens and McNally vacating the bar was Rita's cue to enter so there'd be no chance she'd have to talk to either of them. She strode to the bar and ordered a drink. Jimmy took a long swig of beer. It was time to gamble. He walked over and sidled up next to her.

"Rita," he said, trying to sound like an old friend.

She looked at him but didn't answer. He figured either she didn't recognize him or didn't want to be bothered. He was about to give her a memory jogger, but hesitated when he noticed a kind of sadness in her eyes. "I'm sorry," she said, her voice a little shaky like she'd been crying. "I just found out about a friend."

"George?" asked Jimmy, taking a chance.

She nodded.

"I'm sorry," he said. "He was a close friend of mine."

She picked up a glass of red wine and drank about half of it. "Fucking people."

The anger in her tone negated any reason Jimmy had to ask her what people. "George helped me with a brief for the conference tomorrow," said Jimmy, thinking this could be the break he needed. He pulled a disc out of his pocket, and asked, "Think you can get this loaded on the conference room computer?"

Rita opened her hand down at her side, and Jimmy slipped her the disc. Without saying a word, she picked up her drink and walked to the table where civilians from NAVSEA sat. Jimmy waited a few seconds before following her and taking the only remaining empty seat across from her. He avoided meaningful conversation so he could watch the theater unfolding at the head table only a few feet away.

Stevens sat next to the old man with the look of a Russian roulette player about to take his turn. High-ranking officers fawned over Foley like star-struck teenagers. Gold wristwatches gleamed from shirt cuffs as their forks stabbed slices of sirloin. Jimmy picked at his own meal while he observed them audition for future jobs.

When only a few scraps remained on Lawrence Foley's plate, Jimmy decided it was time to shift the momentum. He got up, took a few steps and stood at the backside of the retired admiral's chair. He waited for Foley to finish telling the shipyard commander how much he looked forward to hearing good news about the superheater tubes tomorrow before he leaned down and offered his hand.

"Hello, Admiral Foley."

The admiral took the napkin from his lap, dabbed his lips, and looked up. He squinted at Jimmy while extending a hand. "Have we met?"

Jimmy was pleased to see a hint of recognition on the admiral's face, especially considering it was from a middle-of-the-night encounter on the Saratoga a year ago in Mayport. He resisted the impulse to remind the admiral about the way he chewed him out in the trailer, deciding it would be better to

336

let him figure it out for himself. And if he didn't remember, it would definitely hit him before he left the table.

"Jimmy McKee," he said, and bending down ever so slightly, added, "I was close friends with Tommy Homes." He leaned even closer, and just above a whisper, said, "You know, one of the guys who got killed in the car accident while he was in Mayport repairing the superheater tubes your company fucked up."

Shocked, the admiral turned and looked at his stepson, then back at Jimmy. "I'm sorry," he said, in an uneasy voice.

"So am I," said Jimmy. Captain Stevens shifted uncomfortably in his chair and was about to get up, but Jimmy placed his hand on his shoulder keeping him down. "Don't get up, Captain," he said. "Spend some time with your stepdad. You two don't get the chance to bond like you should." He stuck a business card in the captain's breast pocket, then walked toward the rear exit.

When Jimmy got to the door, he turned and watched the two staring at George Sputz's business card. The captain's face was ashen. The former admiral no longer looked like he was riding on the top of the world. Jimmy disappeared into the night.

~

Screaming came from behind the closed doors of a small reception room next to the shipyard commander's office. "I told you to take care of that welder MacIntyre!"

"Jesus Christ," Stevens shouted back, "that was yesterday!" Inside the room the captain's face was inches from his stepfather's. "What do you think, you say to take care of someone, and I snap my fingers and he's dead?"

"Keep it down," Foley gasped.

Stevens's gaze radiated hatred, and in a cold, deliberate tone, he said, "Go to hell." And at that moment, he decided he would get his money's worth out of the gun he bought to finish off Louis Smitt in Forksville but didn't get to use until he murdered George Sputz. "I'll take care of it," he said, in an eerily controlled voice. "MacIntyre won't get into the QPR tomorrow, and when the meeting is behind us, I'll take care of him."

Foley looked at the captain, and said, "Okay, son. Good."

It didn't get by Stevens that it was the first time his stepfather had ever called him *son*, but it didn't matter because he'd had enough. Enough of the old man. Enough of the Navy. Enough of living a lie.

He'd take care of MacIntyre for sure, and Smitt, and anyone else who got in his way.

Fuck them all.

~

Stevens ordered Commander McNally to get him a copy of the guest list, and when he found no MacIntyre on it, he told him to call the head of shipyard personnel for the contact information for welding foreman named Freddie MacIntyre. McNally got back to him an hour later and told him the only MacIntyre in the shipyard was a seventy-eight-year-old woman who worked in the cafeteria.

"Bad intelligence," Stevens said to himself, "again." He didn't bother telling the old man, because according to him, the old man no longer existed.

~

A warm breeze wafted Jimmy's face as he sat on the riverbank less than two hundred yards from the Officer's Club. He could hear the whine of massive tugboat engines beneath the surface of the Delaware River as they thrust ships weighed down by thousands of tons of oil and cargo eighty-eight miles to the Atlantic Ocean. The self-contained steel cities had fascinated Jimmy from the time he boarded his first vessel as an apprentice. He remembered stories Colin had told him about the ingenuity of the Native Americans who carved canoes from trees. They were a precursor to welding steel plates together into ships with boilers that produced steam to turn shafts and propellers, supply power plants that produced electricity for lighting, navigation and refrigeration, and pumps that forced water to showers in berthing areas and sinks in the galleys to cook for the crew.

Three hundred yards south from where he sat was the welding school where he took his first test as an apprentice on carbon steel plate. A few years later, he passed the X-ray test on chromoly pipe certifying him as a specialist qualified to weld superheater tubes. If he walked one-eighth mile, he'd reach the office where he was promoted to foreman. It was just another quarter mile to Pier #6 where the painter was burnt to death, and Dry Dock #3 where the rigger was crushed wasn't much farther. In less than five minutes, he could walk to Dry Dock #5 where the Saratoga was docked when the Maestro Fusion automated welding process caused cracks that led to the death of his four friends.

Shipbuilding was in Jimmy's blood, his marrow. The water-front was his refuge, and the shipyard his sacred space. The men he worked with building and repairing these great vessels were his brothers. The greed and indifference of people in powerful positions violated his sanctuary.

Jimmy never conceived that his benign protest against the robotic welding process would lead to the death of Tommy and three other fellow-shipbuilders. He didn't take a tougher stand because he thought he'd be overruled the way Joey Strunk had been overruled. Now, sitting on the bank of the Delaware one year after his friends were buried, with the homeless man's rebuke ringing in his ears, *Good men can't walk away from the truth,* he felt complicit. Restoring his dignity had become a more powerful force than any scheme devised by corrupt admirals and captains. This was a new battlefield, a battlefield for truth and justice, and now that he knew the truth, he would bring the culprit who connived the Navy into investing tens of millions of dollars in their faulty welding process to justice.

In less than twelve hours, he would be in a stately conference room five hundred yards away. He looked down at his forearm and rubbed a scar from a long-ago burn where hair would never again grow, prepared to restore the valor and honor of labor to his world.

A lone bird glided in from the east, wings spread six, maybe eight feet. It descended gracefully, long stilt legs extended in its wake, its belly barely skimming the water glittering under a full moon. The majestic egret reminded him of the Pelican six feet from his balcony twelve floors above the beach in Florida, staring at him through orange-ringed eyes, as if emancipating him of burden and petitioning him to act for those who could no longer act for themselves.

Jimmy was startled when a pair of feet appeared alongside of him. He looked up. "What are you doing here?" he asked, incredulously.

"This came to my apartment over the weekend," said Jackie, handing him the package. "It's from George."

Between Jackie finding him on the dark riverbank and the package she held from a dead man, Jimmy was too stifled to respond.

"Don't you want to know what it is?" she asked.

He stared at the manila envelope feeling uneasy, unable to process her words, and not knowing what to tell her. There was a long silence before finally, he said, "You don't know about George, do you?"

"Know what?" she asked, tentatively.

"He's dead."

Jackie doubled over like she'd been punched in the gut. She folded down next to Jimmy and sobbed. It took several minutes before she was composed enough to talk. "How did you find out?"

"That homeless guy we saw in the underground led me to him. George was going to blackmail Captain Stevens to get to the old man. I planned to meet him at his apartment in Crystal City Friday night, and when I got there, I found him with a bullet in his head."

"Why didn't you tell me?"

"I didn't get home until after midnight. I called Saturday morning and didn't get an answer."

"I was away for the weekend."

They sat in silence for a few moments. Jimmy lowered his head.

"How'd George know your address?" he asked, timidly.

Jackie was sitting with her legs propped and arms wrapped around her knees looking absently out at the water. "We exchanged Christmas cards every year," she said. Her forehead wrinkled. "Why?"

Jimmy didn't answer, and he didn't look at her.

Her curiosity turned to disbelief, then anger, and then full-out pissed. "Why do you want to know how George knew my address?"

Jimmy had trouble talking. Finally, he stuttered, "I meant…"

Jackie shot to her feet and cut him off. "Don't be a coward, Jimmy. What do you really want to ask me? Do you want to know if we were sleeping together? Is that what you *meant* to ask?" She clinched her fists. "I can't believe you," she said, spewing anger. "I was actually worried about you. I thought you were in danger." Jimmy stared up at her, unable to defend himself. "First you tell me that George was murdered, and the next thing you want to know is how he knew my address? You know what, Jimmy McKee?" she said, "Go fuck yourself," and then turned and walked down the waterfront.

"Wait!" shouted Jimmy, jumping up and hurrying after her. "Wait, Jackie. Please."

She stopped and turned around. "What?" she said, sharp and hard.

"I'm sorry. I just…"

"You just what?" she continued. "You just don't know how to talk to a woman? You don't know how to express your feelings? You going to give me the shit about losing your father when you were a kid again?" She stopped, looking as if she wished she could take back the last remark, then broke down crying. He held her for a long time, and when she stopped, she said, "I just wish you'd grow up, Jimmy."

Jimmy held her a little tighter, lowered his cheek on the top of her head, and said, "Okay, Jackie. I will."

Jackie rested her head against his chest and worked her arms around his back. They remained locked in the position until they turned and walked up the hill toward Broad Street, each with an arm around the other's waist, neither of them saying a word. When they got to Jackie's car, she said, "Good luck tomorrow."

Jimmy looked into her eyes. "Jackie."

"Yes?"

"Thanks for telling me off." He stood watching her watch him. "I mean it."

Jackie took his hand. "Listen," she said, "I know you can take care of yourself, Jimmy, but these people are powerful, and ruthless. Be careful."

Jimmy put the package on her hood and ran his hand up and down her arm tenderly. It was the most intimate he'd ever been with a woman. Jackie looked as if she knew it. Neither of them said a word.

Neither of them had to.

Chapter L

QUARTERLY PRODUCTION REVIEW

L awrence Foley never would have risen to one of the most powerful positions in the United States Navy had it not been for his cunning, ruthlessness, and ability to compartmentalize. These were the qualities he employed to eradicate from memory his confrontation at the Senior Leadership Reception twelve hours ago.

He was also a master delegator. His stepson assured him that Freddie MacIntyre wouldn't get into the meeting, and that he would take care of him when it was over.

Nothing would interfere with his plan to showcase the project he funded as the senior Pentagon official with control over the Navy Research & Development budget and steered to the former Secretary of the Navy's company to pioneer a robotic welding process for high-pressure superheater tubes. In the time since the Graybeard Panel concluded that the Saratoga leaks were caused by shoddy workmanship at the Philadelphia Navy Yard, Maestro Fusion Corporation had reengineered their preheat process, and the NAVSEA technical manuals were updated to mandate that the company's process be used on all naval ships. All evidence of shortcuts the company had taken, and their neglect of metallurgical science had been destroyed, or so he thought. As Chief Operations Officer, Lawrence Foley planned to market the robotic welding process for applications beyond the Navy's 520 ships, opening it up to new frontiers, such as the power industry, nuclear and coal-fired plants, refineries, and a myriad of other industrial applications. Foley fashioned himself as a visionary, a self-made millionaire rubbing elbows with industry elites on a trajectory to the Fortune 500.

~

The commander's conference room was designed to project power. Dark walnut paneling went from ceiling to the navy-blue carpet woven thick enough to swallow dress shoes. All the fixtures and hardware were gilded, the smell of leather covering posh chairs permeated the air. The maple conference table was long enough to accommodate a state dinner at Windsor Castle.

A history buff might mistake the room for a museum. There were thirty-by-twenty-four inch framed black and white photos of ships: some being constructed during World War II, others showed warships moored five-deep from pier to pier jutting into the Delaware River. One commemorated the launching of the battleship New Jersey. Glass cases housed such artifacts as the ship's bell from the USS Wisconsin and the helm wheel of the USS Washington. Each place setting at the table was complimented with a distressed leather-covered notebook, fountain pen, coffee cup, and saucer. Place cards reserved seat assignments, most beginning with ADM, CAPT, or MR, or ending in RET, three with PhD, so that rank, credentials, and importance would not be mistaken. A video camera was mounted to the ceiling. It was aimed at a ruby curtain on the far wall that opened to a roll-down screen where charts and graphs illustrating trends, estimates, truths, and half-truths would be projected. Microphones inlaid in the conference table captured every utterance, and a small, closed-circuit camera hidden in a corner of the ceiling recorded every movement. Captain Stevens's defense attorneys would one-day file a motion at trial not to allow the audio and video of the meeting to be entered as evidence.

Maximum capacity of the conference room was forty-eight, five short of the attendees invited to the QPR. Folding chairs were shoved into corners for the unfortunates considered of marginal importance. Lawrence Foley socialized with dignitaries in the shipyard commander's suite before the meeting and would enter through a private entrance. Captain Stevens stood by the main entrance waiting to see if a guy his old man told him was named Freddie MacIntyre tried to get in. He patted the small of his back for reassurance from the pistol he'd hid under his belt. At eight-fifty, the deputy commander of the shipyard walked up. "Captain, your presence is requested in the commander's suite."

"I'm waiting for someone," said Stevens.

"I'll take care of it. What's his name?"

Stevens looked as if the name got stuck in his throat. He'd never been good on his feet and looked increasingly nervous. The deputy stared at him waiting. "MacIntyre," Stevens finally said. "If he shows up, he's not to be admitted."

"Of course," said the deputy. "Now get up there before they think I got lost."

Jimmy had been waiting around the corner down the hallway, and as soon as Stevens left his post at the door, he approached the deputy with an open hand, introduced himself, "Jimmy McKee," and walked into a crowded room.

The clock on the wall read eight fifty-two.

His adrenalin started pumping, remnants from the confrontation with Foley and Stevens last night. He measured up the room and put his folder on an empty chair along the wall near the back, far enough that people seated at the table would shield him from Foley's and Stevens's view who would be in prime seating up front.

As the minutes ticked toward nine o'clock, Jimmy became increasingly preoccupied with making sure his brief was loaded onto the conference room computer. A short, balding gentleman came up and introduced himself. Jimmy made small talk with him while he surveyed the room for Rita. He wanted to remain anonymous, at least until he took control of the briefing and shifted the tailwinds of Foley's victory parade into a monsoon of evidence implicating him in a conspiracy that cost four shipyard workers their lives.

Maxine Loch, marketing manager for the shipyard, walked in wearing a dark blue business suit. Commander Rommie Davis, the shipyard production officer stood behind his chair two seats from the corner of the table flipping through the book, scribbling notes here and there. Lead Counsel Harvey Goodman, analyzed Sunday's Eagles win with Harry Blunt, Chief of Security. Foley entered from the commander's suite chatting with Johnny Neumann. Executives and officers took turns introducing themselves to Foley and making small talk, addressing him as "Admiral," which made the corner of his mouth curl skyward. Captain Bradley Stevens stood across from his stepfather, looking as if he wished he were elsewhere. Captain Crosby walked up beside him.

"Are you okay?" he asked. Stevens jumped, startled. "Your color's not good, Captain, and you perspiring awful. You ought to get checked out."

Five minutes to show time, and Rita still hadn't arrived. Jimmy fidgeted scouring the room, waiting. Three minutes before nine, still no Rita. Commander McNally walked in with two minutes to go. Stevens approached him, handed him a disk, and said something that appeared to be of great importance. McNally nodded, waited for Stevens to walk back to his seat, then looked around before loading a disc onto the computer.

Fuck! The veins in Jimmy's forehead throbbed the way they did the night Mick Kelly tested him at McGill's. *Training and preparation. If you're not ready, they'll eat you alive.*

The lights flickered off and on the way they did when a train was approaching the Crystal City Metro station. Jimmy closed his eyes and was transported to the underground where he saw the homeless man. *You're on your own.* A sudden calmness enfolded him, and the emancipated feeling returned. His corner man guided him to center ring for the battle of his life.

Good men can't walk away from the truth.

~

At precisely nine o'clock, a photo of the USS Forrestal flashed on the screen. The room hushed when Captain Flask walked in with Admiral Maxwell, Commander of the Atlantic Fleet, who came at Lawrence Foley's request, a power move to provide Maestro Fusion Corporation with absolute credibility. Everyone waited for Admiral Maxwell to sit before following his lead.

"It's an honor to have Admiral Maxwell here with us today," said Captain Flask. He handed off to Maxwell, who told the audience how good it was to be in Philadelphia. "I'm looking forward to hearing about the progress of the robotic super-heater tube welding machine," he said, then nodding toward Lawrence Foley, added, "Thanks to the forward thinking of my good friend Larry Foley, the new Chief Operations Officer of Maestro Fusion Corporation, the Navy will be saving tens of millions of dollars on future ship construction and overhauls." Foley swelled with pride.

Jimmy sat camouflaged on a folding chair near the back, suitably hidden by more than a dozen officers and executives at the table, yet with a good view of the proceedings. Foley sat with his back to him, third from the front of the table next to Admiral Maxwell. Captain Stevens was across from his old man wedged between two other Captains.

The lights dimmed. A video of the 60,000-ton aircraft carrier steaming through the ocean filled the screen, radars spinning, sirens blasting. Fighter jets catapulted off the flight deck spewed waves of condensation that distorted the air as it screamed toward space. A narrator with the voice made for gladiator movies described the scenes using words like "power" and "liberty" and "dominance" and "world order." When the lights came back on, Foley's chest appeared two sizes larger.

Quarterly Production Review in navy-blue lettering replaced the video, as if to notify anyone who'd wandered in by mistake that they were in the wrong room. Maxine Loch positioned herself behind a podium and introduced the principals at the same time a chart appeared with their names, ranks, and titles. After she went through the list and offered a general greeting to the remainder of the attendees, she took a moment to congratulate the Mr. Lawrence Foley on being named COO of Maestro Fusion Corporation. Eight minutes had passed before she relinquished the podium to Rommie Davis. The dog and pony show was officially underway.

~

Reality replaced marketing when cost and schedule graphs came up on the screen. Charts for structural installation didn't spark much discussion because the work was tracking in positive territory, indicating they were ahead of schedule, as was pipe installation. Mechanical and electronics installation were tracking close to the baseline, meaning those categories of work were on schedule. Rommie fielded questions about negative trends for sandblasting and painting and laid out the shipyard's recovery plan to get them back on schedule.

Jimmy suppressed his working grunt instincts while he listened to senior managers and high-ranking officers skirt difficult topics and downplay risks. He'd lived the story behind every trend line and knew that problems existed where others spoke optimistically. He'd spent months inside sandblasted tanks, crawled through piles of shot, chewed black grit, saw the painters' fatigue working twelve-hour shifts sandblasting and painting their hundredth tank. He restrained from commenting to preserve his energy.

Boiler work was the lone standout at three weeks ahead of schedule. Retired Admiral Foley stroked a sleeve of his suit jacket and straightened his tie like a man prepared to accept the Medal of Honor. Jimmy figured the former admiral was expecting clear sailing for the company, especially after pinning the blame on the shipyard for the leaking tubes on the Saratoga and destroying evidence linking them to a job gone bad.

"Boiler tubes are installed, and welding is ahead of schedule on all boilers," said Rommie. "Maestro Fusion Corporation projects they will cut welding time by seventy-five percent over the traditional manual method at an estimated cost savings of more than five million dollars."

Admiral Maxwell looked across the table, and said, "Good work, Larry." Captain Flask winked at him. Jimmy wrung his hands, watching the old man guzzle the praise, and when he looked down at his damp palms, instead of seeing sweat, it was blood that dripped through his fingers. A metallic taste permeated his saliva, reminding him of Enterprise Car Rental on Atlantic Boulevard in Mayport, the butchered Impala, and Tommy's blood-soaked work boot. Inertia more powerful than a tsunami pulled through the conference room, billions of tons of current below the surface, undetectable by sight, yet overwhelming in its devastation, so slowly that nobody could feel the havoc unfolding. Jimmy closed his eyes and saw a homeless man trekking the Loyalsock Trail, alone and free, surviving, a vision so clear that he reached out to touch him.

You're on your own.

He opened his eyes, and said, "Can we have a moment of silence?"

People shifted in their seats, looking this way and that trying to figure out where the voice had come from. Captain Stevens leaned to his right to see past the principals, and when Jimmy made eye contact with him, he looked ill. Rommie scanned the row of seats along the wall, and not knowing who had asked the question, he said, "Excuse me?"

You're on your own.

"Four shipyard workers sacrificed their lives to make this all possible," said Jimmy, straightening in his chair. "Their dedication and hard work enabled Maestro Fusion Corporation to win the sixty-million-dollar contract that is the subject of all these accolades. I'm simply requesting a moment of silence for those brave young men who were killed."

The moment swallowed the room and sucked every second that had elapsed since the meeting began into Jimmy's realm.

Retired Admiral Foley rotated in his chair, and when he saw Jimmy hidden in plain sight, his jaw tightened. Scant familiarity glimmered in Foley's eyes: a flashback to their brief encounter last night or perhaps from the foremen's trailer in Mayport. He glared at Jimmy. "What the hell's that supposed to mean?"

The momentum had shifted.

You're on your own. The longer the homeless man's words lingered, the deeper they penetrated Jimmy's psyche, and the clearer it became that being *on your own* strengthened character and made you fearless, because you had to be. He fought an impulse to walk over and pummel the old man in front of the entire crowd. Instead, he waved his hand at the screen.

"This is all a mirage. You buried good, hard-working men under flashy charts, just like you buried the Strunk Study that proved the Maestro Fusion process caused the boiler tubes to crack on the Saratoga."

Nobody at the table had ever heard of the Strunk Study because Foley had destroyed it. He was too arrogant to presume Mr. Strunk kept a copy, the one he caught George Sputz with during his early-morning raid of the Saratoga in Mayport that wound up in Tommy Homes's hands. If his inept stepson had recovered it from Tommy's Atlantic Beach hotel room after the accident, it never would have ended up in Jack Reddi's mailbox, and now in the folder on Jimmy's chair.

"Who the hell do you think you are?" Foley demanded.

Foley's reaction charged Jimmy's confidence, and Jimmy's visible contempt caused Foley to balk.

"Okay, gentlemen," intervened Captain Flask, attempting to defuse the confrontation. "Sir," he said, addressing Jimmy, "how about we have a moment of silence at the end of the meeting?"

The principals at the table murmured to one another, head-bobbing consensus supporting Captain Flask's suggestion.

Simmering his distain, Jimmy nodded, giving the impression he agreed. He was pleased with the change in course the meeting had taken, the elder Foley distracted by the sniper along the back wall, no longer in friendly territory. He was fumbling with the pages in his book, looking out the corner of his eye, fighting not to turn around and look at him. The old man had nowhere to hide.

"Next chart," said Captain Flask.

Jimmy would have been waiting for the next chart if Rita had shown up to load his version of the briefing onto the conference room computer, because the next chart would have begun the avalanche of evidence revealing Maestro Fusion's corrupt scheme. Instead, he'd have to improvise, muscle the podium from Rommie, and plaster the evidence he'd brought with him onto the screen with his hand. But he had no backup, no witnesses to corroborate his story. He *was* on his own and would either convince the audience or be ejected from the room, bounced out on the street, surely ending his career with the Defense Department. He was about to veer into uncharted waters, follow a plan he'd write as the meeting progressed.

Rommie appeared confused, looking between his copy of the brief and the chart that had flashed on the screen. "This chart isn't in the book," he said. His head swiveled back and forth while he paged furiously through his copy of the briefing. He stared at the screen, and said, "I don't know what this is."

Jimmy knew exactly what it was: a chart he'd added when he went into the office Saturday morning from the papers he found scattered in George's ransacked apartment. He just didn't know how it got on the conference room computer without Rita to load it, but he didn't care. All that mattered was that it was there.

"What you're looking at," said Jimmy, getting up from his seat, "is an original inspection record from the boiler tube welds on the Saratoga." Everyone watched him walk to the front of the conference room. "On just this single record," he continued, pointing at the screen, "you see a lot of rejected welds. A total of fifty-six welds made with the Maestro Fusion machine were rejected by an NDT inspector and validated by Joey Strunk. Fifty-six rejected welds!" he repeated angrily. "Look at the date," he said, stabbing January 1983 with his finger. "Admiral

Foley knew the boiler tubes were faulty before the Saratoga went on sea trials." People at the table looked at one another like they didn't know what to make of the charges they were hearing.

"Next chart," Jimmy ordered. The following chart was a replica of the first inspection record, except the boxes looked different. "If you look closely at this record," he went on, "you'll notice the X's in the accept boxes aren't quite centered. That's because this isn't an original record. It was forged. On the original document, the rejects are clearly marked." Jimmy paused so everyone could process what they were seeing. "The forged copy was signed by Captain John Crosby."

Crosby twitched in his seat. Captain Stevens looked nauseous sitting next to him. Principals at the table were becoming increasingly irritated.

"Who the hell do you think you are?" exploded Lawrence Foley. "Coming in here and disrupting our meeting with your propaganda." He leaned over, eyed his colleagues up and down the conference table to garner support. "Maestro Fusion is proven technology," he said, forcefully. "It performed flawlessly in San Diego and Hawaii, not one defect on eight consecutive boilers including the two destroyers we did in Philadelphia."

Jimmy stepped forward glaring at him. "What's the average temperature in San Diego and Hawaii?" he challenged. "Seventy-five? Eighty degrees? Is that why the boiler work in Philadelphia was scheduled during the summer?" Jimmy turned to the audience. "But the superheater headers for the Saratoga were delivered late from the manufacturer and weren't installed until

October. Welding didn't begin until December. Those tubes were destined to crack the minute the robotic machine preheated the frozen two-and-a-half-inch thick chromium headers and then welded with a ten-thousand-degree welding arc."

"The Maestro Fusion process was approved by NAVSEA chief metallurgist," Foley said, desperately. He looked to Captain Crosby for support, but Crosby sat quietly avoiding eye contact.

"Captain Crosby?" Jimmy coughed, like he'd swallowed a fly. He went to his chair, pulled the Strunk Study from his folder and walked behind the conference table holding it out for everyone to see. "This is a study commissioned by Mr. Joey Strunk, head welding engineer and chief metallurgist at the Philadelphia Navy Yard. Nobody's ever seen this study because Admiral Foley squashed it." He walked to the head of the table, and as he paged to the conclusions, a paper fell on the floor. "Let me read you something…"

"That's enough!" shouted Foley.

Jimmy ignored Foley's outburst. "This is from the conclusions of the study," he continued, "*The Maestro Fusion automated welding processes results in Hydrogen Embrittlement, a condition that causes moisture from inadequate preheating to imbed in the metal and work its way to the surface causing cracks.*" He pointed at Foley. "This man, a former admiral in the United States Navy, buried an engineering study that proved the process he authorized and funded was faulty, then he hired a colleague who owns a consulting firm in Alexandra, Virginia to do a study that concluded the leaks were caused by shoddy workmanship at the shipyard. The study the admiral commissioned was done under the direction of Captain Crosby, his metallurgy guru."

Jimmy pointed at Crosby and asked, "Tell us, Mr. Crosby, what is your background in metallurgy?"

When Crosby didn't answer, he said, "Let me help you out. You graduated the Naval Academy with a degree in Business Administration." Principals at the conference table leaned in to get a better look at Crosby. "Captain Crosby signed the study endorsing the Maestro Fusion process. And," Jimmy paused until everyone returned their attention to him, "he is retiring at the end of the month to become chief metallurgist at Maestro Fusion Corporation." The people around Crosby looked pissed.

"An interesting footnote," said Jimmy, "Mr. Joey Strunk has a PhD in metallurgy and welding science from Drexel University. He was given a choice to retire or be fired for insubordination after the Saratoga failures."

"Who the hell let this man in?" said Foley.

Jimmy bent down and picked up the paper that had fallen on the floor. It took a few seconds for him to digest what it said, and when the date at the top registered, his eyes lit up. Holding it for everyone to see, he said, "This is a memo from Joey Strunk dated January 1980, warning Admiral Lawrence Foley that the Maestro Fusion process was unproven and required more analysis." He took a deep breath and blew out a stream of ire. "That's three years before welding on the Saratoga began."

"Get this lying bastard out of here!" shouted Foley.

Naval officers in their dress uniforms looked between Foley and Jimmy, both wearing civilian clothes, neither with rank: one in control, the other out of control.

"Get me out of here?" Jimmy mocked. "We didn't get to the

good part yet." He walked to the podium and Rommie retreated for an empty seat. "Next chart!" he demanded.

Columns and rows of numbers filled the screen. "This is Maestro Fusion Corporations Annual Report," said Jimmy, stepping close enough to stroke his finger down a row. "Follow the revenue column, and you'll see the company reported less than five million dollars a year between 1979 and 1982." His finger stopped at the following year. "In 1983, revenue jumped to thirty-million dollars. That was the year they won the contract to weld four boilers on the Saratoga, the year their robotic welding process caused fifty-six tubes to fail." Attendees watched Jimmy's briefing with heightened interest. "The shipyard sent a tiger team to Mayport Naval Station to replace the leaking tubes in August of that year. Senator Hawkins, the ranking member of the Senate Arms Service Committee, was scheduled to visit the workers in October to boost their morale. Admiral Foley found out that an engineer named George Sputz planned to give the senator a copy of the Strunk Study, so he sent him back to Philadelphia. But before he left, Sputz gave the study to a boilermaker named Tommy Homes to get to the senator." As Jimmy was speaking, a photo of a conglomeration of twisted metal, broken glass, and bloodstained asphalt replaced the Annual Report on the screen.

"What the hell is that?" came from a random voice.

"That was the car Tommy Homes was driving when it was broadsided at ninety miles-per-hour the night before the senator's visit," said Jimmy. The mood in the room turned somber. "Tommy Homes was killed. So were three other men.

Kenny Essington, Jerry Yorko, and a young Golden Gloves boxer everyone called Cajon. They were the four shipyard workers I requested the moment of silence for." Jimmy looked back at the screen. "They never had a chance."

Retired Admiral Lawrence Foley couldn't take it any longer. He stood, looked out at an audience that was part military, part retired military, all committed to national defense, and never hesitating to exploit patriotism as a front to advance his own interest, he said, "I served my nation for thirty years as a decorated military officer. I dedicated my life to the defense of my country."

With those few words it looked as though the audience might sway back in his favor, but then the old man strayed to a topic he had no business addressing, one for which he had no authentic connection. "It's a tragedy these fine young men were killed in a car accident, and my deepest sympathy goes out to their family and friends." And then, tone-deaf to his own disingenuousness, Foley made a fatal error. "But everything this man said is circumstantial."

Circumstantial! The word electroshocked Jimmy's brain. *Circumstantial,* the term Mick Kelly used the night in McGill's when he told Jimmy he needed an eyewitness, someone who would testify under oath against the conspirators. Jimmy knew he had presented a compelling case, but his theory that the homeless man with no legs living in the underground Metro station was Louis Robert Smitt, the man who murdered his four friends, was just that—a theory. *Circumstantial.* And even if he was right, Smitt had cut him off, vanished. Jimmy lost his silver bullet. He *was* on his own.

But Foley wasn't satisfied with persuading his fellow military officers and executives that his service to the nation gave him impunity from wrongdoing. His instinct was to crush people, destroy them, and in the time between basking in accolades and being accused of conspiracy, he became a defective relief valve on a twelve-hundred-pound boiler about to explode. "How can any of you sit here and listen to this," he trembled, pointing his finger at Jimmy, "this... this fucking welder?"

Fucking welder shook loose the piece of evidence that got lost in the emotion of reliving the death of his friends. Jimmy bored his laser gaze into Foley, who tightened his jaw the way he had countless times during his military career when dressing down a junior officer. He broke stares with the former admiral, pulled a paper from his suit jacket and waved it high in the air.

"This is a Maestro Fusion stock certificate for ten thousand dollars issued October 14, 1983, the day before the fatal accident. It's made out to Bradley Stevens for Services Rendered."

A long, drug-out *Jeeesus* escaped from a wide-eyed Admiral Maxwell.

"Get this liar out of here," Foley screamed.

Jimmy stepped forward and stood toe-to-toe with Foley, baiting him. "Tell me, Foley," he said with contempt, shaking the paper in his face, "why would your stepson be paid ten thousand dollars for services rendered the day before the man who had information to undermine your sixty-million-dollar contract was killed?"

"Who the hell do you think you are questioning me?" Foley snarled, his voice quivering in distain at being interrogated by this man who was once a welder. He looked to his colleagues, expecting backup.

Instead, judgmental eyes stared back at him.

"Where the hell is security!" he yelled. "Get this lying piece of shit out of here."

Nobody moved.

Jimmy shifted his attention across the table at Stevens. "How about you, Captain? What services did you render?"

Sweat poured from Stevens's forehead, down his face onto his uniform. "I…I had nothing to do with it," he said, his trembling hand reaching around to pat the small of his back.

"Don't say another word, Bradley!" Foley ordered.

Admiral Maxwell, looked over at his former colleague, and in a calm, even tone, said, "The captain can speak for himself, Mr. Foley."

Jimmy remembered Cajon describing the feeling he got when he backed his opponent into the corner in his Golden Glove title fight. *A shark smelling blood, go in for the kill, tear him apart.* He had Stevens against the ropes, and he knew it. So did Stevens. He scowled at the captain for several seconds, then panned the room, methodically connecting one-on-one with select attendees: Captain Flask, Admiral Maxwell, Commander McNally. Jimmy looked out at the audience.

"With Mr. Strunk and George Sputz out of the picture, and Tommy Homes dead, the final link was a sailor named Louis Robert Smitt, a boiler tech under Captain Stevens's command, and the driver of the car that killed those men. Smitt lost his legs, his left eye, a chunk of skull, and wound up on life support. If he died, which was a safe bet at the time, nobody would get in the way of the Forrestal contract." Jimmy paused. Every eye in the room glued to him. "But here's the kicker: he lived. The sailor who drove the car that killed those men lived and Tommy Homes's widow got a package in the mail with ten thousand dollars in it. Cash."

"This man's story is a fabrication," charged Foley. "A fantasy. There is no such person as Robert Louis Smitt." Lawrence Foley might have been retired, but he still had connections in the Pentagon, one of whom was head of Navy Personnel Command and had all of Smitt's files destroyed. There was no record that Robert Louis Smitt ever served in the United States Navy.

The bell to the fifteenth round sounded. Jimmy was at center ring in an arena full of spectators against a heavyweight who had just landed a devastating blow. He was depleted of evidence, against the ropes. He knew he was right, but he didn't have a silver bullet.

Jimmy was on his own. Abandoned. An orphan, once again.

~

A crash that sounded like a bag of baseball bats thrown across a dugout came from outside the conference room. A crutch shoved open the door, and a man scuttled in on prostheses. He stopped before he got ten feet inside the room and scanned faces with a single good eye. He honed in on two people sitting up front, tucked one of his crutches under his armpit, raised it the way a hunter aims a rifle, and centered the scope squarely on Captain Stevens's forehead. He appeared to take great pleasure in the terror that filled the captain's eyes before he jerked the crutch, as if firing a fatal round. The captain looked like he might vomit. His stepfather couldn't look away from the man's disfigured face. The triggerman lowered the crutch and made his way to the podium.

Jimmy had never seen him wearing anything but a brown trench coat. Never saw him bathed, or his beard trimmed. The black turtleneck he wore flaunted the contours of his muscular torso, the product of months of rehab and weightlifting. In their last encounter, he had told Jimmy that he was on his own, yet here he was. And at that moment Jimmy remembered the last words the homeless man had spoken that night in Thirtieth Street Station—*I am truth.*

"I'll take it from here, Mr. McKee," he said.

Lawrence Foley glowered at Jimmy. "McKee," he said to himself, realizing he'd been duped by Huey Kortez.

The homeless man leaned his crutches against the podium and took a position across from Jimmy. He looked out over the audience, and said, "What Jimmy told you is true, but it's not everything." He narrowed his one eye at old man Foley. "And it's not circumstantial."

An unnerving stillness filled the room.

"Captain Stevens was chief engineer and I was a third-class boiler technician when I met him on the USS Mehan," he continued. "I lost touch with him when he was promoted and didn't see him again until I was transferred to the Saratoga. One night he came into a bar I used to go to hustle pool, a place called Skeet's Café in Atlantic Beach. He said he needed to talk to me about a top-secret mission. We went to a booth in the back of the bar, and he told me about a left-wing radical named Tommy Homes who was going to give a study full of propaganda discrediting Maestro Fusion Corporation to a senator on the Senate Arms

Service Committee. He said if the company lost the contract on the boilers, veterans would be deprived of tens of millions of dollars in health care and benefits."

The once powerful admiral stared blankly, as if recalling the early morning meeting in the captain's stateroom onboard the Saratoga where he shared the scheme with his stepson.

"I was naïve," the homeless man continued. "I was looking for purpose in life, and when he told me it was my duty to eliminate the threat, I found that purpose: a patriot. Captain Stevens promised to fast-track me to first class and said there'd be a financial reward. But it wasn't about promotions or money to me. It was about patriotism." He paused, rubbed the dent in his skull like he couldn't believe he'd been scammed. "Imagine, my CO, a captain in the United States Navy, recruiting me, a lost kid, for a covert mission. One minute I'm a third class boiler tech chipping brick in a firebox, the next I'm in special ops. I felt like I was inducted into the Navy Seals. I was honored."

There was a slow but noticeable change in the attendees' expressions, more attentive and favorable toward the speaker. Except for Foley who looked at the man with trepidation, and Stevens who was frozen in fear.

"Captain Stevens had the whole thing worked out," said the homeless man, pointing at him. "He told me that Tommy Homes went to a place called the Farmstead every night at midnight to pick up dinner for the guys working the backshift. He said he went alone and that the parking lot was dark, the perfect place to eliminate the enemy. I left the ship early and bought a bottle of tequila even though I never drank in my life.

By the time I got to the Farmstead, half the bottle was gone. My judgment was impaired. I went in the bar and drank beer while I waited."

The homeless man's speech turned slow and monotone. "Tommy showed up with a bunch of guys from the shipyard that night. I had planned to take him out with my hunting knife, but there were six of them. I ran out and waited in my car trying to think. I didn't know what to do. I was nervous, conflicted. Tommy came out of the restaurant last, and when I snuck up behind him, one of the other guys saw me and I took off. I got back to my car and followed them when they pulled out. They stopped at a 7-Eleven on Third Street, so I drove past and waited in a church parking lot a couple blocks away."

He squinted at the far end of the conference room like a drunk driver trying to see out of a windshield. "As drunk as I was, I remember feeling dread. I polished off the bottle of tequila and threw it out the window, then pulled onto the street and waited for them to come out of the store. The last thing I remember when they pulled out of the parking lot was punching the gas pedal of my Dodge Charger to the floor, and yelling," he paused, leaned toward Captain Stevens, and screamed in his face, "I'm a fucking patriot!"

An eerie silence settled into the room, a presence, like the spirits of the four dead men were among them. "Patriot," he repeated, sarcastically. "That's the word they use to trick people into getting what they want. It has nothing to do with God and country. It's a buzzword. Anyone who is willing to support the schemes that advance their interest they call a patriot. Even people who kill for them."

Jimmy had known the homeless man was Louis Smitt since the night he jumped out of bed sweating after seeing him in the Crystal City underground. He stared at him now, imagining the courage it took for a fugitive, an orphan, to stand in front of admirals, captains, and executives, and implicate himself in the deaths of four people in order to bring the conspirators to justice. He knew Tommy would have approved.

"A part of me died in that accident," he said. The words sent a chill through the crowd. "At my sentencing the judge said I already served a life sentence losing my legs and my eye, and he granted my attorney's request to let me go home to see my family before I spent the rest of my life in jail. Only I don't have a family. I was a foster kid, bounced from one lousy place to another growing up. When I went into the Navy, I felt like I finally had a family." Anger oozed from the pores of his face. He lifted his arm and pointed at Foley and his stepson. "Admiral Foley and Captain Stevens took that away from me." He looked back out at the audience. "I deserve to be dead or spend the rest of my life in jail for taking the lives of Tommy and those guys, but I couldn't let these no-good bastards get away with their role in the murders. They don't care about the Navy, their ships, or the people who work on them. All they care about is money and power."

"I've had enough," said Foley, getting up from his chair.

"Sit down, Foley," snapped Admiral Maxwell.

"I'm done here," Foley scolded the admiral, and just as he started toward the back of the conference room, four FBI agents stormed in, spun him around, forced his chest onto the table and slapped handcuffed on him.

"How dare you!" he shouted. "Get your hands off of me."

"Lawrence Foley," said one of the agents, "you are under arrest on four counts of conspiracy to commit murder." A man in a gray suit and woman in dress pants and open sport jacket walked in and joined the FBI agents. The woman identified herself as a Security Exchange Commission agent and added securities fraud and forgery to the charges.

Foley hadn't thought about the stock option since the day he had it issued to his stepson, but after hearing the SEC charge, he regretted the process he had used to pay him. He'd persuaded Johnny Neumann that he needed upfront money to lay the groundwork for the Forrestal contract, so Neumann, the brains of the outfit, an engineer, steered Foley to his Chief Financial Officer. Foley had the CFO issue the stock certificate for services rendered in the amount of ten thousand dollars to Bradley Stevens, making no mention that he was a captain in the United States Navy, or that Stevens was his stepson. The retired admiral was so conditioned to living by his own rules that he'd become arrogant, felt he was above the law, and only now did he regret his careless error, an error traceable back to him.

Foley looked across the conference table, gestured toward his stepson, and said, "He's the one who paid that sailor to kill those poor men."

Two of the FBI agents circled the front of the table, but before they reached Stevens, he pulled the gun from under his coat, stood and aimed it at them. "Back up," he cried.

Everyone in the room froze. The agents raised their hands slowly. "Easy," one of them said.

Stevens slid a finger onto the trigger, and the agents backed away. He pivoted toward the homeless man, his hand trembling, and just as he pulled the trigger, a crutch slammed into his arm, the gun fired. A bullet burst through Lawrence Foley's forehead, splattering blood and brains on the agents who had handcuffed him. The other two agents lurched forward, tackled Stevens, flipped him over, and handcuffed him.

"Bradley Stevens," said one of them as he pulled him to his feet, "you're under arrest for the murder of George Sputz, for four counts of conspiracy to commit murder," he stopped, looked at the body on the table, and added, "and a whole lot of other shit."

The attendees sat transfixed by the blood oozing from Foley's disfigured skull onto the floor. Admiral Maxwell inspected the red splatters on his jacket, shook his head at his deceased colleague, clicked his tongue, and said, "How about we take a break?"

Chapter LI

AFTERMATH

Foley's corpse was long gone, FBI agents had taken their last statement, and Admiral Maxwell had Captain Flask assemble the senior officers in the shipyard commander's suite to finish the production review. The conference room was roped off as a crime scene. Jimmy McKee stood in a deserted hallway with Louis Smitt.

"Well, you had your chance, McKee," said Smitt.

"What are you talking about?"

"Last time we talked, you said you were going to track me down and kill me." Jimmy smiled remembering the night at Thirtieth Street Station. "Stevens fired his gun to finish me off, and you had to go whack him with one of my crutches."

Jimmy lifted his head as if to laugh, instead he looked contemplative. "You know this isn't easy for me."

Smitt gave a slight nod like he knew what Jimmy meant, but he asked anyway. "What do you mean?"

"Standing here talking to the guy who killed my friends."

Smitt seemed to think about that. "If it helps any, what I said in the conference room is true. I deserve to be dead for killing those guys. They were good men."

The hallway was quiet. Two guys, alone in their thoughts. Jimmy looked to be struggling with his emotions. Finally, he broke the silence. "And now you're a fugitive."

Smitt put his fingers to his lips. "Those FBI guys had other priorities. Besides they don't talk to the NIS, and vice versa." He looked around. "Still, I shouldn't hang around too long."

Something resembling a smile came to Jimmy. "Okay, Bobby."

"Bobby?" Smitt repeated, looking like he'd just been picked out of a police lineup. "Where'd you come up with that name?"

"Griz," said Jimmy. "He told me he calls you Bobby because your middle name is Robert. Louis Robert Smitt."

"Griz, huh?" he said. The mention of the man who saved his life long ago opened Smitt up. He told Jimmy about Griz's old street corner buddy, lawyer H. W. Brockton who was granted the motion at his court martial that let him return home for the weekend before serving a life sentence. "Griz drove me back to Forksville after the trial, and I spent the weekend hanging around the store and saying goodbye to friends. On Monday he dropped me off at the Greyhound bus station in Scranton, and I bought a one-way ticket to D.C. I had work to do in Crystal City, so I rented a garage apartment at Forty-four Fern Street."

"So that was your place," said Jimmy, grinning as he realized George had deceived him by playing dumb every time he mentioned the homeless man.

"Yeah. I knew I'd be spending a lot of time in the underground, so I wanted to be close. The underground was my office, my laboratory. That's where I learned how Navy contracting worked, where the decision makers hung out, how deals were made. I spotted Stevens the day after I got there, followed him everywhere he went. I met Rita down there. I found George wandering around, lost. I recruited him, put him to work and let him stay at the garage." Smitt paused, his tone turned remorseful. "That asshole Stevens showed up early the night you guys were going to blackmail him. I hid in the bedroom. They started arguing. Stevens told him if there was another copy of the Strunk Study, he'd kill him. George told him he didn't have the balls. Next think I know I heard a loud bang, and when I looked out, Stevens was standing over him holding a gun. I grabbed my crutches, threw them out the back window and took off." Smitt smirked. "The pussy couldn't even catch a guy with no legs."

Jimmy wanted to believe him, but something wasn't adding up. Then it hit him. "But you were at Thirtieth Street Station that night."

"I remembered George saying you always took the train to D.C., so I took the Metro to Union Station and hopped the train to Philadelphia. I got in around ten o'clock and waited. I knew you'd be coming."

Jimmy rubbed his chin, then slowly began shaking his head. "Tell me about the ten grand."

"The payoff," said Smitt. "When Griz visited me at Walter Reed, he sweet-talked the nurses into letting him take me to the Navy credit union. I withdrew the money and told him to mail it to Tommy's wife. Cash."

That explained the Forksville postmark while Smitt was still in rehab at Walter Reed in Maryland, but Jimmy still wanted to know why a man who killed a woman's husband would send her his payoff.

"I don't need money. She's got a kid, no husband. I don't know. I suppose guilt has something to do with it. And restitution."

Jimmy scratched his head. "How the hell'd you get Tommy's address?"

"Griz is from South Philly. He's got connections. He can get anything."

Jimmy thought all the pieces had finally come together, except one. "So how'd the SEC get involved?"

"You know what? I didn't know that either so I asked the guy from the FBI."

"And?"

"He told me a guy named Mick Kelly tipped them off."

Hearing Mick's name come from Smitt's lips nearly knocked him over. "Let me get this straight," said Jimmy, putting out his hand and flicking fingers. "George Sputz, Rita, the FBI, Mick Kelly, SEC, me." He smiled. "You orchestrated this whole thing."

Smitt smiled. "I guess I did." He seemed to think it over for a few seconds. "It wasn't hard once I found out Stevens didn't have any friends. Rita hated him. McNally despised him."

Jimmy's eyes widened. "Are you the one who gave McNally the disc?"

"What disc?"

"Come on," said Jimmy. "The disc with my briefing that McNally loaded on the conference room computer?"

Smitt shook his head. "I have no idea what you're talking about."

Jimmy waited for Smitt to come clean, but it didn't happen.

"I better get the hell out of here," said Smitt.

Jimmy nodded in agreement. He extended his hand. "Good luck."

"Between me and you," he said, lowering his tone, "Admiral Maxwell offered to help get my sentence commuted."

"Are you going to take him up on it?"

"Haven't decided," he said, and grabbing his crutches, added, "I'm kind of liking this Bobby Schmidt gig."

"Bobby Schmidt?" said Jimmy, realizing that Louis Robert Smitt had assumed an entire new identity.

"Forget I said that," said Smitt, leaving Griz's South Philly counterfeiting connection untold, the reason his trail turned cold when the FBI and NIS tried to track him down after his court martial. The train tickets and garage rental were transacted with fake ID. He winked at Jimmy.

"Keep that Bobby Schmidt thing between me and you," he said, tapped his crutches on the floor and scuttled down the hallway.

~

Jimmy walked outside and stood on the steps looking up at a clear blue sky. After a few minutes, he started up Broad Street. It felt like years had passed since he walked into the conference room a couple of hours ago. A smile came to him when he noticed a familiar face coming toward him.

"Judging from all of the cops and paramedics, it must have been a lively meeting," said Jackie.

"You could say that."

"So things fell into place?"

Her tone raised Jimmy's suspicion. "You know something I don't know?"

"About what?" she said, feigning ignorance.

"Oh, I don't know," said Jimmy, looking skyward. "How about you start with how my briefing got on the conference room computer."

"How would I know?" she asked.

"All right. Give it up."

Jackie smiled, then went on to tell him about the message on her phone from Rita when she got to the office this morning. Captain Stevens had gone to her hotel room last night, suspended her for insubordination and ordered her to go back to Crystal City. Rita couldn't get to McNally because he was staying at the officer's quarters on base, so she left a message for Jackie to meet her outside the shipyard this morning and gave her the disc to get to McNally before the QPR.

"Son of a bitch," said Jimmy, realizing that Jackie had his back all along. "You're the one who got McNally to put my brief on the conference room computer."

Jackie shrugged. "It didn't take much convincing. McNally might be a loyal squid, but he knows the difference between right and wrong."

"How about we walk?" said Jimmy. They headed in the direction of the river where Jackie had told him to go fuck himself less than twenty-four hours ago. He smiled when it occurred to him that she'd told him that more than once.

"What do you think will happen with the automated welding machine?" she asked.

"It's inevitable they'll use it," said Jimmy. "But with Foley out of the way, it'll be done right this time. They'll validate the engineering, be more stringent with the preheat and testing, and train more welders on how to operate it." He exhaled. "It's just sad that four guys had to die to make it happen."

When they got to the river, Jimmy sat down on the grass and Jackie sat next to him. The dock for the ferry to New Jersey was to their left, a destroyer moored to Pier #4 to their right. They watched the water flow toward the bay. Jackie reached over and rubbed the back of his arm.

"You did good work, Jimmy," she said.

Jimmy wasn't good at accepting compliments and looked to change the subject. "You know what Wednesday is?"

Jackie thought for a moment. "The first day of August?"

"One year since we left for Mayport."

"I'm sorry," she said, sounding solemn. "I know you were close with those guys."

"Thanks," said Jimmy. "And thanks for everything you did for me."

"What'd I do for you?"

"You woke me up." He thought for a few seconds, and added, "And I'm better for it. From now on when I got something to say, I'm going to say it. Straight up."

Jackie smiled. "Glad I could help."

"You know, after Tommy became a father, he told me if I didn't watch out that one day I'd wind up married to the shipyard."

Jackie seemed to ponder the advice. "Hmm. A sound piece of wisdom for someone so young."

Jimmy looked at her. "How'd you like to grab something to eat some night?"

"Not wasting any time, huh?"

"Well?"

"Can I let you in on something?"

"Sure."

"I don't usually date."

Jimmy narrowed his eyes at her, "Seriously? The pretty woman who chewed me out about how to treat women doesn't date?"

"Wow! Pretty woman. You think I'm going to fall for that bullshit?"

Jimmy laughed. "Why don't you date?"

"Face it. Men are pigs."

"Wait, you have four brothers."

"Except for my brothers."

"Oh," he said, weighing her reasoning. "So except for your brothers, men are pigs."

Jackie smiled. "My brothers," she said, sliding her hand under Jimmy's arm, "and maybe you."

"How about this then?"

She looked at him with anticipation.

"How about we take a long weekend next weekend and go up the Poconos?"

"Jesus," Jackie laughed, "a transformation." She leaned her head against his arm, pulled back and looked Jimmy in the eye. "That sounds like a plan."

The End